I0774968

<u>List of Authors</u>

Christopher Badcock
Craig Brownlie
Rebecca Cuthbert
Heather Daughrity
Jason Daughrity
Savannah R. Fischer
Douglas Ford
Joshua Loyd Fox
Emma J. Gibbon
William F. Gray
Justin Holley
Caleb Jones
Bert Lestrange
Marie Lestrange
Sirrah Medeiros
Briana Morgan
Susan H. Roddey
Cassandra O'Sullivan
Sachar
Cat Scully
Katherine Silva
Ali Toothman
Patrick Tumblety
Steve Van Samson

HOTEL

OF

HAUNTS

EDITED BY

HEATHER DAUGHRITY

Parlor Ghost Press

Parlor Ghost Press

The Grand Old Dame
{Heather Daughrity}

Tall the Hotel Ethel stands,
Stately, elegant, and grand.
Her front doors open, welcome in
Each guest, each secret, and each sin.

The lobby rings with echoing cries,
The corridors with ancient sighs.
Each room holds sorrow, panic, tears,
A litany of hidden fears.

On marble floors soft footsteps creep,
Down velvet walls the horror seeps.
Lullabies linger in the gloom,
Touched by love and loss and doom.

Beneath it all, the old foundation
Drinks the blood of Ethel's victims,
Absorbs the screams and magnifies
A century's worth of sacrifice.

Come in, come in, she welcomes all
To walk her lush, decadent halls.
To dine and dance, to lust and love,
To drown in wine and bathe in blood.

No soul too stained, no past too dark.
She calls to all with open arms,
And graciously she does her best
To welcome every sordid guest.

So, drink the tea and sign the ledger,
Commit your soul to her forever.
She hides your sins but steals your breath:
The price for secrecy is death.

Beneath the glamour and the gold,
Old Ethel many evils holds.
A grand façade masks dreaded hosts;
The Ethel holds onto her ghosts.

Table of Contents

FOREWORD ~ Lindy Ryan ... i
1910 ELEVATION DIAGRAM ... v
WELCOME ... 1
THE HIGH LIFE
BEAUTY HAS HER WAY ~ Susan H. Roddey ... 7
JUST ONE DRINK ~ Cat Scully ... 21
INDEMNIFICATION ~ Rebecca Cuthbert ... 39

24/7 CONCIERGE
BEHIND THE MUSIC ~ Craig Brownlie ... 73
UNFOLDING ~ Katherine Silva ... 95
BROKEN DREAMS ~ Bert Lestrange ... 107
BLOOD, TEA, & WHISPERING WALLPAPER ~ Marie Lestrange ... 127
HEARTLESS HUSBAND ~ Ali Toothman ... 149
FALSE WALLS ~ Caleb Jones ... 165

YOU LIVE IN A HOTEL?
SEE THE TRUTH ~ Savannah R. Fischer ... 183
TEMPLE ~ Justin Holley ... 199
THE INFERNAL SHADOW OF DWIGHT FRYE ~ Douglas Ford ... 213
DID HE FLY, GOSH DARN IT?! ~ Joshua Loyd Fox ... 235
A MOTHER'S SACRIFICE ~ Sirrah Medeiros ... 253
JANIE'S GOT A GUN ~ Emma J. Gibbon ... 273

WHAT TIME IS CHECKOUT?
POSSESSED MUCH? ~ Cassandra O'Sullivan Sachar ... 291
DEVOURED BY SHADOWS ~ William F. Gray ... 307
A BATH OF MERLOT ~ Steve Van Samson ... 319

SERVICE WITH A SMILE
LEFT BEHIND ~ Christopher Badcock ... 339
THE COST OF MOTHERHOOD ~ Briana Morgan ... 361
THE BLACK LEDGER ~ Patrick Tumblety ... 385
BOILER ROOM HOT ~ Jason Daughrity ... 401
THE RECIPE BOOK OF LILLIE HITCHCOCK COIT ~ Heather Daughrity ... 423

FAREWELL
ABOUT THE AUTHORS

Foreword
Lindy Ryan

If you've spent any time with me—or my fiction—you'll know I'm a believer in haunted places. Houses with creaking stairwells. Hospitals with echoing corridors. Roads where headlights disappear into the fog. But of all the haunted places, it's the hotels that have always felt the most alive.

A house may hold one family. A hospital, one kind of grief. But a hotel? A hotel is a churning mass of humanity. It's a place that has seen *everything*—and *remembers* everything. Secrets slipped between the sheets of its beds. Arguments reverberating off its wallpaper. Dreams won and lost in ballrooms and lobbies and dining rooms. Love, lust, violence, despair— they all pass through the same revolving door.

And then there's the **Hotel Ethel**.

She isn't just a building. She's a hostess, a confidante, a predator, a seductress. She remembers everyone who's ever crossed her threshold. She doesn't forgive. She doesn't forget. She is, in every way that matters, *alive.*

I should probably admit something: Ethel was my great-grandmother's name—the given name behind the nickname Ducey, who later became the namesake of Ducey Evans in my *Bless Your Heart* series. When Heather

Daughrity first invited me to write the foreword for this anthology, I laughed out loud. Here was a haunted hotel anthology, its Grand Dame named Ethel. It felt, in the most uncanny way, like a family summons.

So perhaps this isn't a foreword. Perhaps this is me writing a letter home.

The anthology opens with a verse that describes Ethel as "stately, elegant, and grand," her marble floors and velvet halls steeped in blood and secrets. She is described the way you might describe an aging debutante—one who has traded her satin gloves for something sharper, one whose beauty has not dimmed so much as it has darkened.

Reading these lines, I thought: *Yes. That's her.*

Because Ethel is a woman. Not merely in name, not merely in metaphor. She is matron, widow, vamp, and ingénue, depending on the guest she's entertaining. She welcomes every sort of sinner, and she hides them just as quickly. She's equal parts confidante and executioner. And, like so many women of a certain age, she has learned the power of discretion.

The stories in this collection trace the many faces of Ethel, each one a different reflection in her gilded mirrors.

Consider Susan H. Roddey's "Beauty Has Her Way." In this story, the Ethel is a Hollywood lounge, where glamor and predation drink from the same glass. Here Ethel is complicit, providing both backdrop and accomplice to Cormac Atlas—the so-called "Vampire of Hollywood"—as he drains starlets in the name of protection and obsession. Blood and beauty, lust and exploitation. Ethel has seen it all before, and she'll see it again.

Then there's "Blood, Tea, & Whispering Wallpaper" by Marie Lestrange, which casts Ethel in a distinctly Gothic light. Here she is a Victorian parlor, her walls murmuring with secrets. Tea is poured, but it's steeped in blood and whispers. If Roddey's Ethel is a predator, Lestrange's is a gossip—an old crone whispering behind her hand, reminding us that even the wallpaper remembers.

And in "The Black Ledger" by Patrick Tumblety, we meet the hotel's bookkeeping side—Ethel the accountant, Ethel the record-keeper. Every sin tallied, every debt entered into her ledgers. There's something chilling about the bureaucracy of it: sins not just remembered but *archived*. A reminder that memory itself can be damning.

Many of these stories return again and again to Ethel's hunger. Not just for blood, though there is blood aplenty, but for devotion, for attention, for company.

Briana Morgan's "The Cost of Motherhood" reimagines Ethel as a devourer of maternal love, a place that demands sacrifice from those already giving too much. It's a story about the weight of caretaking in a world that never stops hungering for women's bodies and time.

Sirrah Medeiros's "A Mother's Sacrifice" pairs with Morgan's piece beautifully, both circling around the question: how much must women give, and when is enough *enough*? In both tales, Ethel is more than setting—she's the one demanding payment, the one asking mothers to bleed themselves dry.

Contrast this with "Temple" by Justin Holley, where Ethel becomes a site of worship, a literal temple. Here the hunger is divine—or infernal, depending on how you look at it. The guests are both parishioners and sacrifices. Ethel, it seems, likes to be adored.

What fascinates me most about hotels is the tension between their glamour and their rot. A shining lobby may mask a moldy boiler room. A ballroom chandelier may glitter just enough to distract you from the shadows in the corner.

This tension is everywhere in *Hotel of Haunts*.

And in Douglas Ford's "The Infernal Shadow of Dwight Frye," Ethel becomes a cinematic specter, her halls haunted not only by ghosts but by the echoes of horror history itself. Here she is a projectionist, replaying reels of madness and shadow until the line between screen and flesh collapses.

In "Just One Drink" by Cat Scully, indulgence takes a deadly turn. The promise of leisure becomes a trap. In "Unfolding" by Katherine Silva, the very walls conspire to unravel the body. In "False Walls" by Caleb Jones, the hotel reveals what it's hiding—because Ethel's walls are never just plaster and paint, but skin stretched tight over bone.

And then there's "Boiler Room Hot" by Jason Daughrity, which drags us into Ethel's underbelly. Here she is sweating, heaving, working hard to keep her upper floors polished. The hotel is never more alive than when you realize how hard she works to keep up appearances.

Not every guest checks out. Some stories remind us that the Ethel collects her tenants the way some women collect pearls.

Christopher Badcock's "Left Behind" imagines those abandoned by the world finding a place in Ethel's grasp. William F. Gray's "Devoured by Shadow" suggests that shadows themselves are tenants, chewing at the light. And Steve Van Samson's "A Bath of Merlot" proves that not even luxury is safe; Ethel's wine is always redder than you expect.

Joshua Loyd Fox's "Did He Fly, Gosh Darn It?!" brings vengeance into the mix, a reminder that Ethel doesn't always deal in undeserved terrors. Sometimes she delights in retribution against the same sins she otherwise forgives, leaving guests wondering whether to scream—or cheer.

Emma J. Gibbon's "Janie's Got a Gun" takes the familiar notes of rock and roll and turns them into a ballad of revenge, the kind of guest Ethel might actually admire: one who fights back, who demands to be heard above the static.

And then there's "Possessed Much?" by Cassandra O'Sullivan Sachar, a tongue-in-cheek reminder that sometimes Ethel just wants to have a little fun with you—just enough to make you question who's really in charge of your body.

Heather Daughrity's ending story "The Recipe Book of Lillie Hitchcock Coit" roots Ethel firmly in San Francisco lore, reminding us that this Grand Dame was born of local legend and firelit myth. Recipes become spells, kitchens become altars, and Ethel proves that her appetite is as old as the city itself.

When I think of my great-grandmother, Ethel, I think of a woman who was sharp, resilient, and enduring. She outlasted people who underestimated her. She laughed loudly, lived fully, and left her mark on everyone she met. In many ways, the Hotel Ethel feels like an echo of her—unyielding, unforgettable, a woman who refuses to be invisible.

And that's what I find most compelling about this anthology: that Ethel refuses to vanish into the background. Too often women are cast as scenery, supporting characters in their own stories. Not here. In *Hotel of Haunts*, Ethel is the story. She's the setting and the subject, the walls and the whisper.

What you hold in your hands is more than a collection of ghost stories. It's an invitation to spend the night with a woman who will seduce you, terrify you, and maybe even devour you.

She will show you the way the rich and scandalous live ("Behind the Music"). She will bind you with contracts you never meant to sign ("Indemnification"). She will break your heart in ways you never imagined ("Heartless Husband"). She will pull you into dreams you can't escape ("Broken Dreams"). She will force you to face truths you've tried to deny ("See the Truth").

And once you do, she will never, ever let you go.

As you turn these pages, you are checking into a hotel where the concierge is a ghost, the bellhop carries your coffin, and the maid has blood under her fingernails. You are walking into the arms of Ethel herself.

She is beautiful. She is terrible. She is eternal.

And she has been waiting for you.

Welcome to *Hotel of Haunts*.

Lindy Ryan
North Carolina
August, 2025

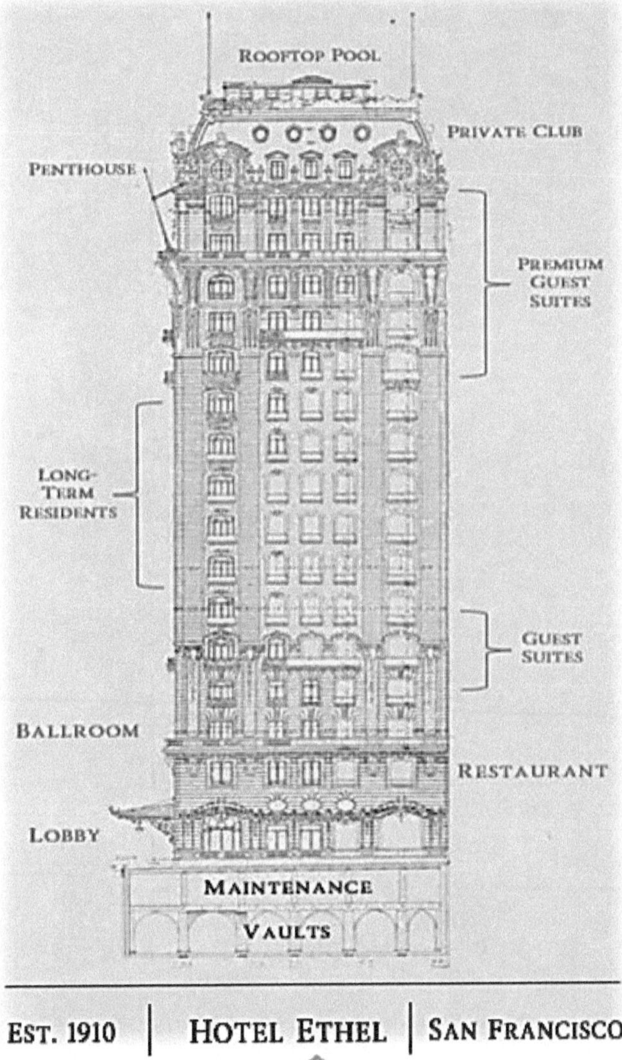

EST. 1910 | HOTEL ETHEL | SAN FRANCISCO

Welcome

It's nighttime, approaching midnight, as you make your way through the curving thoroughfares and steep inclines of San Francisco. The streetlights cast circles of yellow light against the pavement; the shadows between stretch long and dark, perfect hiding places for criminals or wild animals.

Or worse.

When you started out on this walk, when that overwhelming urge to wander swelled up inside you, there were still other people about. You passed families out for evening walks, laughing friends grouped on balconies, restaurants and shops and bars busy with the comings and goings of diners and patrons and those seeking any kind of relief from their loneliness.

It's been awhile, though, since you've seen another soul. The restaurants closed long ago, the shops even longer. A few bars still flash their neon signs against the darkness, but anyone lingering inside is likely there for the night, quiet and somber as they drink away their memories and their pain.

It's just you now, you and that strange feeling in your gut that urges you onward.

The air smells damp; it *feels* damp against your skin. That infamous San Francisco fog is rolling in off the Bay. Before long the streets will be so thick with it that you'll barely be able to make out your own hand in front of your face.

There's a giant hill up ahead, and from beyond it you can hear the gentle lapping of the ocean and the occasional call of a distant seagull. In your mind you imagine the poor bird flying, drifting in circles across the wide expanse of the Bay, and you feel a strange kinship with the animal.

You, too, are drifting aimlessly. You don't know why. It was that urge, that impulse, that sudden irresistible pull that dragged you out of your dingy little hotel room and down what feels like a thousand unfamiliar streets.

You take a right turn off Chestnut onto Montgomery, your eyes on the daunting cliff face that marks this side of the hill, on the strange tower that sits atop it, a finger of pale stone against the night sky.

The ground opens up in front of you. You nearly fall in.

Some sixth sense of self-preservation pulls you back from the edge, teetering for a moment, your heart pounding double-time, until you steady and look down.

An enormous hole, big enough to hold a building, spreads like ink before your feet.

What's this?

In the pale glow of the half-full moon, a strange sight comes into focus.

The hole *is* big enough to hold a building. And it does.

You look around, confused. You've seen earthquake damage before; whole city blocks crumbling, teetering, disappearing into enormous cracks in the ground. But you've never seen a sinkhole—is that what it is?—that contains, quite neatly, without disturbing anything around it, one single building.

There's a sign ahead; a foot to the right and it, too, would have disappeared into the crater. You walk toward it, carefully, and squint through the fog at the words written there.

THE ETHEL HOTEL
EST. 1910

The name rings the faintest of bells in your head, though you can't recall just why.

There's one thing, however, that you know for certain.

This is where that urge, that compulsion has led you. This is the destination of your strange wandering journey.

This is where you're supposed to be.

A sound makes you turn quickly to your left—a loose pebble disturbed, skittering across the ground and falling down, down, down into the chasm before you.

A shadow skips toward the edge of the hole.

Jumps across.

You know it's a bad idea—stupid, dangerous, absolutely crazy—but your feet follow in the shadow's footsteps, finding the narrow gap where one corner of the sunken building's rooftop, now just below street level, leans close to the edge.

You step across.

The dark world of San Francisco explodes into light around you.

Laughter fills the air. A hand, cool and damp and nebulous as the fog, grasps your own and pulls you forward.

The High Life

Hello, there.

Welcome to the Ethel. She's a beautiful old girl, isn't she?

I always was impressed with her—not that anyone cared about my opinion.

Oh, she's an old broad, that's true, but she's got life in her yet. The heart of the Ethel still beats; blood still flows strong and steady through her pipes.

What? Oh, no, not actual blood. Figure of speech, you know? More like—oh, I don't know, oil and axle grease and electrical wiring. Don't ask me. I'm not the construction type.

Not that anyone up here is either; know what I mean? Those salt-of-the-earth types never make it this high up, not unless they're here to do maintenance or something. This is where the hoity-toity socialites mix and mingle. It's the high life up here.

Are you checking in? Oh, well, of course you are. Why else would you be here? You don't look like you're here to fix the plumbing! I'm afraid you've got a long way to go to get to Reception, though. Would you care for company on your way down? Perhaps a little tour of old Ethel's many wondrous attractions?

Yes? Fabulous! You'll just love it here. Oh, wait till you see these top few floors—they're where all the wicked and wealthy congregate, don't you know?

We'll head straight over to the rooftop pool. No, no, it's fine that you don't have a swimsuit—trust me, you wouldn't want to spend too long with this crowd anyway, unless you're one of those types who'd just absolutely kill for fame.

Then it's down to the private club. Admission is by invitation only, but you're with me, so you're good. The drinks are cheap, but the price is steep. Hmm? Oh, never mind. I say strange things sometimes!

Then we'll stop off and sneak a peek at the penthouse suites. Lots of hush-hush things happening there, where the rich and infamous hide their dirty deeds. It's fabulous fun.

Oh, no, I don't mind. It's not like I have anything better to do with my time. Quite frankly, between you, me, and the dog, I'm bored out of my mind here, and you look like an interesting individual. Which is good.

Ethel needs new blood.

Rooftop Pool
1981

Beauty Has Her Way
Susan H. Roddey

November 14, 1981

Her tiny moan trickled down his spine, just as the blood trickled from the gash in her wrist. Deep crimson, viscous and shining in the dim lounge light, slid over her tawny skin like a caress, the faint *drip, drip, drip* of it barely a ripple through the stillness as it fell into the glass clutched in his hand. Her head lolled to one side, a mixed symptom of blood loss and the hefty dose of methaqualone in her system.

Her eyelids fluttered. Unconsciousness had lasted less than an hour.

She was a fighter, this little starlet. He had to give her that. Strikingly beautiful, with an inquisitive mind, and intuition enough to know he was dangerous… yet sorely lacking a sense of self-preservation.

"Are you sure we're allowed to be in here?" she'd asked him as he pushed open the door to the abandoned lounge. The lights were dim, the furniture stacked neatly along the walls to clear a wide berth beneath the pair of rotten wood panels hanging from their respective frames in the ceiling. He'd reassured her with a smile that she gently returned. Her toes touched the threshold and he cast a quick glance behind him to make sure they were alone, only...

A flash of movement at the edge of his vision caught his attention. Pale skin, a tattered—was that blood?—t-shirt on a lean body. Whoever—or whatever—it was, it was already gone, seemingly having not seen him.

Cormac shuddered at the thought of the unspeakable things lurking in the dark corners of this building and turned his attention back to the beautiful woman at his side.

"Of course, doll," he'd cooed, curling his arm tighter around her shoulders. She didn't flinch, but instead leaned into his side, as if chasing away the chill in the air. "Not a soul will question why the Ethel's concierge is giving a private tour to the famous Indira Arya."

Her laughter rang in the silence like the most perfect bell, wiping away any lingering thought of the stranger on the stairs. "Oh, Cormac... all these years and you still haven't changed a bit!"

Oh, but he had... she just didn't know it yet.

His glass sufficiently full, Cormac Atlas wrapped the puncture wound on her wrist in a clean handkerchief and lay it atop her belly, the dark crimson quickly soaking through the linen to stain her pale dress. She moaned again.

He lifted the glass, wafting it beneath his nose to scent the bouquet of her blood—rich and tangy, slightly sweet—then touched his lips to the rim and let the warm liquid flow over his tongue. She tasted *divine*.

His heart thumped once, harder than usual.

The bouncing lilt of Blondie's "The Tide is High" reverberated through the ceiling from above, a sudden shock to disturb Cormac's peace. He'd hoped to have at least one glass before they turned the music up, but alas, it was not to be.

The party, it appeared, was finally in full swing. Thirty-five of Hollywood's beautiful hopefuls (now minus his current companion, of course) had come out tonight to court some predatory hack wearing a producer's skin, out to exploit the youth of the day.

He'd experienced the man—Sebastian Hunter—before, since these parties were a regular occurrence, and knew the pig would be fucking his promise of stardom into at least two of those girls before the night was over. Maybe more if the whiskey didn't incapacitate his dick first.

Upstairs, alcohol flowed freely while music masked the whispered rumors. Lips and legs were loosened. Inhibitions lowered. And every pretty girl around that pool would be a victim in some way or another before the night was through.

Down here, however, he'd begun his night's worship. His next step in the plan to dismantle the Hunter Productions empire.

Cormac glanced back at his companion, her beautiful body arranged along the bartop like the world's most decadent piece of living art. He'd done her a favor, removing her from that mess, even if she might not see it that way.

At nearly thirty, Indira Arya was older than the average starlet-in-training-wheels upstairs, and still without steady employment in the film industry. A few commercials in childhood, one flash of stardom as a ten-minute B-movie scream queen, and a dozen nepotism-fueled single-line walk-on roles had been the extent of her career. Never the lead.

Except to him.

He'd loved her from the first moment he laid eyes on her. With skin the color of rich milk tea and eyes like shimmering night, this *Mona-Lisa*-made flesh had stolen his heart on the set of a cigarette commercial when they were children. At nine years old, Cormac had known that he'd always, *always* protect his beautiful Indira, because he would always and forever love her… even if she couldn't love him back.

Which was how he justified his actions this evening. Hunter had set his sights on her, and in Cormac's experience, there was no escaping it.

Whether Indira loved him or not, she'd been the one to approach Cormac in the lobby, to slip her graceful arms around his neck and press her ruby-red lips to his cheek with an expression of unbridled joy on her face. She'd offered him that invitation to catch up—*"Gosh, has it really been two years? Time flies in this crazy world!" she'd said, clutching at his right hand with cold fingers*—and he was not about to miss the opportunity.

The wolf-in-producer's-clothing upstairs would no doubt scent her desperation and draw her away with pretty promises, only to fuck her raw and leave her weeping when he was done. But Sebastian Hunter was not one to take and be done.

No... he liked to break his victims. He'd leave her wasted in a bed not his own with the reminder that her skin—older than any other in the room by at least five years—would soon lose its shine. He would remind her that the filmgoing public would never be interested in a mixed-breed Indian whore such as herself, regardless of the fact that her mother was the late great CoCo Milan, the blonde-haired Hollywood bombshell who rivaled Marilyn Monroe for sheer sex appeal.

What Sebastian *wouldn't* tell Indira was that he was the same man for whom CoCo had spread her legs for the promise of a career so many years previous, all without knowing her darling husband had already greased enough palms to ensure her stardom.

Or... perhaps he would. That knowledge would certainly break a more delicate constitution.

Her blood had been just as sweet as her daughter's, and her death remained one of Hollywood's greatest mysteries. Exsanguinated, dismembered, and artfully arranged on a lounge chair beside the pool in this very hotel after one of these raucous parties ten years previous, CoCo Milan's murder was rivaled only by the Black Dahlia herself in curiosity and gore.

Cormac smiled at the memory. CoCo had been the first, awkward and messy, but she'd made him feel powerful for the first time in his life. She'd been his initiation. His fall into darkness.

Over the years, his confidence had grown, and through it, he'd gained himself quite the moniker: the Vampire of Hollywood.

Up and down the coast of California, he'd delivered beautiful hopefuls to the Great Beyond, partaking of their lifeblood and thus transferring some small part of their vitality to himself, all in the name of protecting his beautiful Indira from whatever fate attempted to throw at her.

All these years later, she still had yet to realize the trail of bodies left by the serial killer were indeed left in her wake.

Not that it mattered. She'd never once been a suspect. No, Cormac had been careful to always direct suspicion toward Sebastian Hunter himself. Always investigated, never indicted. After all, it had always been after one of *those* parties.

Surely the attendees upstairs would, in their drunken reverie, remember seeing their darling Indira moving between them, entertaining the masses as if she were a queen holding court. They would remember her smile, remember the sparkle in her eyes and the sway of her hips, the glass of wine perched in long, dark fingers, and the trilling bell that was her laughter. They would talk of her as if she were a shining star out loud while whispering of her deserved fate in shadow, all secretly relieved that their competition had thinned by one.

Cormac drained his glass, the liquid inside coating the surface in a thin, red sheen as it cooled and began to coagulate.

"Oh, my darling," he crooned, rising to his full height so he might look down upon her beautiful, drowsy face. "I should love to drain you dry, to take your entire life into myself. Then you would be with me forever."

He swirled the last drops of her blood around, watching how they dragged in his glass. "I would very much love to keep you at my side forever. I'd have married you, you know"—he drew one long, steel-claw-tipped finger along her cheek, enjoying the softness of her skin—"but, my darling, you never truly saw *me*."

Her head rocked from one side to the other, another low, hazy moan spilling from her slightly parted lips. Her eyes rolled beneath fluttering, half-mast lids, fighting against the sedatives in her system to focus, but it was no use. He'd dosed her well enough that, even though she may have built a tolerance to the drugs, she shouldn't wake for quite some time.

Shouldn't, he told himself, *yet she'd not fully fallen under its spell yet.*

Another pill, perhaps? This one crushed and placed under her tongue?

The dose might turn lethal, but that hardly mattered. After all, he didn't want her to suffer, even at his hands, with what he'd need to do before the night was over.

His head tilted to one side as he considered her. "You could have learned to love me, I think."

Her legs twitched, drawing his attention toward her beautiful body. The stain of blood bloomed from her wrist like moist rose petals across the flat plane of her belly, and her fingers stuttered as if the sedative were somehow beginning to wear off. The bottle of wine he'd used to administer said drug sat at the far end of the bar, well out of reach. She'd already been intoxicated, so two well-measured glasses were all it took.

He caught his own reflection in the mirror behind the bar, his visage broken up by sparkling liquor bottles, and his lip lifted in a snarl.

There was nothing *physically* wrong with him, aside from the thin scar that ran along his jawline—a gift from none other than Sebastian Hunter when he was twelve and tried to stop the producer from putting his hands up Lizzie McQueen's dress on the set of a Doublemint Gum commercial—but that incident had been enough to remove Cormac permanently from his dream of stardom. Not because he was disfigured, but because he'd been labeled a *difficult* man. Blacklisted permanently by a man with the power of a god.

As it was, he could still stop traffic with his face alone. Women gave anything he asked of them. Others swooned, asking why he wasn't the most famous man in Hollywood.

Because of Sebastian fucking Hunter.

"I've practiced, you know," Cormac continued, lifting Indira's hand into his own as he refocused his attention on her face. "Perfected my technique. Honed my skills until I was certain I was worthy of you."

Her fingers were cold, dangling limply across his palm. Long and slender, beautiful.

"For so long, I've worshipped you. I'd have given you anything. *Anything,* Indira. My heart, my blood… my soul." The pulsing warmth in his chest turned to a shivering chill. His eyes narrowed against his rising fury.

"But I was never what you wanted. I had no power. No sway. No ability to boost your career the way *that man* could. He never gave you what you wanted, yet you hung on his arm like his own personal diamond."

Cormac slammed his open palm against the bartop. "Never. Again," he snarled, then cleared his throat and pulled his anger back into himself.

He smoothed a stray lock of hair away from Indira's face. "You, my darling, shall be my masterpiece. Flesh made divine. Transformed into the goddess you were meant to be. And a fitting punishment for the louse who saw fit to keep you under his thumb."

Thirst rose in his throat; the need to taste her again.

Soon, he told himself. *He would slake his thirst soon.*

Pulling the handkerchief away, Cormac twisted her hand in his, tearing loose the clots forming along the line in her skin so he might fill his glass a fourth time to the gentle warble of Stevie Nicks' "Leather and Lace" from above.

The clock on the wall over the bar ticked steadily along, announcing the time as 11:47 p.m. The party should be winding down soon. Certainly Sebastian had chosen his favorites by now and vanished from sight to do whatever it was he did. By twelve-thirty, staff would clear the pool and lock the doors.

Then…

Then his ritual would begin.

It was well into the latter half of the midnight hour and the air around the pool was thick enough to chew.

The stale odors of sweat, cigarette smoke, and alcohol hung around him, creating a haze through which dim moonlight filtered. The glass ceilings, installed during the renovation two years previous, *looked* classy enough but in reality did little to add to the ambience of the space. If anything, they added a layer of stuffy humidity, the very same humidity which had fueled the rot that caused the ceiling collapse below.

A fitting analogy for society, he thought blandly. A sparkling facade coating a layer of decay.

Glass champagne flutes, small gold-rimmed china plates, and empty alcohol bottles lay scattered across the various surfaces—chairs, tables, the floor itself—and a scrap of fabric Cormac was certain belonged to the top half of one of the recently-vacated Hollywood hopefuls floated near the deep end of the pool. A dozen different perfumes, all cloyingly sweet, wove in and out of the tobacco-and-reefer funk, but none could compare to the scent of flowers and blood wafting from the beauty cradled in his arms.

One by one, the seconds continued to tick steadily away. The sound echoed through the quiet, reminding him that he would need to work fast if he were going to avoid detection by the cleaning crew. He'd scheduled them to come in at three o'clock, but the party had run long and a proper ritual took time.

The sedatives had completely incapacitated Indira, but only for a short time. It was no secret that all of Hollywood operated on Quaaludes and

Valium, so it shouldn't have surprised him that she'd metabolized the drugs so quickly.

Lucky for him, she was far-enough gone that she could not resist when he lifted her body, but the tiny, breathless moan as she hung limp in his arms now told him that his time was short for more than one reason.

He couldn't be *too* upset, though. The feel of her body moving against his ignited something in his soul. Finally, after twenty-two years of soul-crushing longing…

Cormac lay her gently across one of the lounge chairs nearest the pool, arranging her limbs and clothing so her dignity remained intact, then touched his lips to her forehead. One kiss. One sweet, damning kiss was all he would allow himself before he moved on to set the stage for his performance.

Indira gave another of those tiny moans, but didn't move. The sound made his head swim.

No time, he told himself, shaking away a wave of lightheadedness, and moved away from her. *Work to be done.*

First he retrieved the pool cover and the tools stored inside the supply closet near the far end of the room, then from the pool's skimmer basket he plucked a tightly wrapped parcel containing needles and tubing. Then, a lounge chair.

Finally, with the scene sufficiently set, Cormac lifted Indira's limp form into his arms.

Or, rather, he attempted to. As his biceps engaged, a wave of dizziness clouded his mind and he pitched forward, catching himself by the palms on either side of her. She whimpered again as she bounced, her head twisting and her eyes rolling as if she were trying desperately to wake up.

The moment passed, and as he righted, Cormac told himself it was the humidity and residual pot smoke in the air. Just a contact high.

He took a deep breath and tucked his arms beneath Indira a second time. She came away from the lounger easily, one arm caught between their bodies while the other—the mangled one—dangled limply beneath her. Small, round droplets created a trail across the slick tile floor as he carried her to his makeshift altar.

She was radiant. Even in the dim moonlight, she shone like a star in his eyes. Cormac's chest constricted as he gazed down at her in silent wonder. His vision narrowed, coming into sharp focus on her face as the rest of the world warped around him.

When he reached for the needle and tubing, a second wave of dizziness overtook him, this one stronger. Longer. This time he *did* topple to the side, hands too engaged to catch himself.

Someone wailed. A high-pitched, banshee-like shriek that cut through the fog clouding his mind. Someone else was here. Someone was *watching*.

The thought that he should be terrified ripped through his mind, but his body couldn't get on board with the idea. His heart rate didn't rise. His eyes didn't dilate. His breathing didn't quicken. Cormac languidly turned his head from side to side, looking around as he struggled to sit up.

Indira moaned. Her fingers flexed against his thigh, stronger this time. When he looked down at her face, her eyelids fluttered. She was waking up.

Through the muddy haze in his head, Cormac struggled to think. The blood euphoria didn't usually set in so quickly. By the time he lost himself to the exchange of life, he was always well beyond the ritual. Not... not in the middle of it.

He looked at the clock. It wobbled, swimming in and out of focus, taunting him with the stark truth that it was nearly two o'clock in the morning.

Another of those wails sounded. He turned again but found nothing. The sound was so real... so very real. And so close.

Wait.

What was happening?

Indira made another sound. He looked down at her. She was so beautiful. So inaccessible.

A tinny buzz filled his ears, wiping all thoughts from his mind.

The click of stiletto heels against the pool tile drew his attention, but the sound echoed around him without a source.

Cormac looked down at his hands. Blood seeped from Indira's wrist into his palm. When did he pick up her hand?

Why was she bleeding? Was that his fault?

Hold on a minute...

He'd miscalculated something.

No... nononononononono... no... not yet... not yet...

It was too soon for the blood euphoria. He wasn't done. Hadn't even started yet. He needed to drain her. Needed the rest of her blood.

Needed to...

Needed...

What did he need? He couldn't remember.

The tang of metal rose in the back of his throat. Rested on his tongue. Teased him with its bouquet. He wanted more.

Her wrist was in his hand. He just had to... had to... what?

Not yet. Oh, Lord of Darkness, not yet. Not yet... not yet...

"Cormac."

The sound of his name whispered in his ear raised the hairs on the back of his neck. He turned too quickly and toppled over, and in the flash of muddy scenery, he thought he saw something.

Someone.

The back of his head connected with hard tile. Even through the layers of tarp, it shot ribbons of sparks and stars across his vision. It didn't *hurt*. Truth be told, he couldn't feel much. But he was more concerned that someone had found him.

The cleaning crew, perhaps?

No. Couldn't be. It wasn't time.

Something moved. A sharp dart of activity off to his left. Cormac turned his head, only to find himself dangerously close to the water's edge.

Indira groaned. Her legs slipped along the tarp.

No... no, no, no...

Cormac forced himself into a sitting position, clutching at the back of his head. His fingers came away sticky and blood-bright. Warmth trickled down the back of his neck. What had he landed on?

"Cormac..."

The voice again, reverberating on the air and this time accompanied by the slip of delicate fingers along the ridge of his shoulder. He shrieked, the undignified sound of fright tearing from his throat without warning, and turned toward the sensation.

Nothing.

He'd...

Miscalculated. Waited too long to finish the ritual and the euphoria took hold too soon. It was the party.

The party.

The party.

Too long.

Hunter. Fucking Sebastian Hunter.

Arrogant prick.

The party went too long.

He drank too much.

"Oh, my darling..." came the gentle, maternal coo.

He knew that voice.

So long. So long since it spoke. So long since it haunted his nightmares. She'd... fought. She was gone. Sacrificed. He'd taken her life for his own. She shouldn't be here.

His head rolled to the side, and through the milky haze covering his eyes he saw the impossible.

Blonde hair. Long, pointed nails drifting across a tawny cheek. A glittering gold dress wrapped around the most delicious curves to ever grace a woman's figure. Solid and spectral all at once.

A woman ten years dead turned her graceful neck in his direction.

"No…" The word left his lips as the breath rushed from his lungs. "Not real, not… real, notrealnotreal…" he muttered against a sharp inhalation and slammed his eyes shut. It wasn't possible. When he took, they stayed gone.

But…

Not… not her.

Not CoCo.

She turned her gaze on him. Dark, dead orbs rested in the sunken pits where her gentle blue eyes once shone. Blood red lips peeled back from straight, white teeth, not in a smile, but in a snarl.

"You…" The word echoed through his skull, a damning reverberation which promised a slow and painful death.

Behind the beautiful phantom, her daughter stirred again.

The movement grabbed Cormac's scattered attention, and when he looked back, those sharp white teeth were closer. Too close. Red-tipped fingers reached for him, the nails no longer adornments of beauty, but weapons of a predator.

"You…"

This time, the word issued from the atrophied throat of the dead woman before him. Those black pits glared down at him. She reached.

Cormac scuttled backward, slipping on the bloody tarp. His arms and legs would no longer cooperate.

Too much blood.

Too much time.

Her talons hooked into his shirt. Through his shirt. The first bite of pain was muddled, buried under the mask of drugs. He looked down at his chest where she held him and his jaw fell. Her fingers were not in his shirt. Not in his skin. But… *inside* him. Sunken to the second knuckle into his chest, then deeper. He could feel the pinpricks of her nails as they closed around his heart and began to squeeze.

He tried to scream, but his lungs no longer worked. The constriction of his inner organs held him at bay. He couldn't breathe. Couldn't see. Couldn't *think.* And as the specter of CoCo Milan hoisted him into the air by the rotten muscle in his chest, he knew.

Knew that *this* was his eternity. His first drink had come back to him, come to bring his immortality.

He smiled.

With or without the blood of his final victim, the Vampire of Hollywood would live forever.

Club
1925

Just One Drink
Cat Scully

You could say Roderick Foley knew people. Roderick—his friends called him Roddy—could read a room and know the motives of every person in it with one glance.

Roddy could size up anyone who walked into his establishment, something he had developed over years of bartending. He could spot the cheap drunks, which customers would drink their weight in liquor and pay handsomely, which would try to stiff him, and which ones had something special to offer him in exchange for his services.

You could also say he just plain liked people, or rather, liked watching from his position as head bartender. He liked knowing what people were thinking sometimes before even they did. He found them endlessly fascinating.

Tonight was different. There was something in the air at the Hotel Ethel club bar.

Something wrong.

Some kind of ill wind.

He scanned the room and could smell the fear on the girl sitting next to her angry gambler beau—he had just lost another hand of cards. That wasn't it.

Roddy could also sense the heartbeats of the couple in the back corner of the club quickening, the one with his hand up his girl's dress and her hand down his pants. That wasn't it either.

Something stank, and he was going to find out what.

Roddy did have heightened senses; that was the standard package deal with being made a vampire. Still, he liked to think he had another sense altogether, and that sixth sense was a-tingling.

Roddy tried to throw himself into his work. He enjoyed serving drinks to folks who looked like they needed it. And they always needed it.

Still, he couldn't shake it. Someone here didn't fit no matter how hard they tried to force their way in, like a bad puzzle piece. He could smell them—something rank and foul, like turned meat. He was going to find out who or what had gotten into his club and toss them out right quick. He was more than ready for a fun little hunt.

Roddy poured round after round of drinks. It was harder than usual to tell people apart. The place was particularly crowded for a summer night.

He hadn't expected Marty to part the crowd and walk up to his bar, but he didn't need to read Marty to know why he was there.

Marty was dressed in his usual buttoned-down striped shirt and brown work pants. His outfit positively screamed artist-turned-betting-bookie, but this time his hair was a little wet from perspiration as if he had been running to get here.

Roddy could smell the fear practically dripping off him. Then Roddy noticed what was in Marty's arms and knew why he was sweating.

"Evening, Marty." Roddy lingered on the name with his thick Texas drawl. "What delivery you got for me this fine evening?"

Marty carried with him a handsome wine box with a small envelope on top. The package was tied together with neat red ribbon.

Roddy shot a glance and a knowing nod to his neighboring bartender, Jules, a black kid barely out of his teens who had only started working Hotel Ethel six months ago but had already moved up to the club level on account of his talent for not only serving but smuggling in liquor.

Jules took over for Roddy, no questions asked. Roddy moved down and joined Marty at the darkened corner of the bar.

Marty immediately heaved the box and letter over to Roddy, who received the package by slipping it back under his counter and out of sight of any prying eyes.

"Frank West sends his regards," Marty said as quietly as he could in the loud bar.

"He does, does he?" Roddy slid the wine box open. "Château Latour a Pomerol. Quite a nice bottle."

Roddy moved to open the letter, but Marty grabbed his arm with such force it startled him, and he wasn't easily startled.

"Don't." Marty licked his lips. The dark rings around his eyes were deeper than usual. "You won't want to let it out."

Roddy shrugged a shoulder. "As long as what I think is in there is actually in there, we're good."

Marty nodded but didn't let go of Roddy's hand until he had tucked the envelope into his dress coat.

"Looks like the West family has been keeping pretty busy lately," Roddy said, storing the shallow wine box with the other high-end wine bottles on the shelf behind him. "I'm surprised you were able to slip away all the way across the country from New York."

Marty reached into his jacket pocket and pulled out a set of keys. He flipped through them until he found a red one with a gnarled handle that looked like it had melted in a fire and was barely holdable. The pin was sharp enough to slit a man's throat. It was unlike any key Roddy had ever seen.

"Jesus, what is that thing?"

"Traveler's key. Latest upgrade from Raymond, our concierge. Allows one to travel between hotels no matter the distance. Much better than taking the train in the past to come and see you. Good thing too; I need to be back by eight to take bets."

Roddy snorted. "They still have you run ragged taking bets on everything imaginable at the Grand Hotel?"

Marty wiped his face hard with his hand and let out one hell of an exasperated sigh. "Every damn night. Horse races. Dog fights. Even chickens. But at least I get to paint during the day. Not many can say that."

Marty leaned across the table, and his eyes were hungry. "Do you have Frank's request?"

People had come to Roddy ever since he learned how to conjure up cocktails that could do more than just quench your thirst. It was why the Baking Circle—the women who financed the building of Hotel Ethel—had paid so much money to keep him mixing drinks for their exclusive club on the top floor since it first opened.

He could mix power, shake up a cocktail of success, or make a cordial that could make your beloved instantly fall in love with you. He could even bottle fear if given the right, nasty ingredients.

But it came with a price. A drink for a drink. The way he saw it, if his customers were happy and also willing suppliers of the blood he needed to survive, it was a win-win. Before long, Roddy found himself with an endless list of clientele and positively stocked up in blood supply. What other vampire could say that?

"Yeah, I got Frank's request. It's in the back." Roddy left Marty without another word.

The back room was a space Roddy kept all to himself, and it looked more like an herbalist witch's lair than a vampire's typical collection of fine wine and expensive liquor. Not that he didn't also have those things in the back, but the nice bottles were mainly for club guests.

Most of these ingredients were left over from his warlock ex, Maverick. The endless shelves full of dried herbs like lavender or rosemary were pretty typical, but there were also sections with samplings of bat wings, snake bones, and lizard eyeballs. Those ingredients never gave Roddy pause. He had seen his share of nastier dead things in his younger years back in the Texas desert.

Roddy ran a hand along the jars and the stacks of books, which held all manner of magical texts and grimoires meant for conjuring. He had learned all of Maverick's tricks, how to read his books, and how to make a damn fine drink. If that meant he had to be swimming in his ex's old things, then so be it.

He had barely scratched the surface of Maverick's library, but lately he was in the habit of only looking up what he needed and leaving it at that. As he ran a hand along the shelves of delivery bottles looking for Marty's request, the smell of gunpowder and old tobacco lingered in the air.

Maverick.

An unhelpful memory of his lover resurfaced and dug into him like a wave threatening to pull him under. He closed his eyes to shut it out, but he could feel Maverick's hand on his again, guiding him along these bottles. Roddy could have sworn his husky voice whispered in his ear.

Roddy shook his head and opened his eyes to an empty room. Maverick was *gone.* He had been unceremoniously dumped so Maverick could go around the world searching for alchemic texts or some shit that was more important than their relationship and growing business.

Roddy thought he was over it. He thought he was better. The past few months this place had even started to feel like home and ceased being a painful reminder of happier times. Now, instead of sorrow, the sour bitterness of longing for his lost love had turned to a blazing anger. He felt enraged over the decade he had lost loving and losing Maverick.

Roddy straightened his jacket and checked again for the envelope. It was fine. With Maverick gone, Roddy had started having more clients than he could keep up with. And if he ever came back… well, now Roddy had just the gift to give his ex-boyfriend.

Roddy plucked a tall, green bottle off the top shelf. "Bottled high demon. Hell of a request," he muttered to himself. "Hope Frank isn't going to drink this himself."

He grabbed an errant wine bag and slid the bottle carefully inside. He brought it back out to the main club for Marty and presented it to him with a flourish and a wink of his eye. "Took some effort acquiring the ingredients for this. Hope Frank likes it."

Marty took the bag and opened it, peering in to be sure the goods were there. "Much appreciated. Frank will most certainly be pleased. Now, about what's in that envelope…"

Roddy raised an eyebrow.

"I don't know what you've got planned." Marty licked his lips. "Don't open it, whatever you do. What's inside that envelope is said to give bad luck, nightmares, possessions. That's one particularly nasty poltergeist if you ask me. One would have to hate a person as deeply as their worst enemy to inflict something that evil on someone."

Roddy ran his tongue over his canines. "I know damn well what's in that envelope, and the rules. It's exactly why I asked for it."

Marty shivered. "It gives me the willies."

Roddy grinned wide enough that he could bare his teeth while still smiling. "And I happen to hate the bastard that much."

Marty sighed and looked suddenly bored. "It's for your ex, isn't it?"

Roddy's face fell. "Does it matter?"

"You don't even know where to find him. He could be in some alternate dimension for all we know."

Roddy leaned across the bar. "Well, he has to come home sometime, don't he? For all his spell books and all his little trinkets and oddities. And when he does, I'll have just the thing waiting for him. There's one thing that's true about Maverick—he never could resist opening a surprise."

Marty swallowed hard.

"Now, about my payment…"

Marty's brows knit together in confusion. "But, I gave you the box. What more do you want?"

"You know my price," Roddy gestured with two fingers for Marty to follow him to the back. "A drink for a drink."

When Marty got up from his seat, the worry on his face concerning what was about to happen was evident. Roddy could tell here was a man who was on his last rope. Marty had been run through by his job as a bookie, by his boss who made him work keeping account of every bet in the Grand Hotel, and now a vampire wanted to suck his blood.

Roddy didn't feel the least bit guilty. He was working for the man too, and they all had to eat. It was a dog-eat-dog world, and they were both more blessed than most to be a demon and a vampire through it all.

He gave Marty his best smile, the one that showed all his teeth. "It's okay. I'll be real gentle… at first."

Roddy returned to the bar some time later. Marty hadn't tasted that good and it left a foul feeling in his gut, but the surge of power he got from drinking demon blood never got old.

He rejoined Jules and helped sling through a couple rush orders, including a round of gin refills to the big party in the back.

"You okay, boss?" Jules asked. "You're looking a little… green."

"Really should know better than to drink demons," Roddy said and swallowed back some bloody bile down his throat. "Couldn't be helped. At least they give a little extra boost."

"What kind of boost, boss?"

"When you drink someone supernatural, you get their powers. For a little while."

"Demon powers? Sounds nasty." Jules laughed it off, but there was still concern lingering in his eyes. "If you want I can cover for you a little while longer. If you're still… sick."

That's when Roddy saw her.

The blonde flapper was younger than most in his bar, and her dress more daring. Even across the room he could tell the beadwork was painstakingly detailed—hand-sewn, exquisite.

Her smoky eyes surveyed the club, landing on everything but Roddy as she made her way to his bar. Her figure caught more than one eye as she crossed the room, and she was very aware of how her presence caught attention. She slid into the farthest seat available at the end of the bar and waited patiently for Roddy to look her way, but he didn't and wouldn't for several moments.

Roddy busied himself with the latest requests: whiskey, gin, several Aviations, a couple of sidecars, and one bottle of wine. He waited until the last drink order was fulfilled before making his way down to the petite belle.

"Evening, ma'am." He was well aware he was laying on the southern charm real thick. "What can I get you?"

She wrinkled her nose, and he couldn't help the flush that crept up the back of his neck. It was rare a customer did this to him. Her blood must be real sweet.

"What's the house special?" She batted those long lashes of hers and recrossed her legs to show the full length of her gams, and what was between them.

Roddy couldn't believe himself. He was getting turned on by her.

He let out a laugh that he worried revealed how attracted he really was. "That would be gin, and not the bathtub stuff, neither. The real deal."

She smiled, showing all of her perfect teeth and dazzling blue eyes. "I'll have a gin drink then…" She leaned across the bar. "Can you help me out? What should I order?"

Roddy grinned but made sure not to reveal too much of his teeth. The fangs were out, and with how hot and bothered he was getting, there was no chance of them sliding back in anytime soon.

He set his focus on mixing her a Bee's Knees. Roddy liked to let himself fall into the rhythm each time he made a cocktail. He was something of a scientist about it, measuring each portion carefully and exactly as if he were making an explosive weapon that could go off with one drop of the wrong fluids.

He twisted the lemon garnish and ran its silky rind around the rim of the coupe glass. He only made eye contact with the girl again when he set the full coupe on a black napkin.

"What's your name, sweet?" he asked.

"Marigold," she said.

He chuckled. "Of course it is."

She reached for her drink, but he wouldn't slide it over to her. "Do you know how payments work around here?"

She glanced left and right at her fellow patrons, who were all rather inebriated. "Um, I have some dough. And a little more back in my room."

He and Jules exchanged a glance and a knowing smile. "We don't take money in this here club. Surely they told you the conditions of your membership?"

She shook her head, and her shoulders tightened, giving her the appearance of a lost child rather than the confident young woman she had been only moments ago. "What do I need to do?"

Jules slunk back out into the crowd while they were talking.

"Not anything too terrible. But all drinks come with a price."

Roddy waited until Jules was standing behind her. That's when Roddy flashed a smile—his real smile.

"A drink for a drink," Roddy said. "I can collect the payment now, or after you drink. Lady's choice."

Marigold turned to leave and found herself face-to-face with Jules. He grabbed her by her shoulders and forced her back down into her seat.

"Choose," Roddy said. "What is it going to be? Should I collect my payment now, or later?"

Marigold's hand shook as she reached for the coupe glass full of the golden cocktail, but Roddy let her have it.

"Liquid courage it is," Roddy said.

Marigold took her time with her drink. Each sip was a measured taste. She would lift the coupe carefully to her mouth and set it gingerly back down on the counter. Jules never left her side, and never once lifted his hands from her shoulders, not even when more requests started coming in and Roddy had to address the new orders.

"Hurry it up," Roddy said, returning after sending out another batch. "I have all night, but I'd rather not take it. Neither would my man here."

Marigold glanced at the couple who took their drinks back to their seats with them. "Do you drink from everyone here?"

Roddy grinned. "Every last one."

Marigold swallowed hard and her face flushed. She grabbed the coupe glass with renewed vigor and downed the rest of the cocktail. She had over half of the Bee's Knees still swirling around the glass, but she took it all with a strong gulp.

Jules guided her back behind the counter and into Roddy's waiting arms.

"We won't be long," Roddy said.

"You got it, boss."

Roddy guided her to the back room and found her body surprisingly strong for such a little thing. He leaned in once to get a whiff of her, hoping to place the scent wafting off of her. It was so familiar, so intoxicating, but he couldn't place where he had smelled it before. Her perfume or natural musk was definitely floral somehow, and it reminded him of the herbs Maverick left behind.

When they entered the library and apothecary, she let out a soft gasp she immediately stifled with her hand. "You're not just a vampire?" she said. "You're also… a witch?"

Roddy laughed. "Hardly. My ex left all of this stuff."

Marigold circled, taking in the room. She ran her hands along the small bottles filled to the brim with alligator teeth and cat dew claws. "You kept all of your ex-witch-girlfriend's things?"

His good mood soured, and he could feel his expression darken. "No. He left them here for me to take care of."

She spun back to him and clasped her hands behind her back. "Do you miss her?"

"Him," Roddy corrected. "And no, I don't miss him. Not anymore."

Marigold frowned, considering the information he had just handed her. "Sounds like your hatred is justified."

He shook off her question. "That's none of your business. You're stalling, and it's not going to work."

Roddy reached where she stood in two large strides. She didn't cower like he expected, but he grabbed her arm hard to keep her from running all the same.

Marigold met his eyes defiantly, and there was something about her look that was so familiar to him, but so out of place. Looking in her baby blues reminded him of that sinking feeling he had earlier in the evening, that someone was here that shouldn't be. Maybe it was her. Only one way to tell.

He used his other hand to grab a fistful of her hair and pull her head back until her neck was exposed. Roddy was careful not to do it too quickly and snap her neck.

A little whimper escaped her parted red lips, and he found himself placing his mouth on hers instead. Her mouth tasted of gooseberries, as tart and acidic as dry wine. It was a strange flavor, matching perfectly with the warning that rose louder in his gut than ever, but the growing urge in his pants overpowered every other thought.

She kissed him back, harder and harder until her tongue was down his throat and playing across his canines. When they both came up for air, their bodies were so pressed together her dress was tangled in the zipper of his pants, but she didn't seem to care.

She locked her smoky eyes with his. "I want you."

This was it, his moment. He better take it before he thought better of it, before he lost his senses completely and devoured her in the sexual sense instead of the literal one. Roddy drew back his mouth, exposing his canines. He brought his mouth closer to her neck.

"It's good to be home," she said.

Roddy stopped cold. He was so taken aback, his fangs retracted a little. "What do you mean?"

She shrugged. "You kept the place so nice for my return. Even restocked all the bottles. What has it been, a year? And everything is freshly stocked. I appreciate all the hard work and effort you put into our business."

"*Our* business?" Roddy roared and flung Marigold—Maverick—away from him. "The one you abandoned?"

Maverick, still wearing Marigold's golden curls and flapper dress, laughed in her laugh. "You like this form? One of the new tricks I picked up out in the world. Like I said, Roddy baby, there was so much magic to learn out there. Wearing new faces will help us out so much."

Roddy wiped his mouth with the back of his hand until he was sure all the lipstick was gone. "This is low. Even for you."

Maverick got to his feet and teetered on his heels. He gave a little twirl and a curtsy before snapping both his fingers and letting his disguise fall away like old clothing onto the floor.

Marigold's skin landed in a heap like a dirty rag. He kicked it away.

"The trick is, you really have to skin them *for real*." He grimaced. "Nasty work, walking around as someone else. Not easy, but she was more than willing. Trouble is you can't get the host's smell out. Luckily, she smells like something barely tolerable, but I still had to add my own floral perfumes to get the rest of the stink out."

So that explained her strange smell. He knew there was someone in the club that didn't belong, but his ex-boyfriend wearing the face of a girl he had skinned was not something Roddy ever would have guessed.

Roddy opened his mouth to call Maverick a sick, evil, fucking bastard, but stopped himself. Something was different about him.

Not in his dress or manner. Maverick was wearing, as he always did, the most incredible tailored outfit. This time it was a black and gold suit with cufflinks that bore his family crest surrounded by little diamonds. His blue eyes were a sharp contrast to his slicked-back, jet-colored hair and thick eyebrows and chiseled jawline. His look had made Roddy fall hard, quite literally, off of his bull at the local rodeo the first time he saw Maverick.

Even now, with hatred pumping through his veins, Roddy had to admit Maverick never looked better. Then again, Maverick could afford to always look good.

Roddy shifted his weight, testing to see if the letter was still tucked away in his official hotel coat. The letter prodded him in return. "Why are you back?"

Maverick waved a hand, gesturing at the room. "I had always intended to come back. We built this place together. I told you that before I left."

"What you told me is that you were going away to visit family. You still doing whatever they tell you to?"

Maverick sniffed and his perfect nose wrinkled. "You never did like how close my family is."

"No, I didn't like how you would jump every time they said leap. No matter what I thought or what I wanted. It didn't matter. What your parents wanted for you, that's what was more important than anything. Than me."

"Yes, well," Maverick ran his finger along the spine of one of his books. "They do foot the bills."

"If *my* family were not only witches and warlocks," Roddy said with a sneer, "they were also wealthy because they made bank as healers, doctors, and lawyers, I guess I'd feed off the family coffers as often as possible. Every time I ran into even the smallest bit of trouble."

Maverick sniffed. "You never did like my family. I'm sorry it was a life which was such a far cry from your hard-working, bootstraps, prairie past."

Roddy clucked his tongue. It was now or never, before his anger over past hurts got the better of him and he said something really stupid. "Either way, you arrived at the perfect time. I have a gift for you."

He slipped the envelope out of his breast pocket and held it out for Maverick.

Maverick's eyes lightened. His fingers gave the barest flicker of excitement, the sort of gesture anyone might miss, but not Roddy. He knew how tempted Maverick would be to open a gift.

"Go on," Roddy said. "Take it."

Maverick reached for the envelope and hesitated. "What is it?"

Roddy shrugged a shoulder. "Guess you'll have to open it and find out."

Maverick gave him the same delighted smile that used to bring Roddy to his knees and snatched the envelope out of his hands. He started to open it and stopped.

"What is *this*?" Maverick shrieked. "You planned on giving me a *vengeful ghost* as a present?"

With a wave of his arm, Maverick sent a rush of air at Roddy that was so strong he was flung backward. Roddy went wheeling into the ingredients shelf and hit the wooden bookcase with a smack that sent him and half of the ingredients tumbling down.

Roddy hit the floor and so did all of the glass bottles. They smacked and popped all around him as he instinctively covered his head.

Didn't matter. Some of the shards still got through and cut up the backs of his hands real good.

"It's a real shame too," Maverick said. "I was so happy to see you. I thought the girl was a nice touch too. A little seduction and then, surprise! I'm home! I'm back to help with our business we started together! And you took such good care of it all this time. I thought you'd welcome me back with open arms."

As a vampire, Roddy could take a beating, but he could take one before he had been turned too. He was one of the best bull riders and whiskey slingers West Texas had ever seen. Being thrown once wasn't going to keep him down, no matter how hard Maverick tried.

He'd never faced off against a warlock before. He might be immortal, and make magical cocktails, but he didn't have any magic of his own besides brute force.

At least, he didn't until Marty.

He was going to have to be smart about this.

"Sorry about that, honey," Roddy said, making a real show of getting to his knees. "Wasn't real nice of me to play a trick like that, but neither was pretending to be some woman to seduce me. Call a truce?"

Maverick raised one of his thick eyebrows. "Perhaps. For now."

He raised the letter between two fingers. At first, Roddy didn't know what he was doing, but he felt the wind rush all around him again and the letter went flying.

A soft "no" escaped Roddy's lips before he had a chance to think better of it, and he really shouldn't have reached for the letter when it whizzed by his head. It flew across the room and slid easily right into one of the open air vents.

"Now that little letter will be buried somewhere in the hotel," Maverick said. "But you won't be able to find it. No matter how hard you look."

Roddy took a step forward. "I thought you said we were calling a truce."

Maverick looked at his nails. "Now we have a truce. Although, I would call it a shaky one. I saw how you reacted when I sent the letter away."

Roddy wanted to kick himself, but it was too late now. Better to see what Maverick's next move was so he could figure out his own. "What now?"

Maverick gestured to the center of the room and snapped his fingers again. He muttered something quickly beneath his breath in a language Roddy didn't understand. A dining room table fully laden with food, lit candles, and wine appeared before them as if it had always been there.

"Have dinner with me?" Maverick offered. "I realize you can't partake, but perhaps after? A drink for a drink? By the way, are you still offering that deal to our patrons?"

"I am." Roddy knew what to do. He smiled, played the affectionate and wounded boyfriend, and intended to fool Maverick to the best of his ability. "Just one drink."

In the year since Maverick disappeared, Roddy had studied all of the books that he could on those shelves, and he had learned quite a lot. While lately he had been neglecting his studies, there were many weaknesses that he had found in those pages.

Roddy joined Maverick at the table and took the seat across from him with care. He had to keep up appearances. Didn't want Maverick to suspect anything. He sat there while Maverick droned on about his exploits. He suffered through his various trysts in France, and his experimentation in Brazil.

The more Maverick talked about the magic he learned and the people he slept with to gain their spiritual knowledge, the more the blood inside Roddy burned. It was a side effect of drinking demon—unchecked rage, aggression, and the inability to care about the consequences of one's own actions. He needed to hold it together a little longer and just hoped that certain other side effect would appear soon.

"And you would have just adored the spot in Singapore. The food was divine. But of course, you wouldn't be able to taste it. Can't eat food and all that." Maverick smirked at the knife-twist comment.

It had always been a point of contention in their relationship—the things Roddy couldn't do. He was never enough. Would never be.

Roddy raised his glass. "I propose a toast. To your travels, your newfound knowledge, and your safe return home."

Maverick got up from his seat in one fluid motion. He sauntered over to Roddy, hips swaying seductively as if he were the golden-haired flapper again. He leaned against the table in front of Roddy, not caring that he sent Roddy's plate of food onto the floor with a clatter.

"I missed you."

Maverick leaned in until his lips were on Roddy's, and that was the moment he felt it, the sudden pain in his right hand. The one that always came when he drank demon blood and acquired their powers for a little while.

Roddy leaned into the kiss, giving his body more time to accept the physical transformation that was happening to his hand. He sent his tongue deep into Maverick's mouth and played while the sharp prongs swelled and grew into rows of teeth in his palm. It wasn't his favorite side effect, but right now, he could kiss Marty full on the mouth for the perfect timing of his awful gift—the growth of a second mouth.

Once he was sure it had fully grown, Roddy slammed his fist straight into Maverick's groin. Maverick howled as Roddy's second mouth, full of jagged teeth, chomped down on his tenderest bits. Blood splattered across Roddy's shirt, his face, his hotel-official dress suit, shirt, and tie.

Maverick squirmed, tried to blast him with the air trick again, but there was no fighting the strength of Roddy's second mouth and he was losing blood fast from a main artery in his leg. He paled and fell back, taking Roddy, who refused to let go, with him.

"Why?" Maverick asked. Blood spluttered out of his mouth. "I love you."

Roddy let the mouth in his right hand have its own mind about where it wanted to feed next.

Demons all had second mouths appear somewhere on their body. For Roddy, every time he drank demon blood, it would appear in his right hand. He normally hated how hungry he would get, how the hand was a kind of possession and pain that ran deeper than the hunger for blood he knew as a vampire. But this time? He wanted this moment to never end.

"You did love me," Roddy said. "And I loved you. For a time. But that time is over. Now, I'll see you in hell. It's only fair."

Maverick smiled with blood between his pearly white teeth. "A drink for a drink."

Roddy didn't stop the second mouth from feeding, not until there was nothing left but a smear where his ex-lover used to be. And he did feel bad, but only for a moment. After all, it was a world full of predators, and it was nice to finally be back on top of the food chain.

19th Floor – Penthouse Suite
1964

Indemnification
Rebecca Cuthbert

Evelyn held her careful smile in place as the handsome young doorman in the sharp purple uniform welcomed her into the lobby. By the time she got to her floor, that smile was breaking.

Inside her penthouse suite, she wanted to collapse. But there was the bellhop, setting down her cases and smiling, expecting a tip, and a maid with her hair in a neat French twist, murmuring something about extra blankets in the closet as she pushed past them both into the hallway.

So Evelyn waited—nodded at the maid, handed cash to the bellhop, said her thanks. And finally, *finally*, the door clicked shut. She leaned back against the floral wallpaper, then slid to the floor.

Alone, for better or worse.

She didn't cry. The last of her angry tears had been shed on the cab ride over, absorbed by the collar of her wool coat, evaporated into the frigid January air.

Arthur had been at the club when she left, still ringing in 1964 three days after everyone else's New Year's hangover had faded.

At least, that was this week's excuse, but Arthur was always at the club, and always at least half cut.

Evelyn had timed her departure for when she knew he'd be two-thirds of the way into his first Scotch bottle—which he'd definitely finish before sinking another, then stumble home past midnight, where his routine was to fall into bed next to her and fumble with the straps of her nightgown.

Except tonight, she wouldn't be there, and his clumsy fingers could fumble with himself.

The thought almost made Evelyn smile.

Almost.

She lost track of time, sitting there, but eventually she noticed the light had changed: afternoon to evening. She blinked and stood, looking around her temporary home.

The Hotel Ethel, nineteen floors up.

The same penthouse suite in which she and Arthur had spent their honeymoon nine years before. Back when she thought he loved her.

Not long after, she found out he only loved her inheritance.

Had she booked it because it felt safe, familiar when everything else was strange? Or had she booked it to torture herself?

She walked across the room and past the kitchenette to step onto the balcony. Two lounge chairs, a few potted plants, and one sturdy iron railing. She rested her arms on it, looked out over the city. So many people moving around down there, living their own lives, feeling their own heartaches. She spent a few minutes breathing in cold night air, then went back inside.

Evelyn felt tired but restless—what was she supposed to *do* with herself?

Realizing she still had it on, she shrugged off her coat and hung it in the closet—noting the overflowing basket of blankets, right where the maid said they'd be—then carried her suitcase to the bedroom. She put away the few things she'd brought—two or three days' worth of outfits, toiletries, a pile of cash. All her jewelry, too. Because if she'd left it, no doubt Arthur would have pawned it for booze and cigars, or given it to women whose affections were for sale.

She looked into the gilt-framed mirror over the dresser. Was she really so wretched? Even if Arthur loved her money the most, why couldn't he have loved *her*, too, even a little? Her blonde hair hadn't yet faded to ash. Shallow crows' feet barely marked the skin near her eyes. She hadn't let her figure go. At thirty, she was still an attractive woman, or at least put together. Well kept.

But Arthur? Rich food had plumped him up, and years of drink had broken all the blood vessels in his nose and cheeks. For the life of her, she couldn't even recall why, at nineteen, she'd thought he was such a catch. Back then, he'd been handsome. But handsome men with good table manners were as common as cigarette butts on a sidewalk. And that's all she could remember liking about him.

But shallow gets what shallow is.

Not *is*. *Was*, Evelyn reminded herself. *Had been*. She *had been* shallow. Now she was deep—deeply, deeply regretful.

Her stomach twisted, reminding her she hadn't eaten since the day before. Or maybe the day before that? She kicked off her heels and strode across the marble floor to the telephone in the parlor. Before she dialed, her eye caught on the oil portrait above the console table; a man and a woman, their clothing two decades out of date. A small plaque affixed to the frame read "Warren and Harriet Osgood."

She remembered the painting from her honeymoon. The suite was named for them: the Osgood Rooms. The husband's family had been robber barons of some sort—the kind of old money for which origins are hard to trace. People who lend establishments like the Hotel Ethel prestige just by spending time there.

People not so different, really, from Evelyn's family.

She looked closer at Warren Osgood. Like Arthur, he had a sandy moustache and eyes too pretty to trust.

His wife Harriet looked solemn next to him—lovely but stiff in her fitted evening gown. Her dark hair was piled on top of her head to show off high cheekbones and small ears studded with huge pearls. Warren's left hand clutched her waist. His right hand held a pipe.

Something about Harriet's face made Evelyn sad. Like having her likeness captured in oils was a grim challenge to bear.

Evelyn herself was tired of bearing. She'd borne all she could, including too many salads.

She ordered roasted chicken and a slice of cherry pie from the hotel's dining room. When they were delivered—on bone china and a silver tray— she ate them with her hands and licked her messy fingertips.

She woke from her nap after dark, the aftertaste of sugared cherries lingering in her mouth.

She'd fallen asleep on the sofa—but what had woken her? A sound, coming into and merging with her dream world. There it had been some sort of bird—a great black bird, with wings so broad they blocked the sky, and the sound was the beating of those powerful wings against glass, pounding until the glass broke…

Except she was awake, and her brain told her now that the sound had been real. She hurried to flick on the nearest lamp—nothing seemed out of place in the parlor.

She got up, telling herself she must get used to being brave as a single woman, and walked around the penthouse on silent feet to check for trouble room by room.

She found it on the marble floor of the small kitchenette. A blue vase of freesia, lying there smashed, wet petals already wilting. It had been on the counter—she remembered that from when she'd first arrived—and nowhere close to the edge.

Unless she was remembering wrong. It had been a long day. The past weeks, all the planning and stress, all of it had wrung her out...

Then a different noise. The record player in the parlor, starting up a jazz album.

Evelyn left the glass and turned to see the record spinning. Maybe someone had left it plugged in, and the needle fell...

She shut it off, went back to the couch, left the lights on, and sat there, awake, until dawn, when she moved into the bedroom and locked the door. She needed sleep. That was all. Quiet and stillness and sleep.

It was past noon by the time she woke again, and housekeeping had been in. She'd slept through their visit. The pillows on the sofa had been plumped; fresh towels hung in the bathroom. The mess on the floor was gone like it had never been there.

Even the vase and flowers had been replaced. Fluted cobalt glass, sprays of freesia.

The record player's dust cover was in place, all albums stored beneath it in a cabinet.

It made her wonder if she'd dreamed the whole thing. She considered ringing the front desk to ask for the maid—ask if there had ever *been* broken glass and spilled flowers, if the record player was on the fritz—but how would that sound? Better to leave it alone.

She shouldn't draw attention to herself, she knew. Lie low and decide her next move. That was her plan.

But her plan was shot to hell just hours later, when she saw the ghosts and screamed the entire Hotel Ethel awake.

Evelyn had only meant to close her eyes for a moment, but sleep had taken her. On the sofa, again, after finishing a bottle of room-service burgundy.

There had been a tapping. *Tap tap. Tap tap.* And she came back to consciousness, but slowly, like sinking in reverse.

They were in the room with her. She hadn't thought to leave any lights on, and their faces were cast in deep shadows, but Evelyn could see their shapes clearly enough to swear it—that Warren and Harriet Osgood had returned in spectral form.

He sat in the chair across from her, tapping his pipe against the wooden armrest, head bent low, eyes glinting with malice. Harriet stood behind him, hands on his shoulders.

Evelyn would have liked to absorb more details, so she could parse them later. Pay attention to their clothing. Ask something. Tell them to leave her alone. Go away.

She didn't have time to think it through—what she should have done or said, because she closed her eyes and the sound that ripped from her throat and filled the penthouse and leaked beneath the door and reached for the ears of anyone awake or not awake was the pitch of a hot tea kettle and the volume of a July Fourth firework.

Folks came running. First knocking and shouting, then pounding into her parlor, taking her up in a tangle of arms, shaking her, more shouting.

The first face she saw was the maid's. The thoughtful one who'd left her so many extra blankets. How much overtime did they make this girl work? Then she noticed the night manager, and a custodian, and a couple others in silk dressing gowns who were probably hotel guests.

Humiliation and fear jockeyed for first place within her; still, her eyes roved behind her huddle of rescuers, searching for the Osgoods.

Someone dumped brandy down her throat. She sputtered and choked, tried to tell them to please let her go, but one voice was hushing her while another called for a doctor, and these people didn't understand; she didn't *need* a doctor, but she couldn't get a word out now around the sobs that plugged her nose and stole her breath.

She couldn't stop. Her consciousness split in two—one self howled while the other hissed *"Quiet, be quiet, pull yourself together…"*

It seemed like only a second had passed when a different man was standing over her, listening to her heart, saying she'd be fine, just a touch of the nerves, but she wasn't really listening, though she was trying.

The crook of her arm stung; had they given her a hypodermic? Of what?

Then someone was carrying her, laying her down on her bed like a bouquet on a grave, and soon her eyes closed again, and everything was dark and everything was quiet.

She didn't dream. A minute or a year of blackness passed and when she woke she was alone.

No, not alone.

She heard humming outside the bedroom, and shuffled that way, opening the door to see the maid. The same one from last night.

"What are you doing here?" Evelyn said.

Her whole body throbbed. Cotton gauze had replaced her brain.

The woman turned around and, plastering on a smile, said "Feeling alright, then, Mrs. Robins?" and turned away to straighten a bowl of potpourri on the coffee table.

"Fine, I'm fine," Evelyn said, wishing she'd checked in under a fake name.

She needed aspirin. Coffee. Something to settle her queasy stomach. "But I—"

"You saw *him*, didn't you?" the woman said. Her features were now more solemnly arranged, her voice grave. She stepped closer to Evelyn. "It happens sometimes…"

"What?"

"Mr. Osgood. Warren. His *ghost*."

"Ghost—"

"Such a *tragedy*."

Evelyn wanted the woman to shut up and also to keep talking. How did she know? Had Evelyn said something after all, the night before?

"What happened?" she asked, neither confirming nor denying what she'd seen.

"Hard to get an exact story," said the maid, clearly happy to gossip. She had straight teeth and a pretty smile. "The Osgoods' money kept it out of the papers, so rumors are all we got. But what I heard is that Mrs. Osgood died here during a burglary. Came back from a party early and surprised the thief. He stabbed her before she could even scream, and she bled out all over the floor, poor lady."

Evelyn looked at the portrait; she saw Harriet's face differently now. Not grim or stoic, but braced for horrors.

Though of course that was in her head.

"And Mr. Osgood?"

"Heartbroken. Wouldn't leave the suite. Well, after police let him back in. Threw himself off the balcony a week later."

"Oh," said Evelyn. She sat down on the sofa, pulled a pillow into her lap.

"Don't worry," said the maid. "About Mr. Osgood. He's not dangerous—not as far as anyone's told *me*."

She smiled again and left. When the door clicked shut behind her, Evelyn rushed to lock it, then remembered the problem—the ghosts—had been *in* the suite. But at least she could shut out that maid, whose cheerful face and gruesome talk gave her the creeps.

A glance at the gold clock on the side table told her it was past noon. She hated this sleeping all day—so disorienting. And why was she letting herself get so distracted?

Because ghosts were distracting.

Evelyn *felt* like a ghost sometimes. But she wasn't dead, just miserable. A lonely, miserable woman, who needed to see her lawyer about a divorce.

First, she called downstairs for coffee and sweet rolls and aspirin. Then she called Tom Cybart and told him to come as soon as he could.

She didn't like what Tom told her.

Gray haired, tough and leathery, Tom had been trusted by Evelyn's family for more than four decades to keep their secrets, protect their interests, and give them good advice.

And that afternoon, sitting across from Evelyn in the same chair where, the night before, a ghost had sat, if Evelyn could trust her mind—and maybe she couldn't, all Tom had to offer was bad news.

"It's like this, Evie," he said, setting down his coffee cup on the silver tray between them. "There's no prenup. I wanted you to sign one, if you'll remember, but you were in love."

His tone wasn't scolding, it was the same as always—no nonsense, no pretense. Evelyn felt the sting anyway. How could she have been so stupid?

"Therefore," he continued, "to get the divorce granted and retain a sizable portion of your assets, you'd have to prove infidelity beyond a reasonable doubt, or get *him* to admit in court that he consorted with prostitutes and these other women you say he stepped out with. And you and I both know that Arthur, for all his blunders, is more careful than that."

Evelyn put her head in her hands.

"It's only the money." She looked at Tom. "It's only ever been the money."

"Of course it's the money." He sighed, then his eyes turned steely. "Does he know where you are?"

"No," Evelyn said. "Or, at least I don't think so. I sure didn't tell him…" She decided not to mention the ghosts, or whatever she thought she'd seen, nor the half-dozen people who'd stampeded into her suite the night before.

"Good girl," said Tom, relaxing a little. "I've never liked Arthur. Your father hated him. Your mother was too zonked to tell the difference between him and a potted plant."

"Tom—"

"You know I'm right. Plus, you don't pay me to blow smoke. Your family never has. So listen to me now."

Evelyn sat up straight.

"Hang tight. Let me make some inquiries: find out how he took the news of you leaving, see what he's done about the accounts you haven't emptied. If I have to I'll get some photos of him and his fancy women, go through my usual channels—"

"So you'll need money for bribes?"

"Whatever I need to do and whomever I need to pay, I'll add it to the tab. Now, Arthur's never been violent. A sharp wind could blow him over after he's been at the

Scotch bottle. But that doesn't mean you play fast and loose with your safety. Men have killed for a lot less than what's coming to him should you expire young, missy. Keep that in mind—just what your life, what your *death*, is worth to a cad like your husband."

"Shit," said Evelyn. It wasn't that she hadn't considered it, but hearing Tom *say* she could be in danger made it feel real.

"Shit for sure," said Tom. "Like I said, I'm not here to blow smoke. But you know I'll do whatever I can to help you, kid."

She did know that, and offered him another sweet roll, though she knew the doctor had told him to ease up on fatty foods, because of his heart.

He took it, because he never listened to his doctor, and they chewed together in thoughtful silence.

Evelyn was bored out of her mind by eight p.m.

She'd listened to most of the albums the hotel kept in the room, not finding a thing wrong with the record player. Peter, Paul & Mary. Elvis. The Beatles. Bob Dylan. More Beatles. She'd skipped the old jazz record that had played itself the night before: Billie Holiday.

Even though it was all still neat enough, she'd straightened up her clothing and the vanity in her bedroom.

Then, feeling restless and caged, she pulled on a sweater and walked out to the balcony to lean on the railing, trying not to think of what the maid had told her. Trying and failing.

A cherished wife, murdered. Her husband so distraught over her death that he threw himself over the edge, thinking his last thoughts right where Evelyn was standing.

She looked down. A sidewalk, an awning, a street. She imagined what it would be like, the feeling of falling, the wind in her ears. The unforgiving pavement getting closer and closer.

She shivered.

Her knuckles were white where her numb hands gripped the railing. She pried herself away, backing into the suite, shutting the sliding glass door and locking it.

Thinking like that wouldn't help. It was too depressing. Or maybe too tempting.

She wandered into the kitchenette, rubbing her arms to warm up. The clock read ten to nine. How long had she been outside? It felt like minutes.

But time didn't matter when you had nothing to do and nowhere to go.

Might as well go to bed, she figured. Her head still hurt, anyway. Whatever the hotel's rented doctor had shot her up with, it left her with a hangover aspirin and coffee couldn't cure.

Fumbling in the dark room, she found the light switch and flipped it up. But what she saw didn't make sense.

The closet doors, gaping wide. Her clothing pulled from the hangers, thrown haphazardly into her open suitcase, mixed with her grandmother's pearls, her mother's diamonds.

She'd left her suitcase, zipped closed and empty, on the closet's high shelf. Her clothes had been hung up neatly, arranged blouses to sweaters to skirts.

She'd definitely shut the doors.

Her daywear jewelry had been lined up on the vanity: watch and small hoop earrings. Her heirloom jewelry—pearls and diamonds, sapphires and onyx—folded in silk handkerchiefs and set aside.

None of it made sense. She'd barely left the suite. The balcony opened off the parlor. Anyone coming in would have to cross the parlor to go into the bedroom. She'd have seen them, even out of the corner of her eye. But she'd seen nothing, heard nothing—

She'd heard nothing. But she was hearing something now. The record player starting up, volume low. Not Billie Holiday, this time. Some big band orchestra, a song she didn't recognize.

She crept out to look at the record player—dust cover off, record spinning. Then she ran to the suite's front door to check that it was locked— it was, and she knew for sure she'd locked it because Tom had yelled "Lock it!" through the door after she'd walked him out. He'd waited to hear the click before calling goodbye.

What to do? She couldn't call down to the front desk. They'd send Doctor Needle again, or worse, haul her to a hospital she'd never get to leave. Not if she told the truth.

She could pack her things and check out—find another hotel—but that would mean going back in that bedroom, which was out of the question.

She called Tom, dialing with shaking fingers.

He answered.

"Can you come?" she said, hearing her voice crack. "Please come. Please hurry."

"On my way," he said, and she hung up and waited for him with her back to the door, eyes roving around the suite, terrified that every closed drawer would open, every glass ornament smash, every lightbulb pop and fizzle.

The big band sound came through the speakers and got louder, like someone turned the volume up.

By the time Tom arrived thirty minutes later, panting and pulling at his necktie, Evelyn had stopped shivering—her breathing was almost normal, though her heart still pounded too hard, like it wanted to break out of her chest.

Tom's face was red verging on purple.

"Your heart!" was the first thing she said, forgetting for a moment why she'd called him.

"I'm fine!" he told her, his voice gruff enough to prove he was. "I've got my pills anyway. Now what's going on?" He marched to the record player and shut it off.

Evelyn was grateful—she'd been too afraid to touch it.

"Okay, first, I didn't put on that record. But look in there," she said. "It's in there."

He raised one eyebrow but didn't argue.

She followed him across the room, his presence like a torch in a forest.

He stepped through the doorway and gave a low whistle, then turned back to her and, with a hand at her elbow, guided her to sit down on the sofa.

"Am I to take it," he asked slowly, "that you are not the one who cast your personal items into such disarray?"

"Correct," she said, folding her hands in her lap.

"And when this happened, you were…"

She told him about the balcony. That she'd only stepped out for a moment, then lost track of time.

"And you didn't call hotel security?" he said.

"And say *what*?" Evelyn said, sounding sharper than she intended. "That my room is messy? Nothing was taken, or at least I don't think so. What kind of thief makes a mess but leaves diamonds on the floor? And the door was still bolted. Like I said."

"Yes…" Tom said. "I suppose that does sound wackadoo."

He pulled on his lower lip and stared at the carpet. After a moment, he asked, "Do you sleepwalk?"

"Sleepwalk?" Evelyn repeated, then understood what he was insinuating. "You think *I* did this? I wasn't a*sleep*, Tom!"

"Are you sure?" he asked. "Evie, I'm not blaming you. I'm just asking. Are you sure you didn't nod off? You told me you've been keeping odd hours."

His thick gray eyebrows drew together—she knew that look. He was worried.

"Why would I trash my own room?" Evelyn said, quieter. "Asleep or awake?"

"I don't know," Tom said. "But your things in there—it looks like you were packing in a hurry. Evelyn… You don't want to go *back* to that louse, do you? You aren't thinking of—"

"No!" Evelyn said. Then, "I mean *no*, I do not. Well, I *do* want to go home, but not until he's moved out."

"That's reasonable," Tom said. "Okay. Good. Just checking."

They sat in silence. She was about to offer to call down for late-night room service when he spoke up again.

"Evie, I was going to call you tomorrow, but… I'm glad I'm getting a chance to talk to you tonight. While we're on the topic of Arthur…"

"What?" She didn't like his tone. The worry was back.

"No one has seen Arthur since Monday morning."

"Monday morning?"

"Yes."

"But that's the day I left. I mean where could he…"

"I drove to the house after I left here this afternoon. I was gonna give him some line about needing to talk to you about insurance, you know? Just to see what he'd say, what he might give up. But he wasn't there. The place was dark."

"Well in the afternoon I'm sure he was at—"

"I went to his club. Of course I looked there next, talked to some of his drinking buddies. They haven't seen him. I don't like it, Evie."

She twisted her fingers in her lap. Did Arthur take off on some vacation, realizing he was free of her? Was he on a bender, high as a cloud in the sweaty arms of one of his side women? She thought of what Warren Osgood did when he lost *his* wife—but no. Arthur didn't love her. He wouldn't end his life because she left him.

"You should come stay with me," Tom said. "But it's late. So for tonight, I'll doss down on your sofa. I'm not leaving you alone. Shut the closet doors in there and ignore the mess; you're safe with me here."

Evelyn didn't argue. Exhaustion weighed on her like a heavy cloak.

"Thank you," she said. "I'll get you some blankets."

Glad for the stack the maid left her with, Evelyn went to the coat closet and pulled out three blankets, handing them to Tom.

"I'm off to bed then," she said, trying to stifle a yawn. "Thanks again, Tom."

"Sure thing, kid," he told her, then draped his tie and suit jacket across the chair—Warren's chair, as Evelyn thought of it now.

She picked up her jewelry and rewrapped it, set some stray cosmetics back on the vanity, and closed the closet doors. Then she turned off the bedroom's overhead light but left a small porcelain lamp burning on the nightstand. Between its weak glow and Tom's snoring, she felt safe enough to close her eyes and sleep.

Until sometime later, when cold hands on her bare shoulders shook her awake.

As she came to, one of those cold hands moved to cover her mouth, and following some instinct, Evelyn didn't scream, even when her eyes adjusted to the dim light and she saw the person attached to the hand touching her face was indeed Harriet Osgood, that she wore a beautiful yellow gown covered in a dark stain at the midsection, and that she was slightly transparent.

Evelyn's world halted while she took all this in. Then it restarted, and her heart pounded and her stomach dropped and she inhaled through her nose. She didn't have to decide what to do next—she'd likely have fainted back to unconsciousness—because Harriet put a finger to her lips and gestured toward the door with her head.

The sound was faint, but Evelyn heard it—a struggle, a thump, muffled cries.

A dilemma. Stay put, lose her mind over the ghost in her room; or see what was happening in the parlor, though she already knew it was something bad and that it was happening to the last person in the world who cared about her.

She could process her latest paranormal encounter later. Time was of the essence.

Harriet pointed to the lamp. Evelyn didn't understand. Did light hurt ghosts? Was that why she'd only seen the Osgoods the second night, in the pitch-dark dead hours of the early morning?

"Shut it off?" she whispered.

Harriet rolled her eyes; she made a bashing motion with both hands.

The lamp was to be a weapon, then.

Evelyn nodded, unplugged the lamp, and held it like a club, then tiptoed to the bedroom door and eased it open. Harriet moved to get behind her.

Weak moonlight filtered into the suite through the balcony doors, allowing Evelyn to see the tableau well enough: Tom on the sofa, a man standing over him, pressing a pillow against his face.

A man with a sandy moustache in an old-fashioned suit.

Warren Osgood.

Evelyn heaved the lamp—threw it overhand, with as much force as her two arms could muster, adding a grunt-scream-howl to help it along.

The lamp connected, glancing off Warren's head and rolling to the carpet. Evelyn felt Harriet's hand squeeze her shoulder and turned in time to see the woman smile and fade out. Evelyn looked back and Warren was gone, too. She rushed to Tom, flinging the pillow off his face and putting an ear to his chest.

He wasn't dead. *Thank God*, he wasn't dead.

But he also wouldn't wake up, though she shook him and called his name: "*Tom!* Tom, it's me! Please! *Please* wake up!"

It took a moment for her brain to catch up to her panic and tell her what to do. Turning on her heel, she dashed across the room to the phone and dialed the front desk.

"Please help. Call a doctor. Nineteenth floor, Osgood Rooms. Please hurry. My friend's barely breathing." She hung up without waiting for an answer and ran to the suite's front door, unbolting it and flinging it open.

Moments later, the night manager was there, along with someone from security and that damned maid, again. Evelyn barely spared them a glance; her focus was on Tom. They made her get away from him, though, told her to give them room.

She found herself clutched and drawn away by the maid, pulled into the kitchenette. She called out for the third or fourth time, "He has a heart condition!"

"Shh," the maid hushed her. "Shh now. They heard you."

"You," Evelyn said.

"Calm down, Mrs. Robins," the woman said, smiling that infuriating smile. The one that said "Go to hell" louder than words could. "Let these nice men help your boyfriend."

"Boyfriend!" Evelyn said, indignant. "He's not my boyfriend!"

"Whatever you say," said the maid, not letting that smile drop for a second.

As the adrenaline faded from her system, Evelyn felt nauseous. She pulled her arm away from the maid and took a seat at the kitchenette's counter.

"Can I get you anything?" asked the maid. "Water? The doctor? Maybe he can give you another sedative—"

"I'm fine," said Evelyn, too loud and too angry. She wasn't some hallucinating madwoman who needed sedation, though perhaps that's how she seemed to the staff of the Hotel Ethel and the doctor they kept on call. *He* arrived shortly after the paramedics, and in what felt like just minutes, they had Tom loaded onto a stretcher and were filtering out of the suite.

All but the night manager and the ever-present maid.

"Now, Mrs. Robins," he started, and again Evelyn regretted booking under her real name. "If you could just explain what happened here, in case the hospital calls."

"Well, I was—" She realized then that she only wore a thin nightgown, and ran to her bedroom to get a robe, saying "Just a moment" over her shoulder.

In her bedroom, she looked at herself in the vanity's mirror. She was a mess. Wild hair. Smudged mascara.

Important that she not contribute further to whatever reputation she was building with these people. So she put on her robe and fastened it, ran a comb through her hair, and wiped away the stray makeup with a tissue. When she walked back out to the parlor, closing the bedroom door behind her, she felt more in control.

"There," she said, matching her smile to the maid's. "Where were we? Of course..."

She looked at the maid. "No need for you to stay, dear. You must have work to do! You're such a busy little bee. I wouldn't want to keep you from what the hotel pays you to do." At this she dropped her smile and gave the manager a pointed look.

"Yes, Ruby," he said. "I can manage perfectly well here."

So Ruby was her name. Ruby the Solicitous. Ruby the Always Here. Ruby the Ghost Story Teller.

Ruby walked out, smiling smiling smiling, swinging her shapely hips and shutting the suite's door behind her.

"I'm afraid there's not much to tell," Evelyn said to the manager. "I woke when I heard Tom struggling to breathe. He's got problems with his heart, as I said, so I was concerned. By the time I got to him, he wasn't responsive, so I called you. You know the rest; you were here." She smiled and spread her hands as if to say "That's all."

"So nothing out of the ordinary, like last night?" the manager asked. His little gold pin read "Mr. Hastings."

"Oh," said Evelyn, and she gave a little laugh like the night before was just so silly. "Nightmares, nothing to worry about. I have them sometimes. I'm so sorry for disturbing your staff and your other guests, Mr. Hastings." She beamed at him, as if she were grateful that strangers had barged into her suite and drugged her.

He looked pleased with himself. A dog who'd gotten a pat on the head.

"That's good to hear," he said. "Good to hear. Well then. They took your friend—your friend, you said he was? To City General."

"Oh—did I say friend? He's my uncle, actually," said Evelyn. "Just in town for a few days."

"Uncle" was boring. Not worthy of gossip, like the kind the maid was probably already spreading around about a May-December romance.

"I see," said Mr. Hastings. "Yes, well, the medical personnel took your uncle to City General, and you can visit him tomorrow. Dr. Ashley said your uncle was already coming around before they left, but of course they must be careful, and he told me to tell you visiting hours are ten to noon."

"Thank you," said Evelyn. "It's wonderful to hear they don't think it's serious. I'll be sure to bring him some flowers during visiting hours."

She walked to the door and opened it.

There was nothing for Hastings to do but say goodbye and leave, pulling his blazer straight and smoothing the hair on his half-bald head.

As soon as he was gone, Evelyn untied the sash of her robe so she could breathe easier.

Then her legs gave out and she collapsed onto the carpet, staring dumbly but seeing nothing, too shocked to cry.

Would Tom be okay? Why had Harriet helped her? Why had Warren attacked Tom? The first time she'd seen the Osgoods, they'd done nothing, barely moving but for Warren tapping his pipe on the armrest. Harriet had seemed cozy enough with him, then.

Something tickled at her subconscious. Something about Harriet.

She closed her eyes. They'd only been silhouettes, but when Evelyn woke to find the Osgoods in the parlor the night before, Harriet had been perfectly put together. Hair piled on the top of her head, dark gown flattering her figure. The Osgoods both looked like they did in their portrait.

But the Harriet Evelyn had seen tonight didn't have perfect hair. It had been half-loose, messy. And her gown was pale, not dark. That's why Evelyn could so clearly make out the blood stain.

And there in her bedroom, Harriet had been a bit transparent. The figures in the parlor had seemed solid, as did Warren while he attacked Tom...

She opened her eyes, her gaze landing on the lamp, which had lost its shade and rolled or been kicked under one of the chairs. Evelyn crawled over to pull it out.

A smear of blood marked the porcelain base, which was now cracked. Blood.

Ghosts don't bleed fresh blood.

Ghosts don't bleed and Warren had been solid enough that the lamp hit him instead of flying *through* him.

She had an idea. Her voice shook but she did it anyway, clasping her hands together like she could contain her fear, because only courage would do, now.

"Harriet," she said. "Harriet, please come back."

For a moment, nothing happened.

"Harriet, thank you for saving Tom. Thank you for waking me. But I— I need your help again. Please. Just one more question. Well, maybe two."

A swirling mist, lighter than fog, appeared before her. It coalesced into a human form, and there stood Harriet, an expectant look on her face.

Evelyn had to swallow so she wouldn't choke on her own saliva. She took two deep breaths, and didn't speak again until she could trust herself not to scream.

Harriet dipped her head, prompting Evelyn.

"That—that wasn't your husband, was it?" Evelyn asked. Her voice steadied. "Hurting Tom, tonight."

Harriet shook her head.

A thought occurred to Evelyn. "You can't speak, can you?"

Harriet's mouth moved, but no sound came out. Whatever she said was lost—Evelyn couldn't read transparent lips.

"Okay," Evelyn said. "I think I understand. You can speak but I can't hear you, is that right?"

Harriet nodded quickly, like a teacher praising a child who was finally catching on.

And realization bred realization.

"Harriet," she said. "Is Warren even *here*? Your husband? I mean, is he a g—, excuse me, is he a *spirit* here, like you are?" She worried the word "ghost" might be offensive. "Spirit" sounded more dignified.

Harriet shook her head and pointed downward, smirking.

"Oh!" said Evelyn, remembering what Ruby had told her. "Yes, he, um, he went over the balcony's railing and… and he um, he landed on the, on the ground."

Harriet laughed—or that's what Evelyn thought it was, laughter—and shook her head. She crouched lower, pointing down again, exaggerating the motion. Then she straightened up and put her hands by her head, crooking her pointer fingers, giving herself devil horns.

Devil horns.

Hell.

"Warren's in *hell*?!" said Evelyn. "Is that—is *that* what you're saying?"

Harriet nodded even more enthusiastically this time, and smiled bigger. Then her face changed and she looked sad. She pointed at her bloody midsection, which Evelyn had been trying not to look at, for the sake of manners and also the sake of not passing out.

Then Harriet glided over to the oil portrait on the wall, tapped the image of her husband, then pointed again at her stab wounds.

"*He* did that," Evelyn whispered. It wasn't a question.

Harried nodded more slowly this time, holding eye contact. Her eyes were a rich brown color.

"I'm really sorry," said Evelyn. "That's so awful." She didn't know what else to say.

Harriet shrugged, then came back to Evelyn, who hurt for her. How would it feel to have your murderer lauded as some heartbroken lover? To be stuck here, seeing that same portrait, knowing it was a lie?

Evelyn wondered, then, if Warren had actually killed himself. If the story of Harriet's death had been a lie, maybe his was, too? And why had he killed her? Money? An affair? Something else? But it felt rude to ask. Prying, more than she had already pried.

Plus, she had her own problems—living, breathing, *bleeding* problems.

Harriet flickered, like an old lightbulb. Evelyn knew she had to be quick—that for whatever ghostly reason, Harriet's time there with her was running out, at least for the moment.

"Do you know who attacked Tom? Who was here last night?"

Harriet nodded. Then she leaned forward and tapped the bare ring finger on Evelyn's left hand. The spirit raised her eyebrows.

"Yeah," Evelyn said. "I kinda thought so."

Harriet gave Evelyn that sad smile again, and winked out.

The sky got lighter and the suite brightened by degrees, gray to sunny yellow.

Evelyn would have thought that finding out her husband was torturing her by pretending to be a ghost would feel worse than it did. More shocking, more hurtful.

But she only felt hollow, until that hollow space was filled by anger.

She walked out onto the balcony, letting the freezing air cool her burning cheeks.

That son-of-a-bitch. That was why he wasn't at home when Tom had gone to talk to him. He'd been *here*, at the Hotel Ethel, dressing up in an old suit to scare her.

Questions remained. How was he getting in? And who had been posing with him the night before? And what was his endgame? What was this elaborate charade *for*?

She didn't know. But she knew someone who would have some pretty good guesses, if he was awake.

Leaving her frigid perch behind, Evelyn walked back into the suite to get dressed. Then she ordered coffee and sweet rolls and sat down to watch the clock, willing it to go faster.

Evelyn got back to her suite after a visit to City General and lunch at Giardino Della Vite. She was unsurprised to see Ruby there, running a vacuum.

The maid looked up, and Evelyn noted how she assumed that horrible smile—it wasn't instantaneous this time. Maybe the effort was getting to her.

"I'm all set for now, Ruby," said Evelyn in her sweetest voice. "If I need anything else I'll call down. Thanks so much."

She repeated her move of the night before—went back to the door, opened it wide, then looked at Ruby with raised eyebrows.

Without saying a word, Ruby left. Evelyn stayed at the door long enough to watch her push her vacuum cleaner into the elevator and disappear.

Evelyn had some investigating to do.

Tom had been awake and grouchy when she got to the hospital earlier. His bad mood was a good sign, and over coffee he shouldn't have had, she told him about everything.

At first, he didn't believe her. Then, he was angry with her. But after he'd called her a few things: "daft," "idiotic," "reckless," they'd put their heads together and come up with a plan—well, two plans. Tom hated that he was stuck in the hospital, but Evelyn assured him she'd be fine, and that she would call him later.

Plus, he was helping enough.

Back in her suite, she started her search. The lamp was gone, of course, whisked away, no doubt, by Ruby.

She poked her head into the bedroom. The bed had been made, and a new lamp sat on the nightstand.

Then she went directly to where she figured she'd hit paydirt. The front hall coat closet. All those blankets that Ruby had so thoughtfully piled in a basket on the floor. Evelyn kicked them out of the way and then, using her fist like a hammer, she pounded on the wall until she found the loose panel.

She pried at it and looked through the gap: a janitor's closet.

A janitor's closet, which Ruby the maid had access to.

Ruby the maid, who was surely the one masquerading as Harriet the other night.

Evelyn wasn't sure if Arthur's goal was to have her committed or frame her for murder—would he have done that, if Tom had died? Or was he going to trick her into offing herself—like, drive her crazy for real? Was that why Ruby had told her about Warren Osgood's alleged suicide? Was she planting the suggestion?

Perhaps any of the above—whichever came first. Then she'd be out of the way—in an institution, in prison, in a cemetery—no divorce necessary, and Arthur would be left with all her family's money.

What did he promise Ruby for helping him? Was she just in it for the payout, or were they really in love?

Did she *care*?

Not about that last part.

She went to the phone and called downstairs. Asked for housekeeping.

Midnight. Evelyn sat up, waiting. She'd been silent for hours, immobile on the sofa, straining her ears. Folded handkerchiefs lay at her side. Nervous sweat pooled in her armpits and at her lower back, soaking her blouse.

Every light in the penthouse was off. She'd drawn the curtains across the balcony door to block the moonlight. Opening her eyes was the same as having them closed; it was that dark.

A soft scraping noise came first, followed by a pop. The wall panels being pushed out. Then the swish of the basket of blankets as it was pushed out of the way.

Their footsteps made no sound at all.

Evelyn held her breath as they arranged themselves—"Warren" sitting in the club chair, "Harriet" behind him. Then he started up the tapping—tap tap. Tap tap.

Evelyn clicked on the lamp next to her.

Arthur jumped. Dropped his pipe. Then, remembering his character, lowered his head to glare at her from beneath his brows. She saw the bulge of a small bandage at his hairline.

"Your pancake makeup is showing, Arthur," Evelyn said, trying to sound breezy. "Give it up. And that old suit… It's tight across the tummy, isn't it? Too big in the shoulders…"

Arthur looked stunned. Ruby just smiled, like usual, but Evelyn saw it differently now. Saw *Ruby* differently, too.

"Arthur," Evelyn said. "This is what's going to happen. You will grant me a divorce with no objections or complications. I'll give you enough money to live off for three months—though it won't last that long if you drink as much as you do now. You will not contact me afterward. You will fade away, and you will stay gone."

"Oh yeah? Why would I do that?" Arthur said, dropping his spectral persona. "You've got nothing on me! If you tell anyone about this, they'll think you went around the bend! I'd still get what I wanted!" He laughed, arrogant as ever. Laughing at *her*.

Not for long.

"You're right," she said. "You're *so* right, Arthur. I can't tell anyone about this, without evidence. And you were *so* careful and *so* smart that I don't have a thing on you. But Ruby, here? Ruby does."

Arthur whirled around, looking at Ruby like she'd burned him. Now she laughed—at *him*, and Evelyn liked her just a bit more.

Then the former maid—though she didn't look like one: velvet gown, satin slippers, beaded purse—pulled the pins out of her hair and let it fall to her shoulders. She stepped around Arthur's chair and crossed the room to sit next to Evelyn.

"No offense, Arthur," Ruby said. "I just got a better offer."

Arthur's cheeks turned so red that Evelyn could see the color beneath his pale makeup.

"No!" he sputtered. "This was as much your plan as it was mine. We came up with it *together*! If I go down for this, so do you!"

"Ooh. Not quite," Ruby said. She shook her head. "The love letters you wrote me? The notes you left here at the hotel, telling me when and where to meet? Even the receipts from the secondhand clothes shop and the drugstore where we got that makeup… Yeah. I sold them all to wifey, here."

"*Sold* them? Sold them! For *what*?! She can't come close to paying you what you'll get if you stick by me! If you just see this through with me, Ruby baby, it'll just be you and me, living high on the hog! Just—"

"No thanks," Ruby said. "I'll take my independence instead."

She held out her hands. Evelyn picked up the stack of silk handkerchiefs and handed them all over. Her grandmother's pearls, her mother's diamonds, Great Aunt Ida's sapphire bracelet, even her own wedding set—all well spent.

"Pleasure doing business with you," said Ruby. She stuffed the jewels into her purse. "I hate to run, but I've got a train to catch." She stood. "And Evelyn?"

"Yes?"

"For what it's worth, it wasn't personal. I've been a maid since I was sixteen, picking up every shift I could. It was never enough. I was just over it. I met Arthur, and, well… It was my chance to get away from all this."

Evelyn stood.

"I don't forgive you," she said. "You two would have had me committed. Women don't come out of those places, Ruby. They rot. But… I don't know what it's like to have to work the way you did. Maybe I would have done anything to change my circumstances, too."

"Thank you," Ruby said.

"Likewise."

They shook hands, and with one last smirk at Arthur, Ruby left.

"So that's it, then?" said Arthur after a moment. "A humdrum divorce and a pauper's life? That's what I've got to look forward to now?"

"Don't pout," Evelyn said. "And let me get you a towel. Take that ridiculous makeup off. You look more like a clown than a ghost."

"Evie," he called after her as she walked into the kitchenette. "Evie, I want you to know. I never loved Ruby. You're the only woman I ever loved. All of that? It was madness."

He chuckled, as if that would sell the lie. "I—I don't know what I was thinking. I wouldn't have really done it. What do you say? Do you think we could give it another shot? You and me. Just like old times."

"Hmm," she said, smiling. "Now that *is* tempting. Let's have a drink while I think about it."

"Really?" he said. He wiped his face with the wet kitchen towel she'd brought him while she poured them measures of his favorite brand of Scotch. His glass was filled to the top. "That's great, baby! I knew you'd understand. These things just happen in a marriage. We've got to get through them, that's all."

She clenched her teeth together. Counted to ten. Then said, "Let's get some fresh air, shall we?"

She took her glass and walked to the balcony doors, drawing back the curtains and sliding the door open. She stepped out. He followed.

She took a sip of her drink and looked out at the nightlights of the city. The cold air felt good on her skin.

"Beautiful, isn't it?" she asked, watching her breath fog the air in front of her.

"Sure," he said, then drained his glass in three gulps and set it on the little table, fumbling a bit in the dark. "But not as beautiful as you."

The Scotch was already having an effect on him. She wondered how much of his liver was dead. She ignored his cheap compliment.

"So," she said. "Arthur. Husband of mine. You had a plan, and Ruby was your accomplice."

"Let's not talk about it, anymore, okay, honey? Let's just put it behind us and—"

"You had a plan," she said louder, her tone sharper. "Ruby was your accomplice. But I have a plan, too. And I have an accomplice."

She laughed, first quietly, then louder. "Actually, *three* accomplices." She sat in one of the patio chairs.

He laughed too, and she could tell he thought she was joking.

"Oh yeah?" he said in a playful voice, like this was banter. Like they were flirting. He moved to stand across from her, back to the railing. "And who are they?"

"Well, you know Ruby, of course. And she helped me to understand." She took another sip of whisky. "Women who are for sale never *want* to be for sale. They just want to get to a place where they no longer have to sell themselves."

She stopped smiling. He didn't. "You said *three*."

He reached for her glass. She handed it to him and he sunk what was left.

"Yes. Well, secondly, there's Tom Cybart. The man you've had dinner with, played golf with. The man you tried to smother because you 'panicked.'" She made quotation marks in the air with her fingers. "Ruby told me—how you went off script. Didn't stick to the plan. Naughty, naughty."

His jolly face fell. Turned angry. "I didn't know he was gonna *be* there!" Arthur said, as if he had been cheated out of something. "I *did* panic, okay?"

"Well, no. Not okay. He's gonna be fine, by the way. Actually, I need to phone him shortly..." She glanced at the open doorway, then grinned at Arthur. "And here's my third accomplice! A new friend."

Arthur looked up, froze. Dropped the glass he was holding and didn't seem to notice when it smashed at his feet.

In front of him Harriet Osgood materialized: glowing vapor taking shape. Her wide smile matched Evelyn's, but her eyes held something terrifying.

"Arthur Robins, meet Harriet Osgood. Harriet, Arthur."

Harriet rushed forward. Arthur was so stunned he didn't even scream until he was halfway to the pavement. Side by side, the two women looked over the railing. If he made any noise when he hit, the wind stole it away.

She had to be put through to his room.

"Tom?" she said. "It's done. I've already called the front desk—I didn't want them to see I'd called you first. But they'll be here any minute."

"Good girl," he said quietly, then louder, for the benefit of whomever was in the room with him: "Such a shame that when I saw him the other day I didn't take his threat of suicide seriously. He was so busted up that you'd left him. Said he was going to find you and make you take him back. I guess it didn't go his way."

"No," said Evelyn. "No, it did not go his way."

She hung up, looked at Harriet next to her.

"Thank you," she said. "Arthur never would have given me a divorce. But I think you know all about that."

The transparent woman looked at the portrait of herself and her murderous husband. Nodded.

"And now I'm free, or will be soon. Ruby too. It was hard not to tell her the whole plan—I think she would have approved."

Harriet laughed.

"But that's only two out of three. I wish we could somehow save you, too."

Harriet shrugged. Her sadness returned. How could Evelyn help a ghost?

She had an idea.

"I could stay a little longer. Keep you company? Well, after the police let me back in. Maybe come for visits now and then? Hang out?"

Harriet nodded enthusiastically and pointed to the record player.

"Yes, we can listen to music," Evelyn said. She was getting good at reading Harriet, understanding her gestures. And something else. "It was you, wasn't it? Playing the records? Not them."

Harriet smiled.

"Did you smash that vase?"

More nodding.

"And throw my stuff around?"

Harriet rolled her eyes and pantomimed grabbing things and throwing them down.

"You were packing my suitcase. You were telling me to leave. And the vase—you were trying to scare me, but not to be mean."

Harriet smiled.

"Thank you," she said again. "When I come back, I'll bring more records."

There was a frantic knocking.

"Mrs. Robins! Mrs. Robins!" It was Hastings.

"Showtime," Evelyn whispered.

Harriet faded.

As she hurried to answer the door, Evelyn set her face into something like resigned sorrow and wiped at her eyes, smearing her makeup.

The March winds weren't as cold as January's had been.

On the balcony of the Osgood Rooms on the nineteenth floor of the Hotel Ethel, Evelyn Robins drained her wine glass. The Beach Boys' "Don't Back Down" streamed through the open door behind her, with the record player's volume turned as high as it could go.

She danced.

Harriet Osgood danced beside her.

24/7 Concierge

Hello again!

Wasn't that fun? Spirits and spells—what a hoot! And cranky bartenders… oof. Am I right?

Yes, the folks on the top floors are something else. Especially that Mrs. Osgood. Thinks quite highly of herself, I'm afraid, with her whole "helping the damsel in distress" schtick. Personally, I don't buy it. I think she's just upset she wasn't part of the original Circle, and so she does her best to ingratiate herself with the guests so they'll like her better.

The Circle? Oh. Hmm. Best not to talk about that. Pretend I never said it.

Anyway, moving on.

Let's visit the Premium Guest Suites, shall we?

You know what "Premium" means, don't you?

Come closer, let me whisper it to you. It means *rich enough to think they're too good to mingle with the common folk down below*.

Yeah. You get a lot of that around here. Excuse me while I roll my eyes.

Anyway, there's some interesting characters on these floors.

That weird girl on Seventeen certainly raises some suspicions—she's got a paper-thin alibi, if you ask me. For what crime? Oh, I don't know. Any of them. Ha!

Beth and Todd are probably fighting again down on Fourteen. Between you and me, I think they deserve each other.

You can stop off on Thirteen if you want. That's Housekeeping, so there's not much glamour to be found there. If you do decide to poke around, ignore the claustrophobia. I promise, it's for your own good.

But first, stop by Eighteen for a visit with Sid—I mean, Mr. cHang. Goodness, the names these young kids come up with these days. He'll sing you a tune if you like. See if that old Dixieland jazz is still creeping into his voice and let me know, will you?

Be careful on Sixteen… and even more careful on Fifteen. Calvin's a pushover, but Agnes and Alma are not to be trifled with.

Agnes. Sigh…

Oh, don't mind me. Just… old wounds, you know? It was good while it lasted, though, I must say.

Go on now, don't let my melancholy stop you from having a good time.

Me? No, no. I'll just hang around here a little longer and meet back up with you in a bit.

Yes, go on. Just to the elevator there. Old Boris, the attendant, will take care of you, get you where you need to go.

Boris? Oh! Ha! I don't know his real name. I don't think anyone does, actually. But when you see him, you'll understand.

Now go on.

Go.

18th Floor – Premium Suites
2022

Behind the Music:
Hank "cHang" Moore's
2023 Grammy-Winning Ragtime Album
Craig Brownlie

Unscrewing the top of the hand lotion, Parker Compinche sniffed orange and lavender with a hint of fennel. She set it on the furthest corner of the bathroom counter along with the other complimentary soaps and salves.

She extracted selections from a baggie of acceptable mini bottles collected thus far on tour and arrayed them in order. She opened two favorites and inhaled—so much better than the bowels of urban arenas with their scent of game-worn jock straps, unflushed toilets, and wall-crack mildew.

Parker could reach out her arms and touch opposite walls. But no one from the tour could barge in on her tonight. She had forty-seven messages on her phone since leaving the arena, but she only had to respond to three of them and she could relax.

A quick test confirmed the shower produced hot water without scalding.

Afterward, she sat on the bed and flipped through the channels on the television. Lingering over the stupidity of late night cable, Parker sipped a bottle of water.

Traveling for business might not be so bad if your nights could be spent with a little privacy and time to decompress. Maybe a quick call home to reassure your spouse and children—when you remember their existence— before you slip away to peaceful oblivion.

Parker had no one to call. With luck, the only person whose ringtone she could not silence would leave her alone.

Almost seven hours earlier, Parker spoke into her cell. "Is this the Hotel Ethel? I'd like to make a reservation for tonight, the penthouse if possible."

She had found the most private closet in the quietest corner within the bowels of Chase Center.

"You don't? You have room on the floor below?"

A premium guest suite might evade the paparazzi and the fanatics even better than the obviousness of the top floor.

"We'll take it. And I need a room on a lower floor, preferably quiet and not terribly close to the other room. Great. You can put them both under the name Sidney Jolson."

Parker wondered where cHang came up with his aliases. Of course, he had adopted a professional name which no two people ever pronounced the same.

"Confirming we will be checking in late and checking out late tomorrow morning. Thank you."

Parker glanced at the countdown on the mobile screen: an hour until Hank went on stage. Many of the eighteen thousand rabid ticket holders filing into the arena over her head did not know cHang had a pedestrian name once upon a time.

Parker corrected herself. A disturbing number of them carried a frightening amount of knowledge about the life of cHang and his sustained dominance of the American music scene over the last decade and a half.

She had time to breathe for one minute.

Parker held the title of tour manager, but the tour had become a well-oiled machine. After three months back on the road once COVID had backed the hell off, the crew, the musicians, and the venues all had found their groove. Nowadays, when things ran smoothly, Parker served as personal assistant to the man, the myth, the legend, cHang.

And now he wanted a break from a bed which rolled and a hiatus from seeing his support band at breakfast and a pause from the ever-present groupies who knew most of his aliases.

The door of the supply closet flew open.

Maurice grunted.

"You found me," said Parker, looking at the head of tour security.

Maurice tugged a young woman into view and shoved her forward. "I found this one backstage again. She made it further than Knoxville, but not as far as Orlando."

"Hello, cLover," greeted Parker. "Do you enjoy buying a ticket and then not seeing the show?"

"Why do you hate me?"

cLover had dyed her hair bright orange and tinted her skin a light shade of blue, mimicking cHang's appearance on the cover of his David Bowie tribute album.

"Why does he hate me?" The young woman pointed a thumb at Maurice.

"Hate's a pretty strong word," said Maurice. "You're not so important to me."

"See?" pleaded cLover.

"What do you want? He's not going to sleep with you," said Parker.

"Don't be disgusting." cLover considered her audience. "I bet you never saw, neither one of you. He picked me to come up on stage. We danced together. He nuzzled my neck. He whispered in my ear."

"I'm always here, cLover. And he's danced with a million girls."

"It definitely happened," added Maurice.

"What did he say?" asked Parker.

"He called me the perfect young American."

Parker studied the young woman and then looked at Maurice, who awaited direction.

"There's the boss lady," came a famous, soft voice from the hallway. "Did you reach the Ethel?" cHang could hold the attention of a stadium with a whisper. "Hey, Cynthia," said the diminutive pop star as he saw cLover for the first time.

Parker's jaw muscles tensed. "Your Aunt Ethel… is doing fine after her… surgery."

For the hour or so before going on stage, cHang tended to move in place. On this subterranean concrete floor, his platform shoes produced rhythmic dense thuds.

"Aunt Ethel," he spoke to the tattoo of his steps, "is all set." His sudden smile raised the lumens in the room. "Excellent." He considered the other three as though taking their temperatures. "As you were in your unique confab." He backed out of the room and disappeared from view.

Silence filled the gap he left until cLover ruined the respite. "He smells like lavender and kiwi tonight. Isn't it wonderful?"

Parker turned on the fan. "I can put you in a chair in the wings, obstructed view. You remain in the chair until thirty minutes after cHang has left the building."

"Unlimited bathroom breaks, popcorn, water, and Pepsi. Plus tickets to Wednesday's show in Portland."

"Unlimited bathroom breaks in the city jail starting when Maurice hands you over." Parker poised her finger over her cellphone.

"Water and bathroom breaks?" pleaded cLover.

cHang did the briefest of walkthroughs in the green room after the concert. The pandemic provided a ready-made excuse for reducing backstage passes. Parker hovered nearby, bobbing in and out of each interaction ensuring no conversation produced a quotable moment. No personal history, political commentary, or questionable photos needed to create a firestorm on Twitter. Hearts and banality made for the ideal tour.

When cHang took Parker's elbow, she led him through two halls and three staircases on a route which Escher would have appreciated. Suddenly they stepped outside beside a sedan in a boring shade of brown.

"Was Sidney Jolson a real person?" asked Parker.

"You absolutely checked Wikipedia."

"You scribbled the name and Hotel Ethel. You handed me said slip of paper at six p.m. Of course I have not had time to look him up."

"Dixieland superstar," said cHang.

"No, you are not." Parker had survived every twist and turn of cHang's career. After hitting it big with an auto-tuned ballad (released as Hang), he next unveiled his actual phenomenal voice with a selection of Bowie tunes.

He also added the c to his stage name in honor of his best-selling remake of "Changes." Then he self-produced the funk album. The next ten years became a blur of musical styles, fluctuating degrees of social consciousness, and a *Sybil*'s worth of onstage personas.

The current arena tour served as a warm-up for the kick-off of the stadium tour in the spring. "You are not bringing back Dixieland."

cHang chuckled like a mischievous elf. "A hundred years ago today."

"Jazz does not sell. People do not go to stadiums to hear the fucking clarinet."

"Kenny G would disagree." His eyes went out of focus.

Parker had observed hundreds of similar lyrical bursts.

cHang repeated the line after activating the dictation function on his mobile.

"Artist knows best," Parker ended the tiff.

"Sidney Jolson played piano with Frisco's Incredible Dixieland Originals. He wrote their biggest hit, "The Dirty Bottom Rag"—maybe the biggest Dixieland hit of them all. He disappeared in 1919."

"F.I.D.O.? Really?"

cHang smiled enigmatically. "Kenny G played the saxophone, not the clarinet."

As Parker drove the directions described by her phone, cHang changed clothes, becoming the Hank she befriended in college.

By the time they arrived at Hotel Ethel, they looked like a fashionably relaxed mogul and his assistant in need of a relaxing night at the Grande Dame of San Francisco hospitality.

Still, Parker steered them toward the employee entrance in a dark corner by the dumpsters. They took turns pressing the intercom button and waving at the questionable overhead camera beside the door.

cHang had worked out the first verse of a song called "Bored, Bored, Bored, Tired, Very Tired" by the time an irritated voice asked them what they wanted.

"The bowels of Ethel require examination," intoned cHang as they walked past employee announcements and a rusty punch card clock.

Suddenly Parker walked without her companion. Turning back, she saw him pointing at the top of the cinderblock wall. Moving beside cHang, she read the words scratched into the paint right below the ceiling: "The Vampire of Hollywood lives."

"Methinks Johnny Depp has walked this passage," joked cHang.

"He's not that tall. And before you run through all the members of Hollywood Vampires, they're all vertically challenged. Now follow me before we spend the night in Ethel's colon."

The front desk clerk looked annoyed and relieved as they emerged from the service door. "My shift ends when all the reservations are closed out," she said.

"Frankie will be here overnight. They hired me with the Covid reboot, but he's been with the Ethel forever. Since we reopened, he's been helping out here in addition to handling overnight laundry. So, don't be surprised if he takes a minute to return your call. But he will. And Frankie is the walking Wikipedia of the Ethel."

The phone vibrated and rang at the same time which meant it had to be Hank. Parker wanted it to stop, but her arm would not move. Worse, she had sharp prickles from the elbow down. She kicked out and rolled toward the antagonistic device. Parker suppressed a scream when her sleeping hand flailed at the cell phone. As feeling rushed back into the sleeping limb, she used her other hand to answer the phone. "Yes?"

"I'm hearing voices," said Hank.

"Makes two of us. Mine keeps coming from my cell," responded Parker.

"Did I wake you? Do you have to entertain thousands of people by holding their hearts in the palm of your hand later today? Also, I haven't been able to fall asleep yet and I might not be at my best? Like later, when I have to perform and hold…"

"I caught it the first time," interrupted Parker. "Have you tried pounding on the walls?"

"Do you not recall Montreal?" asked Hank.

Parker sighed. She could always gauge Hank's desperation by how long it took for him to mention Montreal. "I'm on my way." She hung up before he could say anything else.

Montreal had been a local politician and his mistress. By the time Parker had arrived, Hank stood in the hall. He had adopted a poor French accent in an argument with the couple. None of the three wore any clothes. Parker's exchange semester at McGill and subsequent fluent French had saved the tour from untoward publicity.

Returning to her role, she took a one minute shower, dressed in clean clothes, and prepared mentally to manage whatever situation awaited. Most likely, cHang had failed to come down from the performance.

She had dealt before with a band member's audible hallucinations by sending a roadie out for earplugs. Only the star merited a late night visit from Parker. If necessary, she would sit with him while he fell asleep. Hopefully his room had a comfortable chair.

The plush carpet of the Hotel Ethel hallways and elevator absorbed the sound of her passage to the fancier floor. They had taken advantage of the Covid closing to update the carpet and wallpaper.

Parker smiled tiredly. She had always hoped those design classes in college would come in handy. The designer must have looked up the Arts and Crafts movement and lost her mind. As she ascended in the ornate box, Parker's mind grew muddled from the exhaustion built up by the road.

Parker's fist grazed cHang's door and it opened. His haggard expression caused her to wonder how poorly her own face must appear. "You look like shit," she said.

Retorts rose to his lips but he swallowed them in order to have her save him. "Enter the inner sanctum and tell me I'm not insane." His voice was rough as he gestured for her to follow. He had a hot tea waiting beside the bed.

They passed from the sitting room into the bedroom. Parker stood in the center and silently counted to a hundred.

"I don't hear anything." She turned on her heels. "Have a good night."

"Wait," rasped cHang. "Please," said Hank. He raised a finger in the air.

Parker went to the nearest window and gently spread the curtains. A trio of pigeons flew off into the night. "They didn't cry, but…"

"I heard voices."

Parker's eyelids longed to close but she fought them open. Exhaling through her nose, she settled onto the edge of his bed. "Five minutes. No voices and I vamoose."

"Vamoose." He grinned like he had won the round, which he had. "Kid Ory and Jelly Roll Morton might have played downstairs here. They played ragtime which caught on like wildfire."

"So, we're off the Dixieland? Please be off the Dixieland."

"Relax, it all goes in here"—he motioned to his ears and then scribbled in the air—"and comes out here as another thing entirely."

Parker did a much more dramatic air writing. "There hasn't been very much of this lately. The label wanted new songs a year ago."

cHang settled in cross-legged on the mattress. "Sidney Jolson might have played his last gig here."

Parker gave him her where-are-you-going-with-this look. "The real Sidney Jolson? Not you, right?"

"He's one of the great lost musicians of early jazz. A historian at Indiana University wrote about it on his blog. He found a story from a 1919 San Francisco *Examiner*. Sidney's wife said he went to play a gig at the Hotel Ethel even though he felt sick as a dog. Can you believe people have been saying 'sick as a dog' for more than a century?"

"A lot of people probably got lost ," said Parker. "The flu epidemic all those soldiers brought home from World War I."

"Takes a college professor to find the details after a hundred years though." cHang played air piano and sang, "I'm sick as a dog and nobody will give me a bone."

"The world should wait for your blues record," commented Parker.

"You keep me grounded, Parker, but maybe you ought to let me fly a little every once in a while."

She leaned toward him and held his eyes with hers. "Hank, you're a once-in-a-generation talent and I am honored to be on this ride with you, but I am damned if I am going to let you go out in front of tens of thousands of fans and play shit like 'Darktown Strutters Ball.'"

cHang zipped his own lips shut. He attempted meditative. Finally, he cracked the quiet. "Do you hear it?"

"The humming?"

cHang frowned. "I swear…"

Parker shushed him. She studied the baseboard vent, barely visible under the wingback chair.

The voice reverberated nearby.

"Can you hear me, cHang? Can anyone hear me? I'm really scared. I'm not alone in here."

"I told you I wasn't crazy," hissed cHang.

"What do you want me to say? This makes up for all the other times no one spoke to you from inside the walls?"

They glared at one another.

The voice carried into the room. "Is someone with you, cHang? I swear I didn't tell anyone else where you went."

"Fuck me," said Parker. "Do I hear cLover?"

"Cynthia!" exclaimed cHang.

"Yes!"

cHang leapt to his feet as if claiming the stage. "Leave!"

"I don't know how."

Parker stood beside cHang. "How'd you find your way in there?"

"I walked through an opening in the hall."

Parker backed toward the door. She motioned to cHang to keep the girl talking. Carefully, Parker stepped into the hallway after propping the door open with the Do Not Disturb placard.

The wall between cHang's room and the next one had to be somewhere between the doors for the two hotel rooms. Parker arrived at the door to cHang's next door neighbor without coming upon anything unusual, such as a person-sized hole in the hallway wall.

Parker turned around. As she paced back to cHang's door, she dragged her fingers over the wallpaper, looking for seams or indentations or any indication of a panel. She tapped from top to bottom—no hollow echo and no voices.

Parker slipped back into cHang's room and placed herself where she had a clear line to measure the distance from the door to the talking wall. She stepped the distance. Then she returned to the hallway and recreated the measurement. She removed a shoe and placed it to mark the spot.

"I have no idea what I've accomplished," announced Parker to no one in particular. With crossed arms, she considered the hall. The rooms were not aligned. They matched on either side until you reached cHang's room. Past it, the rooms on her side slid an extra yard or more away.

Parker returned to the room and asked, "I don't suppose you have a hammer? There might be a crawl space without a door."

"The hammer is with the shovel and the pick axe on the tour bus," deadpanned cHang.

"Did you say there's no door?" called cLover.

Before cHang could shush her, Parker answered, "You climbed in there, Cynthia! Why not leave the same way?"

They waited for a response.

"cLover? Honey?" called cHang. "Is there something you're not telling us?"

The girl's voice cracked on her first attempt at an answer. After a moment, she shouted, "I'm not alone in here!" before stifling a cry.

"What are you talking about?" demanded Parker. "Who'd you bring with you? You said you didn't tell anyone else?"

"I can't say," defended cLover.

"You're fine. Tell us who's with you," asked cHang.

"I'm afraid."

Parker and Hank gave one another the look of do-you-want-to-say-it.

"Do you have your phone with you?" asked Parker.

"Wait!" cHang surprised them all with his exclamation. "Is he threatening you? Have you seen any part of him?"

"His shoes," said cLover after a pause. "He's wearing dad shoes. They're brown. He's wearing an old brown suit. It's raggedy."

"Cynthia, talk to us," said Parker.

"I can see his head, but my battery is dying." She sounded on the verge of tears. "If the battery dies then I won't be able to show you the lyrics I wrote."

"What does he look like, Cynthia? Does he have brown hair? Blue eyes?"

"He doesn't have any hair. Or eyes."

cHang stopped working on the grate. "What are you talking about?"

"He's a skeleton. He's trying to talk."

cHang settled back onto the floor. "What's he saying?"

"He's grinding his teeth."

"It's the wind," whispered Parker. "It's not a crawl space. It's a vent."

"Are you feeling a breeze, Cynthia?"

"Cynthia, is this guy between you and the door out of the crawlspace? Does it mean you…?"

"I crawled over him! Apparently." She sniffled. "It felt like wood slats. I spent a summer putting up dry wall."

An instant passed and then she cried out, "No, no, no, no!"

"Hey, buddy!" cHang shouted. "You leave our girl Cynthia alone in there!"

Parker shoved the chair out of the way and clawed at the grating on the wall. "Find me tools," she insisted.

cHang crouched beside her and twisted the screws. "Ask a guitar player when you need powerful fingers."

Scraping and quaking sounds emanated from the opening.

"He's moving," Cynthia barely produced the words.

As they heard rough drumsticks dragged over a dehydrated xylophone, cHang worked at the grate and freed the metal rectangle which clanged to the floor.

"Do you have space to move away from him?" asked Parker.

"I'm trying."

cHang grabbed at the top of the opening and tugged on the plaster. A rain of dust fell on the floor. Parker worked the other end. After a few minutes, they cracked a wooden slat and pulled the broken piece free. Light from the room poured into the opening.

As they scanned the interior, a skeletal forearm appeared, as if its owner crawled along the floor. A ragged brown sleeve hung loosely over most of the bone. Muscles like beef jerky flexed with the weary movements of the fingers and wrist.

cHang reached into the abyss and grabbed the arm. He rolled back and away from the aperture. A hideous crack filled the room.

cHang lay on his back clutching the hand, wrist, and a few inches of arm. Inside the hole, the empty sleeve had given way and the skeleton toppled to one side. Its head rested near the ground and faced Parker. The empty eye sockets considered her.

cHang sat up. Still clutching the desiccated arm, he said, "I am Sidney Jolson."

"I remember," agreed Parker. "I used the alias to book the room."

cHang held up the ulna and radius. "I am Sidney Jolson."

"Okay, maybe you should go lie down and I'll deal with cLover."

Parker watched cHang stand. "Why don't you leave the bones?"

"Never sick. Why do people believe I died of the Spanish flu?" cHang made no move for his bed.

"The skeleton is moving again!" cried cLover.

"Hank, I really need to deal with this." Parker motioned at the hole in the wall.

"Mrs. Boudin booked the Incredible Dixieland Originals but they insisted on turning down the gig. Our cornet, Chester, had an unpleasant experience when we played here the previous New Year's Eve. He thought he had a way with the ladies. Mrs. Boudin desired those ladies not include her daughter."

Ignoring the sound of bones dragging across wood from behind her, Parker scrambled to her feet. She went to place her hands on cHang's shoulders.

Backing away, cHang continued, "I had mouths to feed. Mrs. Boudin offered a nice chunk of change, so I pulled together other friends once my regular boys backed out. Before the first note, the lady took me aside and made it clear she recognized my subterfuge. She still paid better than my substitutes could make anywhere else on a Friday night, so we let stand her insistence on a steep discount. Plus, she would have her vengeance on one in lieu of all."

Parker's hands had fallen to her side and she had backed away from cHang. "What's happening, Hank?"

A scream from the hole ripped through the room like a breaking guitar string. Parker stopped breathing while the oxygen refilled the space around her.

"Fuck!" screamed Parker. Maybe she meant to shock Hank back to being cHang. Maybe she needed to shock herself into a better reality. Maybe she needed to scare the world back to normalcy.

None of those happened. "cLover?" asked Parker.

"I want out," the forlorn voice came from the hole.

"During our first break, the Lady Boudin sent word how I could still make full pay plus a little more if I played a private gig for her and a few friends after the public performance. The Governor had come to town and Mrs. Boudin hosted the evening. With him in the penthouse, the private performance would be here in this intimate space."

cLover wept.

"About a dozen luminaries filled the two rooms, getting up to no good business. They had me at a piano in the sitting room and I kept my head down to avoid seeing the coming and going back here. Mrs. Boudin invited a few girls up to keep company with the Governor, the Mayor, and what have you."

The tears inside the crawl space grew soft.

"Nobody recognized me until a knock came at the door. A pretty young thing had brought fresh drinks and hors d'oeuvres for the party. She pushed the cart right over beside me and I smiled at her—my last smile ever, I suppose."

"Hank, are you even in there?" Parker could only stare.

The sobbing in the walls sounded farther away than ever.

"Madame Boudin never missed a trick. I said, 'How are you, Miss Cynthia?' and the poor girl called me by name. 'Simply fine, Sidney.' I knew Cynthia's husband as a sometime banjo man, a little heavy on the drone, but adequate."

Parker's eyes closed. "Are you telling me…?" She shook her head until the weight of her eyelids released. "I don't understand."

"'Now it's time for everyone to retire for the evening,' announced the hostess with the leastest. She herded everyone out except the muscle. She told Cynthia and me to wait for tips."

Parker turned to the wall. "Cynthia!"

cHang's voice rose. "They took us in here and laid us on the bed. Mrs. Boudin explained how her daughter had died from the flu and she blamed Chester. To be honest, she likely had the correct malefactor. Ideally he would be present, but I would do as a stand-in. Poor Cynthia's only trespass had been recognizing me and ruining their alibi for my demise."

Parker kicked at the edges of the hole. More plaster crumbled. Cynthia grew louder but her voice failed to drown out the slow drag of bones.

"One of the thugs handed a knife to the lady in charge while others held us down. I've had plenty of time to acknowledge I'm not much of a man because I fainted as soon as she carved into my chest."

Continuing to break fragments of the wall, Parker shouted, "What do you mean you've had plenty of time to acknowledge it?"

"Sitting in the dark for so long…"

cLover's wail hit a higher note.

"Too dark to see she was in there with me," said cHang. "We remained so alone… and only a few feet apart."

Parker banged her head into the wall. "I can't break through!" she shouted to cLover. "I'm going down to the front desk and grab a sledgehammer or whatever they have!"

She ran for the door, pursued by cHang. "I don't want to be alone anymore," he said as the door closed in his face.

"Shit, shit, shit, shit," chanted Parker on the offbeat to pressing the call button for the elevator.

The whoosh of the opening doors gave her pause. She stepped aboard like reentering the womb. Leaving the floor… for safety.

Except the car did not budge. And Parker was not alone.

"Your destination, Ma'am?" asked a gaunt, pockmarked man in something like a bellhop uniform. Seeing her confusion, he added gently, "I man the elevator from time to time. They say it is a blessing to have a place to be when you reach a certain place in life."

By the time the car bottomed out on the first floor, Parker had regained her breath. Offering a grateful nod to the operator, she edged out of the car.

The quiet of the lobby enveloped her. A bell sat on the front desk and she tinkled it. After her second ringing, an elderly man stepped out of a hidden office. Pulling on a suit coat, he eyed her suspiciously. Her first question did not improve his expression.

"Do you have a pickaxe handy?" asked Parker.

"Let me check," said the clerk and turned back to the office. Returning a moment later, he announced, "We do not."

"A shovel? A hammer?"

"Might I enquire as to what this might be in the pursuit of?" The old man stayed a little back from the counter.

"For Christ's sake!" Parker heard a stirring behind her. Given the moment, she considered her next few words. "I'm sorry. I'm very tired."

The front desk clerk had undoubtedly seen a great deal. His eyes showed pity while his forehead offered emotional support. "I believe you are Ms. Compinche?" He motioned behind her. "This young lady has been trying to ring your room for the last hour. She claims to be your sister."

cLover tapped Parker on the shoulder. "Hiya, Sis."

About to tumble to the ground, Parker clutched the countertop. She massaged her temples and tried to focus on the current moment.

"You would not believe how cold it is outside," said cLover. She glared at the clerk. "Nobody is checking in a tourist without a reservation."

"It is policy across the city with the reopening after the pandemic," He sounded nonplused. "I provided a blanket while she waited for you to answer."

Parker held up her hands to silence both of them. She turned on the clerk. "She is coming upstairs with me."

"The Hotel Ethel provides a fifty dollar surcharge for an additional guest," he commented to her back.

Parker led cLover to the elevator. Once the doors had separated them from prying ears, Parker ran a hand through the air by the floor buttons. Catching the worried look on cLover's face, Parker shrugged, "It's been a weird night." Shifting tone, she asked, "Sister?"

"He wanted to throw me out. I didn't lie about how cold it is outside."

"You didn't make a reservation when you bought the concert ticket? Anywhere within driving distance?" Parker pulled out her cellphone. "Don't bother answering. I'm unexpectedly relieved to see you. I've been walking through a nightmare for the last hour."

She pressed a saved contact. "Maurice? I need you at the Hotel Ethel. The eighteenth floor. Without delay. Bring a large hammer, but subtly. No, this is not Minneapolis all over again."

cLover pasted a smile on her face. "I really admire you."

"Let's do silence until the elevator dings."

When the doors opened, Parker led them down the hall. Outside cHang's room, they could hear a conversation within though the words did not come through clearly. Parker barged in, afraid of explaining any of her night to cLover while standing in the hall.

cHang sat on his bed. He pointed the arm bone at Parker. "You left me." Then he rose to his feet and walked right past her. With his arm around cLover, he returned to his perch on the mattress, now joined by the glowing young woman.

"Maurice is on his way over because…" Parker stared at cLover. "What the hell were you doing downstairs? You're supposed to be inside the wall."

cLover attempted an answer, but cHang held her hand in a very distracting manner.

The musician spoke. "She's right. You're supposed to be inside the wall with me."

cLover worked her hand free of cHang. "What's he talking about?" she asked Parker.

"We thought you had been trapped in the wall," repeated Parker. "You called out to us."

"But I'm not in the wall." cLover slid across the bed. "I'm right here."

Scrabbling sounds came from the hole.

"I heard the rats were bad in the Bay area," commented cLover.

A skeletal hand emerged from the aperture. Leather-like flesh and tendons held it together. Its fingers snapped.

cHang knelt beside the extended hand and placed the other forearm on the open palm. After a little maneuvering, both arms disappeared into the hole.

Parker patted a muted cLover on the back. "Like I said, it's been a long night and you might want to consider going back down to the lobby and sleeping all this away."

"No way." cLover displayed the enthusiasm of the youngest person in the room. "The skeleton moved. Besides, the creepy front desk guy waits below. He does have a pickaxe in the backroom because he definitely had a whole I-bury-dead-guests-right-outside-the-city vibe."

"Let's not let our imaginations run away with us," said Parker. Then she shrugged. "Too late I suppose."

Crouching beside the opening, she used her phone to illuminate the interior. "Maybe we ought to talk to that guy or anyone who works here because this sort of space doesn't exist between any other rooms on this floor."

Parker sat beside cHang. "How are you? Back to yourself yet?"

"I'm grateful you brought a friend back with you," said cHang.

"No, no, no, no," muttered Parker. She grabbed cLover. "You have to leave right now."

"Have you seen Mrs. Boudin?" responded cLover. "Something awful has happened. So tired, I sat down for a minute. Mr. Jolson told me to go on home but when I spoke to Mrs. Boudin, she wanted me to stay."

"What's your name, dear?" Parker asked.

"Cynthia, thank you for asking." cLover sat. "I have been so lonely. Would you sit and have a conversation with me if I promise not to take up too much of your time?"

"Cynthia, how do we fix this? What has happened to Hank and our Cynthia?" Parker trembled with exhaustion. "Are they all right?"

A definite knock came from the other side of the wall.

Parker spun and hushed the other two in the room with her. "Hank? Cynthia?"

Two knocks came from distinct parts of the wall.

Parker ran along the wall and knocked once at either end. "Are you in there now?"

She ran back and forth between cHang and cLover. "You have to let them out! Hank and Cynthia can't stay in the wall forever! I'm terribly sorry for whatever the hell happened to you, but you need to let them out!"

"Hello!" Maurice called from the doorway.

"Thank God." Parker ran to Maurice and tugged him into the bedroom. "You need to break them out of there. Do you have a hammer? Break up the wall around the hole."

With practiced silence, Maurice studied the occupants of the room. After a minute, he crouched beside the hole. He tapped around the edges of the opening until cracks spread like a punk song transforming into a free jazz jam.

Using a room service menu, Parker scooped wall pieces into the trash. Before long, she had filled the receptacles in the room and made one trip to the bin by the elevator.

Returning from the elevator end of the hall, dangling the plastic trash can from one hand, Parker walked right past cHang's door. Another thirty feet, she stopped and turned. The walls and doors looked like an endlessly repeating pattern. Parker reached out for the wall, but it fell away as she toppled to the ground. Her last conscious thought: *I used to be able to stay up all night.*

"Miss Compinche?"—the voice attached to a persistent jostling.

Parker opened one eye and groaned at the sight. Looking harried and concerned, the front desk clerk stood over her. Then her eyes caught sight of his hand. Her arm shot out and intercepted his arm and stopped the naloxone he planned to administer.

Peeling her drooling lips off the carpet, she slid upright against the nearest wall. Placing a thigh over the spittle stain, Parker ventured a wry smile.

"One of our other guests called down to say a woman had fainted in the hallway." The clerk glanced toward a nearby door. "They suspected you had overdosed like they have been reading so much about online. Please tell me you don't need the naloxone."

Parker stared at him. She wiped her lips. "I wouldn't be answering if I needed the naloxone."

He lowered to the carpet beside her. "I'm familiar with a difficult employer."

Parker read his nametag. "I appreciate it, Franklyn. You've been working here long?"

"Decades," said Franklyn. "My grandmother worked here briefly. She died in the great flu epidemic soon after giving birth to my mother. According to my grandfather, Grandma went to work one evening and never came home. The Hotel Ethel sent word she had collapsed and died."

"So, you took a job here to solve the mystery of her disappearance?"

"Not even on a bet. I grew up around the corner and old Ethel paid well at a time when the city got busy tearing down neighborhoods and making the alternative a rental across the Bay."

Parker gestured down the hall. "Does anything look off?" Back on her feet, she helped the old man upright.

"Can't say."

They walked back to cHang's door.

"This isn't right. There was more space between this room and…" said Parker. The opposite door aligned perfectly with the door she faced. The entire floor had been restored symmetrically. "Franklyn, does Ethel fuck with people?"

"Language, ma'am."

Parker pushed the door open though she hesitated on the threshold.

Quiet had filled the room.

Parker walked inside. Through the bedroom door, cHang and cLover lay on the bed, adorned in rumpled clothes, atop the mattress cover, as though they had been overcome and fallen backward. Parker went to them and adjusted the bedclothes to keep them warm.

Behind her, Maurice leaned against the wall. He had dramatically increased the hole. Mounds of plaster, dust, wood shards, and white smoke snaked along the floor at his feet. The back of the sitting room wall now stood less than a foot away, providing a setting for the visible dead.

Parker's chest seized as she took in the tableau uncovered by Maurice's labors.

One desiccated corpse, mostly bones, clothed in the remains of a brown suit. Another dead body, only slightly less preserved, wearing the tattered uniform of a hotel waitress. Their hands clutched one another as though they had been deprived of any touch for a century.

Maurice used the hammer to free a large dangle of plaster. He sighed, stepped back, and pointed at the revelation. "What do you make of the third one?"

A little shorter, a little more flesh on the bones, familiar attire.

Parker screamed, "Franklyn!" as she ran for the hall. Out in the empty hallway, she stumbled over the naloxone packet lying on the floor.

17th Floor – Premium Suites
1990

Unfolding
Katherine Silva

There is a sound. A thing. A noise.

It pulls at my attention. A knock. A sharp ticking and I can't concentrate anymore. These papers are sucking my life away one letter at a time, one letter at a *fucking* time. Stuck in this room until I get each page of this contract proofed. Until it becomes legible, filled with pomp and puff. Then every dried-up suit that's flown in for this conference can pretend to read it, sign it, and drink their champagne.

But I can't finish proofing it because of that damn… thing.

I shove up from my chair and search for the origin of this incessant sound. Maybe if I make it stop, I'll finally be able to finish. My legs are stiff when I stand and my feet tingle as I take a few tiny steps away from the corner desk toward the middle of the room. With each one, my blood remembers that it's supposed to help me keep moving and with it, my imagination conjures.

Maybe it's something in the walls getting ready to scratch its way out? Something broken in the vents or heating ducts that I can't reach. But I look. I look because I can't sit there anymore. Feels like I've been there in that one spot for weeks.

It hits me now how beautiful this room is. All the bold colors, the gold accents, the flourishes in the moldings. Like stepping into a by-gone era. *The Great Gatsby* or some shit like that… I had a similar thought when I arrived but that didn't last long.

Within minutes of setting my suitcase on the floor, my boss appeared at my door and pushed his way in like an over-inflated party balloon searching for more space to encroach on.

"Fucking pretty, eh?" he'd said, drifting from one thing to the next, touching this, caressing his hand over that. He had to touch it all, had to get his slime on every little thing…

But I kept it in. I stood there prim and plain as I always did and nodded and fiddled with my glasses and said nothing because that's what I did. That's what I got paid to do. I chose a job where I could fold myself into a neat little shape like an origami crane.

At night, I unfolded.

"We need the final draft by Friday." He spoke toward the ceiling; not to me.

"These fucks will be going over everything with a fine-toothed comb. It needs to be pristine." Into the mirror; not to me.

"So, I want you on this day and night." Into the ripples in the curtains by the window. To the clock on my bedside table. The shadows on my wall.

Not to me.

I didn't say anything because I'd begun to imagine him as more of a housefly than a visitor, a voice settling into a drone as it alit all over my space. The kind of housefly that couldn't save itself by flying out the open window. It flew deeper into the room instead propelled by some dizzying stupidity. Maybe it wanted death. Maybe it wanted to be slammed against the countertop by a big, flat swatter…

"You listening?"

He'd been talking at me then and I regurgitated what he wanted to hear: that I'd get the proofread done. I always got the job done. And because he had begun to fix me with a look that questioned my ability in spite of all my assurances, I added that I'd get it done by Thursday at midnight.

It's Thirsty Thursday. Eight thirty-three p.m. and I am officially in hell. I've stayed dry as a stack of firewood since I started work on this and as much as I want to call down to room service for a smooth, luscious Cosmopolitan to take the edge off... I'll miss some*thing* if I do.

But the noise... That's taking precedence now. Like the sharp tick, tack of someone drumming their nails on a desk or... I stop close to the door and frown. It's almost like it's coming from outside. Someone is clicking their fingernails over and over in repetition on my door.

I peer through the peep hole, my breath fluttering out like a candle extinguishing. Nothing in the hall. No *one* in the hall.

Rocking back onto my heels, I frown in the newfound silence. That's odd, right? No one in the hall this early at night? Not one person leaving or entering their hotel room?

They're probably all at the club, I realize. Maybe some drunk dipstick was playing around before he got in the elevator or took the stairs back to his room. *Wouldn't I have heard a door though?*

Brush it off. Rinse it out.

I hear my partner's voice in my brain. They're always right. They always put it in perspective.

I make myself turn around, make myself return to the desk and sit down. There are forty-one pages left in a stack on my right to read. The number alone practically bounces me back out of the chair almost as soon as I've made contact with it.

There's no way I'm going to do this in time. No way I'm dropping this off at my boss's hotel room in—I peer into the bedroom at the clock on the side table—three hours and five minutes.

My stomach grumbles. I haven't eaten since this morning. Had buttered toast, a poached egg, fancily cut fruit. Black coffee. I'd worked straight through lunch, propelled with the understanding that I'd put myself in this stupid position and only I could get myself out of it.

Food. I could order room service again. The company is strict about its budget but... if they are willing to put me up in the Hotel Ethel on the seventeenth floor... Well, they won't care if I tip the scale a little in order to get the job d—

I freeze.

The sound.

The *scritch, scritch, scritch...*

Tack, tack, tack, tack, tack...

The *something* is back.

I'm out of the chair like a skipping stone, across the room and at the door, chin lifted, toes pointed to lift myself to the peep hole... I stop.

The tiny prickle of fear swimming through my brain. Like a polliwog. Undeveloped. Chaotic. Vulnerable. But I allow it to melt when I remember what's at stake. If I don't finish... So, I look.

And there is nothing.

I open the door and lean out into the hall. The seventeenth floor gapes back at me in all of its majesty: all of its doors, its length of carpet, its ornamental flourishes and its emptiness.

At the end of the hall, I notice the elevator doors closing on a couple kissing. Funny. She's dressed in something I haven't seen anyone wear in years. Could they have been the ones making the noise outside my room? Maybe. Maybe not. While I'm tempted to say something, I scuttle back inside and shut the door again.

Anger strikes hot once I'm inside and I realize what's happening. It's my fucking boss. When I've stated that I can get things done in half, sometimes a quarter of the time the company is giving me, he calls it showing-off. He tells me no one can do the job that well. And adds more to my plate in an effort to prove me wrong. And when I do, he gets even more livid.

Sure, it was a risk. Him upsetting me and not letting me finish by midnight. But in his eyes, I have a whole other day to work. It isn't supposed to be done until Friday. So, he'll get his laugh, he'll disrupt my work until the midnight hour and then he'll swoop in and say something undoubtedly conceited and misogynistic about my work ethic.

Just needing to be that goddamn fly again.

I need to catch him in the act. Show him up. He's being childish.

I stay where I am and stare at the door and wait. He's bound to start that fucking noise again soon, whatever it is. The thought of him scraping his nails on my door is confusing because he doesn't have many nails to scrape.

My boss is obnoxious but he is also a nervous man, the kind of man who never learned not to bite his nails. And they look horrible when he does, the nail bitten down so that all that show are these awful stumpy rectangles below the flesh.

Maybe he's using his room key.

Scratching up a luxury room door at the Hotel Ethel? Geez. Hope he's willing to pay the damages for that.

One minute goes by. I watch the door, unblinkingly, as though I might miss something.

Two minutes.

Three.

Impatience tugs at my anger.

This is how he gets you to waste your time, I say to myself. *This is more of a procrastination than if you were sitting over at the desk. Or ordering something to eat.*

As if on cue, my stomach gurgles again.

Fuck. I cross the room to the phone and pick up the cardstock in-room menu on the table there. The restaurant is on the second floor, only a short elevator ride away. I hadn't eaten their once since I'd arrived but I'd investigated late one night after unfolding. Impressive to say the least. Eating in there would make anyone feel like they were royalty dining on things like crudités and amuse-bouches.

I settled for the chicken. In the middle of my order, the noise began again and it took everything I had not to throw down the receiver and shriek like some kind of bat. What I wouldn't give for my Walkman. I'd left it behind at home, right on the dining room table.

I decided I wasn't going to go to the door. I wasn't going to look. Somehow he knew. Somehow my boss was able to hide every time and it would only give him a sense of gratitude knowing that he could hear me coming, knowing he'd interrupted me.

Scritch, scritch, scritch...

The television. It was the only other thing I had in the room that could distract me, that could be played loud enough over that *something*. Even if it wasn't my idea of white noise, it would have to do the trick.

It has always been notoriously easy for me to get sucked into whatever is on the screen, no matter how boring the subject. My partner once famously put on the television just to have some other noise in the house while they made dinner and found me half an hour later glued to the screen as I watched a how-to public access program about replacing drywall.

I can do this. I can focus on the driest contract this planet has ever seen and not get sucked into whatever is on television. Because I have to. Because if I don't...

I grab the remote for the television and the scratches turn into bangs. Great thumping bangs that reverberate through the walls and shake the pictures. I throw the remote across the floor and it tumbles beneath one of the chairs there.

Charging. My heart thrashes in me as I stamp across the floor to the door, as I swing it in and take the biggest lungful of air I have to—

The waiter jerks back and I do the same. How could he be here already? Wasn't it just a moment ago that I... I must have deliberated longer than I thought about the television.

I let him wheel the cart in, take the tureen cover off the steaming plate of chicken and vegetables, all bathed in a delicate gravy, and he's back out of there in less than a minute.

The clock in the bedroom now says nine-thirty. The entire night is running away from me and there are still forty-one pages sitting there requesting my eyes on them.

The chicken is bland, the vegetables bland, the gravy thin. But it settles my stomach and satisfies the growls that have emanated from it. I return to the desk, to the chair, and plant myself in it. Scrutinizing the top page on my stack, my nerves jangle with anticipation. Any moment, that noise will start up again. It's a wonder it didn't while I was eating, that blissful fifteen minutes now just a reminder of the peace I was missing.

The first two paragraphs go by without a thought. No thought at all in fact. I've been so preoccupied listening for a noise that I haven't paid any attention to what they'd said at all. I'll have to start over again. I inhale deeply, shake out my fingers.

Brush it off. Rinse it out.

Brush it off. Rinse—

Sssssssscrrriiiiiiiitch.

Every ounce of my chicken wants to come back up my throat and onto the desk. That elongated whisper of a scratch hasn't come from the door.

It came from the wall next to me. The outside wall of the hotel, where nothing but cold air and the distant sounds of traffic and people and sirens reign.

As insane as it is for there to be something outside poking at the wall, I glance out the window. Telegraph Hill gapes at me from beyond, a strange scrape of rock that feels prehistoric in the midst of San Francisco's urbanity. On the cliff's edge is a shape: tiny, wobbly. A child.

I divert my attention to the side of the building, hoping for a bird or scaffolding or something that will explain the sounds and there's nothing but the air.

When I look back to the cliff, the strange child is gone. What. The. Fuck?

I pull myself away from the window.

A rat.

It has to be a rat.

Or some small critter clambering through the walls making a racket as it follows the internal maze of pipes and studs and plates behind the drywall. That stupid how-to program I'd watched is staying with me until the end of time, it seems.

It's funny. When it was at my door, it had sounded so rhythmic, and now it's almost softer, longer… a hiss escaping out of a crack, a talon being dragged across wood…

I grab the papers from the desk and take them into the bedroom. This is even riskier than turning on the television. Every person in their right mind understands that separation of work and play are a must. Play in this instance meaning sleep.

No one takes work into their bedroom unless they are an insomniac, single, or both. It's like polluting your clean air with the filth of expelled toxicity. All the engines turning and billowing smoke in your brain as you make them work, and then when you try to sleep, you can't help but be haunted by the gears grinding.

Or vice versa. Sleep overpowers and drags you down into the mire of oblivion. Those pages might as well be another shifting blanket to wrap myself in as I fully lose myself beneath the downy comforters and high-thread-count sheets.

I opt to sit on the floor, cross-legged, the pages in front of me. It's going to be hell on my back but at this point, I'm running out of options. The clock is closing in on ten. At this rate, I'll have to proofread a third of each page a minute. It's doable but it's rushing. We're talking about some dense paragraphs here, sentences with the heft of a stone wheat cracker slathered in cement and nearly as appetizing to read.

I'm using my pen to follow the lines on the page, to go back and re-read before continuing on. As I flip a sheet and finally take on page forty-two, I hear something that makes no sense.

Shlllllk.

Shhhhhhhlllllllk.

It's coming from beneath me. Under the rug. On the floor. *Under* the floor. The vibrations tingle against my calf like the feeling of a feather drifting across me.

This is not a rat.

This is not my boss.

I stand and take a large, ballerina-esque leap toward the bedroom doorway. Upon landing, the scraping resumes directly below me and soon enough, on either side of me in the door jamb.

"No." The word drops from my mouth without me meaning to.

I skirt along the edges of the room and the sound follows me. Sometimes it's in the floor, bumping the boards beneath my feet before it slides up into the walls and starts to POP! POP! I run, hands over my head, toward the door.

And I can't open it.

I yank on it, jiggle the knob, the desperate shout swelling in my lungs before I remember that I had locked it before. Unlatching the hook and flipping the deadbolt, I fling the door wide and throw myself into the hall, practically barreling against the wall opposite me.

The silence is drowning.

Standing there, heart pounding, skin slick with perspiration, I watch the rectangle of light from my room in the dimness of the hall and wait… just… wait.

Fuck the contract.

Fuck the conference.

Fuck that sound. Whatever it is.

How quickly could I book a plane back home? I can't. I don't have the money. I've flown here on the corporate dime, sitting in first class next to my boss as I watched him down nip after nip. It's night. Going anywhere after dark alone in this city is risky. Without my purse. Without my luggage?

Maybe I can ask the front desk for another room? Maybe they'll be okay with a switch. This late in the week though? We were only here for another day. We checked out on Saturday. What if they charge extra for that? What if the company questions it?

Not to mention what I'll have to tell my boss. He'll laugh at me for swapping rooms because I've heard a noise, a noise that I can't explain, a noise that could be anything from pipes to loud neighbors to unwelcome rodents or even all three.

And in all this time that I've been here in the hall trying to get my breath to return to a normal cadence, the scratching and the bumping in the walls and floor haven't followed me.

Standing there in my tank top, my sweatpants, and barefooted, the anxiety of being completely exposed out here begins to weigh on me. How many people are watching me silently from the safety of their rooms, through their tiny peepholes?

How many of their eyes are tracking along my body wondering if it's the right moment to call the front desk or the police?

As all of these thoughts cram down into my brain, I can't stop obsessing over the sound. The scratching sound from the bedroom. It had been so familiar. Not a tapping, not a knocking, not a scraping...

Slowly, unassured, I return to the doorway and stand in it.

Brush it off. Rinse it out.

Christ. I need a cigarette.

I need to *unfold*—

No.

Not yet.

I can't enjoy the process with the weight of this assignment hanging over me. It's too insistent on my thoughts, too all encompassing.

But... I can't deny this need growing inside of me. The itch that comes with unzipping, with *unfolding*. I want to leave the daily burden of the nine-to-five workforce drudgery behind and become anything other than the shrew who collects, assembles, monitors, and brings everything together for the office day in and day out.

So, we're going to rush this motherfucking job.

Still no noise in the doorway. The fizz of apprehension calms down in my head as I take a few more steps inside.

One step at a time, I find the center of the room and turn to face the bedroom where I've left the contract in a heap on the floor. Sitting on top of the stack is a small shape, a small *something*.

I move toward it as if my own body is outside of my control, focusing on the tiny object until I'm close enough to bend over and take it between my fingers. It's a small origami crane.

The sound.

Now I recognize that sound.

I pick up another page from the contract and bend two corners together. With my index finger and thumb, I pinch and crease.

The sound is identical.

Very quickly, I understand two things.

One, I am confined.

Two, I need to unfold *now*.

Nighttime is the best time to play. Nighttime is the best time to let the shroud die, let the professional persona bleed away.

Brush it off. Rinse it out.

I like this body. I like following this strange ritual day in and day out, playing the part of the girl who needs this job, who needs to prove something to her corporate ladder that she can advance, play the game. And at night, I can take it off, brush it off, rinse it out and… wander.

We have an understanding, my partner and I. When I unfold, they fold. Like the sun giving way to the moon or the tides shifting in the ocean. When either of us are folded into a body, we obey its physics, we understand that it has limitations, that its mind can't comprehend the vastness of us. It only understands its basic day-to-day necessities. Eat. Bathe. Survive. And always remember your partner's wisdom.

Brush it off.

Rinse it out.

And that unfolding feels as glorious and as refreshing as sleep.

As a cold shower after a long run.

But the human mind can't fathom the necessity of unfolding because it can't understand it. It will try to delay it, like sleep. And if one of us does this, the other gets… for lack of a better word… upset.

My partner is curling into the hollows of her body when I rise and expand. We have a brief moment to entangle ourselves in one another and communicate our sensory experiences. They are annoyed at the body's lengths to avoid unfolding tonight. They are grateful to get to be the ones to finish editing the contract.

To join the party upstairs in the club.

To commune with the rest of the sweat-laden, slovenly creatures there. Dancing and drinking and laughing and being something that neither of us have ourselves been in a very long time.

And I promise that after I've finished unfolding—after I've drifted from room to room and explored the rest of the ghosts in this ancient space—that I'll join them for a spell. I'll find a willing body to fold into, one that is compliant. One that won't mind going to sleep for a while.

A new body to start the cycle over for a while.

In the end, all we are is paper.

16th Floor – Premium Suites
1956

Broken Dreams
Bert Lestrange

William of Wykeham is attributed with the phrase "Manners maketh man." Which was a wonderful concept should one possess the capability of speaking and acting in accordance.

Calvin, however, was currently unable to recall his own name, much less the intricate pleasantries of high society.

While internally nervous, anxious, and malignantly anti-social, Calvin could generally hold his own in conversation. Especially after a shot of liquid courage. But his mettle was untested against someone like her, and he was thankful to have traveled this last day in his suit. A young man in a snazzy suit tended to enjoy a different side of people, like armor against the judgment of caste.

But this was different. Even in a room of dolled-up pin-ups, she would shine like a dime.

There was no lie he could tell and no amount of alcohol that would save him now.

Her legs were a country mile of Italian marble, complimented by curves that were probably illegal in at least a dozen states. Orbs of captured winter sky glittered with intelligence as they bounced around the Hotel Ethel's smoky bar. Mirthful laughter escaped the woman's lips, infecting everyone within earshot. They were crimson and satin, mirroring her lustrous, traffic-stopping hair. Pearly teeth caged a clever tongue, no doubt honed to a razor's edge from breaking hearts. From the tall baby doll pumps to her veiled pillbox hat, every inch of this woman had been hand-crafted to utterly ruin his life.

Guys like Calvin didn't stand a chance with vixens like that.

But...

Opportunities ignored were lost and long shots paid best.

After straightening his tie and sliding fingers through his ducktail, he swaggered to the seat beside her.

"Sir, I'd have two fingers of your finest whisky, neat, with three drops of water."

The barkeep sized him up with a raised eyebrow before shrugging his begrudging approval.

When she turned, Calvin's stomach squirmed with angry, drunken butterflies.

"Now that's a ginchy order! The drink of a sophisticated man."

As the mustachioed bartender dropped off Calvin's glass, she caught his arm. "Think I could have one of those?"

Her voice was like a lioness's purr; intimate, inviting, and deadly.

With a shrug and a nod, the bartender returned to the rainbow wall of glass bottles.

While he was distracted, she leaned in close to Calvin. Her velvet lips tickled his earlobe. If he'd had a ring, he would have proposed on the spot.

"I don't think you're old enough for that, love."

His heart crawled into his throat to hammer away as she pulled away and winked.

"But I can keep a secret if you can."

The clink of glass on wood pulled him back from the brink of stupor. He gulped his drink in three swigs and grimaced before wiping his mouth on a sleeve.

"Could I pay for that?" He motioned to her drink. "And your dinner tonight?"

It sounded smoother and hipper in his head.

She bit back a giggle and downed hers without so much as a shiver. "I'm a touch old for you, Daddy-O. Just like that whisky, you couldn't handle me if you tried. Thanks for the drink, but I'm not for sale."

Standing, she stretched and turned to leave.

"If a star fell each time I pine for you beyond this moment, the sky would be cold and lifeless before sunrise. Yet even in that darkness, I'd find you shining brighter than Venus herself. An hour of your time is all I ask, to bask in your glow and inscribe your face, your laugh, and voice in memory, so that one day I might testify of your existence to my children's children."

Calvin took a step closer, straightening his road-worn suit, and maintained eye contact.

"Give me your name and I will carve it in the highest mountain peak and shout it for the world to hear. And when my voice cracks and breaks, I will whisper it unto my last breath."

She tilted her head slightly, eyebrows rising with the flush of her cheeks.

"Once more, madame, and only once more will I ask. Would you honor me with your presence at dinner this evening?"

Contemplation sparkled just beyond her long lashes.

In that delicate moment, while his future teetered on the edge between triumph and trepidation, an old woman slipped her elbow around his and nearly jerked him off balance. His grandmother, Agnes, peered at the bombshell as though sniffing something rotten.

"Calvin! You aren't supposed to be here! Sharing hard liquor with harlots before the noon hour? For shame... I raised you better... Now let's get up to my room before the bellboy decides to pull his tip from the luggage."

Her glare narrowed. "And you should have more decency. Preying on the ignorance of youth! Leave this boy's innocence be. This is the infamous Hotel Ethel, girl. You need some proper clothing."

She pecked Calvin's cheek protectively, then just as quickly as she'd appeared, so too was she gone. But the moment was spoiled, and the damage was done.

"No..." The soft shake of the woman's alluring head sent scarlet curls dancing and Calvin's budding confidence crashing through the floor. "I can't. Not tonight, at least. I'm to meet my girlfriends for dinner. But I'm free tomorrow, if the stars can last that long?"

He couldn't believe his ears and pinched himself twice to be sure. Chest bursting, the response slipped free of its own volition.

"Who needs them when I'll have you? Let them wink out forever! Why settle for polished glass with diamond so close?"

She shook her head in surprise. "Alright, Calvin. Best catch up to granny. She's a spicy number... I think we've done enough damage there. It's Victoria, by the way. And I hope you have a chisel to go with that silver tongue. Can't be breaking promises before our first date."

He tried to think of a clever response but was saved the effort by Agnes's screeching impatience.

"Calivn! I swear... It's time to go!"

Calvin had never known his parents, and Grandmother was a far cry from "loving caregiver." She'd raised him with the same sort of stern, sterile callousness as one might offer a houseplant. Watering it from time to time, providing shelter, food, and a grubby little window through which to see the rest of the world. All the necessities of life without so much as an afterthought for emotional support.

She didn't hang his drawings on the ice box, make appearances at his baseball games, or show anything beyond mild contempt for his interests.

This was all while living in a society where men were expected to be strong and resilient. Emotion was for women; best not to look weak. Even when your intestines roiled like snakes from the internalized anxiety in a void of absent acceptance.

As such, he'd subliminally clung to a desperate need for her approval. Perhaps that was why he still pushed so hard for her permission, even after all these years.

It wasn't until recently that she'd acknowledged him as an autonomous person, rather than an inconvenient obligation. When she'd asked him to join her for this annual journey to California, he'd been flabbergasted. She wasn't getting any younger, travel made her bones ache, and she could use his help this go-round.

But that deep-seated compulsion festered into an opportunity to prove himself which, foolishly, steeled his resolve.

"I really wish you wouldn't interrupt when I'm chatting up a gal. That woman could be in picture shows if she felt the itch. She had just agreed to let me take her out before you blustered in like I was a misbehaving child."

Calvin unpacked Agnes's entirely unnecessary amount of luggage with a scowl.

She snorted, glaring daggers above her glasses. "YOU ARE A MISBEHAVING CHILD! That was no woman, Calvin. That was a lady of the night; a predator. Different beasts entirely. Given what she was wearing, she'd have more interest in the contents of your wallet than your thick skull. You're lucky I was there lest you find yourself with something that doesn't wipe off."

He stopped folding shirts to meet her expertly withering gaze. "I AM a MAN, goddamn it! Not every pretty woman is like that."

Her practiced intensity bore though his soul. The connection remained for a few moments before he had to look elsewhere.

"Damn and drat, Calvin! Any woman that looks like that and shows interest in you is like that. Your father's weak chin and watery eyes aren't exactly endearing. No facial hair to speak of. You have your mother's spindly hands to complete the package. Trust my advice. Find yourself a homely girl and settle. Leave romantic fantasy to your poetry books."

Her lip quivered a fraction. "And the next time you raise your voice to me you'll be walking back to Tennessee. You're just another know-it-all rugrat. Never wrong and rarely in doubt. I'll mash your lip long before taking it."

He was staggered from the direct brutality. It wasn't uncommon for her to be dismissive, even rude, but this blunt cruelty was two steps beyond. If his eyes hadn't been watery before, they were now.

"That might have been a bit harsh. I can admit that I'm not the best at sentiment. You didn't have a mother's soft touch."

She sighed and rolled her eyes. "Perhaps I've been too brassy over the years, but bad memories offer bitter seasoning. It's my job to harden you against a prickly world. People might be mostly kind back home, but exploitation is a bumper crop on the Golden Coast. If you aren't careful, you'll find yourself hogtied in the basement with a knife at your throat."

This was as close to an apology as he would get, and they both knew it. The rare crack in her emotional wall emboldened him once more, even if it meant twisting the barely contained venom on his lips into the honey of submission. It was a talent well-honed from years of practice.

"I meant no disrespect and apologize for it. Your wisdom is always appreciated. But if this is a mistake, I'd like to learn it for myself. Let me use the tools you've provided. I'd really, really like have dinner with her tomorrow evening."

Calvin fidgeted with his mismatched cufflinks. The suit, the shoes, even stepping foot in this hotel; each was yet another reminder that he owed her everything.

"Just dinner. I'll be careful. I need to experience such things, even if it ends in rejection, and I'd like you not to harbor hatred for it. But as I'm here at your request, and I recognize that, if you demand I stand her up, I will. But, as you've argued in the past, a person can't grow without risk and hardship. Let me have this chance and watch what happens?"

Setting her jaw and cocking her head, she squinted up at him for a long moment before sighing.

"That's the problem with men; two heads but only enough blood to work one at a time. But you're right. To reap we must sow. Even if the seed is rotten and the soil barren. Fine. Go have your date, but don't fall head over heels into a ditch."

She noted his fidget and sighed. "Lord above, Calvin. You haven't even matched your cufflinks? Poor lamb to the slaughter."

Agnes rummaged through one of her many suitcases before producing a velvet lined box. She snatched something from within and pressed it into his palm. "Here, these were your grandfather's. At least attempt a good show for the sake of the family name."

His eyes lit in wonder at the intricacy of them. Two onyx cufflinks, picturing serpents with ruby eyes, each appearing to devour their own tails. They held a weight deeper than their mass. Calvin thanked her and attempted a hug. She seemed uncomfortable with the show of affection.

It was with a joyous song in his heart that he finished unpacking the last of her things. Calvin thanked her several times before jogging one story up to his room on the sixteenth floor.

Surprisingly, his grandmother had footed the bill for both rooms and had even given him the better of the two. Somewhere in the deeper recesses of his brain, he wondered if this wasn't a strange issuance of challenge. Was she giving him the space and opportunity to step beyond her protective gaze? More likely, she just wanted her own space, but he couldn't shake the consideration.

While her room had peeling wallpaper, his was immaculate, a fine example of the historied opulence of the Hotel Ethel. It was out of character for her.

It took a few minutes to settle in while riding the swell of his emotions, though a low-pitched hum was maddeningly present.

The next afternoon, Calvin spent several hours making himself presentable and hyperventilating.

Thank God he had his suit. And now the cufflinks.

"Painted dapper as a cornbread can hope for, I suppose." He frowned, staring at himself in the mirror.

"Your collar's up," a voice whispered in his ear.

Calvin spun, cocking his wrists to throw a jab. But there was no one except an empty, dripping shower.

"Keep it together, Cal," he muttered.

He turned to go, but something in his reflection caught his eye.

He lifted shaking hands and smoothed down the edges of his collar.

Contrary to his Agnes's expectation, Calvin's date with Victoria went swimmingly. His tongue remained mostly untied and waxed poetic long after the dessert plates were swept away.

To his delight, she was clever and well versed in a range of literature. From the fantastical world of a newer author, J.R.R. Tolkien, to the bleak pessimism of humanity painted by Friedrich Nietzsche, Victoria dominated the conversation with enthusiasm.

Their chat lasted only a few hours, but spanned lifetimes.

He'd learned she wasn't that much older, having seen twenty-four years to his twenty-two. She'd also lost her parents before she knew them. When she came of age, her foster father had attempted to marry her off to a string of oafs with important names and impotent personalities. As such, she'd packed up and begun life on her own terms.

"I must admit, the notion of a single woman on her own terrifies me. I wouldn't have the stomach for it. That you've made it your reality is particularly impressive. But what of money? Do you work? Surely a woman of your tastes and chic elegance can't rely on the generosity of strangers?"

The moment of truth, perhaps. Would she admit to prostitution? His wildest fears emerged at once.

She grinned with a fair hank of smug. "Oh yes, it does take more than a drink from desperate men to keep me bouncing. Turns out I'm pretty nifty at writing. A real hotshot. I travel around and do write ups on what I've seen; those go back to New York for magazines and newspapers. The trick is writing like a man for men. Most of my stuff is published under a nom de plume. It's easier and keeps me swimming."

"A pseudonym? Why not your own? You must be proud of your work and could be an inspiration to so many unheard voices." He sipped from the coffee mug that had been empty for the past fifteen minutes. "I'm certain you're a fabulous writer."

"No offense, Romeo. But you've clearly never been a woman." Her sneer was a smirk shrouded by condescension. "Guess I can't blame you for ignorance on the topic. Women don't get paid. I could do ten times the work in half the time just to get a dime on the dollar and a half-dozen bum pinches for my effort."

Victoria shrugged dismissively. "Nah, love. I like the way you think, but this is a man's world. I'll keep scooping from the shadows, please and thank you. Apparently, there's just not enough dignity to go around."

Calvin digested the sour words slowly. It was delicate ice on which to skate, but Agnes had unintentionally trained him for this exact event. Walking on eggshells was his forte.

Instead of appealing to her sense of logic, he offered his own raw, emotional maelstrom.

"I can't know what that must be like, but I understand enough to hate the injustice of it. You're brave enough to live what you love and clever enough to find a way to do it. That makes you uniquely special."

He inched closer but maintained a reasonably respectful distance. "I'd kiss the tears from your cheeks, but my efforts would be wasted. I doubt you'd let them fall, for one thing, and secondly, you don't want my pity. Finally, your previous experience might lead you to wrongly perceive it as an attempt to slither into your bed. I also understand the futility of the gesture even as my lips shape these worthless words, but I apologize for the whole world and everything in it."

Her jaw clenched before settling in a jaunty angle. "You have no interest in slithering into my bed, then?"

"There are few things I'd like more. Shockingly, I find myself more interested in sharing your company than your bed. But talk is cheap and, as you've made plain, you're not for sale. Additionally, you deserve more than clever words and dirty tricks. A woman of your dedicated determination deserves a proper wooing by a proper gentleman."

He grinned sheepishly, feeling sweat beads trickle anxiously down his back. "Until we find one, I humbly offer my modest companionship in his stead."

Though Victoria masked a mirthful smirk by swirling the last sip of Moscato d'Asti, the sparkle in her eyes gave up the game.

"Alright then."

Cocking his head, already lost once more in the radiance of her, Calvin grinned apologetically. "Alright when?"

"Your company; I accept it. Graciously, if it suits." Victoria shrugged. "And I can expect certain assurances before ink touches paper?"

He beamed like dog with a particularly meaty bone. "Refusing you is like counting grass. I'm sure I could, but I've no idea where to begin nor any interest in trying."

"I want to see if those lips can match that silver tongue of yours, Daddy-O. Let's find a lonely corner and give it our company."

She watched his chin hit the ground before lifting him up by his newfound ego.

He didn't mind that she took the lead, slowly gaining speed until they were running and laughing though the halls. Victoria pinned him against the elevator with passion he'd never known. And when their lips met it was as lock meets its key, as though made for one another.

Her head jerked backward, and she gave him a curious look. "Didn't think you were the type, but I'll admit a little hair pulling never hurt anyone. Next time, slide your fingers in and pull softly from the scalp. Don't rip or jerk. Firm grip, gentle tug. Got it?"

He had no idea what she was talking about but nodded all the same. If she enjoyed her hair being pulled and even offered directions, then he would master it. She whispered something more, but the acoustics of the elevator must have been off because it seemed to come from behind and either side of him. And the voice... voices, rather... were distorted.

The door opened and she dragged him into the third floor Ballroom.

But as they slipped through the silent door the fire abruptly died.

Standing before them, arms crossed, and malignance illuminated by fluorescent bulbs, was his grandmother. Calvin's imagination added fleeing shadows to her already furious aura.

Even before the judgmental tirade that followed, Calvin felt the blistering cruelty in her eyes.

Even if Victoria didn't pack and leave this very evening, she would likely never speak to him again.

"DAMN AND DRAT, CALVIN!"

To her credit, there was no quiver in her lip, nor did she break that violent gaze. Calvin knew that brutal glare all too well. As Medusa, it had a way of turning him to stone, but not Victoria.

Rather than crumpling, she seemed to drink in the fire, swelling with her own indignant rage.

She didn't flee but rather stormed off without a word edgewise.

He endured his own tongue lashing all the way back to his room. To make things worse, he slept fitfully. Waking with no covers, or the tap in the bathroom running full blast. Calvin could have sworn the telephone had been ringing off the hook, but his angry greeting only served to piss off the operator.

"How rude! Sir, you rang me! I suggest you calm yourself and try back later!"

To his bewilderment, Victoria caught Calvin at breakfast and breathlessly demanded to see him again, soon. Apparently, she'd taken the verbal assault as a personal challenge. He was more than happy to oblige.

She noticed the faint tremble as he reached for the coffee mug, the bloodshot nature of his eyes and weight of the dark bags below. No doubt she'd recognized the sluggishness of his responses. This wasn't a woman to miss obvious signs. He muffled a yawn, and she spoke her mind.

"Listen, I'd love a chat somewhere private and all, but you look terrible. Did your granny beat you or something?"

Calvin grinned into another yawn and stretch before answering. "Nothing so bad as that. I cannot begin to describe the respect I have for you after weathering that storm. But no, sleeping was miserable last night. It was like she was watching me, doing little harassments to punish me. I'd wake fighting mad without explanation. I'm fairly certain that I ruined the switchboard operator's day before it began."

"She's in your head, but you're a grown man. It's okay to be happy, even if it pisses her off. You need some shut-eye."

Victoria sighed. "I was hoping for a bit of mouth-to-mouth debauchery, but I wouldn't have you desecrating Granny's future deathbed in such a state. Go have a rest and find me when you're done."

He agreed and ten minutes later found himself beneath the covers of his bed. The warm wave of sleep soon drowned him.

However, just as he reached the veil of twilight at the very edge of proper sleep, the door creaked forcibly against its chain. The sound came clear as day. Next, the door's wood splintered and the chain broke.

Calvin popped up. Bleary vision focused on the only entrance or exit and found it closed, locked, and chained shut. Another saboteur dream.

"Leave me be, Morpheus, save your tricks for Dolos," he grumbled.

Once more, his world faded into a cozy cocoon. This time he managed to straddle the boundary marking unconsciousness.

Victoria was there. He couldn't open his leaded eyelids, but he could taste the heat of her passion and feel the curve of her naked body against his. He'd have clawed through his eyelids if only his useless arms would move.

When the weight of her shifted the bedding...

When she backed herself against his hips...

When she caressed him from low back to inner thigh...

Calvin felt his sanity melting into white-hot lust.

And through it all, he might have been encased in concrete. No part of his body would respond.

When at last he could take no more, he cried out in frustration and wrenched open his eyes to see her. To drink her in and know the shape of perfection.

But this was no Victoria.

Instead, the rotting, nude corpse of a gnarled old woman grinned wickedly back at him though milky eyes. Her smile was insanity. Spiders, beetles, and all manner of crawling life skittered across her gray, sloughing flesh.

She licked her lips, reaching below his waist, only for her slug-like tongue to slither from her mouth and land on the linens. It arrived with a splat and an entourage of maggots. To his abject horror, the abomination lifted of its own accord, scrunching toward his lips.

Her hand held a deep cold, like a slab of concrete in winter or a river rock undisturbed for centuries. It found its destination and he screamed like he'd been branded.

Calvin crushed his eyes closed, begging Almighty God to take it away as hot tears streamed down his cheeks.

A series of sharp, brutish knocks on his door wrenched him from this torture. Upon opening his eyes, there was no undead woman in his bed. Though numb and filled with electric needles, his hands flexed when he bid them to do so.

He also found himself capable of flipping over entirely when the lock and chain shattered, sending shrapnel across the room.

Hadn't that just happened?

Three police officers barreled into the room with Smith & Wessen Model 10s swinging about wildly. When he raised a helpless hand in self-defense, all three locked on his chest.

Johnny Quick-Draw ground his teeth. "Where is she? Swear to God, mister. I'll blow your fucking balls off if you killed her!" The hammer clicked menacingly.

Calvin still fought through the cobwebs of abruptly interrupted dreams.

He wanted to ask who they were talking about and beg them not to castrate him via .38 Special, but his tongue was too thick, and his reaction time found wanting. Instead, he was forced to plead his case into the pillow while slowly suffocating under an officer's weight.

The second ignored his yelps, nearly dislocating both shoulders while cuffing him.

"Check everywhere! He ain't moving." Sergeant Squash shoved his knee farther into Calvin's spine.

The manhunt ended soon after, as the hotel room only had so many cracks and crevices. Only then was he allowed to gasp and sputter properly for air between wheezing out. "What... the hell?"

One of the men glared at him while all three trained their revolvers on him.

"Where is she? Last chance!"

Calvin shook his head in exasperation. "What are you talking about? Who are—"

Three explosive reports echoed, followed by half a dozen more as they fired round after round. At the first muzzle flash, he threw himself backward onto the bed while covering his head with both arms.

But there was no pain, nor were there cuffs restricting his movement.

Upon opening his eyes, he found the door once again fully intact. His shoulders didn't hurt, though his hands were numb and throbbing.

Looking around, Calvin realized that it had been yet another hallucination or night terror or whatever one chose to call them.

The clock offered another hour of rest out of pity. But when he lay on his stomach, hand beneath the pillow, he felt something rubbery and slipped it out.

A maggot wriggled between his fingers.

At first, he questioned his perceptions. How much of what he remembered could be trusted when his dreams felt so real? When he was living a waking nightmare, what haven was left to him?

The week moved by in odd intervals, mostly as half-formed memories. Here he would be laughing with Victoria, sipping wine or sharing intimate moments in dark corners. Then, it seemed, he would rub his eyes and he'd be hauling shopping bags while his grandmother shopped and chatted with Alma, the dear old friend she'd come to entertain.

Agnes and Alma. They went together like piss and vinegar.

Both women were equally callous and left nothing to the imagination when it came to his insufficiencies. He much preferred to be ignored, which was fairly often. If ever he disgraced their ears with his own opinion on a topic, even if it matched their own, he was met with rolled eyes and snide comments.

Each evening was inundated with horrendous nightmares. Rest remained little more than a broken promise to himself.

One night he was so certain that there was a baby crying inside his room's walls that he called the front desk. An orderly arrived nearly half an hour later, but by then the sounds had stopped.

He splashed his face in the sink only to be met with the reflection of a grim-faced man standing immediately behind him. Of course, when he whirled about there was no such specter. Calvin took a mental note to seek treatment when they returned to his beloved Smoky Mountains of Tennessee.

His belongings would randomly strew themselves about his room. One day his shoes turned up missing and he made the long trudge to the front desk in sock feet. There he was greeted by the scowl of his Agnes who refused to believe him.

Determined to prove it, they marched up back to Floor Sixteen. She had no more than walked through the door before scoffing and pointing beneath his bed. All four pairs were in a neat row, though the rest of his quarters were in such disarray that he received a double scolding. One for laziness and the second for negligence.

Calvin began to question reality itself.

One afternoon, he woke to find no strange happenings. The clock marked the hour at ten till one. A quick calculation told him that he'd slept for thirteen consecutive hours. The most he'd managed in the entirety of his stay. More curiously, he felt strangely enervated. For the first time since reaching California, he felt good.

He phoned the operator and, after an apology, was switched over to Victoria's room. Surprisingly, she was not only in, but also interested in meeting, excited at the prospect even.

She mentioned they hadn't seen each other in two full days and had entertained the notion that he was avoiding her. With his sincerest apologies, he scapegoated his grandmother and inquired of her availability that evening.

Not wishing to delay, she asked for an hour to make herself presentable. He obliged thankfully, as he'd need time for himself as well.

Whatever nonsense he was dealing with hadn't burned that bridge. God willing, he intended to follow it as long as she'd allow. If she were so inclined, he would gladly spend years with Victoria. That would undoubtedly require deft diplomacy with his grandmother. She was terribly skilled at setting dynamite and lighting the fuses at critical junctures.

Somehow, she always managed to bugger their little romantic escapes with her presence. But no more...

After shaving, showering, and dressing, he met the wonder that was Victoria in the lobby, and they spent the remainder of the day together. The onyx cufflinks, for whatever reason, doubled his confidence.

They shopped for a picnic, which they took to the beach and shared in a romantic meal. He even bought a candle, though the cool Pacific breeze kept it from lighting. The waters were tempestuous and frigid, a stark contrast to the Gulf Coast.

Victoria's view of the world was like a brawny white stag—too rare to live, too beautiful to die, and far too proud to be refused. She had grand ideas of investing in the future. Her friend, one Ray Kroc, had won her over with his small carhop diner based out of Des Plaines, Illinois. It began as a barbeque shop, but she believed in his fifteen-cent hamburgers and expected it to really take off over the following years. She had a mind to invest early.

Her fiery passion was addictive, and Calvin soon agreed to join this venture.

He couldn't imagine anyone driving somewhere to purchase an overpriced burger when one could make them at home so easily, but matched her excitement with his own. Honestly, if she'd wanted to sell water to fish, he'd start collecting buckets within the week.

It was an ideal day, warm, sunny, and filled with her. The sunset was the most glorious he'd ever seen. She watched it from his lap while he toyed with her crimson locks. He experienced it only in reflection, specifically from her eyes, and found it all the more perfect.

Before it was too dark, they found their way back to society proper and hailed a cab back to the Ethel Hotel.

They weren't so much as through the main entrance before she was dragging him toward the elevator. This time, he did the pinning and a little hair tugging for good measure. The doors opened on Floor Sixteen and she ushered him out.

"Done with me already?" he asked with breathless disappointment. "That was the best day of my life and I'm not sure if I'm ready for it to end just yet."

Victoria bit his earlobe as a response and whispered, "I was hoping to see your room from the inside."

He dropped the keys half a dozen times between nerves, her roaming hands, and his excitement, but eventually managed the lock.

She had his shirt off before they hit the bed.

They rolled together, entwined as one for an indeterminate amount of time before she bit him again. This time it was hard enough to hurt. Then she jerked his head awkwardly to the side.

"Hey, not so rough," he grunted.

Twisting back to her, his stomach fell away entirely. Her eyes had rolled back into her head, and surrounding them was an umbra of black veins which tendrilled across her suddenly terrifying face like an infection of shadow.

She grinned, revealing too many rows of teeth like tiny daggers. Her purple tongue writhed like an eel. Even the walls pulsed, breathing like a living nightmare.

The struggle that ensued must have made quite the commotion because through the door burst both Alma and Agnes; they appeared ready for a fight.

Calvin was mortified for a variety of reasons, but for once he was grateful for her intervention. "Help me with her! She's hysteric!"

"I told you not to get involved with things you don't understand, Calvin!" Agnes growled even as she tugged at Victoria's arms.

As though expecting such a curious situation, Alma overturned a bag filled with a battery of occult objects ranging from crosses and holy water to a bone-handled blade of chipped black stone and herb sprigs twisted into a pentagram.

The moment Alma began chanting, Victoria stiffened, and her head twisted around one-hundred-and-eighty degrees to glare back at her.

Agnes started next, joining in the words that vibrated with ancient power. Victoria's face twitched back and forth between them, sneering with malice.

Whatever they were doing was working, because after initially lashing out at his grandmother, Victoria's arms twisted back against her sides as though pinned by an intangible fist. She writhed, floating upward until none of her was touching anything at all. It was as though she were suspended by spectral wires. The sounds that came from her lips were black acid, perhaps half a dozen voices in unison.

Calvin scrambled back against the head of the bed, unsure how to help.

Alma raised an obelisk of clear quartz toward the possessed woman and black ink seemed to drain from her to fill the crystal until it looked no different than obsidian. A moment later, she dashed the obelisk against the floor, where it shattered into a thousand smoking pieces before dissipating entirely. Victoria fell back to the bed limp as a noodle.

"What the hell? Jesus Christ Almighty, what in God's name was that?" Calvin sputtered.

Agnes glowered, still muttering incantations. Alma answered him instead.

"Hell, indeed. Demonic possession. Your dear grandmother sensed the darkness early. Always had an eye for such things."

He wrung his impuissant hands. "What do I do? How do I help her?"

"*You just need to wake up,*" a chilling voice whispered.

Snapping around, he once more found himself lying in bed, this time drenched in sweat.

Calvin's sanity was held together by two frayed knots, and they were grinding against one another.

The phone rang and he answered by swinging his pillow like a baseball bat. Heart pounding, he meekly collected it from the floor.

"Jesus... You sound like two pounds of shit in a half-pound bag. I rang to see if you were free, but..." Victora's good-natured jab stung, but it was laced with genuine concern. "If you need the night to take care of yourself, let me know. I could bring some soup. Isn't that what people do?"

Calvin rubbed his burning, red-rimmed eyes. "No. No soup. I'm fine. I'd love to see you."

"Wonderous!" Victoria cooed. "I have positively momentous plans for this evening!"

"Can't wait to see you," he added, but there was a click, then silence, eventually followed by a dial tone.

Knowing he needed to get a grip, he took a quick, frigid shower. His teeth chattered and his fingers quivered as he readied his best suit. His grandfather's cufflinks were there, and he'd certainly need them tonight.

~~ to be continued ~~

15th Floor – Premium Suites
1956

Blood, Tea, and Whispering Wallpaper
Marie Lestrange

Agnes

The trouble with living long enough to see your secrets turn into wallpaper was that more often than not, that wallpaper yaps for all of eternity. Quite dreadful, honestly.

"Pipe down, girls!"

A loose, tattered flap of wallpaper unexpectedly peeled free from the wall and flapped in Agnes's general direction like a ragged, spectral hand waving for attention. The whispering chorus of her sister spirits, swimming among the sun-faded, floral-patterned walls of the Hotel Ethel, usually presented as a low buzz. But this was intentionally flagrant. The old bats were becoming bolder.

If only she had known that immortality came with drafty windows and the unpleasant stench of mildew—well, the Baking Circle probably wouldn't have their very own "Agnes" as a fringe friend.

Down the once-grand hallway, a tall figure in a black trench coat and fedora strode past, leaving a faint chill in his wake. The Baking Circle fell instantly silent, every whisper pressed flat against the faded wallpaper. Even the boldest old bat knew better than to cross paths with the likes of him—for he always walked alone, and always, somehow, in a hurry to somewhere else in time.

The man now gone, the whispers started up again.

Agnes the accomplice.

Agnes the agitator.

Agnes the apoplectic.

Agnes the absolutely-over-this-shit.

"Well damn and drat!" she cried, crossing the parlor to close the wide open window that was letting in far too much sea breeze. Nearly set her up for an uncomfortably damp afternoon indoors, it had. Couldn't be having that. Not at'all.

Agnes rubbed her arms to stave off a bit of San Francisco's October chill, but mercy be, it had already seeped in. The cold drilling deep into her bones, settling into the marrow. In times like these, she felt her age.

Too close to the sky up here, that was the trouble. Ought to be in the vaults, where the real power lay.

She moved through the suite, a gilded cage that had once been the height of Art Deco fashion. Now? A stage set for a play long past its prime. Gold leaf peeled from the walls, exposing the bare plaster beneath.

Just like my skin, shedding its taut finery, bit by bit.

The plush carpets were threadbare, their intricate patterns faded with time and neglect. The aroma of damp stone and forgotten secrets lingered, seeming to drink in, then vomit out, her cinnamon-and-vanilla potpourri before dismissing it entirely.

It always lingered.

Secrets were power. A firm mantra repeated over decades. *And we, the Baking Circle, held the greatest secret of all.*

Well… *they* did. But she did, too, by association.

Her gaze snapped to the murals. The six founders of the Hotel Ethel, their painted eyes following her. Or did they? Agnes narrowed her gaze to consider the portraits more intently. Sometimes, in the quiet hours, the eyes held accusation rather than admiration. Pure judgment at other times (especially from Corrine).

They were just paint on plaster for most of the year. Except for the days leading up to the anniversary, and with this year being a sacrifice year… well, the old bats had been quite active for weeks!

You'd think she'd be used to it after all these years. One by one, their living numbers dwindled and the spectral ranks bloomed, or, in language for the simpletons: as the women of the Baking Circle died, their spirits infested the walls of the Ethel Hotel.

Still, it rattled her every now and again.

She reached for the silver kettle, its surface tarnished with age. The metal felt cold beneath her fingertips. Reminiscent of the vaults far below, where the real work, the real blessings, and real abundance happened. Where it would happen again, very soon.

This kettle had been present at every Baking Circle meeting; a silent witness to their pacts and promises. As the water bubbled, the rising steam begged to coalesce into matronly forms.

"Not yet, dears. We must wait for Alma, as you well know."

She could almost see their withered faces swirling within the vapor: Ethel, pragmatic, unyielding; Lillie, flamboyant and impulsive; Louise, gentle but fiercely loyal; Maud, the fiery rebel, and, of course, Corrine.

Her heart winced. The pain never really went away. Corrine, the most cunning and deadly of them all.

Agnes glanced at a newspaper clipping on her vanity, its edges yellowed and brittle. "Local Couple Still Missing," the headline screamed. Calvin's birth parents. Their stupid, hopeful smiles.

Collateral damage. A necessary sacrifice.

But such guilt was wasted.

She opened the velvet-lined jewelry box, revealing the tarnished silver locket. Inside, nestled against faded silk, rested a lock of Corrine Carrington's golden hair. Stolen after her death, a piece of her essence captured and preserved. Agnes traced the delicate strands with her fingertip, a jolt of energy surging through her. More than a memento. A key.

The fog-shrouded cityscape didn't deter Agnes from making her way to the window, looking further beyond where San Francisco sprawled beneath. The neighboring Coit Tower's imposing silhouette cast a long, foreboding shadow across the Bay, a silent tribute to Lillie Hitchcock Coit. A reminder of what had been accomplished and maintained all these years.

The kettle whistled, the shrill sound startling her. Agnes poured boiling water over tea leaves, the familiar scent of bergamot filling the air. Stirring the mixture slowly, she tightened her fingers around the locket, knuckles white.

"Thirty years, Corrine," Agnes whispered. "The boy is ready."

Agnes checked her reflection. Not too severe? Not too… eager? A touch of rouge to brighten the cheeks, a severe chignon to emphasize the bones. This morning was about business, not beauty, although she never truly discounted the power of appearances. Especially when dealing with the dead.

The grandfather clock in the hall, one of her favorite pieces here on Floor Fifteen, chimed ten o'clock. Prompt as always. Good. There was nothing worse than a tardy ghost; they tended to bring a draft.

She adjusted the lace tablecloth, ensuring the floral arrangements were precisely centered. Lilies—Lillie's favorite, of course. A subtle nod to the past.

There came an unmistakable tapping down the hall; the slow, deliberate rhythm was a melody as familiar as her own heartbeat. "How very Poe," she chuckled.

She poured a second cup of tea; her favorite black, of an imperial-spiced blend, with just a drop of honey, and waited.

A sharp rap at the door. Agnes inhaled deeply and straightened her spine. Show time!

The heavy oak door creaked open with a reluctant groan, and Alma stepped inside, the faint scent of embalming fluid trailing her like a shadow. Her gloves, ink-stained and stiff, clutched a small shard of quartz—an earthquake relic from 1906, smooth and veined with delicate fractures. Agnes nodded to it briefly, a silent acknowledgment passing between them.

"Alma, darling! Punctual as ever." Agnes pulled the door wide, greeting her old friend with a practiced embrace. Alma de Bretteville Spreckels, a titan in her own right, and the last of the living Baking Circle besides Agnes herself.

Well, she was more of an honorary member... a replacement after the first ritual, but still. By association, right?

Even at this stage of their years, she could still see clear up Alma's nostrils to count the flecks of dry skin peeling off from the scarring. Such a tall and poised woman, Alma was.

Too many "pep pills," one could wager. Mother's little helper, indeed.

A small and highly unladylike chortle nearly escaped Agnes's lips. *Grandmother's little helper* was more like it these days.

Alma slouched a bit to plant a kiss on both cheeks, her gaze taking in the suite with sharp appraisal.

"Agnes. You've kept it nice. Although, I liked the place when we were younger; more virile—a palace for ladies of the night. Truth be told, I assumed the worst, but you've done as well as could be expected. Hotel Ethel still shines despite the circumstances."

Alma settled heavily onto the settee, her cane thumping against the floor.

"One does what one can." Agnes gestured toward the tea service. "Care for a cup? Darjeeling, your usual."

Alma nodded, accepting the delicate porcelain cup. "And the others? Are they... joining us?"

Agnes smiled, a thin, brittle expression. "They wouldn't miss it for the world." She glanced around the room, lingering on the vacant chairs, fingers closing tighter still around the locket of Corrine's post-suicide hair.

"Ethel? Lillie? Louise? Maud? Corrine? Ladies, you will each forever have a seat at this table. Please, join us."

A chill swept through the room, the temperature plummeting several degrees. The scent of lilies intensified, becoming almost cloying. Shadows along the wallpaper deepened, swirling and coalescing in the corners of the room. The air crackled with static electricity, like the coming of a storm, raising the hairs on the back of Agnes's neck.

Alma shivered, clutching her teacup. "They're already here, then."

"Always." Agnes opened the window to give her spectral guests a little more room to make themselves comfortable.

A faint, ethereal voice echoed in her mind: *Agnes... it has been too long.*

Ethel. Practical, efficient, always to the point.

"Not long enough, Ethel. However, such is the case, and such we must do. The details of the anniversary, the guest list..." Agnes tapped a manicured nail against a stack of papers on the table. "We need to finalize everything. Ensure the... necessary arrangements are in place."

Another voice, laced with laughter and mischief: *Oh, darling, you always were so wonderfully morbid.*

Lillie. Her favorite and the only one who spoke to her as an equal. *I trust you've selected someone... suitable this year? Someone with spirit? Someone with youth?*

Agnes ignored a shiver that flowed down her spine. "You already know exactly who I've selected, and why. He will be here soon enough. The chessboard has been set, now it's just a matter of moving pieces."

A dry, rustling sound, like leaves skittering across a tombstone. *The ball must be spectacular. A distraction. A feast for the senses, so they don't notice the... main course is missing.*

Louise. Kind, gentle Louise, forever haunted by the events of the past.

The final voice, a whisper of ice and ambition: *Ensure the boy is ready. The ritual is everything.*

Corrine. Oh, how the years had changed her, both in the flesh and now beyond it.

Agnes turned back to Alma, who watched with a mixture of fascination and unease. "We are all in agreement and understand the stakes. The ball must proceed. Everything must be perfect. For Calvin, for all of us."

Agnes looked longingly at the photo on her desk. The face of an innocent child seemed to plead back at her. A boy whom she had long ago condemned to the ritual.

But it must be done…

Alma swallowed, her clouded vision darting around the room, desperate to look upon the faces of her Baking Circle sisters again, even though she couldn't. "And the sacrifice? Are we certain… is there no other way?"

Agnes's smirk was devoid of any hint of warmth. "There hasn't been another way since 1910, Alma. You know the terms of the pact. This hotel…" She gestured expansively. "…our legacy… it demands a price. And that price must be paid. Every. Single. Time."

"Of course," Alma murmured, poured more steaming Darjeeling onto the table runner than into the delicate porcelain cups, but such was the life with her failing eyesight. The tea's scent curled upward like smoke, mingling with the faint musk of aged paper and lavender potpourri. She set a pitifully filled cup before Agnes, who accepted it with a nod, the porcelain wincing beneath her ink-stained fingers.

"Foundation's weakening," Alma said, voice low, eyes sharp beneath heavy lids. "East wing's cracks deepen. We'll need to reinforce."

Agnes smiled thinly, fingering the silver locket at her throat. Inside, Corrine's hair writhed, coiling like a serpent trapped beneath glass. "Last time we patched it, the 'Carrington Incident' left its mark." Her words were smooth, but the cold edge beneath them was unmistakable.

Alma's fingers twitched. "Richard's blood soaked the walls, but the cracks remain. Careless work. The heir grows restless."

She withdrew a pearl-handled hatpin, sharp and gleaming in the dim light. With a practiced motion, she pricked her finger. A bead of blood welled, trembling as it fell into her tea. The liquid darkened instantly, thickening, congealing until a rusted vault key emerged, suspended in the black depths—the very key last used in the 1933 sacrifice.

Agnes's breath caught in her throat. The key was a grim talisman, a poignant reminder of unpaid debts.

From the murals, the painted eyes of the Baking Circle's founders gleamed unnaturally. The room's golden glow dimmed, shadows pooling and deepening. The air chilled, carrying whispers that seemed to rise from the walls themselves:

"Blood for the foundation, heir for the cracks."

"The heir's blood seals the pact."

The locket burned fiercely against Agnes's skin. Corrine's hair squirmed, desperate to escape its prison.

Alma's voice dropped to a whisper., "The boy must be ready and the sacrifice flawless."

Agnes reached into a velvet box, lifting the cursed cufflinks—gold serpents devouring their own tails, ruby eyes glinting with ancient malice. They hummed softly, resonating with the dark promise woven into Calvin's stolen bloodline. She'd stolen them back after their first night, to show her sisters.

"He will wear these to the ball. Both as symbol… and shackle."

Alma smiled, sharp and knowing. "At midnight, the vault will open. The foundation will drink again."

Agnes nodded, eyes fixed on the twitching hair in the locket. "And the Circle will endure."

The seven women nodded concurrently, some more solidly than others, of course.

"The Circle will endure."

Calvin

The sharp sting at the back of his head throbbed with every blink, a dull ache that blurred the edges of the room. He sat before the tall mirror in his suite, the golden light of the late afternoon filtering through the heavy drapes and gilding the polished wood.

The onyx cufflinks Agnes had pressed into his palm earlier caught the light, their black surfaces gleaming like twin pools of midnight. He turned them over slowly, mesmerized by the cold weight and the intricate serpentine engravings curling around each one.

His reflection stared back, eyes glassy and unfocused, but then something shifted. The reflection's lips parted, mouthing words he couldn't quite hear at first. Then the melody came, soft and haunting, threading through the room like a whisper only he could catch.

"Sleep, dear child, your future calls,

Cradle ash to stitch the walls,

Six souls seek what time forgot,

Crimson vows or castle rot."

Calvin's breath hitched. The lullaby was impossibly old, a song his grandmother sang. Said to be the base for "Hush Little Baby." Yet there it was, slipping from the lips of his own reflection, in none other than Victoria's voice, the haunting melody curling around him like a shadow.

The reflection winked.

Calvin jerked back, heart hammering. His fingers clenched the cufflinks, the cold melting into his skin like a sickness. He tried to shake off the dizziness and steady his racing thoughts. *It's just nerves. Just the bump on your head. You're imagining things.*

But the lullaby lingered, echoing faintly in his ears.

"B'cuz if you don't... the walls'll come down."

The room seemed to tilt. He gripped the dresser edge, knuckles white, and forced each breath. In for eight, out for four.

Breathe in...

One...two...three...four...five...six...seven...eight...

Breathe out...

One...two...three...four...

Whew.

The hope that had flickered all day—the possibility of something good, something real—felt fragile, like a candle struggling against a room full of birthday partiers intent upon blowing their wish out into the world.

Maybe he should make a wish.

Tonight.

Agnes and Alma

Far below, in the hotel's vaults, the air was a different kind of bone-cold—chilling and absolute. Agnes stood stiffly beneath the flickering gaslight, the shadows swallowing the corners of the stone chamber like a starved beast, eager to satiate. Alma sat at the heavy oak table, her ink-stained gloves clutching a fountain pen and bleeding darkness onto the brittle ledger before her.

The ledger was ancient, its pages yellowed and worn, but the ink still flowed thick and dark as Alma carefully inscribed a name below three others:

Richard Carrington

George and Etta Roberts

Calvin Roberts

Dry paper drank ink like a tick left to feast and fester. The pen's nib leaked, dribbling a pool of contained midnight onto the page. It was as though the grimoire and quill worked in tandem to hide their secrets within each other. As though they, too, understood the power and danger of clandestine knowledge.

Agnes's gaze was hard, unwavering. "Are you certain this is the right time?" she asked, voice low but edged with steel.

Alma's eyes flickered with doubt, but she nodded. "The boy is marked. The bloodline demands it. We cannot delay any longer. Ethel crumbles as we speak."

Across the vault, elevator doors creaked open with mournful reverence, as though they remembered what would soon follow. From within, another memory, this one an attendant, emerged as silent as a coffin nail in grave dirt.

"The Circle always collects," he rasped, voice dry as sawdust and sand.

Agnes was transfixed by his disfigurement, as always, but remained resolute. "And we always pay our dues."

"A debt owed by all, soon to be paid by one. May the Circle remain unbroken." The attendant's lips twitched in what might have been a smile or a grimace.

She nodded, and added, "May the Circle remain unbroken."

He vanished back into the shaft, leaving the vault even colder and darker than before, if that were possible.

Alma dabbed at the spreading ink, but it was no use. The blot grew, somehow... alive, creeping across the page like night devouring day. She looked up at Agnes, and when she spoke, her voice was barely a whisper. "This ledger is more than a mere record. It's prophecy."

Agnes nodded slowly, her fingers tightening around a small velvet box. She opened it to reveal the original set of onyx cufflinks, their black surfaces etched with serpents swallowing their own tails, ruby eyes gleaming faintly. Identical to the cufflinks Calvin now wore.

They were the same as his grandfather had worn on the night of his murder.

Calvin

The lullaby drifted again, carried on the faintest breeze through the suite's open window. Calvin's head swam, the room blurring around the edges as he steadied himself against the dresser.

"Sleep, dear child, your future calls."

Drawn by the sound, he moved toward the ballroom doors, the amber light of his suite on the sixteenth floor fading behind him as he stepped into the shadowed and hollow heart of the Ethel Hotel. The grand room was empty, save for moonlight spilling through tall windows, casting shadows across the polished floor.

Victoria stood alone in the center, her back to him, her voice soft and clear as she sang.

"Cradle ash to stitch the walls."

Her words sent icy tendrils dancing down Calvin's spine. This was no innocent song, no proper childhood lullaby. This was a summons, a curse. The lullaby of Corrine Carrington—the woman whose bloodline had cursed his own, whose legacy was woven into the very walls of the Hotel Ethel.

He'd heard the stories around town. Eavesdropped on Agnes enough to know… something was unnaturally, supernaturally, wrong with the Ethel Hotel.

His breath caught, panic rising like a blistering magma begging to erupt from his jaw. The room spun, the shadows deepened, and the haunting melody echoed in his mind.

He was trapped between hope and horror, caught in a blissless experience he hardly understood, other than to know there was no longer an option to escape.

A curse!

Calvin woke with a start, his neck stiff from the horridly awkward position he was in. Must have fallen asleep in the armchair again. He rose, consumed with an unrelenting feeling that he needed to find Corrine.

Wait… no. Victoria.

Not Corrine.

He crossed his suite, marching for the lift to take him down to the ballroom. Against all better judgment, he knew without a shadow of a doubt he'd find her there.

"Damn and drat, indeed."

The grand ballroom of Hotel Ethel lay empty, save for the soft moonlight filtering through the tall, arched windows. Just as his dream, but this time in reality.

The freshly waxed floor gleamed like a dark mirror, with the faintest of shadows cast by the ornate chandeliers overhead. Calvin's head still throbbed from the earlier bump. Each new wave of pain scattered his thoughts all over again. He blinked, trying to steady himself as he stepped further into the room.

Victoria stood in the center, waiting. Her silhouette was sharp against the pale light, the delicate curve of her neck, her back, her hips exposed beneath the soft waves of her much-too-thin but oh-so-wonderful satin dress.

She smiled with a slightly furrowed brow and reached for him. "Calvin? Are you all right? You seemed… distant."

He swallowed hard, forcing a smile. "Just a bit dizzy. The room spun for a moment."

She stepped closer, her perfume drifting to him—a scent like freshly turned earth, damp and rich with decay. It was unsettlingly familiar yet intoxicating. He finally took her hand, the warmth of her skin grounding him.

For a moment, everything seemed normal. The music of their conversation flowed easily, laughter bubbling between them like a fragile spring. But then, as the candlelight flickered, something shifted.

Calvin noticed the flicker of movement on the floor. His eyes bulged when he looked down.

Victoria's shadow peeled free from beneath her feet, sliding forward like a living thing. It bowed deeply, then rose, curtsying with a grace that was both elegant and grotesque. The movement was an exact mimicry of a habit he'd read about in old journals—Corrine Carrington's signature gesture.

His breath caught in his chest.

Victoria's smile faltered, her eyes darkening with a strange light. Then, in a voice that was no longer quite her own, she whispered, "Once more, madame, and only once more will I ask…"

The words sent a chill through Calvin's spine. The voice was different. Sinister. Unlike Victoria's usual tone.

It was Corrine's—silken, cruel, and ancient.

Victoria pressed a slender hand to his lips, producing a cigarette stained with deep red lipstick—the unmistakable shade his grandmother Agnes had worn since 1933. He barely had time to react before she tilted his head back and pressed the butt to his mouth.

The smoke curled into his lungs, tasting of bitter almonds and roses— sweet, deadly cyanide.

His eyes widened, panic rising, but Victoria's gaze held him fast, hypnotic and unyielding.

She leaned in, her lips brushing his cheek—a kiss so cold it burned like ice. The touch left a frost that spread through his veins. Her breath smelled of grave soil and wilted petals, a scent that clung to him like a shroud.

The murals along the ballroom walls flickered, the painted faces twisting and shifting. Calvin watched in horrified disbelief as his own face replaced Richard Carrington's in a noose, the rope tightening with every heartbeat. The image burned into his mind, a silent warning etched in shadow and paint.

Victoria's voice dropped to a whisper, low and venomous. "She should've let me keep Richard."

Calvin staggered back, the room spinning wildly. His heart pounded in his ears, drowning out everything but the echo of that cruel promise.

The shadow at Victoria's feet bowed once more, then merged back into her as if it had never left.

She smiled again, but the warmth was gone, replaced by ice that seeped into the marrow of his bones.

"Are you feeling better? Let's get you back upstairs and in bed, darling," she cooed, but the edge in her tone made his skin crawl.

Calvin nodded reluctantly, though terror churned beneath his calm facade. He knew, now, that the woman beside him was no longer entirely Victoria, and he didn't wish to anger her.

The night had turned.

A haunting at the Hotel Ethel had begun.

The elevator rattled and groaned as Victoria led Calvin down to the Vaults, her gloved hand cool and insistent on his arm. The brass doors parted with a sigh, and the air changed—thicker, tinged with the scent of burnt almonds and wet stone. Calvin blinked, the world swimming, his cufflinks burning against his wrists as if they'd absorbed the fever of his nerves.

Victoria's heels clicked down the stone corridor, her silhouette sharp and elegant. But the shadows clung to her strangely, stretching and twitching in ways that defied the golden hall light. Calvin's own reflection in the glass was pale, sweat beading at his hairline. He tried to steady his breathing, but the further they walked, the more the air felt wrong—heavy, like the hush before a funeral hymn.

They reached the center vault. Victoria's hand lingered on the arched door frame, her smile brittle. "You trust me, don't you, Calvin?" she asked, her voice made of velvet and razor blades.

He nodded, not trusting his own.

Inside, the Vaults were cold and ominous. All the trappings of hotel storage had been cleared out, revealing a low altar cobbled from jagged hunks of blackened stone. He recognized the look of it—San Francisco's old bones—he'd seen some very similar in a local memorial made from the 1906 earthquake rubble—repurposed for something unholy. Candlelight flickered, casting oily shadows that slithered up the walls.

Calvin's shoes stuck to the floor. He looked down to watch as black sludge up from the cracks in the stone floor, thick as tar, sluggishly creeping toward the altar. The stench overwhelmed him: sweet almonds, rot, and something metallic, maybe copper? No, iron. It reminded him of biting his tongue. Blood. He gagged, covering his mouth.

Victoria's skin looked pale, almost translucent in the candlelight. As she moved, Calvin saw cracks spiderwebbing up her neck and jaw, fine as crazed porcelain. She turned, and for a heartbeat, her face split. Beneath the surface, Calvin glimpsed something gray and sunken—Corrine's corpse-smile stretching impossibly wide.

He stumbled back, clutching the altar for support. The stone was cold, rough, and sticky with the black ooze. The moment he touched it, memories surged—Agnes's voice, chanting in a language he didn't know, standing over his crib as a baby.

The memory was sharp and sickening: Agnes's hands, red to the wrist, covered in his parents' blood, the circle of women chanting, the taste of iron in the air.

The shadows upon the walls began to move. Faint, elderly, feminine whispers slithered from the curling edges, wretched voices layered and overlapping:

"Blood for the cracks, heir for the foundation."

The voices grew louder, the words burrowing into his skull. Calvin pressed his palms to his ears, but the sound only grew sharper.

Victoria's shadow stretched behind her, impossibly long. Her skin cracked further, flakes drifting to the floor like wilted rose petals. She smiled, and Corrine's voice came out: "Your grandmother always was a clever woman. But she never fully understood the price."

Calvin tried to pull away from the altar, but the tar held him fast. The cufflinks burned, searing his skin, and he cried out, the pain white-hot and electric.

The walls bulged and split. The faces of the Baking Circle sisters— Ethel, Lillie, Alma, Louise, Maud, and Corrine—emerged, their eyes hollow and hungry. They slid from the walls, trailing black ooze, their mouths opening in a chorus of whispers that filled the room.

"Blood for the cracks. Heir for the foundation. The Circle endures."

Victoria—no, Corrine—leaned close, her breath cold as the grave. "You were meant for this, Calvin."

He squeezed his eyes shut, trying to block out the ghosts, the pain, the memory of Agnes's hands, the chanting, and the blood. But the voices pressed in, relentless, as the room spun and the altar pulsed beneath his hands.

When he opened his eyes, the ghosts of the Baking Circle were all around him, their fingers reaching, their eyes wide with malicious intent.

The Circle always collects.

The altar of earthquake stone pulsed with a sickly light. Calvin, wrists burning beneath the onyx cufflinks, stood encircled by the assembled Baking Circle—Agnes at his side, Alma trembling, Victoria radiant and cold. The ghosts materialized from the walls, their eyes hollow, yet eager.

The air vibrated with overlapping chants, each spectral woman's voice muffled but insistent. It was a cacophony: the scrape of stone, the hiss of tar, the desperate thrum of Calvin's own heartbeat. Agnes's locket writhed at her throat, Corrine's hair inside twisting and knotting with anticipation.

Victoria's shadow peeled from her feet, bowing low before the altar. She smiled at Calvin, but her eyes were Corrine's.

"It's almost time, cousin," she whispered, her voice lilting with a secret joy.

Calvin's cacophonous mind balked at that. "Cousin?"

The word echoed, absurd, impossible.

Alma's pen scratched Calvin's name into the 1910 ledger, black ink pooling and running, as if the page itself wept.

The ghosts pressed closer.

Corrine's laughter erupted from Victoria's lips—a sound that was not human, not living. "Did you really think you could hide from me, Agnes?" A malicious blend of Corrine and Victoria's voices rang out, mocking and triumphant. "Did you think the results of your little tryst with Richard would go unnoticed… Agnes?"

Agnes froze, the blood draining from her face as she stepped back from the circle. "No-no, that was years ago. No one knew—"

"Oh, but I did." Corrine's voice was everywhere: in the flicker of the candles, the drip of the black sludge, the very stones beneath their feet. "You thought you'd gotten away with it. You thought the child was safe. But the Circle always collects, Agnes. And tonight, it collects your grandson… Richard's grandson… and you."

Calvin staggered, bile rising in his throat. "What are you saying?" His voice was a raw scream, barely audible over the chanting, the laughter, the scraping of spectral feet.

Victoria stepped forward, her face shifting, flickering between Corrine's corpse-smile and her own. "You're not just the heir, Calvin. You're the payment. Agnes's blood, Richard's blood—bound together. And… well…

Granddaddy knocked up ole Granny Agnes before he went for his little swing, now didn't he?"

She winked at him, eye color changing in a flash. "That's why when Grandmama CiCi asked for my help with this year's ritual… I simply couldn't refuse her."

The truth crashed over him, suffocating. "No. No, that's not possible… but we—"

"Blood is thicker than water, dear cousin." She cackled. "And tastes much better with a side of sacrifice, I like to think."

The Circle's ghosts pressed in, black tar oozing from their mouths as they chanted, "Blood for the cracks. Heir for the foundation. Agnes for the Circle."

Calvin screamed, the sound swallowed by the rising symphony of sorrow. The altar vibrated beneath his hands, the stone growing hot, then blistering cold.

Victoria—no, Corrine—leaned in, her lips brushing his ear, her breath grave-cold. "You were always meant for this, cousin. Your grandmother's sin, your father's blood, my vengeance. The Circle endures."

Agnes's hands shook as she clutched the locket, Corrine's hair inside now a writhing mass of black snakes. The ghosts reached for her, their fingers sharp as knives, their lips tearing open as they howled her name.

"No!" Agnes shouted, voice ragged. "You can't have him. You won't have me, either!"

With a cry, she ripped the locket from her neck and hurled it to the ground. The glass shattered, Corrine's hair spilling out in a writhing, smoking heap. The Circle's chant faltered, the ghosts recoiling as if struck.

Corrine's laughter turned to a shriek of rage, echoing through the room. The altar cracked, black sludge pouring from the fissures, swallowing the ledger, the pen, the names.

Calvin fell to his knees, gasping for breath, the world spinning in a maelstrom of screams, gold thread, and broken covenants.

Above it all, Agnes stood defiant, her eyes blazing. "The Circle ends with me!" she spat, as the ritual collapsed in chaos and darkness.

Floor Fifteen

Agnes's hands trembled as she shoved the last of her precious items into a battered leather satchel—the splattered ledger, the onyx cufflinks. Her suite, once stale, now stifled her breath, the golden light now a cruel mockery of safety. She needed to leave, to disappear before the Circle's shadows closed in for good. She'd sent Calvin to gather his things from Floor Sixteen.

A sudden gust slammed the door open with a violent crash. The heavy wood rattled against the walls. Agnes whipped around, heart pounding, to see Victoria sauntering in, her silhouette framed by the hallway's dim light. Her eyes gleamed with cold fire, and the faintest curve of a cruel smile played on her lips.

"You really thought you could run?" Victoria's voice, all hers this time, was silk and poison.

Agnes gritted her teeth, clutching the satchel tighter. "This ends tonight."

Victoria stepped forward, her shadow peeling free at her feet, curtsying mockingly before the portrait of Corrine. "Precisely, homewrecker. Corrine didn't forget. And neither do I."

Before Agnes could react, a blade flashed, cold steel slicing across her neck.

No chance to run.

No chance to fight.

After all these years of penance and guilt… the Circle had come to hold her accountable anyway.

Pain exploded, hot and sharp, a warm wetness spilling down her blouse and gushing onto the floor. She sank to her knees, vision blurring.

Through the haze, she saw the hotel's façade crack, fractures spiderwebbing across the textured ceiling just like in 1933. The building groaned—its thirst for blood finally quenched.

Victoria's shadow bowed low to Corrine's portrait, the lips of the ghostly woman turning up at both corners in silent approval.

Agnes's last sight was the shattered locket on the floor, Corrine's hair writhing like serpents.

Victoria's voice, cold and final, echoed in the dark: "The Circle endures."

The ritual recipe was complete, one ingredient substituted, and the Ethel Hotel's hunger was sated for another twenty-three years.

14th Floor – Premium Suites
1994

Heartless Husband
Ali Toothman

The elevator door arrives at our floor with a loud ding, yanking me out of whatever daze I had fallen into. His normal aggravation level is amped up thanks to the couple who were making out in the corner of the elevator.

They dressed like they were from the 1930s or so. Maybe they were at a themed party before stumbling back into the hotel, unable to keep their hands off of each other. I'd give anything for a relationship like theirs. Unfortunately, I'm stuck with the asshole walking ahead of me.

I snap to attention and follow my husband, Todd, onto the fourteenth floor. I keep my eyes trained on the floor until Todd is a few paces ahead of me then try to get a good look around.

Along the light floral wallpaper, there are portraits hung with gold plates beneath. Each painting features a different woman, possibly the founders of the Hotel Ethel. I faintly recall hearing it was created by a group of women who called themselves the Baking Circle.

Before I can catch myself, I'm staring at a picture of Ethel W. Sperry. As I take in her features and the stern look upon her face, Todd snatches my hand and pulls me in the direction of our suite. He shoots me a vicious glare then tugs me along, causing me to trip over my heels.

When I right myself, I catch sight of a housekeeper at her cart who quickly averts her eyes to the floor when Todd turns her way. Though he gives her a curt nod and faux smile, she knows he's not as kind as he pretends to be.

As he leads up to our room, I catch glimpses of the portraits. It feels like the women's eyes are following me with each step and a tingle runs up my spine, raising the hairs on the back of my neck.

Todd stops at our door and I nearly run into him as I continue to stare around the halls. He turns and I catch the death glare he shoots me over his shoulder. I ignore his annoyance and wait for him to get the door opened. Motion in my peripheral catches my attention as Todd grumbles and curses as he fiddles with the lock.

I whip my head in the direction of the movement and am surprised to see a young boy, likely around five, running toward me with a bright smile. I can't help but smile back his way as he zigzags down the hallway without a care in the world. My heart gets hit with a sharp pain.

I've always dreamed of being a mom but there's no way in hell I'd even consider having a child with the monster of a husband I have. As I turn and watch the little guy pass by, the door comes unlocked and Todd lets out a huff of frustration.

My mood is instantly soured as I'm dragged from my short-lived daydream and back to reality.

He reaches for my arm and I step away before he can grab me once again. A huff of frustration leaves him, then he gestures for me to enter the room. I hold my chin up high in an act of defiance as I cross the threshold.

A sharp pinch hits the back of my arm, causing me to yelp. I chance a look at Todd and catch a smirk on his face at his accomplishment in harming me.

In a chance to get away from him, I head straight to the en suite, shutting and locking the door behind me. I pull myself up onto the marble countertop, landing in between the twin sinks, and swing my feet back and forth. I tap my fingers on the edge and stare at the wall ahead of me, nothing particular on my mind except the incessant need to be away from Todd.

A few minutes have passed as I count the flowers in the rows on the wallpaper when I hear a thump against the door. My head drops between my shoulders and I let out a breath of exasperation, knowing it's Todd about to demand my presence.

"Bethany, you can't stay in there all night," he says in a sweet voice.

I roll my eyes but don't reply. Instead, I kick off my shoes and let them fall with loud thuds to the floor. Todd sighs and I hear his footsteps as he retreats from the door. I pull my feet up and sit crisscross on the counter, then lean back against the large mirror behind me. I know he'll be irritated with the smudges I cause but I can't seem to bring myself to care.

Time ticks by and I allow myself the chance to open my mind and think freely. The one thing I keep coming back to is the various portraits along the hallway leading to our room.

From the looks of each of the six women, I don't believe they're related, but they all seemed to have the same look about them. They exerted a confidence I don't think I could ever feel while also keeping a hard look on their faces. I imagine they demanded respect, even from men.

The way their eyes followed me as I passed still gives me the chills. It was like they were trying to keep watch over me. That's what I tell myself anyway.

Todd pounds on the door, clearly over my ignoring him, and I relent. I drop from the counter and grab my shoes before making my way to the door. As I open it, Todd shoves forward, smacking me in the shoulder with the heavy wood, the knob hitting me in the stomach.

I let out a huff as the air is forced from my body and I know it will leave a bruise. Todd seems pleased with himself and lets a grim smile touch his lips.

Ignoring the fact he thinks he's getting the best of me, I stride into our suite and place my shoes by the door.

Despite Todd being nearly forty years my senior, I rarely give him the respect he believes he deserves. Respect is earned, not given, and he certainly hasn't proven he deserves mine. It infuriates him to no end.

"Bethany, it's our anniversary. Can't you pretend to be happy to be with me?" Todd asks, a pleading in his voice. He and I both know he couldn't care less about how I feel.

I shrug and ask, "Why would I do that? It's not like I asked to be married to you."

Todd strides forward, stopping in front of me as I sit on the end of the king-sized bed, and takes a rough grasp of my chin. He forces my head up so I'm looking him in the eyes, the anger evident.

"You should be grateful you're here! Do you know how many women would kill to be in your shoes?" Todd's grip grows more harsh with each word and I struggle to keep a straight face.

"Then why don't you marry one of them and let me go?" I ask, squinting my eyes, my rage matching his.

"Oh, sweet girl, you forget your place," Todd says, lowering himself to my height. He places his hands on my knees, and I flinch on instinct. "You are mine."

I attempt to stand and walk away but he grabs my shoulders and shoves me back down onto the bed. Before letting my anger get the best of me, I take a deep breath, then smile. I lean forward, nearly nose-to-nose with Todd, and say, "But I don't want you." Each word clipped, ensuring he knows I mean every one.

Todd squeezes my knees and shoots up to walk away in seconds. He growls his frustration and I wish I could pat myself on the back for getting to him.

While he stares out the window, looking upon the bustle of San Francisco, I notice the bellhop had brought our luggage to our room before we arrived. In an effort to spend as little time with Todd as possible, I head for my bag and grab my novel. I make myself comfortable in the bed and pick up where I left off.

Most nineteen-year-olds don't spend nearly as much time reading as I do. They also aren't likely married to an abusive old guy.

From the corner of my eye, I see Todd look over at me. Instead of bothering me like I anticipated, he grabs his briefcase. He sits it on the table by the window and pops it open, grabbing whatever papers he was after, and starts working. I breathe a sigh of relief in knowing he'll leave me be for a while.

After reading fifty or so pages, Todd slams his briefcase closed. I chance a look over at him and note sunset is upon us. As much as I'd love to head out to watch the sunset over the city, I know my request would be shot down in an instant. I try to ignore Todd and go back to my book, but he stands at the foot of the bed and stares at me. When I turn the page, he clears his throat as if I don't know he's standing there.

"Are you planning to read all night?" he asks with a look of annoyance.

"I planned to. That's why I brought two books," I say, raising the one in my hand.

Todd rolls his eyes and props his hands on his hips. He stares at me as if his glare will get me to change my mind. It's a wonder he still thinks he can get to me. He may hit and hurt me, but I won't back down. I didn't want any part of this marriage. My father forced me into it simply because Todd has money. He wanted me to be cared for. Love be damned.

"I'm going to order food. What would you like?" Todd asks, his tone coated in anger.

"Well, that depends. I don't even know what there is," I say, closing my book and sitting it on my lap.

"Are you aware of where we are? Just pick whatever you want," he says, gesturing toward the room phone.

"I thought we would go down to the restaurant," I say, a bit of hope in my words.

Todd lets out a bark of laughter that doesn't hold a hint of amusement. "Absolutely not. Look at you. Do you really think I'd want to be seen anywhere with you looking like that?"

I sigh and rattle off a few of my favorite things, and with a roll of his eyes, Todd places an order with room service.

The sunset is breathtaking, from what I can see of it from my seat on the bed. I set my book on the bedside table then walk over to the large windows overlooking the city. When Todd hangs up the phone, he comes up behind me and places his hands on my waist. With my back to his chest, my face screws up in disgust. I force my fingers to unclench from the tight fist they're in, one finger at a time.

As I stand stark still, staring into the horizon, I feel a trickle move from my palm and down my middle finger. I notice droplets of blood on the beige carpet below my hand and cringe. Imagining the reaction Todd will have if he sees, I tuck my hand and pull myself from his clutches and head for the bathroom.

The door snaps closed harder than I intended, causing me to cringe as I hide behind the locked barrier. I grip my hands together against my chest and take a deep breath before stepping up to the sink.

As I run cold water over the half-moon-shaped cuts on my palms, a stranger looks back at me in the mirror. I turn my face side to side, trying to figure out who I'm looking at until I accept that it truly is me looking back.

My lackluster, flat hair matches well with the porcelain skin and dark circles around my eyes. It's like the life has been zapped from my body. I can't remember the last time I took a good, hard look at myself but I could swear I've never looked this rough.

A sharp knock at the door jolts me from my thoughts and I hang my head. There's no escape from this life I've been roped into. I run through ways I could run away but nothing seems to be feasible. Still, getting away from my heartless husband is the only goal I have in mind.

"What the hell are you doing in there, Bethany? It's been nearly twenty minutes. Get your ass out here and eat," Todd says behind the door.

The only thing left to do is fluff my hair, straighten my spine, and lift my chin with defiant confidence. I steel myself before opening the door. Todd is waiting on the other side, hands on his waist with a look telling me he's ready for a fight.

Todd gestures to the feast displayed on the small dining table in our room and says, "You always have to be difficult, don't you? You certainly don't need to be eating this much. Since it's a special occasion, I'll allow it, but don't think this is going to be a usual thing."

He stares at me, waiting for a response he won't get.

Instead of continuing to let my food get cold, I take a seat. The moment my ass hits the chair, Todd snatches a handful of my hair, yanking my head back to look up at him.

"When I speak to you, you will respond. With. Manners."

I stare up at him, lips locked. A few moments pass until he realizes I'm not engaging with him. Todd throws my head forward, releasing the death grip he has on me. I straighten and fix my hair, brushing off his abuse like I always do. The only way to get through it is to keep pushing forward, hoping I don't lose myself in the meantime.

Various plates of steak and lobster, shrimp cocktail, grilled cheese, pizza, stuffed mushrooms, and calamari sit before me. It's not the most traditional dinner but I couldn't decide what I wanted so I got it all.

Todd sits across the table, straightening his shirt and loosening his tie before cutting into his steak. Seeing him with a weapon always makes me nervous. I try to make it inconspicuous as I eye his movements, flicking my eyes in his direction every few seconds.

He takes his time cutting his food, instilling more discomfort within me. When a sly smile creeps across his face, I wonder if it's intentional to mess with my head.

"So, what do you think of the hotel?" Todd asks in between bites.

I shrug one shoulder as I finish chewing. "I suppose it's fine. It's not like I've gotten to see anything."

He slams both fists on the table, shaking the dinnerware, causing me to jump. The death grip I have on my fork and knife tighten as I prepare to fight if I need to.

"Nothing is ever good enough for you, is it, Bethany? I bend over backwards to make you happy but you're never happy. What more do you want?" Todd says through gritted teeth.

"Out of this marriage," I say under my breath as I pop a shrimp in my mouth.

I chance a look at Todd and see his knuckles, wrapped around the knife and fork, are turning white. His jaw is locked so tight, I'm sure his teeth will break under the pressure. I keep a stone face but laugh on the inside.

Todd throws the knife in my direction, forcing a small scream from me as I tuck into myself. "You're not going anywhere! You are mine! Your father agreed to this marriage! He wanted his precious daughter taken care of. I guess he didn't know what a little ungrateful bitch he raised!"

He jumps out of his seat, rushing in my direction, and I prepare for impact. Instead of slapping me as I expected, he brushes his hand through my hair and down my back. I don't dare move or relax under his touch, knowing how it could change at any second.

Todd drops down to my level, getting so close to my ear, I can feel his hot breath wisping my hair. "You. Are. Mine." Each word is clipped and dripping with violent venom.

He stands and runs a hand along the top of my head then rests it on my shoulder. Todd's grip tightens and pain bursts through my body from my ribs. Before I can catch my breath, I realize he's held me in place and punched me with a force I never expected.

Slapping, grabbing, and hair pulling are usually his go-to. Until now, he's never hit me like this. Of course, it's where no one will see. Todd usually avoids hitting me in the face. God forbid anyone sees what a monster he is behind closed doors. The world only sees the charming, kind businessman he portrays.

I gasp for air, begging for more like never before. Before I can move from my seat, I lean over and vomit on the floor, some landing on Todd's dress shoes. He grabs my hair once again and throws me into the puddle at his feet.

"You disgusting piece of shit! You ruined my shoes! Do you even know how much these cost me? Clean this shit up and get yourself together! I didn't even hit you that hard!" he yells before stomping away.

The agony of his punch is exasperated every time I heave against my will. I feel snot and puke dripping from my nose as fast as the tears I couldn't hold back. My lungs beg for air but I feel like I'm breathing through a straw. No amount is enough.

When I get my body under control, Todd has left the bathroom and returned to eat his meal. He watches out the window while I drag myself up from the floor. I stumble past without him giving a blink in my direction.

By the time I make it to the bathroom, I can finally take in oxygen at a steady rate. Once I get the door shut and locked, I take off my vomit-covered clothes and drop them in the trash can. I look around the room and notice a closet tucked in the corner. Fluffy robes hang along with a surplus of towels and wash rags.

After I cover myself, I grab a handful of towels and walk back to the main room of the suite. I kneel beside the mess I made and begin slopping it up. Once I get all I can, I lay a towel over top of it.

"You're really just going to leave that there? What is wrong with you?" Todd asks in disgust.

"There aren't any cleaning supplies in here. I didn't know what else to do," I say in a voice barely above a whisper.

"Wow! It can speak!" he says, clapping his hands with sarcasm. "Do whatever. I don't fucking care anymore."

I take the towels to the bathroom and rinse them in the bathtub. The last thing I want is for some poor housekeeper to lift one and be covered in barf. Once I get them as clean as I can, I toss them into one of the sinks.

My confidence, no matter how much I forced it, has crumbled. I feel like a broken shell of a person. The woman I was an hour ago is gone, hidden away. My reflection shows just how far I've fallen in such a short span of time. The circles around my eyes have darkened along with gaining red rings and swelling from crying.

The realization hits me like a semi. My bags are in the main room. I have to face Todd, once again, before I can have another moment of solitude and safety. Safety being my main priority.

I peek around the door before tiptoeing out of the bathroom to my bags. I don't look in Todd's direction for fear of angering him again. Thankfully, my sleep clothes are right on top. I grab them and hustle back to the bathroom, my safe haven in this tiny hell I've been thrown into.

Despite fearing what I'll see, I stand in front of the mirror again. I peel off the robe, cringing at the pain in my side from the Todd's punch to the gut. An angry purple bruise shows itself as I turn for a better look. Fresh tears spring to my eyes at the sight. I can only imagine how much worse it will be by tomorrow.

Turning on the shower, I set it to the highest temperature. I need to feel something other than the agony of what is dancing behind the skin suit I wear.

When I step inside, I hiss as the scalding water makes contact. Needing the pain, I force myself under the spray. I use a wash rag and wipe myself down. By the time I get to my legs, I freeze. My mind goes blank of anything other than the rage and hurt I have toward my parents and Todd.

I crumple into a ball on the shower floor, letting the burn of the water seep into my bones. My eyes sting as I fight back more tears but they win in the battle of wills. It doesn't take long for the silent crying to become violent sobs. I cover my mouth, trying to keep Todd from hearing my weakness.

The last thing I will allow is him thinking he's won.

Three sharp knocks tell me my alone time is over. "Just a minute!" I yell from the shower floor.

I shut off the water then hurry to get dry and dressed. Todd is waiting on the other side of the door, as expected. He looks me up and down with a grimace. "Are you done hogging the fucking bathroom?" he asks as he pushes past me.

My gaze drops to my feet until I hear the bathroom door close. When I hear the shower start, escape plans thrash through my brain and I freeze.

I could walk out the door and run. Would anyone here actually help a girl in her pajamas? They'd probably think I'm drunk and not meant to be here.

Maybe I should wait until we're back at home and Todd's on a business trip. The house staff are off on Sundays. Where would I go? My parents would probably ship me back to Todd.

More ideas flitter around but I can't land on one I think would actually get me away from him.

Todd's large hands clamping down on my shoulders jolt me from my dreaming, causing me to nearly jump out of my skin. I clutch my chest as if it will slow down my racing heart. When I feel him move, my body stiffens on instinct. Todd leans down, so his face is next to mine, and plants a chaste kiss on my cheek.

"Come on, let's lay down. It's getting late," he suggests, pulling me in the direction of the bed.

Todd moves the duvet on what's been deemed my side. I stare at him, befuddled and not knowing what to do. To my surprise, he waits for me to make a move with patience. Once I'm in the bed, he covers me and hands me the paperback I had been reading earlier.

"We have an early flight back home, then I have to leave for Boston the next day. Might as well get some sleep while we can," he says with an uncharacteristic calmness. I nod in response as he turns off the bedside light on his side.

All I can think is *who the hell is this and what have they done with my husband?* I stare at him while he covers his eyes with his arm.

It could've been minutes or hours before I drag my gaze down to my book. I push myself back up against the headboard and try to find a good position to read in.

"Could you stop fucking moving? Jesus Christ, Bethany! I'm trying to fucking sleep!" he yells, throwing his arm off his face to glare at me.

I don't dare make another move as I dive into my book. The words on the page blur as my attention fades from it. I've read the same paragraph countless times but can't recall what the first sentence was.

Freedom calls for me. I stare at the door, willing something to drag me away. Of course, nothing happens. I'm the only one who can make things happen.

I watch time tick by, each second seeming slower to pass than the last.

By two a.m., I'm feeling confident Todd's thoroughly asleep. I watch the wretched man beside me breathe easily in his slumber. My face twists in disgust and hatred as I look him over.

My bags aren't far from the bed. I slip out, careful not to jostle it too much. Todd rustles a bit, leaving my heart in my throat until he settles.

I pad my way to my suitcase, grabbing the first outfit I find, then rush to the bathroom. As desperately as I want to turn on the light, I wait until the door is closed before hitting the switch.

For as far back as I can remember, I don't recall ever being afraid of the dark. Tonight, something feels off. It's as if there's an electrical current running through the air. I'm sure with one wrong move, it'll crack like lightning.

When I get the clothes unwrapped from my tight hold, I realize I grabbed a t-shirt and sundress rather than pants. I drop my head and let out a huff of frustration, staring at the garments. Once I get ahold of myself, I remember it's currently in style for girls my age to wear t-shirts with dresses. I just hope I can pull it off.

As I sneak my way back into the room, I grab my purse and pull out a scrunchie. The rat's nest I call hair can't be tamed with a few swipes of my fingers at this point.

I slip my shoes on then grab the door handle.

My heart is pounding with such ferocity, I worry it'll burst through its cage in my chest.

The only thing keeping me going is the reminder that I'm no one's punching bag. I deserve better.

Before I can talk myself out of it, I turn the knob and straighten myself. I pull the door open a few inches and am greeted with silence. My confidence rises and I take a step to slip through but come to an abrupt halt as a light in the room clicks on.

"Going somewhere, darling?" Todd says, pulling himself up to sit.

Not even a squeak makes its way out of my mouth.

Todd pounces across the bed and toward me like a tiger after its prey. He slams the door, closing it on my foot before dragging me back into the room. His grip on my upper arms makes me wonder if my attempted escape was the last thing I'd ever do. I'm almost certain of it as he slams my small frame against the wall, rattling the art hanging nearby.

"You tried to escape? Really? What do you think would happen? You'd run home to Mommy and Daddy and they'd welcome you with open arms? Oh, sweet girl, no. We signed a contract. You. Are. Mine," he whispers, our noses nearly touching. I can feel his rage building with each word as his hold on me tightens.

Todd releases my arms and grabs a handful of my hair, his hold so tight, I can feel the strands ripping from my scalp. He throws me against the bed, smashing my injured ribs against the footboard and mattress. Before I can snag a breath, he raises my head and grips my face. Todd stares at me and I see the flames building in his eyes as he digs my cheeks against my teeth.

"What the fuck is wrong with you? I give you everything you want and more!" he screams in my face as he pulls at his hair.

I jump back as soon as he releases me, trying to put distance between us. My skin tingles where it doesn't hurt from his harsh touch. I feel zipping throughout my body as the air grows thick. My hands get zapped from the blanket and I chance a look around.

Before I get halfway across the bed, he claws at my legs. I kick out and try to get away, but he wins when he gets ahold of my ankle.

The lights flicker as he pulls me to the edge of the bed. With the speed he rears his fist back, the lamps brighten until the bulbs burst. Todd's hold on me falters, giving me a moment to get away.

When he realizes I've moved, he jumps after me. Todd's body freezes mid-jump, and I throw my arms up to protect my face. The punch I expect doesn't come. Instead, a loud crash comes from across the room.

I chance a peek between my arms to see Todd has been thrown through the wardrobe. I hope for a little bit of luck as I dart across the bed in an attempt to get to the door, but Todd is faster.

"You fucking bitch!" he yells as he charges at me again, causing me to return to my former position protecting myself.

The overhead light flicks on and we hear a crash outside our door. It doesn't faze my husband nor sway his mission to end me.

I put my hands behind me and kick my feet to scoot away when he reaches for me. Before he makes contact, Todd shoots upright with a look of horror the likes of which I've never seen.

His back arches at an abnormal angle, bulging his chest forward. I don't have a second to comprehend what's happening in front of me as I hear a slow tearing sound. Todd's face shifts from fear to pure agony but no sound comes from his mouth.

A lump forms in his chest, pushing forward at a slow, even pace. The wet ripping reaches my ears once more. I sit with my jaw on the floor and my stomach in my throat as I watch my husband's heart shoved out of his chest.

Crimson raindrops explode with the force. In a split second, I'm seeing red. It takes me a moment to realize it's not a burst of emotion; my husband's blood fills my vision. I rub at my eyes maniacally and feel liquid smudge across my face as I do. Droplets make their way to my lips, causing me to absentmindedly stick my tongue out. The taste of copper makes contact and I feel vomit climb its way up my throat.

The organ floats in the air in front of Todd as I notice the hole through his torso. Blood squirts from the arteries and drops onto the floor. Before I have a chance to consider if this is real or not, Todd's heart drops to the ground, landing with a *squelch,* and I cover my mouth to withhold my puke.

Whatever was holding him up releases Todd's body, causing him to crumple to the floor.

An older woman, shadowy and transparent, stands in his place, her hands clasped in front of her. With a kind smile and a nod of her head, she says, "You're free, sweetheart."

13th Floor - Housekeeping
2008

False Walls
Caleb Jones

"The thirteenth floor is housekeeping."

The elevator dinged while the words left the hotel manager's mouth, as if the aging man had ridden this elevator to this floor so many times, it was impossible for him to not know exactly when the bell would ding, when they would arrive.

"Please," the manager said, and lifted an arm out, directing the way from the elevator as his other arm blocked the sensor, keeping the door from closing. The smile on his face was strained.

Carol stepped off the elevator into the dim hall beyond. She'd been told that the thirteenth floor was where housekeeping was—usually the help was ushered into a basement closet, but here, they had an entire floor. Strange, but of course, Carol knew the Hotel Ethel was a strange place. A luxuriant oddity.

She couldn't help picturing the doorman she'd passed, decked out in a handsome purple and gold suit to go with the theme of the hotel–and how strange he would look up here, on this abandoned floor. It all seemed to be a lovely and appropriate metaphor for what she already knew of the Ethel.

It became even stranger as she walked into the hallway and realized that the thirteenth floor didn't appear to take up the full footprint of the rest of the building. It was much, much smaller. She understood the lower lighting, the less-than-refurbished walls and doors, and the aged, uncared-for carpeting. This place was for the maids, so it didn't have to look nice. But why was it so much smaller?

The other floors of the hotel, which Carol had seen many of after her interview for the position, stretched out from the elevator all the way to the far sides of the hotel, and branched off into many hallways. Carol, though, standing on the edge of the thirteenth floor, was confronted by an ugly, nondescript wall only one hundred feet from where she'd stepped onto the crunchy shag carpet that hadn't been updated in at least three decades.

She walked out to where she knew the other floors branched off to other wings of rooms and was met again by walls. This floor was nothing more than three rooms on either side of the hall.

And walls.

"It's much smaller than the other floors," she said as she walked up the wall that faced directly toward the elevator.

"You have superstition to thank for that, my dear," the manager said. He too approached the wall and laid his palm against it. "Thirteen," he said, affecting what he must've thought of as a *spooky* voice. All Carol heard was disdain.

"Right," Carol said. "Thirteen. Many hotels just skip it when they give their floor numbers."

"Never was the case here," said the manager. He tapped the wall and a surprisingly hollow sound rang out down the shortened hallway. "In fact, this was not always the housekeeping floor. This floor was every bit as active as the others. It's, in truth, just as large as any of the others. These," he said, gesturing toward the wall in front of them, then to the other two standing perpendicular to their position, "are false walls."

"So there are rooms beyond the walls?"

"Yes, indeed."

"But why?"

"Like I said, superstition. Management, myself included, began to notice that many people were refusing to book on the thirteenth floor. Even in this so-called enlightened era. It became such an issue that we cordoned the floor off and cut it from our service budget. Less overhead is never a bad thing."

It seemed dramatic to Carol. There must've been at least twenty rooms on the floor. There was no way they couldn't use at least a handful. But who was asking her? She shrugged and said, "One less floor for me to clean, I guess."

The manager thwacked the wall again, much more aggressively this time. "That's where you are wrong, dear. In fact, it might be the most important floor of your upkeep duties. These walls still have rooms beyond them. Rooms that hold dirt, and hold potential to grow mold. Whether it be for superstition or otherwise, throwing up walls doesn't dismantle the reality that lies beyond them."

He ran his hand across the faded wallpaper, was silent for a moment, then went on. "*False* walls. And a room that still stands but goes unlived in, unkempt, has the most potential to cause hazardous conditions. Like stagnant, dirty water. Because, see, the rooms are still connected to the rest of the hotel. Still very much a part of the building whether we like it or not. And that stagnation of life, it must be kept behind the walls. But it also still must be maintained. Hidden, but clean."

"Mold," Carol added, simply.

The manager tilted his head back and forth. "More or less. If anything builds up in one of those rooms, whatever the source, it could spread through the walls or the HVAC and infect the other floors."

Seems like more trouble than it's worth.

Again, though, who was asking Carol? She only smiled and said, "Floor Thirteen will be kept as tidy as all the others."

The manager smiled. "That's what I like to hear."

There was only a monthly cleaning of the closed-off section of the thirteenth floor. Carol hadn't thought of it much after her initial hiring. In the first couple days she was at the hotel she floated a few questions to the handful of other maids, who simply stared daggers at her, or gave a quick shake of the head. It made Carol wonder if the superstition the manager had alluded to was just as applicable to the staff as it was the residents.

On her third week, the maid in charge, a stout old woman named Mallory who looked like she hadn't pushed a vacuum or lifted a feather duster in a couple decades, pulled Carol aside.

"Tomorrow's the day," she said. "You're cleaning no man's land."

"No man's land?" Carol asked, though she already knew. Despite being decidedly non-superstitious, she felt a flutter in her chest.

Mallory rolled her eyes. "You know," she said, pointing up. "The maid's floor."

"Right. Got it."

"Any questions?" Mallory asked, her hefty arms across her chest as if to say *if you do have any questions, don't bother to ask them.*

"Other than how to get there, no."

Mallory set a hand on Carol's shoulder and said, "Good girl."

The next day, Mallory met Carol at the elevator on the thirteenth floor with a load of cleaning supplies. "Have to ride up one then walk down," she explained.

That's exactly what they did, getting off on the fourteenth floor and walking to the nearest fire exit. The concrete and metal zig-zagged the nearly two hundred feet down to the ground level. To Carol, it looked like a dungeon. Mallory wheeled the small cart of cleaning supplies to the edge of the steps.

"You can handle taking this down, yeah?" Mallory asked.

Carol eyed the cart which really only consisted of a vacuum, duster, various cleaning solutions, and a pack of micro-fiber rags. She rolled up the sleeves of her maid uniform dramatically and said, "I think I got it."

Mallory let out a single syllable laugh. She pointed to a wood door jam sitting on top of the cart. "Door locks from in here, so don't let it shut. Emphasis is really on the vents. Get them nice and shiny. That's what management is really concerned about. Don't overthink the rest." She looked down at the fire exit door on the thirteenth floor and turned to walk away.

Walked away pretty fast.

Carol didn't like that. And did she see the old woman stifling a shiver? Maybe. Still, Carol agreed to the job, and the thirteenth floor—all of the thirteenth floor—needed cleaning. She pulled the small cart of tools to the edge of the steps and slowly began her descent, thudding the cart down step by step. When she arrived at the door, she pulled the door stop off the top of her cart, then took a deep breath.

Why are you so nervous? Just get this over with.

She opened the door. Nothing happened. The hotel didn't collapse beneath her feet. There wasn't a fire burning on the thirteenth floor. There was simply a hotel floor stretching out from the fire escape. It was dimly lit, just like the housekeeping quarters, but other than that, it looked every bit the equal of the other fifteen residential floors of the hotel.

Carol nodded, because this was what she expected. Nothing more, nothing less. She walked in, pulling her cart behind her, and stopped to place the door jam. She tested the fire escape door to verify it would not shut, and when satisfied, turned back to the thirteenth floor, ready to work her magic.

By the time she got to the third room, taking extra care to double-dust the air vents, she found herself at ease. She left the vacuum on a full blast and stepped out into the hallway, looking down toward the fire escape. It was still propped open, but more important to Carol, she was undisturbed and alone.

One thing that was made very clear to her was that if she were caught with headphones on while working, there would be dire consequences. The Hotel Ethel needed her full attention, and that included ears to hear what the old girl might be saying.

Cleeeean meeee. Cleeeeeeeeean meeee.

Carol giggled at the ghostly voice playing out in her mind. But if the Hotel Ethel had a voice of some sort, there was no doubt it would be ghostly. What other kind of a voice would a hotel with false walls and a condemned thirteenth floor have?

In one of the rooms, truly adding to the ghostly allure of the place, Carol found a stack of photos, easily a century old. Men and women in sharp attire dancing in what she recognized as the Ethel's banquet hall, a group of musicians clearly getting into the groove, sweat pouring over their instruments.

She shrugged, wondering how many maids had perused these same photos, wondering if they should take it to management—hell, maybe there would be a bonus! All those maids likely came to the same conclusion as Carol, that the manager, and likely Mallory too, would do little more than scold her for taking time on the clock to look at old photos. She shuffled them back in place and figured it had nothing to do with her.

"No ghosts here, at least," she said, just loud enough to be heard over the sound of the vacuum she'd left running.

She turned back to the room and pulled out the iPod and headphones she'd stowed away in her apron. She put the headphones in and cranked the volume. Some generic pop to drown out all the humming and brushing sounds of her trade. In previous jobs it was what kept her sane. It was crazy that they'd expect her not to listen to music at this hoity-toity joint.

The few hours she poked along at each room, dusting the high corners, scrubbing the bathroom floors, and cleaning those all-important air vents that could send bacteria to the other floors, moved at a speedy clip.

Carol was always the type of worker that became completely engaged, losing herself in her work, becoming one with each arm stretch of the vacuum, swaying back and forth with the duster as if it were an extension of her own fingers.

By the time she got to the last room on the last hall of Floor Thirteen, she looked west toward Telegraph Hill and imagined the breeze coming off the Bay in the distance. She was surprised to see the sun beginning its dip behind the hill and into the sea beyond the city. Carol let out a deep sigh. A view like this, even from the thirteenth floor, was something to envy.

BAM!

She clicked off the vacuum cleaner and removed the headphone from one of her ears. Britney Spears, or maybe it was Christina, still belted in her other ear, but Carol was listening intently for any sound that might come from outside the room.

"What was that?" she whispered. She didn't like how her voice mixed with the quiet of the thirteenth floor and the world of pop still blaring in her left ear. She removed the other headphone, embracing full silence.

Carol tiptoed a few steps toward the hotel room door then stopped herself. Who was *she* sneaking up on? She was *supposed* to be there. Whoever had made that bang was the one that should be tiptoeing.

She planted her feet firmly on the ground then stomped out into the hallway, ready to shoo the trespasser—probably some spoiled brat staying there with his parents—back to his proper floor.

She had a clear view from her end of the floor, straight back to the false wall that blocked off the housekeeping quarters. There was nobody there. Not a single person that could've made that sound.

"The fire escape," she gasped, and took off at a dead sprint, praying the jam was still in place.

She rounded the corner toward the fire escape and ran for the heavy door but stopped after only a few paces. It was clearly still open.

She let out a sigh of relief, only then realizing just how nervous she was over the idea of being trapped on this little island of hotel rooms. She walked the rest of the way toward the fire exit, then gave the door jam an extra kick to make sure it was firmly wedged into place.

"What the hell was that?" she asked the empty halls.

Carol slowly paced toward the door closest to the fire exit. She was mentally preparing to go into each individual room and check to make sure they were all still empty.

Just as she was about to turn the doorknob, she thought she heard someone sobbing. It wasn't coming from the other side of that particular door, but somewhere further down the hall.

"Hello," she called out.

The only response she got was more sobbing. She began to move down the row of doors, pausing before each to listen and see if that was the one where her crying intruder might be hiding.

On the fifth door, the sobbing grew louder. The crying was also accompanied by a quiet voice. A feminine voice. "Please," the woman whispered, then again, "P-p-please don't. Just let us—"

"I'm not going to cause you any trouble," Carol said as she turned the knob and pushed the door open.

As the dying sunlight from the window beyond spilled into the central hallway of Floor Thirteen, Carol heard one last pleading cry, this one desperate and loud.

"PLEASE, SIR! Don—"

BAM!

The voice was cut off, and Carol, standing in the doorway, had to let her eyes adjust to the glare of the setting sun, unable to accept what her eyes were taking in.

Nobody was in the room.

She was positive this was where the noise was coming from, but here it was, unoccupied. A red mist floated in the air, though, and there was a splotch that dripped from the side of the bed onto the floor. It caught the fading sunlight and reflected orangish-brown. A stain. A bad one.

"What the…" Carol whispered as she walked forward, letting her words trail off. She'd just cleaned the room, not even two hours ago. Where did the mess come from?

She looked up at the vents and pipes that ran across the room, guessing maybe one or the other had started a serious leak. She dabbed her finger in it and lifted it to her nose, then gasped.

It was blood.

BAM!

BAM!

BAM!

BAM!

The sounds came from the hall behind her at near mechanical intervals. Spaced out by seconds, but timed almost to a four-on-the-floor rhythm. There was a pause, then a few strung together.

BAM-BAM-BAM!

Carol screamed, frozen in place where she stood next to the bed for a moment. She knew the sound. Who didn't know the sound as a blue-blooded American?

Gunfire. Shooting. In the decades that she'd come of age, the prominence of the crazed mass shooter grew from a rare specter to a legitimate concern for public safety. And here she was, frozen in place while just beyond the reach of the door, she could hear the common nightmare of American living coming to life in real time.

The firing came to an end just as quickly as it began.

Carol still found it hard to get her feet moving. She had a nephew who'd recently started having to do school shooter drills and she could still hear his chipper voice as he relayed the three choices one has in a public shooter situation.

Auntie Carol, you have to try to run, or hide, or fight.

She knew running was best, and finally convinced herself to inch forward toward the door. She peeked out and let out a squeaking gasp. Much like the splotch on the bed, there were three red spatters in the hall. Blood spilled everywhere.

If her rational mind had been functioning, it would point out to her the oddity of there being no bodies. But all that was working in poor Carol's brain was her fight-or-flight instinct. That impulse guided her feet to backpedal, to slowly slip herself behind the queen-sized bed, and to crawl beneath. And to pray.

"Carol! Carol!"

She didn't know how long she'd stayed there with her face dug into the carpet. It was long enough that she'd stopped crying and the sun no longer came through the high-rise window.

"Carol, if you're up here I need you to come out."

Before Carol could respond or move, she saw a pair of feet come to stand in the threshold of the room she was hiding in.

"Carol?"

Carol, finally recognizing the voice, scurried from her hiding spot. She ran over to where the chief maid stood and took her hand, dragging her forward into the room.

"Mallory," she whispered. "Did they get him?"

"Get who?" Mallory said. She put her strong hands on Carol's shoulders and guided her back toward the bed, forcing her to sit.

Carol allowed herself to be placed on the bed, but then remembered all that blood. She screamed and shot up to her feet again. She struggled against Mallory, who was trying to force her back down, but still managed to turn and look at the bed. The linen was as white as winter's first snow. Not a drop of blood.

"B-b-but how?" Carol stammered.

"Oh, dear," Mallory said, and placed an arm around Carol, then guided her from the room. Carol almost resisted. She wasn't ready to see the remains that she'd only caught a glimpse of previously. Mallory coaxed her, though, speaking as gently as Carol could ever remember her boss doing.

"It's alright, dear. It's all okay."

They rounded the threshold of the suite onto the thirteenth floor hallway. Carol kept her eyes sealed shut for a moment, but needed to gather her bearings as Mallory guided her forward.

When she finally allowed herself to look, the only thing there was the maid taking the overnight on-call shift. No blood. No bodies. Only the hall that she'd vacuumed so impeccably, just a few short hours earlier, and her terrified coworker.

The other maid opened her mouth to speak, but Mallory lifted a hand and said, "Not now."

Carol was guided away from the floor toward the fire escape, down to the twelfth floor, and onto the elevator. She moved like a prisoner, and perhaps that's what she was. A prisoner to her own shock and terror, unable to move without guidance.

When the elevator doors opened and she saw the shortened thirteenth floor sprawl out before her, she started to squirm.

"No," Carol said. "No, we need to leave."

"It's okay," Mallory said, guiding her once again. This time, off the elevator and toward the one room that the modified floor kept as living quarters. A suite used by hotel staff should they need to stay overnight in order to be on time for an early morning shift. It was rarely, if ever, used.

Mallory forced her, gently, to sit down on the bed.

"What happened?" Carol asked.

Mallory dragged a seat over and sat across from her. She let out a deep sigh before answering, "Absolutely nothing."

"But I—"

"Saw nothing," Mallory said, cutting her off. "I know what you think you might have seen, but then you saw what was really there. Pristine, white walls and spotless carpet that get cleaned once a month."

"What happened over there?" Carol asked. A reality was dawning on her. The question was no longer about what had *just* happened over there, but what may have happened a long time ago. Why the false walls, and a mostly unused thirteenth floor.

"Lay down," Mallory said. "It's been a long day, and you're very, very tired."

Carol wanted to protest, but found herself acquiescing, allowing Mallory to help her comfortably onto the mattress. Then her shoes were taken off, and in the face of what horrible impossibility she'd just experienced, she fell asleep.

"Oh, God! No, no!"

BAM-BAM-BAM!

Carol's eyes peeled open. The red vessels pulsed around her irises.

She ran to the door of the maid's bedroom and peeked her head around the corner. No horrors awaited her out on the hotel floor. Just that lingering plea. And then…

"Carol."

"Oh!" Carol turned with a start, away from the false wall and toward the voice that had addressed her. It was Mallory, naturally, come to check on her charge.

Mallory smiled. "I think you should take the day off."

"That won't be nec—"

Mallory's hand went up. "You're not in trouble, and you won't lose your job. You've had a rough day, and I can assure you that everyone that takes your position has that same rough day. I just don't want you to have it again if you continue to work here…"

It sounded as if Mallory intended to say more but left the words to linger in the air.

Linger like that mist of blood.

"Okay," Carol agreed. "I'll take the day."

"Good. Go home and get some rest."

Rest was the last thing Carol had in mind.

Out on the street before the Ethel, she stopped and turned toward the building. A luxurious oddity.

"You look faint."

Carol startled and looked around. She was a short distance from the hotel entryway, and the doorman in his suit was looking at her, a wide, concerned smile on his face.

"I'm sorry," Carol muttered. "It was a long shift."

The doorman laughed and said, "Don't I know it." He took a few steps toward her, but came to a sudden stop and looked back over his shoulder. Then to her again.

"Why don't you come have a seat?"

His gloved hand motioned her toward a nearby bench. Carol was tempted. But the strained smile on the doorman's face gave her pause. She started to back away.

"I'm sorry," she said as she turned from him. "I have a busy afternoon."

Carol didn't have a PC in her apartment, and she didn't have one of those insane phones that connected directly to the internet that people were starting to carry around.

So, after going home and changing out of her maid's uniform, she headed directly for the library. She found an open computer and opened a search window.

Hotel Ethel Shooting

She typed it out, then her finger lingered over the ENTER button. Did she even want to know? It was a tragedy that was becoming ever more common. Did she have to confirm that such a tragedy happened in her place of employment? This was becoming part of *the American Experience*, so what good would it do just to know it had happened?

"Yeah, but not everyone is seeing ghosts," Carol whispered to herself and hit the search button.

There were plenty of results. On the fifth floor, and the eighteenth floor and a few others. But nothing came up on the thirteenth floor. Nothing that could be replicated by her afternoon of terror on the condemned wing of the hotel. She tried refining her search

Hotel Ethel 13th floor

Nothing.

Ethel Hotel Killer floor 13.

Nothing. And so on and so on. With each further search and nothing to prove there was at least an earthly reality to plant the supernatural she'd experienced, Carol felt her grip on reality loosen.

An hour later, dozens of searches completed, and a deep dig into the far reaches of the internet's darker corners brought out little more than a few articles about deaths in the hotel, but nothing akin to what she was actually looking for.

She'd never been the superstitious type—it's why she hadn't batted an eye when Mallory told her of the thirteenth floor duties she would be required to perform—but she did believe people went crazy, and as she drifted from the library and made the long walk back home, she had to wonder if that was exactly what was happening to her.

The next day, she was back on the cleaning schedule.

As the elevator rose to the thirteenth floor, she felt a chill but was grateful that she wouldn't have to travel beyond the false wall. The elevator arrived, the doors slid soundlessly open, and she stepped out into the dim, shortened hall beyond. She made her way to the overnight room and walked in.

The maid that took her place for the graveyard shift was in her regular day clothes, sitting on the bed.

"Look like you seen a ghost," the woman said. She had a wide grin on her face. One that could keep spreading and eventually swallow Carol whole.

"Yeah, it was a long night," Carol said. There was a body-length mirror, and Carol stepped to it. She didn't want to keep looking at the maid and settled on her own haggard reflection instead. "Then a long day yesterday."

"Who you telling?" her coworker said. "Been a long lifetime. Here we are though."

"Fair enough," Carol said, still running her hands down her uniform.

The other maid appeared in the mirror behind her. "So, you heard it, huh?"

Carol froze in place, other than her eyes, which glanced up toward the woman's reflection.

"H-heard what?" she asked.

The maid rolled her eyes. "C'mon now. You're just like every one of us now that they try to bring to this godforsaken floor. Why do you think they keep hiring newbies like you? Why do you think they keep letting us walk away?"

Carol spun on her. "But what is it? Mallory acted like I was crazy."

"Mallory doesn't think you're any crazier than she is. She's just disappointed that you heard it. She thought there was a chance you might be different. A presence is a presence, though. If it wants to be known, it'll be known."

"A presence?" The other maid smacked her lips.

"Yes, what else do you think it is? Those poor people got killed up here, plain and simple, and now they can't be quiet. Ask me, I'd say any spirit'll be pretty damn loud if you try to put a couple walls up and forget them."

"Why can't I find anything about it? I tried searching old news articles, the internet. Nothing."

At this, the other maid let out a full-throttled laugh.

She said, "You must not know what kind of folks you're working for. Rich. Powerful. They're the kind of people that could have something tragic like that happen in their building and run some walls up, block it out. It's like that manager guy says though. You put a wall up but the truth still exists beyond it. All that dirt still lingers."

The other maid turned to leave as she continued speaking.

"That's true even here at the Hotel Ethel. Maybe especially here."

Carol rushed to follow her out into the hallway. "What do I do?"

The maid kept walking away, but called over her shoulder, "Nothing to be done. Except to maybe avoid the thirteenth floor at sundown. That's when we all think it happens. That's around the time we always hear it. Muted past these false walls."

She got into the elevator and left Carol alone on the shortened hall. Alone to face the rest of her day, to work with all she'd been told rambling through her mind. To make heads or tails of the story.

But later that day, as the sun set, she rode the elevator back to the thirteenth floor, went into the maid's overnight room, sat down, and waited. She wasn't sure why—the phrase *bear witness* kept coming to mind. One hairline crack in the false wall.

She would bear witness to the truth, and flinch with each shot that sounded muffled along the way. She would know the truth even with a false wall thrown up, sit in the dirt that could never truly be cleaned.

Even if she was an audience of one.

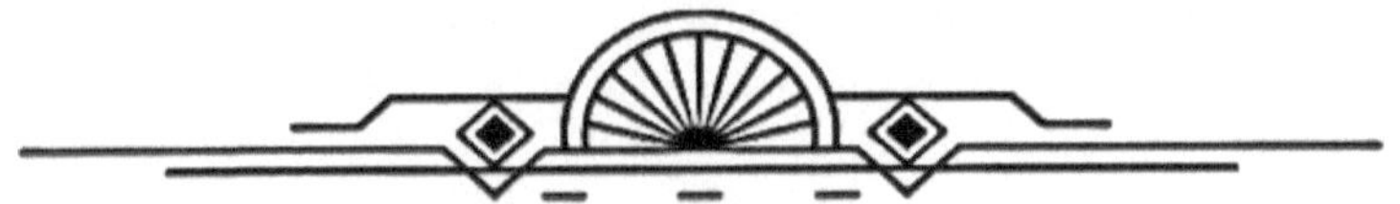

You Live in a Hotel?

Ah! Good to see you still looking well.

How were things with the *Premium* guests?

Did, um…

Did Agnes mention me, by chance?

Ah, yes, I agree. You were wise to observe her from a distance. Best not to interfere.

Anyway, let's not linger on old memories. Onward and upward, as they say! Or, well, in our case, onward and downward, right?

The next six floors are for the Ethel's Long-Term Resident suites.

Yes, that means people who live here.

Who would want to live in a hotel? Oh, you get all types, really. Sometimes people just need a place for a bit while they work a job. Sometimes they do it for the convenience—fully furnished and all bills paid, you know. Some people enjoy the anonymity living in a place like this brings. People coming and going all the time. Easy to blend in and disappear.

At the moment, we've got a mixed bag of residents.

A few warnings:

Steer clear of any strange shadows, especially on Ten. And, uh, keep your baby makers tucked away. No—don't ask. Just… keep yourself to yourself, okay?

You'll probably hear Anna singing on Eight. Yes, yes, she'll sound terribly sad. Don't try to cheer her up. Don't ask her what's wrong. And whatever you do, don't mention Telegraph Hill or *the cliff.*

Beware teenage girls who seem innocent. That's all I'll say about Floor Seven.

Best to keep your mouth closed, your hands to yourself, and your eyes straight ahead on Twelve and Nine—some dangerously shady characters there, and you wouldn't want to get yourself into trouble, would you? We wouldn't want you getting offed unceremoniously, oh no! Only fully ritualistic murders are approved here at the Ethel.

What? Ah, just a little joke.

Now, let's see, who am I missing?

Oh. Her.

Floor Eleven. *Samantha.* Yes, she looks like a helpless little old lady, but she's not. Okay? She's just… not.

Go on. You're doing so well. We'll get to the bottom of this place soon enough.

See what I did there? The bottom? Because we started at the top? A pun!

Well, I thought it was funny.

What's that? The strange couple in the elevator? Yes. Ahem. I've seen them.

Yes, the man looks an awful lot like me. A marked resemblance, yes. Familial, even.

Damn, you, George. And your stupid little Etta. Could have ended the family curse if you'd just stopped sucking face long enough to see them coming.

What? Oh, nothing.

I don't want to talk about it.

I *said* I don't want to talk about it.

Get going.

12th Floor – Long-Term Residents
1921

See the Truth
Savannah R. Fischer

"Well, whaddya think, eh, Rita?"

"It's beautiful, Tony," I gasp, taking in the grandeur of the suite.

Beautiful doesn't begin to cover it.

I'll admit, when Tony told me his boss was setting him up with a long-term residency at the Hotel Ethel, I was irritated. Gone was the dream of a house of our own, an army of little *bambinos* to make Tony proud.

Hotels are for businessmen, politicians, and prostitutes—all important cogs in the greasy wheel of the mob. Worse, they demanded Tony move immediately. He's been here on his own for six months while we waited for our wedding day to finally roll around. It came and went, as did the honeymoon, and now we're finally home sweet home.

Looking around at the emerald-green walls with their gold inlay glittering under the crystal chandelier, the wait sure was worth it. My eyes fall on the beautiful four-poster bed, with matching gold inlaid into the wooden frame. A girl could get used to this kind of luxury. Bare minimum, it's the perfect place to practice making our first *bambino*.

Tony's eyes fall on my chest and heat ignites between my thighs.

"Shall we?" he says, waving toward the bed.

"Oh, Tony. I thought you'd never ask," I moan into his ear as he scoops me into his arms.

Oh yes, life at the Hotel Ethel is going to be perfect.

Our frenzied lovemaking over, Tony plants a tender kiss on my forehead.

"I gotta meeting with the boss in an hour. Those FBI *bastardos* are sniffing around the racket."

"Be careful, Tony. Won't cha?"

"I'm always careful, Rita. We're in the pockets of the *polizia*, the politicians, the judges—ain't no one but those stupid feds care what we're up to."

"It's the feds I worry about."

"Don't you worry your pretty little head." Another kiss lands on my forehead. "No stupid fed is gonna find the stash. Why, our girl Ethel is wrapped up with the bootleggin'."

Oh! Now it makes sense why we have to be here.

"So, you got the operation all set up?"

"Yes, she runs like a charm. The old biddies that run the joint won't let us into the lowest levels, something about permits and keeping things clear in case a' earthquakes. So, we got the still set up here, and we hide 'shine on this floor, and behind some secret walls in the ballroom and the restaurant.

Hell, we got the whole floor to ourselves, although not by the books, of course. Old Ethel is a crafty bitch, helping us operate."

He lowers his voice conspiratorially. "See, the old biddies like getting a cut of that bootleggin' money. They even serve guests some of our 'shine! Now, let me do a line on those perfect breasts."

My heart races at the mention of my greatest vice—cocaine. I'm jealous as Tony uses the crisp business card from the hotel to lay out a line on my chest. He buries himself in my cleavage, snorting the drugs and playing with my nipples. It's an intoxicating feeling of power to feel him go hard again. To my displeasure, he withdraws, tucking his erection into his boxers as he reaches for his suit.

"Now, I'll be back in a coupla hours," Tony says as he continues dressing. "I expect you to be naked in bed waiting for me when I get back. A husband has needs, after all."

"What should I do while you're gone?"

"Maybe take a little nap or draw in that sketchbook a' yours. Stay in the room for now. Just cause Ethel is in on the con doesn't mean we might not have some enemies around. Goin' out on your own could be a death sentence, *mi amor*."

With that, Tony leaves me to my own devices for who knows how long. Sketchbook, my pretty little ass. Once I'm sure he's gone and not coming back, I set myself an important task—finding where my husband stashed that cocaine!

My search of the living area, kitchenette, and bedroom turns up empty. With my luck, that one line is all he had on him.

If I can't find Tony's stash, I might as well take that nap. There's not much else to do.

I wake up later, groggy and alone. It feels like I slept for a lifetime, but surely it was only an hour or two. My throat hurts like it's been rubbed raw on the inside with sanding paper—must be allergies.

Some steam from a hot bath should help. And hey, if I'm lucky, maybe Tony will come back in time to join me. I know this is a working trip, but who says we can't mix business and pleasure? After all, I am the new Mrs. Bianchi.

One step into the bathroom is all it takes to be overwhelmed once again by the grandeur of the place. Black marble counters with two sinks and matching gold mirrors greet me.

The tile is black and gold, but the star of the show is the golden clawfoot bathtub with ruby-colored spigots. Eagerly, I turn the handles, amazed at how quickly steamy water cascades from the spout. I can already breathe better.

A woman's scream, her voice as shrill as nails on a chalkboard, splits the air. Panic roils in my gut, guiding my feet as I leap into the living room. *Tony said we have the floor to ourselves!*

I wrap my housecoat around me as I realize our balcony doors are open. I rub my eyes in shock—there's a woman on our patio!

Black hair, sexily tousled like she's just had a romp in the sheets, cascades down her back. Her robe matches mine—*is she a hotel guest? How did she get in here?*

She turns and fixes her empty gaze on me. Where her eyes should be are two pitch-black orbs trailing matching tears, like ruined mascara melting down her face in thick rivulets. She points a finger at me and beckons me closer.

Sunshine be damned, it's freezing out here. I pull my housecoat closer even as my traitorous feet move toward the woman. My brain screams at me to run but it's like a compulsion. I simply can't turn away.

When we're together on the balcony, she drops her robe, revealing a body befitting a Greek goddess, if only it weren't marred by innumerable burns.

"Who did this to you?" I whisper, reaching for the woman.

She doesn't respond, instead stepping away from me until her naked buttock is pressed against the metal railing.

Even if she's just a figment of my imagination, I have to *try* to help her. I take a few tentative steps forward.

The poor woman shakes like a newborn calf, standing on wobbling legs as she turns her back to me, pulling herself to stand atop the railing.

She turns back, locking those haunting eyes on me. She mouths "run," but I can't. My feet are rooted in place by her magnetic presence.

She jumps. We scream together, my already raw throat ripped bloody as I run to the railing.

The woman splatters to the ground with a sickening thwack. From twelve floors up, there's no way she survived.

The spell breaks and I run to the railing, peering over even though I already know what I will see. Her broken body, a pool of crimson blood blooming around her like the world's most gruesome flower, is barely discernible from this height.

Horrified, I run for the door before remembering Tony's explicit instruction *NOT* to leave the room. Surely, he couldn't have imagined a scenario like this?

Still, I know better than to deny a direct order from my mob-boss husband. Left without a choice, I retreat back to the bathroom.

There's no sound of running water. D*id I turn it off before leaving the bathroom?* The curtain is drawn, too—odd.

I step forward, my heart hammering in my chest. Tony must have slipped something into my drink. I bet he's getting such a rise, knowing I'm alone and hallucinating. *Cazzo.*

With nothing else to do, I pull back the shower curtain and scream.

A naked woman lies in a pool of her own blood, both arms slit from wrist to her inner elbow. Her head lolls to the side of the tub, her skin pale as fresh-fallen snow. Her eyes are open, the same black orbs as the woman from the balcony. A few curls of brown hair escape her bun, trailing into the steamy water—this was recent. *Did this happen while I was outside?*

Revolted, I pull the curtain shut and stumble away. Tears flow freely as I make my way into the living room. My breath comes in hitching gasps.

There's a dead girl. In my bathroom. And I can't leave without risking my life. The FBI, a rival mob, a disgruntled client—being the wife of a mob boss doesn't come without a target on your back. I have to wait for Tony.

Maybe this is some sort of warning from a rival mob—letting Tony know they can get to me right under his nose?

Those poor women. And their eyes. *THEIR EYES!* I cry for what feels like hours, leaving my body frail and weak from the exertion. *Merda.* I thought I knew what I was getting into with Tony, but this is above the pale.

I can't let Tony see me like this. It's my job to be his rock, strong and resolute in the face of danger. I force myself to stand, even though I'm weak-kneed like a baby calf, and stumble my way into the bathroom.

My fingers smooth my hair back into place. I remove my makeup and start afresh, carefully averting my eyes from the desiccated bathtub. Before long, I look just like the flapper girls of New York—perfect.

Soothed to the best of my ability, I leave the bathroom and head for the bedroom. Surely, Tony's on his way back from the meeting now. I strip out of my housecoat, leaving it draped lasciviously across the back of the chaise lounge, and situate my nude form in the middle of the bed.

I close my eyes, working my hand between my thighs. Tony loves when he finds me all revved up.

A creaking sound spoils the moment.

My eyes shoot open, and I see another dead woman, this time suspended by thick rope from our living room's crystal chandelier. Her naked body swings limply, her feet almost touching the couch.

I can't look at her. I mustn't.

The killer is in the room with me!

Blind panic consumes me as I throw on a dress and shoes and run from the room—potential outside danger be damned, there's danger *INSIDE*. I'm almost to the door when the knob begins to turn. *TONY!*

I freeze, my body positioned just under the hanging woman. From here, I can see she has the same haunted eyes as the other two, but something's off this time.

I don't know what it is, but other than the eyes, I can't make out any of her features. Even through the haze obscuring her, she somehow still feels all too familiar.

I'm going crazy!

Tony steps into the door, pausing in the entryway. Surely, he sees her. He *HAS* to see her.

"*Figlio di puttana!*" he roars, shoving his way into the room. "Those damn feds are right up my *coglioni*! Sniffin' around like a bunch a' *bastardos*."

He pauses, looks up, and shakes his head. "You always were a *stronza*, Rita."

He saunters in, ignoring me even as I scream.

Don't you see them, Tony?

I beat on his chest, hysterical, but he brushes past on his way to the bed. I watch in shock as he pulls more cocaine from his breast pocket, dumping the contents onto our bedside table and snorting it up before shambling into the bathroom.

He takes a piss, then comes back out, a fat cigar between his lips as he heads for the balcony. Only then do I notice the split lip, the disheveled hair, and the scar across his cheek. *That wasn't there this morning? What happened?*

My mind reels as he gazes out over the balcony, sighing like the weight of the world rests on his shoulders. Chills set in, raising gooseflesh over my exposed skin.

More than just the dead girls, something isn't right. I don't recognize my own husband. He's never been cold to me, let alone ignored me. Pezzo di merda *didn't even stop to check on me!* Gone is my kind, doting husband, replaced by a stone-faced monster fueled by drugs.

With Tony situated on the balcony with his smoke, I run. Out the door and down to the elevator. It's empty, praise the virgin and all her saints.

The attendee pays me no mind, not even bothering to ask me what floor. His tall, ghoulish appearance reminds me of a pock-marked corpse. Silence is preferable to hearing whatever he may have to say. Regardless, the doors shut, and we begin our descent. We stop at every floor but thankfully pick up no other passengers.

When we get to the lobby, I don't even offer a tip. I take off like a shot fired by a rival mobster, hurtling out of the elevator.

The ivory marble and dangling chandeliers do nothing to dispel my fear. No one bats an eye, not even the beautiful receptionist Tony couldn't keep his eyes off of when we arrived. *Maybe he's been off schmoozing her instead of warming my bed?*

I push thoughts of my husband's potential infidelity aside as I run and crash into the doors. The darkness of the night sky is all consuming as I run, run, *RUN* away from the grisly scene upstairs and the husband that couldn't care less.

I'm back in bed, my head pounding away with the worst hangover of my life. A blinding bolt of pain makes me wince. The last thing I remember is running for the front door in the lobby. *How did I get back here?*

There's a crick in my neck too, accompanying the sandpaper feeling of my throat. I set about massaging my sore muscles, starting at the connection point between my shoulders and my neck, and slowly working my way up. It's oddly tender, and no amount of massaging is helping. *Great. Just great.*

A look around the room reveals no sign of my husband. *Tony.* My heart breaks anew as his words from yesterday come flooding back. How could he be so tender in the morning and so callous upon his return? And how did he not see those girls?

I'm not stupid—I know he's had to do *things* in the name of the mob. But it's never come between us. He's always been the perfect gentleman.

Everything hurts as I force myself out of bed. Fear laces through me like a hit of cocaine, spiking my heart rate. Is *SHE* still here? A quick glance between my fingers reveals nothing out of place in the living area. Whoever she was, the mysterious woman hanging from the chandelier is gone.

What about the others?

Tentative steps sink into the luxurious carpet on my way to the bathroom. Even though I'm terrified, I have to see, to *KNOW*. Blood rushes in my temples, my fingers tremble on the crystal doorknob. I can't bear to look—but I must.

Before I can talk myself out of it, I give the knob a mighty twist and swing the door open. Instead of looking directly at the tub, I fix my gaze on the mirror. The curtain stands open, revealing a perfectly normal tub. No signs of the dead woman or her bloody bathwater remain.

Maybe it was all just a hallucination? Did I fall asleep after Tony left and am just now waking up from the world's worst nightmare?

My breath hitches as I leave the bathroom and turn to the patio. Outside is overcast, like we're on the edge of a bone-rattling thunderstorm. Mercifully, there's no sign of the jumper.

Still unable to fully relax, I grab my sketchbook and pencils, then head for the bedroom. I can't stand to be alone in the living room right now, to sit where a dead woman's feet dangled inches above the couch.

My fingers dance across my pencils, itching to draw something, *anything*, to distract myself. My selection made, I open the clothbound book and scream.

The woman from the bathtub leers back at me with her soulless, scratched-out eyes. The first drawing is her in the bathtub, a side profile like I first saw yesterday. *Or was it today? When did I have time to draw this?*

Next is a close-up of her face, each tendril of hair messily arranged to keep out of the water. The detail is impressive, beyond my normal ability, but those eyes—those damn black weeping eyes.

A close up of the slits of her wrists follows, with realistic drops of red watercolor mimicking blood. A name in the corner catches my eye— Dolores.

"Who are you, Dolores?" I whisper to myself.

"A maid," replies a soft-spoken voice.

The temperature in the room drops so cold my breath leaves patches of white lingering in the air. I wrap the blanket around me, desperate to fend off the chill threatening to worm its way into my bones.

"Look harder," the voice continues, this time coming from right behind me, almost as if she's whispering in my ear.

I should turn around, look in those black orbs, and beg for answers. But I can't. I'm not ready. I pull the blanket closer, crunching my eyes shut, and plead with the ghost.

"Please, leave me alone. *Please.*"

Silence so intense it hurts follows my plea. The temperature of the room slowly returns to normal, but still, I can't open my eyes. Can't move a muscle. The *whoosh whoosh* of blood in my ears accompanied by the slamming of my heart are the only things anchoring me in reality.

I don't know how long I sit there, clutching my sketchbook to my chest under the blanket, before the door to the suite opens.

"Blessed Madonna, let me have peace today," Tony prays.

I open my eyes just in time to watch him cross himself, then look up at the chandelier. With a shrug of his shoulders, he soldiers on, heading for the bathroom. He doesn't acknowledge me as he lays down a line on the counter to snort. Rage surges through me straight from hell itself.

"Tony!" I yell, throwing a pencil at him. "Look at me, you useless *testa di cazzo!*"

He shoots up immediately, eyes bloodshot from the coke. He fixates on me in the mirror but refuses to turn and look at me.

"Fuck you, Tony!"

My primal scream fractures the mirror, slicing Tony's reflection at the neck. I feel a sympathy twinge in my muscles.

"When will you leave me alone, you *stronza?*" he screams back.

We stare at each other, locked in a silent battle of wills. I won't give him the satisfaction of looking away. He's not the man I thought he was, and I refuse to give him the satisfaction of bowing to his will.

"I am your wife," I hiss, "and you will treat me with respect."

Tony blinks once, twice, three times, his motions alarmingly fast.

How much did he take? Has he been mixing it with his 'shine?

Without saying a word, Tony grumbles out of the bathroom, shambles out of the living room, and slams the door behind him. Alone again, I descend onto the bed and weep.

Time holds no meaning anymore. I don't know how long I've been trapped here.

Tony comes back sporadically, mostly to do drugs or sleep, but he never speaks to me.

I flit in and out of consciousness—one miserable day after another bleeding together into a sea of loneliness. *How did everything go so wrong?*

I've tried to leave the hotel, but I always end up back here. My theory is Tony has someone watching me, making sure I don't escape. I don't know why, since he obviously doesn't care one bit about my existence, but I stopped trying weeks ago.

Porters, maids, the other guests—they're all in on his plan too. No one will talk to me or even acknowledge me. My only companions are the ghosts that haunt my waking hours.

Dolores shows up in the bathtub randomly, or behind me, begging me to "see the truth." All I see is dead girls. Betty, the jumper, never speaks—

only looks at me pityingly and jumps. I'm now immune to the sound of her body hitting the ground.

I ignore them the best I can. It's better not to show them my fear; it makes them visit more often.

The true object of my fascination is the faceless woman hanging from the chandelier. I've drawn her what feels like a thousand times, but still her features remain obscured, other than her weeping eyes. She never speaks to me, never moves from her spot. Just dangles there lifelessly, taunting me. I'm sitting on the bed, working on a self-portrait this time, when Dolores begins her frantic whispering again.

"You have to see the truth."

"I don't know what I'm looking for!" I yell back in frustration. "What do you want me to see, Dolores?"

"See yourself," a new voice says, soft and sweet.

I turn and see Betty beside me. Up close, it's easy to see she's been a victim of some pretty nasty abuse. Small, red, twisted welts line every inch of exposed flesh, like someone put out cigarettes on her repeatedly. Her ribs and hips are a motley mass of green and yellow bruises, all half-healed and ugly.

"Betty, what happened to you?"

"Not what. Who."

"You're asking the wrong questions," Dolores grumbles, impatient with my inability to see whatever it is she so desperately wants me to know.

"Why won't you just *tell* me?" I ask, looking between the two ghosts beside me.

Dolores and her slit wrists drip blood and water on the carpet, but we both know it will be gone by morning. Betty wraps her arms around herself, shivering. Neither will fully meet my gaze with their black eyes.

"What am I missing?" I scream, scratching out the eyes on the picture I've been drawing today.

"Look," Betty whispers, pointing at my drawing.

I gasp as everything comes into crystal-clear focus, the harsh edges of the truth sliding into place like a knife to the ribs. I bring an instinctual hand to my neck as I look between the paper and the woman hanging from the chandelier.

The curve of the lips, the gentle slope of the forehead, the crook of the nose—my self-portrait mirrors the third dead woman.

I see it now, even as I recoil in shock.

No, it can't be!

Wordlessly, I walk to the couch and stand on my tiptoes, begging my eyes to tell me a different tale than what I'm seeing. I run a gentle finger down her face, *MY* face, as hot tears spring to life.

"How?" I weep as I realize the truth of it all. My feet levitate as I stare into my own black, weeping eyes—dead.

I'm dead.

"Remember," Betty says, grabbing my hand and joining me in a circle with Dolores. "Remember."

Memories flood my veins much like the drugs Tony and I used to take. Ferocious lovemaking. Tony and cocaine. Me looking for the cocaine.

And then… Tony coming back, drunk and drugged up out of his mind. Another round of sex, only this time, Tony is aggressive. He's hitting me, pulling my hair, grabbing me by the throat.

Whatever *this* is, I don't want it. I'm begging him to stop, scratching at his face and hands. He's *enjoying* this.

Everything goes dim, but I feel a scratching at my throat—rope. I see through Betty's and Dolores's eyes as Tony strings me up from the chandelier, using a chair to support my weight.

When I'm tied up, he kicks it out from under me. My neck cracks at an unnatural angle.

Tony, my husband, the love of my life, killed me in a drug-fueled haze our first day at the Hotel Ethel.

Dolores wipes a tear from my face, her eyes normal now that I can see the truth. They're a lovely green—I wonder if she was Irish? Betty's open eye is blue; the other is swollen shut.

I can't bring myself to ask them what happened. I fear I already know.

Dolores squeezes my hand, using her power to show me. Tony grabbing her, the maid, as she came to clean his room. Her rape. Him drawing her a bath, telling her to clean up after she bled from his assault. And then, once she was in the bath, him leaning over and slitting her wrists, leaving her to bleed out.

Betty is next. I see through her eyes as various members of the mob use and abuse her, the daughter of a rival boss. Tony brings her back here, only to continue the abuse. She jumped off the balcony rather than face another day of pain and suffering. Tony may as well have killed her.

Fresh tears slide down my cheeks as my world comes crashing down. Tony raped and killed us all—and I married this monster! *How could I be so blind?*

"How long have I been… have you… have we?"

Dolores and Betty shake their heads, before answering as one, "Time has no meaning for us anymore. We simply are."

I don't want this! I wanted a husband that loved me, an army of children, a house, time for art—happiness! Tony destroyed me, and he won't get away with it. I will haunt him until the end of his days. I—

Tony bursts through the door, face red from exertion. His eyes widen as he sees the three of us.

"But-but you're dead," he stammers.

"Tony Bianchi, come out with your hands up! You're wanted for racketeering, drugs, bootlegging, and other crimes against your fellow man!"

Tony goes silent, looking around the room for any sign of escape. The front door is blocked, and the balcony is certain death.

Trapped—he's trapped with us.

"Go to hell, Tony," I hiss.

"Rita, I—"

"Fire!" orders the voice from outside.

A hail of bullets rips through the walls of the Hotel Ethel, tearing holes through Tony. Crimson blood sluices from his wounds as my husband slumps to the floor, mouth open in shock, eyes gazing at nothing.

Tony will never hurt anyone again.

Dolores and Betty look at me, an unasked question in their eyes.

I think of the horrors we've endured—all the pain, suffering, and death at Tony's hands.

My heart hurts. Even knowing the truth, I still can't bring myself to hate him. Love and pain intermingle, crushing my heart in a vice.

Tony, you *leccaculo.*

I nod at my newfound sisters. It's time we leave this room.

11th Floor – Long-Term Residents
2002

Temple
Justin Holley

Tessa watched as her auntie, twenty-three years deceased, looked over her shoulder, smiled, then disappeared inside the front foyer of the Hotel Ethel without actually opening the double doors.

She'd been seeing her aunt for about a month now. At first, she had needed to overcome her fears, but once she understood that Auntie had a message for her, Tessa settled in and paid attention.

"This is it, Doug," Tessa said to her cameraman and documentarian. She had established long ago that Doug couldn't see Auntie, so she wouldn't mention it now. For all he knew, this was her own idea.

Tessa allowed her gaze to travel up the column of concrete and brick, twenty floors of pure opulence, all the way to the roofline. Behind, the jagged peaks of the rocky cliff face and the copse of trees the Hotel Ethel sat nestled into jutted out and into the bright blue sky.

"You sure about this?" Doug asked. "I mean, you just got the lead reporter job at the station. I'd hate to see you lose it right away." He always asked and the answer was always the same.

"Just follow my lead. We'll do this right, get all the proper signoffs and permissions. It'll be the biggest story of the year."

Tessa shivered. The tall hotel reminded her too much of the twin towers. Only a year and a month had passed since a plane flown by terrorists took the huge structure down. *Ground Zero.*

Tessa reminded herself not to include footage from the outside of Hotel Ethel. *Too soon—much too soon.*

As she studied the structure one last time, movement captured her attention up on the cliff face behind. A boy ran through the trees, skipping, playing. She watched until he disappeared. Tessa hoped his parents were around; she hoped he wouldn't fall.

"Remind me how this theory works again," Doug said. His dark eyes focused on Tessa. He looked concerned, perhaps for her sanity. "And how did you figure the timing out?" He shook his head. "It makes no sense to me."

Tessa knew she would have never figured things out if not for Auntie, and her little clues about how she died in this very building. She'd told Doug this several times, but he never believed her about the ghost.

She cleared her throat and decided to downplay Auntie's apparition. "My aunt disappeared here twenty-three years ago...tonight. October thirteenth, 1979. I've always maintained a healthy curiosity about what happened. So, now that I have access, I researched in the archives, cross-referenced dates, and discovered after months of cataloguing and collating information, that at least one person has disappeared every twenty-three years on the exact date of October thirteenth."

Tessa hoped that placated Doug, even though he had heard this all before. She supposed his nerves were getting the better of him.

Doug appeared to do the math in his head, though Tessa knew he should have worked things out long ago. "So, tomorrow person number six should go missing. According to your theory."

"Precisely," Tessa said. And she knew that was what Auntie wanted from her, too. To end the history of dark magic and sacrifice. Expose it. Yes, she had heard the rumors about the Baking Circle, the six women who funded the construction of Hotel Ethel. *A coven.* Tessa believed this with all her heart. Auntie had found that out firsthand and now Tessa would put a stop to the practice. She started up the steps.

"Whoa, wait," Doug said, fumbling with his video-camera and backpack full of lenses, his shaggy hair bouncing over his dark eyes as he hurried. "I'm not ready. I need to know the whole plan."

"We're ripping the Band-Aid off, right this minute," Tessa said over her shoulder. "Just follow my lead and keep the camera rolling. My plant should be in place."

"Plant?"

Tessa grinned at him, then continued up the steps to the entrance. She took a deep breath and pulled the doors open. A gust of air rolled out and over her until the pressure equalized.

As she scanned the foyer, Tessa didn't see Auntie, but she did spot Vinnie standing over by the bank of elevators, pizza box in hand, Giovanni's Pizza hat on his head. He was speaking to an officious looking man in a suit and tie. A heated discussion by the look of things.

They needed to hurry.

Tessa scurried by the concierge desk, now empty as the man still argued with Vinnie over delivering a pizza with no official recipient. The Hotel Ethel frowned on uninvited guests.

She waved back at Doug to hurry, then located the door to the service stairs.

Having heard the doors open, the concierge started to turn away from Vinnie.

Tessa's heart sped up. *Come on, Vinnie!* She hurried toward the stairs, praying the caretaker wouldn't see her and Doug. That would ruin everything, defeat their mission before it even got started.

Vinnie shoved the box into the guy's ribcage and said, "Don't ignore me. I have a delivery to make and you're wasting my time. Time is money."

The concierge turned back to Vinnie and pointed an index finger into his face. "Look here. I can't let anybody into the residential floors without expressed permission. You'll have to contact the room yourself and have them contact me."

Thank God for well-oiled hinges! The door to the service stairs opened with a quiet swish, then Tessa was in the stairwell, followed by Doug. His duffel bag caught the doorjamb and he paused.

Tessa grabbed him and pulled Doug the rest of the way in. The door closed behind him. She listened but didn't hear anyone approaching, the concierge still tied up with Vinnie and his insistence on delivering his pizza. They'd done it. They were home free. Tessa took several deep breaths, then glanced up the stairs.

Auntie waved at her from the next landing. Tessa could just make out her light blue eyes. They looked just like her own.

Good, we're on the right path!

"Let's move," Tessa whispered. "We need the eleventh floor. According to the kitchen attendant I interviewed the other day, they don't keep the service doors locked during daytime hours. Better to serve the residents."

"Give me a second," Doug said, trying to catch his breath by the looks of things. His chest heaved and his mouth hung wide open. His hair stuck to his forehead. "You don't have eighty pounds of equipment strapped to your person."

Tessa smiled, looked up the stairway where Auntie waited, then took the first step. "We'll take it slow and steady."

Doug grunted but followed. She could hear his heavy breathing behind her, and his plodding footfalls. He whispered, "Too bad we couldn't find a nice service elevator."

"Too risky," Tessa said as she climbed. She reached a landing and continued. "Just keep moving. If you stop, it'll be harder to get started again." She paused, then glanced over her shoulder. "And use this for motivation. We're about to save a life tonight. We're the only two people on Earth standing between a human being and ritualistic slaughter at midnight."

They continued to climb the steps, Auntie peeking down from every landing on their way, providing reassurance, her blue eyes blazing like beacons. They beckoned to Tessa. She felt closer to her aunt than ever, even more than when the woman still lived.

Tessa remembered the first time, several weeks ago now, when Auntie's ghost appeared to her, standing next to a newspaper with the Hotel Ethel on the front page. *My first clue.* The rest of the clues came via vast research and elbow grease. *Good old-fashioned journalism.* Now, here she and Doug were, finishing what they started all those weeks ago.

At the landing to Floor Nine, they stopped. Footsteps pounded up the stairs behind them. A man, slight of build, dressed in only white underpants and a white t-shirt, raced up the stairs, then squeezed by them. "Excuse me," he mumbled before slipping through the door.

"Good lord," Doug said. "Let's just take a random stroll in our underwear."

Tessa let out a breath. "Was that blood all over his shirt?"

"Probably…? I'm colorblind." Doug shrugged.

"Never mind," Tessa said. "We have bigger fish to fry. Let's go." She led Doug up the next stairwell.

After what seemed to take much longer than the journey should have, they reached the landing to Floor Eleven. Tessa watched as Auntie disappeared inside.

Tessa turned to Doug as he stumbled onto the concrete square, looking as if he had just climbed Everest. Sweat dripped from his chin, his face glossy and wet.

"Thank God," he said. He stood next to her, chest heaving as he tried to catch his breath.

"Let's go," Tessa said. "Auntie is already inside."

Doug looked at her with a sideways glance. "Ah, the Auntie's ghost thing again. Remember, I'm taking this *Auntie* business on a whole lot of faith—faith in you. I mean, if you're suffering from some kind of malady, mental illness, bacterial infection, whatever, now would be the time to tell me. Before we go and disrupt an innocent citizen's life."

With her right hand, Tessa whipped out a plastic card. "I'm a member of the media. That practically gives me the right to interrupt peoples' lives. She'll understand… unless she's guilty."

"Samantha Hitchcock Coit," Doug said as if trying the name out on his lips for the first time.

"Yes," Tessa confirmed. "Descendant of Lillie Hitchcock Coit, member of the original Baking Circle. The women who funded the build of Hotel Ethel."

She paused. "But you see now, right? They were spell-weavers, witches. And tonight, they kill, again. Kill to further their dark musings and purposes."

"And just what are those?" Doug asked. "Because you've been mighty light on those details. I mean, other than some scant evidence to a disappearance every twenty-three years, we don't have much to go on."

He squinted at her, then placed a hand on her hip. "Since the original Baking Circle is certainly deceased by now, are we saying their descendants have carried on the tradition?"

"Of course they have," Tessa said. "Duh. How do you think my aunt died? She disappeared right here, at the Hotel Ethel, the night of the annual ball, twenty-three years ago tonight at midnight."

"The ball is tonight?"

"Yeah," Tessa said. "The kitchen attendant confirmed it. They've been baking for two days. The guest list is quite extensive, she said." Tessa grinned. "And is about to become two people longer. Unannounced."

Doug shook his head but followed Tessa through the door to the eleventh floor. "We just gonna go knock on Samantha's door?"

"Well, yeah," Tessa said. "Element of surprise. We'll barrage her with questions, and she'll crack like an eggshell."

"I mean," Doug said, "if you're right about the sacrifice, wouldn't they have them tied up somewhere? Shouldn't we look around, try to find them? Samantha wouldn't just have the person in her room drinking tea. And once Samantha knows we're here—"

"I got this," Tessa said. "Just follow my lead." She watched as Auntie stood outside a door about halfway down the corridor.

"You see her, don't you?" Doug asked. "Your aunt. She's the one actually leading this expedition." He sighed. "For all I know, you're hallucinating."

"Ha, ha," Tessa said. "Now you're a comedian. Shut it and keep walking. Just a little further."

"Look," Doug said, "I have a nice girlfriend waiting for me at home. Tonight's movie night with popcorn and wine. I better get paid for this. You're gonna pay me, right?"

"I said I would," Tessa said. "Right after we succeed."

"No. Whether we succeed or not. This isn't an official assignment. I can't just go to the network and turn in a timesheet. We're freelancing, perhaps illegally."

"Fine," Tessa said as she approached where her aunt had just disappeared into Room 1107. "Yes. Paid no matter what."

She looked around at the opulence of the hallway, a direct contrast to the spartan décor of the service stairway. The striped crimson carpet, plush beneath her feet, seemed to extend out forever, at least to where the corridor turned, and the blood-colored river of fabric disappeared.

The lights were wrapped in shell-shaped sconces, dim, providing the atmosphere of luxury. The wallpaper made her feel as if she were standing on the platform of an old railway station, complete with train tracks running the entire length of the hall, a forest across the way, people with bags milling about in the foreground. *Fancy.*

"Just remember, this place isn't just a hotel, it's a temple. A place where rituals were born."

"A temple. Yeah, okay. You just gonna knock on her door, or what?"

Tessa stood, hands on hips. She had imagined this moment for weeks now. She studied the solid oak door in front of her. Heavy, gold-colored numbers—1-1-0-7—hung above the door.

Not even a peephole adorned the door itself, the gateway to the one person who might know what happened to her aunt back in October 1979. Who might also know something about tonight.

Tessa nodded to Doug, tightened her ponytail, took a deep breath, and knocked on the thick wood.

"And… here we go," Doug said.

The knocks sounded deadened, and Tessa hoped Samantha would even hear them. She didn't see any other means of announcing their arrival. No doorbell, no camera, no knocker. Tessa looked at Doug just as he looked at her.

"Nobody home?" Doug asked, adjusting his camera and pack. He looked hopeful.

Just then the lock clicked, and the door swung inward slowly. Well-greased hinges didn't allow for even the slightest squeak.

A thin, older woman stood in the doorway. Her dark eyes asked who they were, but she otherwise stayed silent. Her coif of gray hair lay in a loose yet stylish bun on top of her head. The woman wore a yellow dress adorned with what looked like blue stars and swirling galaxies. Auntie would have labeled her as well put together.

"Hello," Tessa started. "Are you Samantha Hitchcock Coit?"

The woman smiled warmly, just exposing straight, white teeth. "Yes, I'm Sam. I prefer the short version. And who are you, may I ask? I don't get a lot of visitors."

Tessa noticed Auntie and her blue eyes peeking from around a half wall just inside. She pried her gaze from Auntie and back to Sam. *Yes, I'm in the right place.*

Tessa smiled. "I'm sure not. And we're sorry to bother you. But we're looking to interview some folks who have lived here at Hotel Ethel, those familiar with the history. We're writing a story on the grand old place."

"No kidding?" Sam asked. "First time for everything. I'm sure there's been plenty written, but never from our perspective. Please. Come in. I have tea, coffee, scones. Might even be able to dig up a bag of chips." She glanced at Doug as if his round belly might enjoy such a treat.

"Thank you so much," Tessa said, then followed Sam into the suite. "We really appreciate your time and hospitality."

"Think nothing of it," Sam said. "Nobody gives Hotel Ethel enough attention anymore. Not since all the fancy hotels went up downtown and overlooking the Bay." She smiled as she disappeared around the corner of the half-wall, where the kitchen must be.

Sam kept talking, voice a little quieter as she rummaged for drinks and snacks. "We were the toast of the town. According to family history, after the grand old place opened its doors in October 1910, it premiered as a luxury destination. Now, well, not exactly shabby, but the old girl could use some polish and good press."

"Well, that's why we're here," Tessa said as she looked around the living room. "To discover some of the history of this place. And the folks here, of course."

More opulence met her gaze. The archways leading from the spacious living room to several adjoining hallways were decorated with beautiful white crown molding.

The floors were hardwood, stained dark. The walls were painted beige, adorned with what appeared to be original paintings of San Francisco scenes from long ago. *A fan of trolley cars and the ocean, for sure.*

One painting was of the Hotel Ethel when first built. It looked extravagant, a shining jewel next to the burned-out shell of buildings just adjacent, evidence of the great earthquake and fire of 1906.

Doug, having dropped his camera and bag to the hardwood floor, perused a tall, mahogany bookshelf, filled with large, old tomes. It spanned the entire distance from floor to ceiling, at least ten feet.

Hundreds of books, Tessa thought. *Impressive.*

Sam walked into the living room with a silver serving tray filled with an ancient silver tea kettle and several dishes and cups. The dishes looked formal, probably old as the hotel itself.

Family heirlooms? Tessa wondered. *Yes, perhaps.*

Sam brought the tray to a serving table in front of a luxurious, velvety couch. The expansive table's flat surface was decorated with old photos, decoupaged in place with a clear gloss. There were too many to look at all at once.

"Please, help yourselves," Sam said. "I would serve but my trembling hands aren't what they used to be." She sat in an armchair on the other side of the table from the couch. The cushion barely receded as she sat, so slight was her frame.

Doug dug in immediately, tearing open a bag of fancy chips. Some brand Tessa had never heard of. He began to crunch.

Tessa turned to Sam. "Do you mind if I ask you a few questions and record?" She took an audio recorder from her pocket.

"Please," Sam said, a small smile gracing her pursed lips. Her dark eyes bore into Tessa's. The older woman's hands sat in her lap, her legs crossed elegantly.

Hand over mouth, Tessa cleared her throat, then said, "Sam, are you a direct descendant of the original Baking Circle member, Lillie Hitchcock Coit?"

"Yes, of course," Sam said. "A granddaughter. Great, great, great, I'm sure you realize."

Doug, still crunching, at least held the presence of mind to film. The camera was pointed in Tessa and Sam's direction even if Doug preferred the company of the food to theirs.

"Ah, yes," Tessa said. "I had guessed as much." She adjusted herself on the soft cushions of the couch. *Sam would probably call it a davenport.*

"So, what do you know about the Baking Circle? Does it still exist today?"

"Only in theory," Sam said, a smirk playing at her lips. "There are a few of us descendants still living here, having had our suites handed down from generation to generation."

A sly look crossed her features. "If you were wondering, yes, we will still have our little gathering tonight. Nothing special. Just a rehashing of old times—old memories. Family stories. You understand, don't you?"

A temple, Tessa thought and took a deep breath. "Yes, of course, I was wondering," Tessa admitted. "The Baking Circle and their annual ball. Your families are famous for them."

"Famous, yes," Sam said, but she didn't sound like the word sat well with her. "For the wrong reasons, perhaps. We know all about the rumors of rituals and dark arts practices."

"Any truth to the rumors, Sam?" Tessa asked with a smile. Even if Sam took offense and grew wary that Tessa and Doug were there to thwart their sacrifice tonight, she could easily overpower this lone old woman with nearly zero muscle structure.

Sam sat silently, as if in wait, her lips upturned in a coy twist of the thin flesh.

"Whoa, look," Doug said through a mouthful of chips.

Tessa turned just in time to witness Doug go from pointing at the tabletop to grabbing at his own throat. His face had gone crimson, and choking noises fell from his open mouth. He begged Tessa for help with his eyes. Then those eyes rolled into his head, and he tipped from the davenport and onto the hardwood floor with a heavy thud.

The camera also slammed onto the floor and skidded toward the bookcase. A plastic piece broke off and skipped across the room in the opposite direction.

"Doug!" Tessa said. "Doug, are you okay?" She bent down to him.

"Oh, my," Sam said but remained seated. "I think he may be dead."

The stain spreading in Doug's crotch indicated such.

Tessa turned to Sam. "We need to call for help. Where's your phone?"

"Oh, help is on the way, my dear," Sam said. "Not to worry."

Tessa shook Doug's shoulder, horrible thoughts racing through her mind. *Sam—Sam killed Doug. Must have poisoned the chips. A temple. A sacrifice.* She looked to where Doug had been pointing at the table and noticed what he had.

A picture of Samantha Hitchcock Coit labeled October 1979. She looked exactly the same as she did right now, in the flesh. "Impossible."

Sam smiled warmly. "Oh, I think you're starting to understand. Trust those reporter instincts. You've followed the clues perfectly to this juncture. We've improved on the spells since the *old* days."

"You—you haven't aged…"

"Ah, a burst of clarity," Sam said. "I have aged and that's the problem."

The door to the tidy suite opened and a group of five women stepped inside, all well-groomed and full of smiles.

One of the women said, "She has arrived already. Several hours before midnight. Excellent."

The woman addressed Tessa, "The guest of honor."

The women walked toward her, their arms outstretched.

"May I introduce the Baking Circle," Sam said. "The descendants anyway. In the flesh."

A temple. A sacrifice! Tessa picked up the silver kettle from the serving tray, felt the tea slosh within, and started to swing at the first woman to approach. She could take out all these old biddies, then run for her life.

A strong hand grabbed the arm with which she held the kettle and pulled Tessa's arm behind her.

The silver kettle hit the floor and dumped tea all over the hardwood.

"Oh well," Sam said from right next to her ear.

"I was meaning to redecorate anyway. Perhaps a nice, light pine board this time. Several decades of dark wood will wear on the nerves."

Tessa didn't know how Sam had grown so strong. But if she really was looking to regain her youth, then anything was possible.

The group approached and began to bind Tessa's hands behind her back. No matter how hard she struggled, she couldn't break free. Panic overwhelmed her. She looked to one of the hallways off the living room where her aunt looked on.

"Auntie," Tessa croaked. "Help."

The women cackled. "Look closer," Sam said.

The visage of Tessa's aunt slowly changed, horns growing from her head, tentacles reaching from her back and writhing in front as if in anticipation.

Beyond the apparition, the hallway grew dark, and Tessa could only see stars in the darkness as if nothing except an alien galaxy existed beyond.

Sam addressed the other five women. "Tonight, we turn back the hands of time. Tonight, we renew the Ethel's foundations… and fix a few cracks of our own. The Ethel endures. The Circle endures."

The others laughed in delight, gathered in a circle, and began to chant in a language Tessa had never heard.

Tessa's mind felt fractured with shock. She had known all along.

A temple. A ritual. Sacrifice.

10th Floor – Long Term Residents
1941

The Infernal Shadow of Dwight Frye
Douglas Ford

Bring that infernal shadow of yours, the telegram said, *and a face to go with it.*

Whatever that meant. Had they confused him with someone else—say, Lon Chaney, who died a decade earlier? That sort of thing happened in the movie business, after all. You never really get who or what you want.

Still, as he explained to his wife, Laura, before boarding the train to San Francisco, if they expected the late Mr. Chaney, the "man of a thousand faces," they could do a lot worse than Dwight Frye, the man who, in true motion picture fashion, died a thousand deaths.

"Why don't you just call up Jack Pierce over at Universal and see if he can fix you up to look like Fritz again?" Laura said, referring to Dr. Frankenstein's hunchbacked assistant, a role Dwight had played years earlier.

"Or maybe you can just carry some crushed beetles in your pocket. Snack on them like that other reprehensible character you played. What was his name?"

Dwight sighed.

"Renfield."

He understood Laura's frustration. Neither of them ever imagined that in just a few years after Dwight acted these parts that Laura would have to work as a salesgirl so they could make ends meet. Dwight himself would rather die a thousand and one deaths than play another such role again.

Making the telegram's offer too intriguing to ignore.

Dwight had never heard of Charles Spektor, nor did he know precisely the sort of work that the photographer created. But Spektor knew of Dwight's reputation and wanted him to appear in a special series of photos. "Along the lines of William Mortensen," the telegram read, falsely assuming Dwight should know the reference.

Disembarking the train in San Francisco, he took a bus to his destination: the Hotel Ethel. His suitcase in hand, he stood outside the grandiose building and felt an unsettling connection to his famous bug-eating character.

The hotel's architecture would certainly look at home in the Carpathian Mountains, which caused Dwight to question his decision to agree to this enterprise. Perhaps he could have learned something from Renfield's fate at the hands of Count Dracula. Certainly, if he encountered Bela Lugosi waiting for him inside, he'd know for certain that someone played him for a fool.

Fortunately, the lobby's Art Deco interior reminded him less of Transylvania, though he couldn't help but sense something darker underlying the gaudiness. If the Great Depression had taught him anything, it was to think of glitz and glamour as an illusion.

The telegram instructed him to bypass the front desk and proceed directly to the lift. Dwight crossed the lobby with purpose, hoping to convey that he knew what he was doing. He received nary a glance, and when the lift attendant asked him floor, he requested the tenth, which housed long-term guests like Charles Spektor.

The lift attendant, a cadaverous man with a face full of smallpox scars, regarded him before complying.

"Are you . . .?" the cadaver started to ask.

Dwight finished for him. "Boris Karloff? Why, yes, I am. Would you like autograph?"

A little joke Dwight liked to pull whenever someone thought he looked familiar. People usually caught on and realized that they were talking instead to the hunchback who tortured the Frankenstein monster.

But the attendant did not catch on.

"No. Thank you," he said, turning to pull the lever that took them to the tenth floor.

Charles Spektor looked nothing like Dwight imagined. Perhaps he expected someone older, a little more bohemian. The man wore a rumpled shirt with the sleeves rolled and sported a thin mustache.

"Can you feel it?" the photographer asked him before they even finished introductions.

Dwight had no idea what he meant. Without an invitation to enter the room, he remained standing in the hallway, suitcase in hand. Behind Spektor, he could see a room transformed into a cluttered studio. A complete suite by the look of it. Dwight guessed that Spektor paid handsomely for it.

A quick glance back down the hallway revealed the scarred lift attendant watching him with a blank expression.

Spektor noticed the glance. "Oh, pay no attention to that scallywag."

Then he called out to the attendant, "Don't you have some old ladies to scare?"

Spektor gripped Dwight's forearm as if afraid his guest might turn and run. When he did, the sleeve rose further on his arm, revealing something inscribed on his forearm. A tattoo perhaps? Dwight wondered if the photographer was a former sailor.

"I apologize for my manners," said Spektor. He stepped aside so Dwight could enter the room. "It's just that I expected you to be—"

"Taller?" Dwight quipped.

As with the lift attendant, his joke fell flat. Dwight, who aspired to act in a comedy someday, wondered if he simply wasn't funny.

"No. How shall I put it? I thought you'd be a magnet for the energy surging through this building. Surely you can feel it, can't you? That energy?"

Dwight considered the suite. On one side, the photographer had arranged a whole wall with photographic prints, dozens of them covering nearly every conceivable space. Under those prints, someone had converted the top of a dresser into a make-shift bar, cluttering it with bottles and used drinkware. A large window took up the far side of the room, showcasing a view of Telegraph Hill and the lights of the city.

Dwight smiled uneasily. "It's certainly full. Where do you sleep?"

"Oh, who has time to sleep? But never fear, if I tire you out, I'll let you have your rest." Spektor pointed toward the corner of the far wall, where Dwight could make out a door. "In there. That's where the bedroom is. It's all yours of course. Only the best for the great Dwight Frye. Here, let's drink while we talk."

Dwight set down his suitcase and followed Spektor to the dresser with the bottles—most of them looking half empty.

"What can I mix you?" asked Spektor, picking up an ice shaker.

"Just water, please," said Dwight, refraining from mentioning his background as a Christian Scientist.

"I didn't take you for a teetotaler. I thought you Hollywood types loved your liquor. Well, more for me."

As he poured, Spektor talked rapidly about the hotel. For instance, did Dwight get a good look at that lift attendant? Before Dwight could answer, Spektor explained how seeing that man's scars and pathetic form made him think of Dwight.

"I considered using him in the photos I had in mind. But then I thought, why use a pale imitation when I could get the real thing? I can afford you, after all. Well, that is, my father can. Not that I'll ever see a dime of that money. He'd rather give it to that damn America First movement."

Here, he paused to drink, and Dwight considered bringing up the advance promised by the telegram.

Before he could, the bedroom door opened and out came a woman.

He brown hair hung loose, a tangled mess covering half her face. More remarkably, she wore not a stitch of clothing. She appeared catatonic, taking two uncertain steps into the room before freezing in place.

Realizing that he'd been staring, Dwight looked away. He could feel the blood rushing to his cheeks.

"I was saying, have you studied Mortensen's photographs?"

With a start, Dwight realized that Spektor had asked this question more than once. Mixing a second drink, the photographer seemed unaware that this third person had entered the room, even though he faced a mirror that likely held her reflection. Either he failed to notice her, or he thought nothing of her presence.

"I'm sorry," said Dwight, gathering his wits. "Who?"

"I mentioned him in the telegram. A pretentious sod." Spektor went on to describe a rival photographer, one who apparently favored occult themes and found some measure of undeserved success.

Despite Spektor's vitriol, Dwight sensed grudging admiration for this rival. He even had the man's work on display, as Dwight discovered when Spektor led him to the prints he kept affixed to the wall.

The subjects of the photos left Dwight feeling both uncomfortable and vaguely aroused. He stole a glance back to where he saw the nude woman and realized that she'd vacated the room as quickly and mysteriously as she'd first entered.

"Have you ever seen anything so audaciously childish?" asked Spektor, drawing Dwight's attention to one photo. "You recognize the model of course."

Dwight tried to place the woman in the photo, nearly missing the objects positioned around her. At first, they looked like heads. It took Dwight a moment before he recognized them as artificial. Masks of some type, and not real victims of decapitation. He didn't recognize the woman.

"Fay Wray," Spektor said. "I'm surprised you didn't know. After all, you were in a picture with her. What was it called?"

"*The Vampire Bat*," said Dwight before noting how different the actress appeared.

"Still photography has a way of revealing secrets that a motion picture cannot. Just look at her expression. You know, Mortensen was carrying on with her while he was married to her sister. Look, I have these displayed as reference because I know what Mortensen was trying to do. What he *failed* to do, and what I will succeed in achieving with your help."

Dwight examined the other photos, all of them as revolting as the first. Still, he found that they did radiate a certain power or mystery he could not articulate.

What Spektor said next brought it home for him.

"The secret of existence itself. Mortensen couldn't quite capture it, but I will. With your help, that is. Immortality, hidden there in light and shadow."

Spektor insisted that photography possessed attributes that no other art form could claim, not even the motion picture. "Nothing else allows for sustained accumulation of shadow. That's why I said I wanted yours. I see the potential to use it as a doorway."

"A doorway?"

Much of what Spektor said sounded like madness. Talk of the doorway reminded Dwight of the strange woman who wandered out of the bedroom. Where had she gone? He didn't want to sound prurient by asking.

"Well, not a literal doorway," said Spektor. They sat in chairs that might have looked new in 1926. With Spektor facing him and working on his fifth drink, Dwight watched the door to the bed chamber, anticipating when it would open again.

When it finally did, a different woman emerged. She wore a robe, her hair fashionably curled.

"Sorry, Charlie," she said before plopping herself down on Spektor's lap, "I dozed off. That headache did me in." Without asking, she took Spektor's glass. She started to drink before pausing to regard Dwight over the rim. "Hello, chum. What'd I miss?"

"Don't you recognize the great Dwight Frye, Betty?"

Dwight stood and offered his hand. Simultaneously, Spektor shifted in the seat and caused Betty to fall onto the floor.

"Goddammit, Charlie!" She used Dwight's hand to assist her to her feet.

Swaying somewhat, she gulped the rest of the liquid before considering Dwight's stature. "You're sure no Clark Gable, are you?"

"Jesus. Be nice, Betty. You'll be posing together."

Hoping to change the direction of the conversation, Dwight said, "I think I saw your friend earlier."

"My friend? Mister, I don't have no friends."

Dwight began to stammer. He let slip the detail about the nude woman.

"Betty forgets her robe sometimes," Spektor said. He made a drinking motion to Dwight.

"Bastard. I'm a lady," said Betty, swatting at Spektor in a way that didn't appear playful. It also left Dwight uncertain about who he'd seen earlier. The room smelled of chemicals, and perhaps they clouded his senses.

Regardless, it became clear that no one occupied the room but them.

Spektor already knew what he wanted, all in the name of upstaging Mortensen with his own series of occult photographs. These staged photographs would succeed as art while telling a story that would startle the sensibilities of bourgeoise society. "I'm going to call it 'The Ethel Series,'" he explained to Dwight, "and your presence will pull it all together."

"My infernal shadow," said Dwight.

"Exactly!"

"What about me?" asked Betty.

"Ah," Spektor said, wagging his finger. "Ah."

They spent the remainder of the day pushing the rest of the furniture to the edge of the room, creating space for a tapestry to cover the exposed floor. For the first photographs, Betty simply needed to lie tastefully across the tapestry.

"Damn right it should be tasteful," she said. "I'm not a two-bit floozy."

Though she glanced at Dwight in a way that made him wonder.

As for Dwight, he would wear what looked like a hooded monk's robe, the cowl worn to convey mystery while keeping him recognizable to his adoring public. Spektor demonstrated to Dwight how he should stand over Betty with his arms upraised, as if calling down a great force.

"A great force?" Dwight asked.

Spektor's tone became conspiratorial. "You've heard of this place, the kind of things known to happen here. Yes, yes, it's had its share of people jumping from the top floor when the crash happened, but I don't mean that. I'm referring to things that were—well, less commonplace."

Betty laughed. "Commonplace, huh? That's rich."

"Will you please shut up?"

Betty shut up, but her eyes beamed with amusement. She winked at Dwight.

Spektor went on. "We're going to recreate the extraordinary events that occurred here. In this very room, in fact. It will take some time. A whole week. More perhaps."

That estimate gave Dwight some pause. Had he packed enough clothes? And the cluttered workspace already made him feel claustrophobic. Not to mention the fact that Betty made him uneasy.

"More than a week?" he said. "I promised my wife a shorter absence."

"I assure you, it's no trouble," said Spektor, "and this room will accommodate us all quite comfortably. Oh, don't look at me that way. No one is going to molest the great Dwight Frye. You can have the bedroom to yourself. Betty and I will make do out here."

Judging by her protest, this news came as a surprise to her. Before Dwight could say another word, Spektor thrust a stack of bills toward him, proclaiming it as the advance he had promised.

Dwight counted the money, determining that he would use a telegram to send word that his return would be delayed.

They needed the money.

And Laura would understand.

Posing for a photograph proved harder than acting in a motion picture. Dwight had worked with many eccentrics in his time, but he found Spektor an even more aggravating taskmaster than, say, Browning or Whale.

Spektor complained that Dwight never stood right, every stance or position simply wrong. Sometimes the cowl hid too much of his face. Other times it didn't hide *enough* of his face. He even accused Dwight of deliberately casting the *wrong shadow*, an absurd pronouncement.

"It should exude evil. You're not trying hard enough. Where is the Dwight Frye who terrorized the Frankenstein monster with a torch?"

Didn't the responsibility for shadows lie with the photographer? Spektor sought to blame his lack of talent on others.

The photographer behaved in an even worse fashion toward Betty. She wore a slip made of thin, paltry material that Spektor kept adjusting lower and lower. Now it hung off both of her shoulders so that she lay at Dwight's feet naked from the waist up. The invectives and swearing added to the unbearable conditions, and the constant drinking made things worse.

Dwight concluded that he must never allow Laura to see the resulting photos. She would get the wrong idea.

The session concluded in the dead of night, with Spektor finally exhausting himself and everyone else. They sat on the floor, instinctively avoiding the strange design printed on the floor covering. Spektor referred to it as a "sigil," a term unfamiliar to Dwight. During a quiet moment, he mentioned that the design gave him the willies.

"It should. It's from the Lesser Key of Solomon," said Betty.

Spektor paused in the middle of pouring himself yet another drink. He rested the bottle between his folded legs and stared at her.

"What?" she said. "Don't act surprised. I've met your pop. I pay attention." She reached for the bottle and drank directly from it. She finished with a burp. "It's the Sigil of Beelzebub or whatnot."

"Not Beelzebub," said Spektor. "Baal." He took the bottle from her and placed it out of reach. "You don't know anything."

"I know the story you want to tell with these photos," she said. "Poor Dwight here has no idea."

"I suppose I should hear it," Dwight said.

"I suppose you should," said Spektor. He took a deep breath. "Baal is one of the leaders of Hell."

"So is Beelzebub," Betty said. "I guess I mixed them up." She shrugged and offered Dwight a smile, which Dwight returned. He felt safer with her wearing her robe again.

Spektor shook his head with irritation. "Baal reigns over childbirth, and that's the theme here. An unusual birth took place in this very room."

Betty leaned forward eagerly, as if hearing the story for the first time.

"It happened years ago, when a wealthy man maintained the lease for this room to indulge in certain, shall we say, appetites. His favorite house servant usually accompanied him, a pretty girl he included in his dalliances. Mostly rituals he liked to perform with other members of the ownership class. Whatever he promised this girl worked. She proved more than agreeable to do whatever he demanded. On the last occasion he brought her here, she looked decidedly unwell. Plus, she was with child."

"His child, I assume," said Dwight.

"Not exactly," Spektor said. "Not that anyone showed enough courage to ask, so long as he paid his bill and kept her out of sight. The truth might have shocked them. Still, rumors spread that the tenant had brought his sick mistress into the hotel, so the cleaning staff stayed away." He regarded an empty bottle tipped on its side. "They still do, in fact."

"But the girl eventually left, I take it," said Dwight.

"Oh, no, she didn't leave. Not in one piece anyway." Spektor's eyes sparkled unpleasantly.

"*She* has a name, don't forget," said Betty. To Dwight, she added, "It was Clara. That's who I'm supposed to be in this photorealistic re-telling."

"Precisely," said Spektor. "And people will finally learn about her, thanks to me. She'll finally have her story told, even if it's not a pretty one."

"But what happened to the baby?" Dwight asked

"It was supposed to take after its father. Its true father, that is. They thought it would emerge from the poor girl's womb all aglow with the light of a fallen star, ready to usher in a new age of untold wealth. Instead they got something stillborn and too monstrous to behold," he said. "They wasted little time in tossing it down the elevator shaft."

"My god," said Dwight. "This is altogether too awful to be true. I suppose I'm dressed the way I am because I'm some sort of priest of this . . ."

"Baal," said Spektor, "and frankly, you could have done a better job of it." He stood and stretched. He froze when, looking down, he observed something on Dwight's hand. "Good god, man, tell me you haven't been wearing that all evening."

Dwight looked at his hand and realized what Spektor meant. On his left hand, he wore a silver wedding band.

"A priest of Baal does not wear a goddamn wedding ring," he said, before adding, too quietly, "Take it off."

Dwight sighed but acquiesced, reminding himself that the full payment of what Spektor promised could take so much pressure of himself and Laura. Spektor watched him place it on the dresser next the smudged drinkware.

"I'd planned something else for you tomorrow," said Spektor.

"Show him," said Betty. "I want to see his reaction."

Spektor nodded. He reached into a pile of clothing heaped in a corner and pulled forth a hideous mask.

Having seen the creations of a make-up artist like Jack Pierce, Dwight incorrectly assumed that nothing could bother him.

"Want to try it on now?" asked Spektor.

The mask looked neither wholly animal nor human, the face long and snout-like, the eyes two white, pupil-less orbs.

"Ugh, please don't," said Betty. "I need to be able to sleep."

The curved horns extending from the forehead added a final horrible touch. Dwight couldn't imagine putting his head into *that.* But Spektor made it clear he must do so if he wanted the rest of his salary.

It fit snugly, but he could see little through the thin eye slits. He could hear Spektor's voice well enough, though.

"Hail to the demon Baal."

As promised, Dwight had the bed chamber to himself. He tried not to imagine what would go on between Spektor and Betty once he closed the door. Before retiring he did his best to rinse out his mouth. The mask left him with a funny taste.

He took some of the Mortensen photographs with him, hoping for a better understanding of the aesthetic Spektor hoped to achieve. He pushed aside the pile of clothes covering the bed, blushing when he noticed women's undergarments. Again, his mind drifted to Betty, so he stretched back to peruse the photographs, hoping they could distract him.

They did the job all too well.

As a photographer, Mortensen clearly possessed a talent for making the imaginary seem real. Dwight just didn't approve of the subject matter. Even when not overtly violent, the images still proved disturbing, even menacing.

A witch flying over peaked roofs on her way to a Sabbath.

A crooked figure with a deformed face.

Most disturbing of all, a hulking gorilla preparing to pounce upon a defenseless, half-clothed woman. The gorilla was obviously a person in costume, but somehow that made it more awful.

He thought back to the premiere of *Frankenstein* and the angry reports about people losing sleep after viewing it.

What would those people say about these images? Dwight wondered.

Miraculously, he found himself growing tired, and sleep found him soon after turning off the light.

That is, until movement on the bed stirred him awake.

Then he felt arms curl around his torso, fingertips touching his neck.

Though awake, he pressed his eyes shut.

No doubt Betty had second thoughts about sharing the outer room with Spektor. She obviously assumed the bed could accommodate them both. He chided himself for so easily removing his wedding band. Had he given the wrong impression?

Perhaps if he pretended to sleep, she would get the message. She would grow bored and leave him alone.

Instead, she began whispering something, words that Dwight struggled to understand at first.

It sounded like, *"He's still here. They tore him out of me, and he's still here."*

Dwight wanted to roll over and ask who she meant. Had Spektor entered the room as well? He needed to express how uncomfortable they made him feel.

He opened his eyes just enough to see shadows on the opposite wall. He felt a draft, and those shadows moved. Had he left a window opened? He shivered, and not just because of the sudden cold.

He watched as the shadows began to coalesce into a shape. Like a daguerreotype slowly appearing on a silver plate, an image formed, the last thing that Dwight remembered until exhaustion finally overtook him.

A tall, cloaked figure with long, curved horns.

When morning finally arrived after fitful sleep, Dwight kept his eyes closed as long as possible. He dreaded opening them if it meant seeing that image still there imprinted on the wall. It came doubly to his relief to find it gone and himself the bed's sole occupant. He also found the window closed and the draft gone.

He found an unused robe in the washroom and stepped out to find Spektor wearing the same clothes as the night before. He looked sullen but sober. Dwight saw no sign of Betty.

"She left," said Spektor when Dwight asked about her. "Because of you. You nearly frightened the poor girl to death. Frightened me out of my wits as well, if you want to know the truth."

"Me?"

"Yes, you. That stunt you pulled. Putting on the mask and creeping about the room. I told you enough was enough, but you went over the line with Betty. Grabbing her like that. If you cost me this shoot, I'll see you in court."

Dumbfounded, Dwight shook his head. "She practically accosted me while I was trying to sleep."

Hearing that, Spektor's mood seemed to lighten. "She's in there? You brought her back then? Thank god, because when I saw you leave after her, I hoped that's what you intended."

The barrage of speculation caused Dwight's skull to spin. Where to start in correcting these confusing assumptions? Dwight chose denial, once again asserting that Betty tried to seduce him and that he never once in the night left the bed. Thus, any suggestion that he menaced anyone by putting on that devilish mask and prancing around simply had no basis in reality. Surely, he could appeal to Spektor with logic and reason.

But Spektor responded with an outburst, a clear sign that alcohol had permanently rattled his senses.

"You bastard," said the photographer. "You came here to ruin everything, didn't you? My father got hold of you. He hates me for meddling into his affairs. He hates my art."

Spektor picked up a glass in mid-sentence and hurled it in Dwight's direction. It barely missed and shattered against the wall inches above his head. A shower of broken glass rained down upon him.

"You lunatic!" said Dwight, brushing glass from his shoulder. "You contacted *me*. Not your father!"

But Spektor already had another glass in his hand, and he let it fly before Dwight could finish his sentence. This one came even closer. Dwight now crouched and did his best to shield his eyes.

"He got hold of you," said Spektor. "Hired you to sabotage me. How much did he offer you? Some nerve of him. Some nerve of *you*. You all want to hide the truth from the world. I'll bet he let you join his order."

Dwight couldn't keep up with the barrage of words or glass. Spektor's next missile grazed his hairline before shattering against the wall. His head throbbed now, but even worse, his chest grew tight. He recalled with dread his doctor's warning about overexerting his heart.

Meanwhile, Spektor stepped closer, reducing the distance between them to only a few inches.

Under his feet, Dwight felt the glass from the shattered drinkware. He chanced a glance through his fingers and saw tiny veins in Spektor's eyes. It horrified him to think that his heart could seize up altogether, and Spektor's face would be the last thing he ever saw. *Forgive me, Laura*, he wanted to say, but he couldn't articulate the words. He could only manage one word.

"Paper," he said with a croak. Quite certain he would die, he wanted to leave his wife a note.

The word froze Spektor in the act of throwing an empty bottle, the sleeve of his shirt pulled back high enough for Dwight to notice something.

The tattoo on his arm, now visible, bore the likeness of the sigil of Baal.

What did that mean?

"You want paper? Very well," said Spektor. He lowered his arm and stomped across the room so he could open a drawer on the opposite side. He began to rummage. "You can write a report to my father. Tell him his son has gone mad trying to access the things denied to him. The occult secrets he jealously guards."

These words meant nothing to Dwight.

Nor did he care. He'd even forgotten about his delicate heart.

Because the door to the bedchamber opened, and there stood the woman he thought he imagined before, naked, with distended belly and blood-smeared thighs, her engorged breasts leaking a milky fluid.

Obliviously, Spektor continued to rummage. Dwight realized he could not see her.

She looked directly at Dwight and smiled.

Then she spoke.

"Have you seen my lord's child? They've taken him from me. He needs his milk."

Still unaware of the presence sharing the room, Spektor turned with his fist clutching the paper Dwight requested.

"Write your goddamn letter," he said. "Tell your secret benefactor that his son doesn't need or want his money. He never understood art. I'll find my own path without him."

And with that, Spektor raised his other hand and struck Dwight in the head with the base of the bottle he still held. The impact made everything go dark.

When he regained consciousness, Dwight found himself stretched out on a bench in the lobby. On the floor beside him sat his suitcase, his hat and coat draped across it. He rubbed his forehead where Spektor struck him and found it tender and swollen. The lunatic nearly killed him. Through the fog, he realized that someone gazed upon him with interest.

He recognized this person by the smallpox scars. The lift attendant.

"I figured out who you are," the attendant said. "Bela Lugosi, right?"

Dwight grimaced. He sat upright and cradled his head.

"I'm sorry, Mr. Lugosi, but Mr. Spektor says you need to leave. Immediately," said the attendant.

"I could have the man arrested," Dwight said.

The attendant's lips formed into a crooked smile. "I doubt it. His family has lots of power, you know. Plus, his father keeps tabs on what goes on here at the Ethel. Oh, don't get the wrong idea. He's a good man. Well, good to me personally. You know, he took me to see that picture you were in back when I was very young. That's how I remember you." A pause. "I've lived here a long time."

The attendant's words chilled Dwight, and he couldn't pinpoint why. He tested his legs, and when he found himself able to stand, he gathered his things. He had no recollection of dressing himself, and he prayed that his head injury wouldn't result in long-term memory loss. He started for the door.

He heard the attendant's voice behind him as he exited the Ethel. "Take care, Mr. Lugosi."

Later, at the train station, it dawned on him what made the attendant's words disquieting.

He said "lived," not "worked."

Dwight thought about Spektor's apocryphal story, that macabre birth he tried to recreate in his photo series.

Dwight didn't want to believe it happened. But what of that strange woman with the leaking breasts? Dwight saw her. He *felt* her. He didn't believe in ghosts, but he didn't know what else to call her. What of the elevator attendant then? Had he been born in the Ethel?

Distracted by these thoughts, he almost missed the train's arrival back in Los Angeles. Reaching down for his bag and coat, he saw his own hand, and he realized with a sinking feeling what he'd left behind.

His wedding ring.

Later, he rifled through his things, already knowing he wouldn't find it. Laura watched him as he tossed around the items in his suitcase, her questions about what happened to him lingering in the air.

Dwight found himself making up a story about a mugging. He didn't want Laura to know what happened to him at the Ethel, though he assured himself that he'd done nothing unfaithful. Still, he felt sullied and unclean.

Several months later, he received a package in the mail. Spektor's name on the return label made him hopeful that the envelope contained the rest of the money promised to him. He could use it, and Laura had never quite forgiven him for leaving town and returning home without full compensation.

But he found no money inside. A letter explained the contents.

Dear Mr. Frye,

It has come to my attention that you began a short acquaintance with my son and participated in one of his ne'er-do-well ventures. Mind you, I neither approved nor disapproved of his artistic aspirations, though I remain skeptical that photography constitutes a legitimate artform. Certainly, as the enclosed prints demonstrate, it most often encompasses a base form of pornography. Thus, should the public learn of it, your appearance in my son's work would prove damaging, both morally and legally. You may have heard that with the help of cyanide, my son died by his own hand. Along with the discovery of his body in a suite our family has maintained in the Ethel, the staff uncovered an item that appears to belong to you. I am returning said item along with copies of the photographs he created. As they reflect the fantasies of a fevered imagination, I nearly had them destroyed. But to prove that I am not holding them for the purpose of, say, blackmail, I am surrendering them to you.

No formal closing after that. Just the signature of Ethan Spektor.

Dwight sighed with relief when he found his wedding band inside the envelope. Placing it onto his finger, he studied the enclosed prints.

He recognized his own features in the first one, his profile evident underneath the cowl that covered most of his head. The sight of Betty elicited a surprising pang in his chest. She appeared in the foreground of the photo, carnally splayed on the floor near his feet, her legs parted as if to receive some unspeakable demon. Despite his years in cinema, Dwight still didn't understand the appeal of such garish material.

The next three prints contained variations on this pose. He recalled how Spektor repositioned them more times than Dwight could count, the photographer never quite sure how to make Betty's body and the sigil share the frame.

Dwight noticed something else in the fourth and fifth print. An odd confluence of shadow looking over his image. These shadows formed a large figure themselves, one with the suggestion of ominous horns. Somehow, Spektor had succeeded in making it appear that Dwight himself cast this shadow. He noticed also the terrified expression on Betty's face, apparently in response to the shadow.

The next photograph puzzled Dwight. He couldn't recall seeing it taken, and it didn't include him.

And he hardly recognized Betty.

She stood naked, feet touching the sigil, both hands protecting her abdomen.

Perhaps she returned after his forced departure. Yet she looked noticeably different, her face gaunt, as if deprived of food for an extended period of time. Her distended stomach suggested otherwise.

She looked directly into the camera lens, her mouth agape as if in the act of speaking.

Dwight stared at the photo, wondering what she was saying when Spektor took the photo. Only then did it dawn on him what the size of her belly suggested.

Pregnancy. In an advanced stage.

With dread, Dwight looked at the next print.

It captured the act of Betty stepping backward, away from a figure moving into the frame. With its back to the camera, Dwight couldn't see its face, but the sight of it seemed to terrify Betty. Whoever it was, they wore the cowl, further obscuring their identity.

Who though? Not Spektor. Presumably, he operated the camera. Besides, the figure looked wrong, its head and limbs out of proportion.

One more photo remaining. Dwight didn't want to see it. His hands shook. He knew it would change him forever.

And it did. Not simply for the way it displayed the aftermath of a womb opened with violence, but because it blasphemed with such casualness.

Set free from the shadows, its face not a mask at all, the horned god stood incarnate over Betty's ruined body. A clawed hand gripped its offspring by the ankle.

Even in the stillness of a photograph, it appeared to squirm.

9th Floor – Long-Term Residents
1956

Did He Fly, Gosh Darn It?!
Joshua Loyd Fox

"Did he just *fly*, gosh darn it?!" the detective asked in a loud voice, to those moving with practiced ease around him. No one answered him back, however. Just the dead body, crumpled and somewhat exploded, lying on the pavement at his feet, cloudy eyes staring up at the beautiful blue skies above.

Everyone was doing their job. Technicians were taking pictures, beat cops were canvasing the scene for clues while other uniformed police officers were keeping the public at bay at both ends of the tight alleyway.

SFPD Detective First Class Mel Jones looked down once more at the broken body of a young man in clothes that had seen better days. Then he looked up at the backside of the Hotel Ethel.

Looking over at the towering cliff face of Telegraph Hill to his right and judging distances, there was no way this kid simply jumped from the ninth story window above to crash against the cliff face.

There was easily forty or fifty feet of distance between the two. And he could see both the shattered window and a large drying explosion of blood on the cliff face directly across from said window.

There was no darn way; the laws of physics wouldn't allow it, and darn it, Detective Jones didn't believe that a body could even be *thrown* that far. Not through the plate glass safety panel and then the dozens of feet of distance.

All the detective could fathom at that moment was a silly mental picture of the young man being shot out of a cannon in the room above, to *splat!* against the gray rock face of the cliff.

He shook his head again and called one of the crime scene techs over. He pointed down at the sprawling body of the young man, feeling a pulling in his chest for the guy. Detective Jones had a young son about the kid's age. He couldn't fathom standing over his own son like this.

"Make sure to get fingerprint cards on all his fingers," he told the technician. "We have to identify him so I can notify next of kin."

The young woman nodded. Detective Jones went back to figuring out how the kid got where he was and forced himself not to focus on having women on the crime scene. *Times were a-changing' sure enough,* he thought, putting it out of his mind.

Which was pretty gosh darn easy, since he couldn't quite figure out just *how* the young man had flown fifty feet through safety glass, against the cliff face, and died on the cobblestones underfoot.

I had better start asking some questions, he thought finally to himself, steeling his nerves against his natural hatred of people and enclosed spaces before going up and into the room above.

Detective Jones walked around to the front of the hotel, and approached a young man in a purple and gold suit. The doorman. Jones had not seen the young man before, but that was the way of things. Always changing.

"I'm Detective Mel Jones with the SFPD," he said to the doorman, pulling out his badge. "Can I ask you a couple of questions about the man who died in the back?"

The doorman nodded, and Detective Jones pulled his pad and pen from an inside pocket.

"Let's start with who you are, and then you can tell me what you know about the guy from the ninth floor," the policeman said.

The doorman nodded again. He seemed nervous.

"I'm Shelly Petrovich, umm, sir. And I just started here as the doorman, two weeks ago."

Two Days Earlier

Norman John Sawyer swore to himself, under his breath. He absolutely *hated* the moniker "The Tenderloin Ripper." He preferred the name he chose for himself, but which the papers refused to use:

The Bay Area Trashman.

Because that's what he was doing. He was helping society, and the City by the Bay, by cleaning up the riffraff, the human scum, in the Tenderloin—that warren of rat-infested streets near Nobb Hill—and its underground grittiness.

Gambling halls, gay bars, and B-Girls all over the place. It practically made him sick.

He almost tore the paper he was reading, folding it back up, in the restaurant of the only place his parents would stay on the West Coast, the Hotel Ethel.

Breakfast was a bagel and coffee, and he set into the food, the paper almost forgotten, thrown into the chair to his right. The bagel was toasted and perfect, as were most things at the Ethel.

The coffee was rich and nutty, the silverware shone with brightness, and the air was that of the most of expensive surroundings.

It was clean, safe, and for his purposes, the perfect cover.

And the perfection of his surroundings, the wall murals, the Art Deco chandeliers, the waiters in bowties, all made him think over what would happen later that evening, and the jarring difference in the two environments.

Here, he was surrounded by opulence and wealth. Tonight, he would be skittering with the rats, seeking blood.

"The *'Tenderloin Ripper,'* for god's sakes…" he mumbled around the bagel and cream cheese in his mouth.

"Why, Johnny Sawyer, you positively look like the wind blew you right to me," he heard from behind him.

Another sigh. Another let-down.

Marcy Blevins, the heiress to the Blevins Dairy farms.

The woman swept right around him and plopped her chubby derriere onto that morning's paper. She smiled a bright, piggish smile at him and he had to control himself from plunging the cheese knife into her stupid brown eye.

"Why, Marcy Blevins, as I live and breathe…" he replied in greeting, pasting a fake smile on his handsome face.

"What are you doing in San Francisco? Last I heard, you were being shipped off to Yale or Harvard or one of those other brownstone bores of a college back east," she asked.

He smiled brighter, remembering the way his parents' throats had opened up as easy as pie.

"No ma'am, taking the summer and fall to travel a bit, see the world before living up to the family legacy," he said in reply. Was it getting hot in there, or was it just him?

"Well, you'll have to come out to the farm and see Mother, she absolutely adores you, you know!"

He nodded his acceptance, rueing the day he had met this fat sow at one of his mother's insistent demands that he attend summer camp in California, making connections and creating "the future," as she would put it.

He took another big bite of his bagel to keep both from answering her and from clenching his hands from around her porcelain neck. Oh, how he hated the upper crust and their incessant chattering and posturing.

John suddenly saw the brightly clad doorman on the other side of the dining room, looking at him, patting his breast pocket.

John nodded his understanding, and moved to get up from the table, and to get the key for the back door of the hotel, which he had bribed the new doorman an obscene amount of money to procure.

He didn't have another thought for the woman he left sitting at the breakfast table alone.

John finished his breakfast without another word and quickly excused himself, to Marcy's chagrin. She had been looking forward to catching him at one of the right-on-schedule breakfasts she had been watching him consume for the last week or so.

He *was* quite handsome, if she said so herself, and she had often said so to her girlfriends. They were practically betrothed in her mind. So, seeing him quickly get up from his seat, so out of character for a man who did everything with precision and practice, made her wonder if her hooks were set in him deep enough yet.

John gave perfunctory dismissives and hurried out of the restaurant.

Marcy didn't like that at all and vowed to catch him sometime later. In the meantime, she felt something under her butt, and reaching, pulled out that morning's paper. It was folded so that the big headlines were pointed right at her. She tsked under her breath as she read them.

Tenderloin Ripper Strikes Again!

Body Count Now at 23!

Low class folks killing each other off, what was it to her?

She quickly refolded the paper to show that week's marriage engagements. *Now, here was something to focus on*, she thought as she read and ordered breakfast from one of the well-dressed waiters skittering about, her mind on her own wedding to Mr. Norman John Sawyer.

It would be in his hometown of New York City, and it would be the gala of the year.

John walked purposefully back to his room on the ninth floor. Long term guest suites. He had checked in under his own name, not worried at all that his 'peculiarities' would tie back to him, here at the Ethel.

The richly appointed hotel left no opulent décor under-done. Gold was present as much as rich purples, deep blues, shiny silvers. The Art Deco standard of the expensive place made part of him happy, and the other part sick to his stomach. He did find himself humming, quickly examining the murals along the hallways to his room.

This was his mother's favorite hotel in the area, and because of that, he took up residence here, instead of a hostel or flop house. That would have suited his humors more, but here was as good a cover for his experiments as any.

He unlocked the cream door with a different golden key emblazoned with the number 966 and, walking into his double room, he threw his breakfast jacket on the divan sofa, walked with resounding footsteps across the marble floor into the adjoining bedroom, and vowed to murder every single person in the entire hotel, one at a time.

He barely saw the shadow that flitted quickly into the bathroom, disrupting his joyful thoughts, out of the corner of his consciousness.

He followed the shadow into the richly appointed lavatory, but saw nothing amiss.

Peculiar, he thought to himself, as he had seen many such shadows out of the corner of his eyes, or dancing on the ceiling late at night after a particularly gristly couple of hours spent in the Tenderloin.

Now he was seeing things, he thought ruefully. Maybe he really was crazed and psychotic, like his therapist told his parents. Freudian psycho-babble indeed.

Anyway, no spectral shadow or bloated heiress would dampen his mood, for he had chosen his next victim with aplomb and, to be honest, genuine excitement.

She was Asian. She was a student. And she was a lesbian.

He would enjoy plunging his Bowie knife into her soft body, over and over again. This very night, he promised himself.

He was rock hard as he took off the rest of his clothing, ran the shower as hot as it would go, and began his scrubbing ritual, already mentally experiencing that night's entertainment over and over again.

He found her quickly that evening.

He knew her name was Amy Chan. She was from across the Bay in San Pablo. He had overheard her telling another young female student on the College Green.

Visiting the campus of San Francisco College, he had followed Amy several times from her classes on the Hill, down into the dark confines of the Tenderloin, specifically at Leavenworth and Ellis Streets.

She worked nightshift at the disgusting Senator Hotel on Ellis.

John had been saving her up for the entire eight weeks he had been in the city. He had spied her the very first night he wandered the streets of the 'Loin. Her long legs and tall, sturdy heels made her stand out amongst the homeless and impoverished union workers like she was lit up with Christmas lights.

She was one of a half-dozen victims he had been studying, but she was definitely his favorite. And this Thursday evening in the middle of summer, he was allowing himself dessert before dinner.

Between the Senator and the building next to it was a greenspace, backed by an extremely dark alleyway topped by several floors of fire escape platforms and stairs. Late at night it was deserted, with only tawdry red light bulbs showing dim brightness down onto the tall trees and overgrown bushes of the greens.

And he knew, halfway through her shift, Amy Chan often walked into the greenery and sat eating a sandwich on a bench at the foot of a stunted redwood tree.

He had a particularly devious plan for Ms. Amy Chan. One that would give him satisfaction for days afterward.

He merely had to make himself go slow.

He was wearing his guise of homeless garb. Layers of stinking clothing he had stolen from vagabonds sleeping throughout the city.

His face was caked with dirt and ash from piles of it lining the back alleys of the Tenderloin. And he sat holding a cardboard sign that read "Anything helps, Jesus Loves You."

Under the layer of clothing closest to his body were strapped leather belts holding various knives and instrumentation, and he had secreted about himself bottles of disinfectant, rubbing alcohol, a pistol, and razor wire between two wooden handles. He had made all of the instruments by hand, and had not purchased any of the other items from any one particular place.

He knew he couldn't be caught, and so, he stood up and limped after Amy when she crossed behind him on Market Street. Just another homeless man amongst thousands across the city.

She was exquisite in her knee-high boots and her tight-fitting clothing, with the stink of pussy wafting off of her like a miasma of wrongness and sin.

The world would not mourn the loss of another lesbian commie bitch who needed to be taught a lesson.

This night, Norman John Sawyer would be her teacher, her guide, and her cleanser.

And, as the full moon shone overhead, purification would be her reward.

The tall, ornate, garishly painted gate was unlocked and slightly opened from the street side, just as John had planned it. He knew that Amy would be inside the green space beyond the gate, having her late night lunch.

He made a wish under his breath that the hinges wouldn't squeak as he opened the left-side gate, and they did not. That boded well, he thought.

John made his way through the underbrush, stepping lightly around obstacles that he could make out through the lights shining dimly against the side of the Senator. The shadows shifted, and once again, he could swear there were shapes of people moving near and around him. As if someone were stalking him as he stalked the young woman in the green spaces.

It was becoming an increasingly frustrating feeling.

He could hear humming coming from somewhere ahead in the dark.

He slowly approached the redwood tree. She was sitting just on the other side. He put both hands against the warm bark, breathing quietly, hoping the sound of his pounding heart wouldn't alert the woman quietly eating her bologna.

He could smell the processed meat, mixed with the perfume she enjoyed wearing. He couldn't place the scent, probably because it was a cheap spray. He only knew the high end smells.

He bowed his head, said a prayer under his breath, and readied himself. If he was quick enough, she wouldn't be able to make a sound.

He pulled his serrated Bowie knife from within the folds of clothing he wore, and quickly darted around the tree, catching Amy Chan completely by surprise.

The blade flashed in the red light, cutting her throat from ear to ear.

As her body fell to the ground, the sandwich stayed clutched in her hand.

He breathed deeply, proud of himself for accomplishing the hardest part first. Now it was time to educate and cleanse her body.

He pulled the still-bleeding, limp body of the young woman through the trail around the greenery and back into the black alley. He couldn't see a thing, and didn't want to. His lessons on Ms. Chan's body would be better in the absolute darkness.

As he pulled her into the shadows and stillness, he took off his pants, the only part of his ensemble that wasn't layered. His manhood stood straight and proud in front of him.

He bent down, cut away her clothing, knowing that he bared her to the world, upon the sun rising hours from now.

He found her taut, flat stomach, traced his fingers down to the split between her legs, and after several stabs with the serrated steel of the Bowie knife in the softest parts of her, he then began to stab her repeatedly with his other weapon, the steel between his own legs.

The squelching sounds of blood and body matter sent him over the top before he could even begin to control himself.

That's okay, he told himself as he climbed off her. He still had several more hours of darkness and further cleansing of her body before he had to make his way back to the opulent Hotel Ethel, only twenty blocks away.

Soon enough, he was on top of her dead body again, losing track of the number of hard stabbings from both steel and flesh.

His agility with both astounded even him.

The service entrance at the back of the Hotel Ethel served his needs perfectly.

The alleyway behind the tall behemoth of a building was tucked almost up against a tall cliff face, which would seem out of place in a sprawling city, but San Francisco had been created by chaos and upheaval, so an earthquake-made cliff face cutting a city street a hundred feet apart made perfect sense.

He snuck into the rear of the building using the key that he had purchased from the doorman several days before, and having discarded all of his blood-stained and stolen rags into the chute leading down to the cellar and its hot boiler, he walked up the back servants' stairs to the ninth floor in just a slightly blood-stained pair of white boxers and a plain white under shirt, without a soul seeing him.

Knowing that the bloody rags would be instantly incinerated in the large boiler, and that the doorman was a good chap, ready to take his cash for anything he would need, John felt all that much more secure in the crusade he had bestowed upon himself.

John had done this same series of practiced movements, except he had paid the previous doorman to prop open the back door, every time he went out cleaning the refuse of the city, and no one had been the wiser for his movements. Not a soul saw him coming and going, practically in his skivvies.

No one, except a single pair of piggish brown eyes, which seemed to lurk around every bend while John Sawyer was in the vicinity.

"I wonder what you've been up to, Johnny Sawyer," Marcy Blevins said to herself, fanning her delicate face against the heat coming from the kitchens here at the back of the hotel.

She had watched his comings and goings almost every early morning since accidently spying him coming in, covered in mud and grit, one morning several weeks in the past.

What are you doing, indeed, she thought, turning, and lining up her chance to meet him at breakfast, once again, as was his usual schedule.

A servant of routine, was one Norman John Sawyer. A servant to *routine.* The line spun around and around in her beady little mind, wondering how she could use the information against the young man, and to her advantage.

As for John, having made his room with no one else the wiser, he stood under the hot geyser of water spraying forth from the shower head above him, cleaning his every nook and cranny as well as he had cleansed the body and soul of the dearly departed Amy Chan.

The memories washed through him like warm butter over hot pancakes, but his body was too exhausted to care.

He had spent longer than he meant to with the body, and he was dead tired. This would be one day that he would disrupt his routine and go to bed instead of down to breakfast. He'd use the excuse of being under the weather if anyone should ask.

His mind was too full of the previous night's entertainments to worry about running into the Blevins girl again, or anyone else for that matter.

He sunk his weary body down into the soft confines of the feather mattress, and with quiet bemusement watched the dancing shadows on the ceiling and walls around him.

With the afterglow of the successful killing that night, and the ease in which he got back to his room and none being the wiser, the shadows, for once, didn't bother him.

Soon enough, he was as sound asleep as a babe lying against its mother's bosom, a demonic smirk pulling up one side of his mouth.

Norman John Sawyer awoke to pounding on both his bedroom door and, it seemed, the windows to his right that looked out over the alleyway floors below and the granite cliff face several yards away.

He was disoriented; darkness swam in at the corners of his eyes and the dusky sky outside the windows confounded him.

The banging seemed to surround him, confusing him even more, and his body hurt, soreness rising from his muscles like he had run miles and miles. He was sweating in a heat he couldn't explain, and the discombobulation wouldn't go away no matter how much he shook his head.

His eyes finally caught movement outside the windows, a swarming maelstrom of shadows coalescing in a gel of seemingly living globs of flesh.

An eyeball pressed into the window, looking back at him, and hands ran up and down the length of the floor-to-ceiling glass. Body parts came and went, the shadows becoming real and then unreal in a blink of an eye.

Between the banging all around him, the colors bursting behind his eyes, the soreness of his body, and the eerie movement outside the window, his brain couldn't keep up with the input.

A whisper beside his ear, however, brought awareness back to his sweating brain. It was a multi-toned voice, a choir of misery and pain whispering into his soul.

"You killed us all, Johnny Sawyer, you killed us all, and now, we are here for you together..." it said. *"YouKilledUsAll... YouKilledUsAll... YouKilledUsAll... Youuuuuu... killlleddddddd... .ussssssss... allllllllllll..."*

The sonorous choir continued chanting all around him, a fog entering his brain with the words.

He grabbed his head, screaming in pain and confusion.

It was his mother and father, standing at the foot of the bed, that brought him finally to his senses. They looked spectral, transparent, in the dusky light careening through the window, motes of dust flying through it, and through them.

"Mom... Dad?" he said in question.

They just stared at him, hatred burning in their eyes.

"Mom, I'm so sorry, Mom," he uttered, the looks on their faces, and the opened maws of their throats making him scared as a small boy.

"Mom… I'm so sorry…" he trailed off.

Her mouth opened wide. No sound came out, but the feeling of disappointment was strong in Johnny Sawyer. His father's reproachful look cut Johnny to the quick.

"I'm so sorr…"

His words were cut off as an arm wrapped around his throat.

It was the woman from the night before. He could feel the fires of rage burning in her eyes. He had no idea what was going on, but they were surrounding him on the bed.

The spirits… the ghosts… the pure, unadulterated hatred and pain like living specters closing in around him…

He was lifted off the bed. He could feel the arms, the fingers, the hands under him, digging into his skin, scratching him, tearing him… he could feel their hatred. He screamed gutturally until his throat was pinched off, fingers digging into the skin around his Adam's apple…

The coalescing spirits outside, all hands and eyes and fire within, blew out the windows in shards of glass and spinning death and pain.

The wind blew into the ninth floor room, drapery flying off of the hooks, pottery smashing, the glass of the mirror over the dresser shattering to the floor. For a split second, stretched out seeming like eternity, everything became eerily quiet and still, calm over an icy pond, the silence of an eye of the storm, the deadness right before a tornado struck… and then all at once, the force blowing inward ripped apart and suddenly changed direction.

Everything rushed toward the blown-out windows… the glass went first, the spirits screaming their pain and hatred… things sliding out the windows like the entire world was tilted to the north…..

And with it, he felt the arms under him flex, the hatred swell, the fires of wrathful vengeance rise up around him, and before he knew it, he was shot out of the window like a cannonball fired at an enemy.

The cliff face came at him at a hundred miles an hour. His body splattered loudly against the sharp rocks.

He was still conscious for several seconds as his body hit the pavement, floors below.

The last thing he ever saw were the faces of all of his victims, smugly and victoriously staring down at him from Room 966 of the Hotel Ethel.

SFPD Detective First Class Mel Jones walked down the opulently decorated hallway of the ninth floor toward Room 966. Several people swarmed around the doorway, trying to peek in and see what all the hullabaloo was about. Uniformed SFPD police officers were keeping the folks back, at least keeping the doorway and the hallway clear.

All except for one man, who walked toward the detective as he, himself, walked toward the dead man's room. This man was tall. Wore a black trench coat, even though it was a warm day outside. And he wore a dark fedora.

Detective Jones wanted to reach for his gun in the shoulder holster under his own coat. The man walking towards him was big, and the shadows seemed to stretch away from him as he moved.

Right about the time the detective was going to walk around the tall man, the stranger reached out a hand and halted the seasoned police officer. He only said one thing and then continued down the long hallway… but the statement stayed with the Detective for a long time afterward.

"It's only just begun, Detective Jones."

If Mel Jones wanted to move after the man, arrest him and dig for the answers this tall man might have, he wouldn't have been able to. He couldn't move at all, his mind almost blank, and time slipped from him like sand through a sieve.

But then he came to himself, the sounds and sights around him returning to his consciousness abruptly.

That was weird, he thought. *Man looked like an exorcist.*

He continued down the hallway, putting the guy out of his mind and focusing on the task ahead.

Detective Jones walked through the cream-colored door and noticed something peculiar.

The numbers on the door, made with three-inch-tall brass numerical figures, were the same as every other door in the hallway. However, the screw holding in the top of the number '9' was missing, causing the number to swing downward, making the room number on the door look like an awkward '666.'

"Shit," he mumbled under his breath.

Already he was beginning to realize that this was going to be one of those cases, like so many others at this particular hotel, that would go unsolved, yet would eat at his brain for the rest of his life.

He walked into the room to be directed to a chubby, pale-faced woman sitting in a comfortable wooden chair, her face in her hands, sobs wracking her body.

He offered her his handkerchief as she looked up at him with red-rimmed eyes. Her tears looked genuine enough, he thought, but her face said something else entirely.

"Ma'am," he offered, "can you tell me what you know about the man who was in this room and died below?"

He had learned a long time ago to just come out with it. Ask the questions, don't beat around the bush, get to the bottom as fast as you could.

It worked really well, most of the time. But this girl seemed quite rehearsed. Like she would hide every secret she would ever know, and pretend to know nothing.

"Well, I didn't know him all that well," she said. "He was a friend from summer camp years ago."

He nodded. The uniformed cop at the door had whispered that much to him.

"Is there anything you can tell me about him, and what he had been doing here at the Ethel, or in San Francisco at all?" Detective Jones asked her.

Her face took on a serious look, her shoulders squared, and her breathing relaxed, all in a few heartbeats. He could see her mind working, figuring out what to say and what not to say.

"I can't tell you much, other than he was a very handsome young man, and lots and lots of weird things happen here at the Hotel Ethel," she said finally.

SFPD Detective First Class Mel Jones just nodded his head, knowing he wouldn't get another thing out of the girl. She put on the appearance of being just another dumb bunny, but he could see the calculating shrewdness in her eyes.

She was right about that one thing though, he thought to himself.

Weird things—evil, horrible things—indeed happened, far too often for his liking, at the Ethel Hotel.

8ᵗʰ Floor – Long-Term Residents
1979

A Mother's Sacrifice
Sirrah Medeiros

Each step landed with a gentle thud, cushioned and faint, almost as if the new thick-pile carpet swallowed the sound whole. A slight brushing as pant legs grazed against each other. Anna thought the movement stealthy—footsteps on clouds—not waking a soul. Subdued, it was the kind of movement used to sneak up on ghosts, drowning in the distant hum of HVAC units and the indistinct murmur of televisions behind closed doors.

Anna took a long drag on her cigarette. She leaned against the wall, peering down the corridor, blowing smoke rings toward the overhead lights as a nearby door clanked shut. Her eyes followed in the opposite direction and lingered for a moment, as if watching someone go around a corner, before she turned toward the sound of muffled footsteps.

"Management is going to kill you if they find you smoking out here."

Meredith from 812 glided toward Anna, wearing plaid bellbottoms and a blouse with the largest collar Anna had ever seen. She swung a vodka bottle as she approached. "Care for a drink?"

"Sure. Maybe it'll make this burnt-orange floral floor look more pleasant."

"I kinda like it," Meredith replied.

Anna flicked ash onto the carpet and rubbed it in with the tip of her mule.

"Anna!"

She smirked at Meredith before turning toward her own apartment, opening the door, and stepping aside for Meredith to pass.

"At least it cuts the noise from people coming and going." Anna said as she glanced down the hallway again. She blew a kiss toward the elevators and stepped through her door. "I'll grab the glasses."

"I can't leave. Don't you understand? I won't leave him." Anna said to Meredith after taking another gulp of her drink. Her voice broke at the end. She groaned and lowered her head as she sank into the recliner.

"What do you mean? Leave who? There's no one here, Anna. The neighbors believe you've lost your mind. Wh… what you're doing to yourself—all these cuts and scrapes. Although today you seem better, you talk to yourself most of the time in the corridor, pulling and punching the air." In Anna's spacious living room, Meredith paced as she spoke, her hands waving about as if she were swatting at flies.

"It's the ghosts. You know they've bothered the work crew as well. They won't leave us alone. I have to protect—"

"Us? Ethel's spirits are nothing new." Meredith said with a dismissive wave. "The ghosts, or whatever, leave us alone just fine. No one knows what happened to the workmen. Don't let the hysteria of a few residents pull you under, too. The workers could have been culpable for those catastrophes— not following safety procedures. We don't know. But you—lately you won't leave this floor. And that damned lullaby! You've been singing it for weeks, even months. Anna, you must stop before the hotel reopens. People will gossip."

Anna didn't respond. Instead, she lifted her eyes a fraction and seemed to follow movement toward her bedroom.

Meredith focused on where Anna was looking. Seeing nothing, she shook her head and turned to her friend. "The long-term residents have drafted a petition to have you removed, by force if necessary. Several have spoken to management already. You must get help. See a therapist. Something. Do something that makes sense, Anna. You can't continue like this."

"I won't. I won't leave. I can't leave Phillip." Anna stretched and glanced down the hall, eyes searching.

"Phillip? Honey, Phillip's been dead for years. What has gotten into you?"

Meredith threw back what remained of her drink and kneeled at Anna's feet. Her eyes searched Anna's tear-stained face for understanding. Meredith hoped to reach her old friend, to stop the madness before a lynch mob came to take her away. "Get a hold of yourself. They want to send you to an asylum."

Several seconds passed in silence.

"When did we drift apart? Why won't you talk to me? Tell me what's happened to you."

Meredith sighed and shook her head as Anna's eyes—riddled with sadness and despair—looked away.

Anna couldn't take the harassment any longer. She wished to be alone. She wanted quiet. Peace. And a glimpse of Phillip, before her eyes gave way to sleep that evening.

She faced Meredith, flushed and full of anger. "You don't believe anything I have to say. Leave me alone. I'll die here before I let anyone take me away from Phillip. You can tell the residents that for me."

Anna glared at Meredith. The two had been close friends, but between navigating around the persistent tension among the hotel residents and Anna's own reluctance to socialize or go out in recent weeks, the two had drifted apart. Anna realized that she played a large part in expanding the fissure in their friendship.

Building renovations had taken longer than residents had expected, and now that the hotel was opening soon to overnight guests again, many felt a new invasion would be upon them. Bothersome vacationers checking in and out each day, with expectations that the hotel cater to them, the visitors, rather than accommodating the residents.

Of course, the history of the hotel's hauntings brought paranormal enthusiasts to peer around corners and sneak through the grounds. Five years of renovations had been a welcome reprieve from the outside world.

Although not without other concerns.

There had always been claims of ghosts roaming the building, lending to Hotel Ethel's old-world elegance and charm, but the rumors had not prepared Anna for what had been haunting her for months.

A shadow in the hall. Anna jerked toward the vision.

The room plunged into sudden darkness and a penetrating cold settled in, their breaths visible in the pale light of a wall sconce. Anna whimpered as she gazed at her old friend.

Meredith grabbed Anna's hands on the armrests and held them firm. "Anna, please talk to me."

"Go!" Anna screeched.

Meredith's grip tightened, determined to help whether Anna wanted her to or not. Black trails dashed through the room. Meredith watched as Anna seemed to pull toward one shadow, following it with her eyes. Something whipped past them, chased by a hiss. Meredith shuddered and turned to speak, but froze at seeing Anna's expression.

Anna's eyes twisted and morphed. Coal-black sockets, deep voids of nothingness, peered back at Meredith as Anna's mouth pressed taut. Deep furrows carved across her forehead. Every feature seemed pulled tight, broadcasting the struggle between whatever contorted her appearance and an immediate, overwhelming terror.

"Wh-wh-what is this?" Meredith asked, pulling away.

Anna's right shoulder cracked as it pressed hard into the chair, and long gashes appeared in her sleeves. Blood poured down her arms as if three jagged blades carved her flesh, creating a crimson river spilling into the seat cushion.

Tears fell from Anna's disturbing, hollowed eyes.

Meredith screeched, scrambling to her feet. Backing away to the wall, she stared at her friend.

Now free of Meredith's grip, Anna fought with something invisible.

"What's in here with us, Anna?"

An explosion of black filled Anna's sight, the room gone from her view. A rank scent assaulted her nostrils, causing her to gasp and choke on the putrid stench.

"Meredith, you must go," Anna urged through clenched teeth. "Get out of here before it's too late."

Meredith cowered and pressed herself into the corner. She couldn't escape as an icy bitterness filled her body. Shivering, yet she could not move. Flickers of death consumed her mind. Screams and pleadings came in waves by blood-soaked and ravaged people reaching up from a dark pit, searching for an exit from evil, a madness Meredith understood meant eternal pain.

Moments after the darkness snatched Anna in its grip, she was suddenly released from its tormenting hold. Anna moaned and collapsed to the floor.

As light filtered into the room, she wept, murmuring to Phillip, whispering for her dead son to come to her side. "It's okay, baby. Come to me."

The darkness lifted and spread out along the ceiling, disappearing into the corners.

"What the fuck?" Meredith shrieked and ran to the door, swinging it open. She hesitated, peering over her shoulder at her estranged friend, watching as blood still oozed through Anna's torn blouse. The icy cold eased as Meredith examined Anna, lying curled in a ball on the floor.

Meredith sucked in a long breath and released it. "I'll get help, Anna. This isn't normal. Whatever's in here is evil."

"Go. I'll be okay now." Anna said in a whisper.

Meredith slammed the door. In the hallway, she shuddered, glaring back at the apartment number and struggling to make sense of what she had encountered. She traced the numbers with her finger—eight, zero, nine. *Nine is definitely an unlucky number.*

Anna needed help, but not in the way the residents thought.

Anna Lawson had called the Hotel Ethel her home for six years. However, the extensive renovations intended to modernize the building had an unsettling effect on Anna over the past few years.

Because of electrical line upgrades, residents suffered extended periods without power, including elevator and lighting outages. Anytime she left the building, she never knew what to expect trekking back to her apartment.

Regularly, she'd climb the eight floors to her apartment, steeped in darkness, with nothing but the gloom and groans of the old building to keep her company.

She'd long ago learned to coexist with the shadows and strange noises accompanying the dark. Mr. Butler, the construction supervisor, offered to accompany Anna, helping to carry groceries or shopping bags to her apartment, toward the end of the renovations. Anna brushed off his suggestions until Mr. Butler refused to take no for an answer.

Renovations were coming to a close soon. As Mr. Butler accompanied Anna one evening toward the stairway, she noticed the workers gathered in a huddle. As they passed by, she was shocked to see what the crew was discussing—and froze mid-stride.

In the far corner of the room, illuminated by the afternoon sun, the words "The Vampire of Hollywood Lives" were carved into the fresh paint. Mr. Butler shook his head, ushering her ahead of him as he closed the door on the lobby and ushered her toward the stairs.

Unusual disasters had claimed the lives of three of his workers in recent months. He would not let anyone traverse the dark stairwells on their own, especially the women. The incidents did not make sense, and he shared with Anna that he believed what haunted the building was angry with the recent upgrades.

The work crew deaths provoked terror in the most nonchalant residents in the building. However, while emotions ran high for most residents, Anna grew numb to the heightened concerns of the others.

She moved two years to the day after the tragedy that robbed her of her son Phillip. He had been her everything, and when he died, she felt her soul collapse, caving into something hollow and unrecognizable.

Divorce soon followed Phillip's death, and she moved to the hotel, where she could look out the window and see the cliff that took her five-year-old son. An accident—they said—but guilt and grief consumed her.

She understood a therapist would say that living near the site of his death was unhealthy, but Anna couldn't let go. The sorrowful beauty of the hotel, its grounds, and the depraved allure of the nearby cliff—it all made sense to her.

Throughout the renovations, the hotel restaurant remained open on weekends to accommodate its long-term residents. On occasion, Anna would entertain dinner guests with her tantalizing voice.

She'd sing a few songs, usually ballads or love songs, as patrons enjoyed their meals.

One stormy evening in late spring, Anna strolled around the almost-empty room, singing as she went.

She inched closer to a rain-drenched family as she ended a ballad. They'd slipped into the dining room, seeking shelter from the storm, and seated themselves in a darkened corner, away from the few residents enjoying dinner across the room.

The man busied himself, wiping the rain from his brow as Anna's gaze moved to each dripping-wet member of the group.

Anna's eyes locked onto a bundle in the lady's arms. Without hesitation, Anna began *his* lullaby.

A dredge of agony clung to each note, tender and moody, as she stepped nearer to the mother cradling her son. The boy, asleep against his mother's chest, tugged at Anna's soul.

So similar to her own child…

She resisted the urge to touch him.

Soon, her voice leveled to a velvet touch as she kneeled next to the woman and sang.

Dream, dream, little one, under the silver light.
Magic dances all around, in the calm of the night.
With stars as allies, and the moon by your side,
Rest your crown, dear Phillip. Let sweet dreams be your guide.

It had been Phillip's favorite. She had sung it to him each night before bed, his small voice at times murmuring along in drowsy harmony. But she'd not sang his lullaby, or any other, since his death. Yet, once started, the words fell from her lips without effort. An eerie peace settled over her tortured heart.

That was the first night she saw him.

She had returned to her apartment, locked the entrance, and turned toward the open bedroom door. There, reflected in the dim glow of a bedside lamp, was Phillip. He stood just beyond the light, his small hands clasped, his face pale and blurred, as if seen through fogged glass. But it was him, her boy, as he had been so long ago.

"Mommy?" he whispered.

Anna fell to her knees, tears choking her throat. But before she could reach him, the reflection rippled and changed. A figure elongated and twisted, its face contorting, its eyes sinking to deep inky pits. The whisper that followed was not her son's voice.

"Magic dances all around, in the calm of the night."

From that night forward, the eighth floor was never quiet.

The phantoms came whenever she sang. Most nights, she glimpsed Phillip—playing in the hallway, peeking from a closet, running circles around the coffee table, or sitting on her bed with his little legs swinging over the edge.

She attempted to touch him, but with each instance, he would disappear. Over time, she learned to stay a distance away—then his visits would last longer.

Her neighbors hated the lullaby. They complained, banging on walls, thumping on their floors, or ceiling, depending if they lived above or below her.

"For God's sake, shut up!" old Mr. Delacroix from 811 would yell.

But Anna didn't care. Every time she sang, she caught another glimpse of her boy. Even if it meant enduring the others—shadowed figures looming in the corners, whispering voices that grew louder each night, or icy talons that gripped her ankles or clawed at her arms as she slept. She'd endure it all for moments with Phillip.

Early on, Anna attempted to flee the darker phantoms and leave her floor or the hotel. But they would follow. There was no escape, and the specters drove home their intentions for Anna to comply one summer afternoon.

Dennis Brown from Apartment 911 was thirty-six years old and having an affair with Rachel, a young newlywed in Apartment 802. He was athletic, healthy, and known for his disarming charm among the ladies who would entertain him.

The long-term residents knew of the affair. It appeared everyone was aware except Rachel's older husband. Although the coroner said Dennis had died of a heart attack, Anna knew better.

The dark ones had taken him.

Anna had run from her apartment, mumbling as she slammed into the elevator door and fumbled to find the button through tear-filled eyes. Panic riddled her frame as she searched for an escape.

Shocked by an invisible grip, she was twisted around to face the hallway. No way to run. Evil held her tight.

Dennis had stepped out of Rachel's apartment and stared at Anna. A flash of shame darted across his eyes before he looked down with a shrug.

Anna shook her head, eyes bulging, her neck strained.

Dennis didn't know she couldn't speak.

The shadows pressed her against the elevator door jamb—to witness.

Darkness took shape around Dennis.

Another phantom hovered outside Rachel's apartment, looming over Phillip, its long, elegant fingers hovering above her boy's shoulders.

Immense ghastly figures with long, talon-like appendages pressed into Dennis's flesh, seeping into his body without a trace.

Dennis clutched his chest.

Anna watched in horror as Dennis thrashed, banging against the wall—the specters devouring him from the inside.

His eyes begged for her assistance.

Yet, Anna would not answer his pleas. She pressed her eyes shut as his gaze met hers. The phantoms then showered her mind with the gruesome interior visage of their operation, wrenching arteries from Dennis's heart, tendons from bone, muscles from ligaments. Blood oozed from organs and cells burst open as if detonated from within.

Anna struggled to catch her breath as the onslaught eased. Terror held her hostage. She could not flee.

As the carnage cleared, and only the wreckage remained, the images no longer overwhelming her, Dennis's insides resembled ground meat. The scene made her shudder.

When Anna opened her eyes, she expected a gruesome sight.

Dennis lay on the floor, motionless, but there were no visible wounds on him.

Shock reduced her to paralysis.

Rachel swung open her apartment door, wrapped in a towel, and screamed.

Anna understood their power. The phantoms would allow her moments with Phillip, but on their terms.

She spent more time in her apartment after that incident.

The morning after Meredith's visit, Anna's doorbell chimed. She opened the door to a stylish woman, dressed in a wide-legged coral jumpsuit with billowing sleeves. Her brunette hair was pulled into a bun, with a thick white streak running along one side from her temple to the neatly pinned collection at the nape.

"Hello, I'm Ms. Boudin, niece to your neighbor and one of the hotel owners." The woman examined Anna from head to toe, taking in her polished appearance, and offered approval with a nod.

"Ms. Lawson, may I come in?"

Anna stepped aside. "Yes, of course. Would you care for coffee?"

She knew Meredith had been right about the residents speaking to management, but Ms. Boudin's visit was sooner than Anna had anticipated.

"Yes, that would be delightful. Thank you."

Ms. Boudin stepped inside and, with a slow, casual pace, walked about the living room, stopping to look at photos on the shelves.

"Do you know why I am here, Ms. Lawson?"

"I believe I do." Anna busied herself with the coffee tray in the kitchen and then returned to the living room.

"You are not what I expected. Based on the residents' complaints, they made you out to be a mess, in need of physical or mental care—and a straitjacket." Ms. Boudin raised an eyebrow as she flashed a quick grin and accepted the coffee and saucer from her hostess. "I'm happy to see they were mistaken."

"It's still early, Ms. Boudin," Anna said with a chuckle. She gestured for her guest to take a seat. "You may change your mind before the day is over. Please, call me Anna."

"Thank you, Anna. I'm Lynda." Lynda extended her hand. Long delicate fingers, almost skeletal, reached out to Anna. "I'm not here to judge. Simply to understand. Our hotel has a long and somewhat unorthodox history. I am open to listening if you'd care to share your story."

Anna shook her hand and sighed. "If you're truly open to listening, I would like nothing more." She took a sip of her coffee. "There's not a living soul who can grasp what I have experienced the past few months."

Lynda sat back in her seat, grasping the note pad and pen she'd placed on the armrest upon her arrival. "Stand assured, there is nothing you say that will shock me."

Anna spent the rest of the morning describing the disturbances inside her apartment that caused noise or a commotion that upset her neighbors, either because of her singing or what she saw and experienced. Recounting Dennis's death left her shaken, and the fear that Meredith might suffer a similar fate was overwhelming.

Lynda sat in silence, taking notes, but she would nod for Anna to continue without interrupting, until Anna stopped and shrugged.

"Is that everything?" Lynda asked after a moment of silence.

Anna hesitated. "Mostly," she said.

"All of this started when you sang the lullaby a few months ago?" Lynda asked.

"Yes. I mean, the phantoms and seeing Phillip started then, but I'd witnessed other things, like most people here, prior to that, but my personal experiences of late have been terrifying and comforting. It is hard to explain."

Anna turned away from Lynda's eyes and picked at her cuticles. "Maybe it's manifested guilt."

"Guilt? Why would you say that?" Lynda sat up taller.

Anna met her gaze. "For letting my son die. For not watching him. Instead, I argued with his father at the top of that cliff, my back turned as he reached over the railing for a toy he'd dropped."

Anna pointed toward the ridge of Telegraph Hill. "Phillip fell from the top. What kind of mother turns her back on her child at the top of *that*? I live here to remind myself every day that I contributed to his tragedy."

"And you think he roams the hotel now?"

"I know he does." Anna stood and walked to the window facing the hill. "I walk these haunted grounds and feel a sense of calm. Even through the horrors of the past few months. I'd do it all, over and over, to stay near him."

Lynda nodded.

"I'm not leaving, Lynda. The residents can petition all they want, but I know what I must do, and I'll die here before I let anyone take me away from him." Anna turned from the window and crossed her arms, defiance in her stance.

"I won't argue with you, Anna. The history of the hotel is rich with mystery and unexplained activity. I'd like to tell you more about it, but first, before I continue, I need you to sign this." Lynda pushed a piece of paper across the coffee table and held out a pen.

Anna stepped closer and looked down, her mouth dropping open. "A non-disclosure agreement? Are you serious?"

"I am," Lynda said calmly, still holding out the pen. "You'll understand once I'm done, but I believe I have a proposal that works for both of us."

"Will you force me out?"

"No, not at all. You'll be able to stay at Hotel Ethel as long as you'd like, in a manner of speaking."

"Where do I sign?" Anna snatched the pen and turned the paper as Lynda pointed to a black line.

"Whichever way you decide, you cannot divulge anything I am about to share. My aunt is a rare exception, but I must speak with her first. Is that clear?"

Anna scribbled her name and handed the pen back to Lynda. "I believe this conversation needs something stronger than coffee. Bourbon?"

Lynda smiled and said, "An excellent idea. You'll probably want the bottle."

Anna learned the remaining truth from her neighbor, Ms. Evelyn Boudin, Lynda's aunt.

The elder Ms. Boudin shared that her sister was one of the original six women who had founded Hotel Ethel. The hotel was legendary, built upon the rubble and fiery ashes from a destructive earthquake. How it remained standing all these years was part of its mysterious allure. Perhaps, Ms. Evelyn shared, it was due to the sacrifices held every twenty-three years. The last of which had been in 1956.

"Why would you consider this course, Anna?" Evelyn asked.

"I am, in a sense, a prisoner to this place," Anna replied with a shrug. "I can't leave my son. The ghosts seem determined to keep me here. I know I have a choice, but I made that long before Lynda spoke to me. I just hadn't realized it yet."

Anna struggled with the idea of sacrifice. Was her guilt and desire to be with Phillip powerful enough to overcome her fear of what came after death? It wasn't death itself that bothered Anna, but the unknown of it all. There was enough evidence in the hotel to confirm that existence—that living—meant more than this life.

But what kind of mother would she be if she abandoned her son again? Abandoning him to these monsters, these phantoms living in the shadows? She had to protect him, no matter what the cost. She owed him that much. No matter the circumstances leading to this moment. She was his mother, and mothers protect their children, however and wherever they can.

1956 was the last sacrifice. Which meant… this was the year, just as Lynda had told her.

Anna straightened her spine. She had never cowered in fear at the thought of death. Not since Phillip had perished. If the hotel needed someone, she would give herself to it. And perhaps, if she did, she could hold her son again. The only love remaining in her life.

The residents wanted her to go. So be it.

Two days after her meeting with Lynda, on the night of October thirteenth, and by the half-moon's light, Anna dressed in a frock—a navy-blue dress Phillip had once loved.

She stood at the mirror as long as she could while peering at Phillip's reflection in the corner of her bedroom. *Will I be by your side tonight, or will this moment be the last time I see you?*

Phillip smiled and waved his hand, holding something with wheels. Anna realized it was the truck, the one he had dropped and leaned over to grab, when he fell from Telegraph Hill. Her heart sank as guilt engulfed her. "I'm so sorry. I let you down."

Tears welled over and toppled down her cheeks.

"It's okay, Mommy. We'll be together soon." Suddenly Phillip was at her side, a step out of reach, his innocent face beaming as he spoke.

She felt the hairs on her arm lift, as if pulled by invisible threads. A chill crept beneath her skin as she reached out to touch the top of his head. A bitter cold wrapped around her—an unseen presence, thick in the air with a hint of the vile stench she'd faced with Meredith.

Her hand rested inches from Phillip as she felt a crawling pressure under her skin. A primal warning flashed in her mind as her skin tightened, alerting her flesh to another presence before her eyes could catch it.

Defiant, her hand moved to rest on Phillip's crown of mahogany-brown hair. In the blink of an eye, she grasped at—nothing.

He was gone.

She stared a yard away from where he had stood, watching as long black fingers, like thin charred branches of a dead tree, snatched Phillip's arms and pulled him into the ether.

Anna stepped out of the elevator with her head held high. As she stood at the corner of the dark underground vaults, the chandelier above creaked, swaying, as if disturbed by an unseen force. An ancient Steinway in the corner, brought here from the ballroom above at some point in the Ethel's history, forgotten and long untouched, emitted a single note.

She walked forward a pace and sang.

"Dream, dream, little one, under the silver light."

The air grew thick, the walls trembling as if the hotel itself drew breath. Shadows slithered from the corners, rising like ink seeping through the cracks of reality. She saw him then—Phillip, standing by the piano, smiling.

"Mommy," he whispered.

Tears streamed down her face. She took a step forward, but something moved beside him. A silhouette. A towering, skeletal thing, its mouth stretched in a fiery grin. One hand clawed with its fingers, reaching for her boy, the other pointed with a crooked finger toward the table in the room's center where a strange stone structure stood.

Anna followed its direction and stood next to the narrow table with deep carvings along the side panels.

Six women gathered from the corners, dressed in long crimson wraps as they circled Anna. Embroidered runes adorned each robed figure. She recognized Lynda, but none of the others.

"Thank you for fulfilling your obligation, Anna. It is unusual that our celebration aligns with someone's personal desires. We appreciate your willingness to be our sacrifice. Please sit."

Lynda gestured to the table and then gazed at the members and locked eyes with each as they nodded in agreement. She turned her attention to Anna and gently swung Anna's legs to one end. "Lie down."

Anna glanced at a rope on the back of a nearby chair. She expected, hoped, that they would use it over the chandelier to ensure a sudden ending, but Lynda shook her head. "You must follow our ritual. It's the only way."

Anna swallowed. "I—I thought this would be quick." Her voice shook as she spoke. Searching for Phillip, a tear spilled into her hairline. Her breathing quickened as she felt straps tighten around her ankles. Her eyes darted to see the women moving to her arms. "Is this necessary?"

"Yes." Lynda said. She stepped back, joining the women in the circle. "You are a willing sacrifice until you are not. We release you from this world, but the other side must claim you as their own. Although from your encounters, I believe they claimed you long ago. But we do not take chances. We will fulfill our oaths tonight, as all members have in the past."

The women pulled half skull masks over their faces and then adorned their necklines with necklaces made of teeth.

Anna gasped.

The women chanted as their hands clasped together, one after the other, voices rising to a rhythmic clamor.

Lynda stepped out of the group. In one hand, she held a blade—obsidian, ritualistically dulled save for the last inch. The first twelve inches covered in runes were for song, not for cutting.

As the chanting reached its peak, the circle broke into murmurs. Not human tongues now—older. Hungrier. The air thickened, soured. Whispers came from the inky shadows that had hovered in the corners. They now stretched above the circle to peer over the altar and give witness.

The blade drifted, then descended slowly, reverent, splitting the sternum with the soft sound of flesh parting from flesh. Anna did not scream. Just breathed—her tempo matching the archaic rhythm of the offering.

Blood oozed from the cavity, over the ancient stone of the table and spread like glaze to protect the surface.

Lynda moved the blade to each arm and repeated the process, allowing the metallic scent to waft through the room and the crimson waves rolling from Anna's flesh to seep into the cracked stones below and feed the spirits' desires. As the flow slowed, the phantoms lowered toward the altar base, wallowing in the overflow. After a moment, they slithered from the table and wrapped around Lynda's feet, cooing in a tongue that made the women shudder.

The ritual was complete.

Anna expected peace. She expected warmth, a soft hand reaching for hers. Instead, she became aware in her apartment that peace was an illusion.

She stood. The walls pulsed around her and something sour clung to the air. She turned—and saw herself. Her body upon the table. Lifeless and destroyed. Yet, a sense of smell clung to whatever remained of her now.

Anna wandered.

The building reeked of endings.

The sharp, acrid sting of smoke clung to every surface, curling in the corners like ghosts reluctant to leave. It was the kind of smell that burned behind your eyes, a choking mix of scorched wood, melted plastic, and something organic—flesh or food, it was impossible to tell. Heat had cooked everything down to its rawest scent.

But beneath the blackened residue was a new, competing rot: the damp stench of water that had come too late. The fire had hollowed the walls, and the hoses had drowned what was not devoured by flames. Mold blossomed fast in the soaked remains, a damp, greenish sourness that slithered up through the floorboards and dripped from sagging ceiling tiles. It mingled with the burned air, creating a scent both wet and dry, ruinous in every way.

Anna realized *they* lived in the wreckage of years ago. They saw the renovated building only as it had been and nothing of the beautiful grandeur its residents enjoyed each day.

Concrete gave off its own mineral tang—dusty, sterile, almost metallic—as if even the bones of the building had cracked open and bled. Tangled wires sparked faintly in puddles, adding the ozone bite of electricity to the toxic bouquet.

Every breath tasted like memory and decay. A place that had died, but hadn't stopped breathing yet.

Anna found herself back in her own apartment with no memory of how she had gotten there.

The door to her room creaked open.

She saw Phillip in the hallway, his small hand outstretched. Relief flooded her. She rushed toward him—but as she stepped into the corridor, the walls twisted, expanding, the light flickering to darkness.

She understood.

The hotel hadn't wanted a simple sacrifice. It wanted another spirit. Another to add to its endless, writhing collection of damned souls.

From the other rooms, whispers rose in harmony. She turned and saw them—her neighbors. Behind each were spectral faces distorted in torment.

Mr. Delacroix from 811, Rachel from 802. Oblivious to the terrors that resided with them each day. Dozens of other specters, trapped, their eyes wide with the knowledge of eternity.

She thought Ms. Boudin had shared the truth, but it was a fraction of reality.

Anna opened her mouth to scream, but Phillip took her hand.

The gesture comforted her. Gave her the peace she'd craved since he fell from the summit of Telegraph Hill. She could endure as long as she was with her boy.

"Dream, dream, little one, under the silver light," she sang as she pulled him close to her side.

Reverberating up from the vaults, the Steinway played a single note. And as the souls joined in her lullaby of longing, the walls listened. Waiting.

For the next sacrifice.

7ᵗʰ Floor – Long-Term Residents
1989

Janie's Got a Gun
Emma J. Gibbon

Jennifer stood behind Faith as she talked to woman at the front desk, and the thought, *Are we going to get away with this?* thrummed in her mind like a drumbeat. She watched Faith put on that charming smile she could turn on like a light switch, on and off, and the woman handing her a key.

Faith turned and winked at her, and Jennifer followed her to the elevator. *We're going to get away with it.*

The elevator smelled bad, and a couple were making out in the corner. *How are we getting away with this?* Faith pressed the Seventh Floor button, making it glow warmly. *We're gonna get away with this.*

The couple got out on the third floor and the elevator dinged as the door closed. Jennifer could feel the panic rising, her breathing labored. *We're gonna get away with this*, she told herself, clenching her fists and digging her fingernails into her palms, an old trick her mother had taught her to get a hold of herself.

Her mother. Where was she now? Jennifer fixed her jaw. *We're getting away with this.*

The elevator dinged for their floor. They walked out into a deserted hallway leading both ways.

Faith took a left. "Check out these carpets," she said.

Jennifer looked down. Dizzying orange and red swirls.

"How long ago do you think they put these in? Wait until you see my grandma's rooms."

"What did you tell them at the desk?"

"Shhh." Faith put her finger to her lips. "It might seem like no one's here, but don't underestimate THE NOSY OLD BITCHES who live on this floor." She grinned. "I've stayed a bunch of times with my grandma and forgot my key. The staff at the desk have known me since I was a kid."

"Did you mention me?"

"God, no." She laughed. "I'm joking. I told them you were my cousin from out of town."

Faith's grandma's rooms were halfway down the hall. Faith turned the key and pushed open the door. "Welcome to your new home, for now."

"Smells like old people."

"My grandma is old people."

"Where is she, again?"

"In the hospital." For the first time that day, Jennifer saw some emotion in Faith's face. Up until that point she had seemed in control to the point of rigidity.

"When is she due out?"

"They don't know," Faith said. "Even if she were to come out, she'd cover for us. She might be old people, but she's fierce as hell. Anyway, check out these furnishings. I don't think she's changed them since the sixties, seventies? She won't let the hotel do anything to her space."

Jennifer followed her in. The musty smell was all pervading, but the rooms were tidy, with only a thin film of dust. She ran her finger across the console in the entryway, leaving a track mark. "Might even be fifties. She's kept it all in good shape, though."

"Yeah, she's lived here for years and years. Seen all the different versions of the Ethel. Refuses to move. Says she'll have to be carried out of here." Faith went quiet.

"I'm sure she'll be fine," Jennifer ventured.

"She won't be eventually," she said. "She's real old. And she's the only one who gives a fuck about me."

"That's not true."

"It is, you don't have to sugarcoat it for me." Faith shook herself like a dog coming in from the rain. "Let's not talk about it. I can't think about it. Hey, do you want to order some food from downstairs? It's on Grandma."

"You can order room service?"

"Sure, what do you want?"

"Won't they find two meals suspicious?"

"Nah, I told them, remember? You're my cousin from out of town."

Jennifer had not even thought of food all day. She'd not eaten at all. After the events of the night before, and their run for it, the idea of it turned her stomach, but she didn't want to show Faith that. She didn't want Faith to think she was weak. They had done the right thing, after all.

"Take a seat." Faith gestured to a stool at the counter, then disappeared into another room. She came back carrying a glass ashtray and reached into the kitchen cupboard, feeling along the top shelf. She retrieved a pack of cigarettes and a lighter.

She lit one as she took the phone off the wall and punched in a short number.

She gestured with the cigarette. "She doesn't know I know where they are. Yes, can you send up the special? Two of them—oh, and fruit cups… and a Coke. Yes. It is good to be back. I'm sure my grandma will be home soon. I miss her too. Thank you." She hung up the phone and took a drag of her cigarette. "How the other half live, eh?"

"Do they all know your grandma?"

"Yeah, she's very popular. Not like me." Faith grinned.

"I like you," said Jennifer, and the awkwardness hung in the air.

They ate in the living room, putting their food on the coffee table as they sat on the floor side by side. "Almost like a sleepover," said Jennifer. Faith grinned at her, her mouth full. She grabbed the remote control and clicked on the TV.

"Time for MTV fortune telling! The mighty oracle will decide our fate!"

"Wait, your grandma has cable?"

"Of course she does. She has everything. Okay, you first. First three videos tell your future."

"Aren't we too old for this?"

Faith laughed. "Never. I'm going to be doing this when I'm eighty. Just watch. Wait, here's the next video."

"I dunno," said Jennifer. She had an uneasy feeling that she couldn't explain.

"Oh, come on. Video one is… '18 and Life.' See, not so bad."

"Are you kidding!? This doesn't bode well at all."

"Come on. It doesn't mean… We're not even seventeen yet."

"Turn the sound down until the next one comes on. I can't deal with this."

Jennifer had a hard time with the game that was *their* game. She couldn't understand why she was so sour about it. Maybe it was the prospect of a future she was having a hard time with. What if they didn't have one after all this?

She tried to push it out of her mind. Of course they had a future. Everyone did. For now, this food was good. She was hungry, after all. Faith was still talking.

"It just means we have to enjoy life while we can."

"That's a stretch."

"Okay, next one."

"Can't we just watch TV, Faith? How about a movie?"

"Oh, come on, Jennifer. Humor me for once. Next one is… 'Head Like a Hole.'"

"Oh, Christ."

"Come on, that's pretty funny. I mean, awful, but funny."

"It is not." Jennifer began to smile. "Okay, it is. We're definitely going to hell."

"Well, duh."

They both laughed then through the rest of the song, the manic, desperate laugh of two people who had seen far more than they should have.

"Okay, here's number three—the deciding factor!"

The backward sounds and blue light of "Janie's Got a Gun" started playing. Suddenly, it wasn't funny anymore. Jennifer felt bile bubble up in her mouth. She gagged and swallowed by reflex. It burned the back of her throat.

"Turn it off. TURN IT OFF, FAITH."

Faith scrambled to pick up the remote and killed the screen. She turned to Jennifer.

"Hey, I'm sorry, Jennifer. I'm sorry. I didn't mean to."

A sob escaped Jennifer's lips. The first since last night. She didn't want the tears to fall. She didn't. Not for him. Not for herself. They came anyway. Sobs wracked her body.

Faith crawled over to her and wrapped her arms around her and squeezed too hard, knocking the plates off the coffee table. Jennifer hiccupped, trying to stop it, but she couldn't. Faith squeezed even harder.

"It's gonna be alright, Jen. We'll be alright. He's gone. You don't have to worry about him anymore."

From above, there was a huge bang. It rattled the light fixture. They sprung apart. Jennifer was shocked out of her tears. "What the fuck was that?" she said to Faith, wide-eyed.

"I dunno. It just sometimes happens."

"It was so loud. What's up there?"

"More residential rooms. We're the first floor of them. It's guest rooms below us."

"Do you know who lives there?"

"No clue." There was a gleam in Faith's eyes. "Did I ever tell you this hotel was haunted?"

That night, in Grandma's bed, big enough for both of them, each wearing one of the old lady's floral nightgowns, Jennifer stared at the ceiling, sleepless. She was exhausted. Maybe the most exhausted she'd ever been, and yet as soon as she closed her eyes… best not to think of it.

You're safer than you've ever been, she said to herself, but her body still seemed to be on high alert.

Over on the other side of the bed, Faith had been snoring lightly. She was a restless sleeper and had tossed and turned numerous times since she'd lain down. She began mumbling:

"Jen, Jennifer…"

Jennifer turned over to face her friend. "What?" But Faith was fast asleep.

"The kid's dead, Jen. Her baby is dead. He's lost, though. We have to find him. Find him. He'll be lost forever, Jen. It's Phillip. His name is Phillip."

Her voice had a panicked quality that Faith never exhibited when awake. Jennifer wondered if she should wake her. Wasn't that bad, though? Or was that sleepwalking?

She didn't have to make the decision, because with a loud gasp, Faith bolted upright in bed, looking around like she was lost. Jennifer touched her arm, and Faith just about jumped out of her skin. She laughed when she saw her.

"Don't do that! I nearly had a heart attack."

"You were talking in your sleep. Who's Phillip?"

Faith laughed again. "No idea. It's weird, I only ever do it when I'm here. Grandma complains about it, but literally no one else in my family believes her. What time is it? Why aren't you asleep?"

It was three a.m. It wasn't unusual for them to be awake at this time, but after the day they'd had? Better if it was just over.

A sound started up overhead. It was a woman's voice, singing what sounded like a lullaby.

"I swear," said Faith, "this place is filled with dementia patients."

The singing stopped.

When sleep finally came, it was filled with nightmares.

He was there. Stood over the bed. She would recognize that silhouette anywhere.

Then she was back home, sitting at her childhood dinner table eating cereal, her legs swinging. Her mother explaining that she had a new dad now, and she would have to deal with it.

Then she was at the bridge, looking down at the water below and thinking about all those people who chose to jump. She dared herself to do it. It would all be over, but she couldn't. She just wasn't brave enough.

Then she was standing in front of the Ethel, Faith's hand in hers, looking up at the massive hotel.

Then Faith wasn't there, and Jennifer was running, frantic, up what must have been the service stairs. She looked down, and inexplicably, she was wearing white undershorts and t-shirt, both blood-spattered and torn.

When she woke, Jennifer was shivering and slick with sweat. It was morning, and the other side of the bed was empty. She could hear Faith rustling around in the small kitchen. Faith popped her head around the door.

"Come on, sleepyhead. I got you breakfast. You like eggs, right?"

Jennifer got up and dressed. She only had one set of clothes. She would have to ask Faith if there was a laundry. She couldn't exactly go home to get more, and they'd left with little money. It hadn't been well-planned, in retrospect. She tried not to think about it.

After breakfast, Faith smoked a cigarette. "Want to do a tour?"

"I guess," said Jennifer, "but haven't you seen it all before?"

"Sure, but you haven't. Maybe we'll see a ghost." Faith made spooky noises.

"Can you stop it with that? You know it freaks me out."

As they walked past the console in the entry, Jennifer noticed that above the line she had made in the dust was the word "Sacrifice." Faith must have done it. Weird thing to do, though.

"Have you ever seen a ghost here?" Jennifer asked as they got into the elevator.

"Oh yeah, loads," said Faith, but didn't say any more. Jennifer wondered where the couple was who were making out the day before. She hoped they were feeling better than she did.

Was it possible to be impressed and disappointed at the same time? That's how Jennifer felt when they walked into the ballroom. It was at once extraordinarily grand and chintzy looking.

It had been beautiful once, she was sure, but now it had seen better days.

The wallpaper was peeling in spots, the gorgeous parquet floor so scratched the floor wax couldn't hide it, and the (fake) gold on the furnishing was missing in spots.

There were tables set out for an event, a wedding, perhaps. Each round table around the edges of the room had a white linen tablecloth with a gaudy floral centerpiece and settings for dinner. The room was empty. It really did look haunted.

Faith pulled out two chairs for them at the nearest table and gestured for Jennifer to sit. Then she lifted her shirt a little and removed something that was tucked in her pants.

"What's that?" said Jennifer. Faith grinned, swept knives and forks aside, unfolded the board and placed it on the table.

"Ouija board!"

Jennifer groaned. "Come on, Faith. Can you leave it alone? You know I freak out about this stuff. Plus, after what happened."

Faith's mouth compressed so her lips were in a thin, straight line. Jennifer knew that it meant she was angry.

"It didn't just happen, Jennifer," she said. "We did it. We. Me and you. I did it for you. I'll have to live with it too, and he was nothing to do with me. What if you were lying, eh?"

Her voice was getting louder. "What if you just wanted attention? What if I killed an innocent man?"

She was shouting now. "Will you just humor me, for fuck's sake? Can we just pretend things are normal and that we didn't murder your piece of shit stepfather last night?"

Jennifer looked around frantically to see if anyone was in earshot. She hoped to God they weren't.

"Shhhh. Shhhh. Okay. Do you want to get caught? Have someone hear your whole fucking confession? Stop yelling. Let's play with the stupid board. Maybe he'll come through and we can tell him to eat shit all over again."

Faith barked a desperate laugh. "Okay, let's do this." She reached over and grabbed a water glass. "See, it's like I planned it."

She put the glass in the middle of the board, and they both put their fingers on it.

At first, it didn't move. "Maybe this hotel isn't as haunted as you think," said Jennifer.

"Wait," said Faith. "I've done this before."

"On your own?"

"Maybe."

Then the glass started moving.

"Tell me you're doing that," said Jennifer.

"Nope."

The glass moved slowly and deliberately. It began to spell out a word.

E-T-H-E-L

"Yeah, we're in the Ethel," said Faith

E-T-H-E-L

"Yeah, we know. Sheesh, whoever this is, they're a dummy."

"Don't insult them!"

The glass started moving faster.

J-E-N

J-E-N

J-E-N

K-I-L-L D-A-D

"Well, duh," said Faith. "You just heard us say that."

D-O-N-T L-E-A-V-E

"We're not staying forever," said Jennifer. "They'll find us."

N-O C-A-N-T L-E-A-V-E

"You mean you can't leave? We don't understand."

S-A-C-R-I-F-I-C-E

S-A-C-R-I-F-I-C-E

The glass got faster.

S-A-C-R-I-F-I-C-E S-A-C-R-I-F-I-C-E S-A-C-R-I-F-I-C-E

Then the glass flew off the table and smashed into the wall.

"Jesus Christ," said Faith.

"Did this happen before?"

"No, just some creeper dude who wanted me to take my clothes off."

Jennifer heard a titter behind her. She turned, and peeking in the doorway, half her body visible, was a middle-aged woman in what appeared to be seventies clothes. She had a bubble perm and was wearing a skintight orange-and-brown sweater. The woman put her finger to her lips in a shushing motion and disappeared behind the door.

"Do they have costume parties here?" said Jennifer.

"Not that I know of. Why?"

"No reason."

Then, from above them and seemingly coming from thin air, an orchestra, playing the song—the lullaby—they had heard the woman sing the night before. They both got up and ran, scrabbling on the polished floor. They left the board behind.

Back in Grandma's room, panting behind the closed door, they assured themselves it was probably the hotel's sound system playing oldies. Nothing supernatural at all that had them spooked. They didn't talk about what the board had said.

When Jennifer walked past the console again, the word had been wiped out.

"Hey, do housekeeping come in?"

"Rarely. Obviously. Why? The dust getting to you?"

"No. Did you write something here?"

Faith looked at her quizzically. "Are you okay? You look like you've seen a ghost." She laughed.

"You're not funny."

For the rest of the day, Faith lounged on the sofa smoking and reading a beaten-up copy of *Flowers in the Attic* that she found on her grandma's bookcase, glass ashtray balanced on her stomach.

Jennifer obsessively watched the local news. Surely, her mother would have found her stepfather by now. She would have to report it. It was very clearly not an accidental gunshot wound that he could have ever done himself, even if he was shot with his own gun, twice.

She shuddered at the very recent memory. She'd panicked and got him in the shoulder. Faith had grabbed the gun from her and finished the job, shooting him in the head. They had the presence of mind to wipe their prints off the gun, but that was the extent of it. They'd just run. Got the night bus, then waited in the station until it was a decent enough time to go to the hotel.

Her mother would have known who did it, no question. She knew what was going on. She'd always known what was going on, and she chose to ignore it to make her own life easier. "Don't rock the boat," her mother had said to her once. "He can't help it."

There was no way her mother wouldn't tell on her to the cops. She would do it just to save herself. Jennifer's only hope was that she would get the blame and not Faith. Faith had saved her. But there was nothing reported at all; maybe one measly murder wasn't enough to make the news in San Francisco.

It was early for Jennifer to go to bed, but her eyes were stinging from the screen and smoke. Faith followed her soon after, and Jennifer was asleep in no time, exhaustion finally taking her.

It was three a.m.—again—when she woke up. The first thing she saw was the red numbers of the alarm clock on the bedside table. Even then, she knew there was someone in the room aside from them both.

She knew it was him. She felt his eyes on her. Hadn't she felt them hundreds of times before? Sure enough, there he was, looming over the end of the bed, the unmistakable shadow of her stepfather. Except this wasn't a dream. She was definitely awake.

She was not as scared as she should have been, she realized. Him alive was infinitely scarier, and he wasn't, because they had killed him. They had killed that son of a bitch rapist, and she wasn't sorry, not one bit. She just didn't want to get caught.

She sat up. "You're fucking dead," she said. "Go away. You don't belong here."

Then that hideous chuckle of his. Her voice got louder. "You're dead, Ritchie. Get the fuck out of here. Go to hell where you belong."

Faith slumbered on, unfathomably.

"You're supposed to call me Dad. What would your mother say?" His voice was worse now, in death, creaky and dry.

"I don't care what she says."

"You say that. What do you care about?" He moved around the bed. Something was wrong with the way he moved. It wasn't human. He moved like viscous liquid, like an oil slick. He oozed around the room toward Faith.

"Don't fucking touch her!" Jennifer screamed and shot up in bed like Faith had the night before.

It took a couple of seconds to get her breath back and to truly believe that she had been dreaming after all. She looked over at Faith who was fast asleep just like in her dream.

As she went to lie back down, something in the corner caught her eye. It was an elderly woman with curly gray hair, walking slowly to the window. She was wearing a nightgown and house slippers that were trod down at the back. There was something about the nightdress that was familiar.

Jennifer realized with horror that she was wearing that nightdress. She looked down to check. The floral pattern was the same. Violets.

When she looked back up, the apparition was standing by the window. The curtain moved slightly, as if there were a breeze, but it was too high up for the windows to open.

Faith's grandma, because that's who it had to be, was suddenly obscured by a large dark mass, opaque like dense smoke. This was far more troubling to Jennifer, but then the mass stepped aside and reconfigured itself into a tall man who dwarfed the old lady.

He was wearing a long black coat and a fedora. The man was gesticulating to Faith's grandmother, imploring her, holding out the palms of his impossibly big hands. Grandma was shaking her head in a ferocious manner, her arms folded across her chest, and her mouth set in a grim line.

Jennifer could not make out what the man was saying. She could only hear faint murmuring. When she leaned forward to hear better, they both disappeared.

She attempted to shake Faith awake, but she was so soundly asleep that it seemed a shame to wake her. Jennifer slept too, eventually, but not until the gray dawn peeked into those same windows.

The next morning, Faith began to outline plans for their next step.

"Obviously, we can't stay here forever. My grandmother wouldn't mind, but she's old and will need to recuperate when she gets back. She'll already have a heart attack when she finds out I smoked all her secret cigarettes. Maybe I could just replace them? My parents will start to wonder where I am. It'll take them an age, but they'll realize eventually. And your mother? I mean, she's got to know by now. Do you think she'll have gone to the cops already?"

"There is no doubt in my mind."

"Jesus. Well. How about Mexico? I know it's a cliché, but all we have to do is drive down the coast."

"Drive?"

"My grandma has a little car in the lot here. Did I not tell you that?"

"No, but wouldn't we be stealing?"

"Technically, yes, but she hasn't driven that car in years. She keeps it up so I can drive her places. Besides, do not underestimate the extent to which my grandmother will cover for me."

"Faith," Jennifer interrupted, and she tried to be as gentle as possible. She told her what she had seen the night before. "Do you think she's still alive? Has the hospital called? Who would they notify?"

Faith's lips made that thin line again, and Jennifer braced for impact.

"How dare you?" she shouted. "After all I have done for you, after all my grandma has done for you even though she doesn't know it. Of all the ungrateful…"

"I didn't ask you to!" Jennifer shouted back.

There was a bang from the ceiling again. Jennifer looked up. "Oh, shut up, whoever, whatever you are."

She looked back at Faith. "I didn't ask you to. Did I tell you what I was going to do after I'd killed that bastard? Did I? I was going to kill myself next, but you turned up. Had to get involved, didn't you? Had to take charge as usual and ruin everything."

There was another massive bang from the ceiling, and a photograph fell off the wall with the aftershock.

Jennifer went over and picked it up, ready to apologize for her outburst, ready to apologize for everything. But when she turned the frame over, there was the woman from the ballroom. The woman at the door in the costume, or so she had thought. She held it up to Faith.

"Is that your grandmother?"

"What do you think?"

"Just answer me. Is that your grandmother?"

Faith nodded.

"I saw her, Faith. I saw her in the ballroom."

"Oh, shut up."

"Faith, I saw her. She was peering around the door. Remember when I asked about costume parties?'

Faith let out an angry sob. "Get out of here. Just get out before I throw you out." She snatched the photograph from Jennifer's hands and started to push her toward the door.

"Okay, I'm going. I'm going." Jennifer slammed the door behind her.

Jennifer didn't know how long she spent downstairs. She was so angry and sad and scared and had nowhere to put it all. She walked over to the ballroom, but there was some kind of event happening. She walked through the lobby, but felt too obvious, too exposed.

She finally went out of a side door to get some fresh air and found her way around the back of the hotel, which she recognized from her dream where she and Faith had held hands.

She paced back and forth in the rain for an unknown amount of time before deciding to go up and apologize. Faith was her friend. Her friend who had committed murder for her. Her friend who had helped her get away. They could go to Mexico; why not? She liked the sunshine.

She made her way back inside and up the elevator.

She could hear shouting before the doors even opened. A swarm of cops screaming to open up. One of them kicked the flimsy door to Faith's grandmother's apartment open.

Jennifer stepped back into the elevator before the doors had even closed again. When she got to the lobby, she ran out of the front doors, her heart pounding.

She ran and ran and ran toward the Golden Gate Bridge, knowing she would never make it.

What Time is Checkout?

Hello, darling.

What, you don't like pet names? But you *are* such a darling. So cute!

Oh, you thought…

Sweetie, how shall I put it? Let's see, how about this?

My door swings both ways.

Got it? Good.

Alright, moving on.

Just a few floors in this section. Regular old people renting regular old rooms for the night or the weekend. Totally innocent people with nothing interesting about them.

I mean, aside from some secrets. But everyone has those, right?

Just, uh—and I'm going to say this as nicely as I can—if you happen to see even the corner of a Ouija board anywhere on the next few floors, RUN.

Also, for the love of all things diabolical, don't go pulling any random letters out of strange places, okay? And definitely don't open them. We've got enough of that mess to deal with already. Thanks so much, Roddy the Rotten Bartender.

Speaking of the bar, would you like some wine? Yes? I'll have a lovely bottle of Merlot ready for you in the ballroom.

Oh, quick question: Boris—or whatever his name is—isn't giving you any trouble, is he? Good, good. I'd hate to have to get his father involved.

Alright, go on. Just three more floors till we see each other again, *darling*.

6th Floor – Guest Rooms
1995

Possessed Much?
Cassandra O'Sullivan Sachar

Lifting her suitcase up at the corner so the wonky wheel wouldn't stick, Jen trailed up the walkway behind her friends.

"Oh my god! Look at this place. It just screams haunted!" Michelle said.

Jen raked her eyes over the old hotel's facade. A grand, stately dame in a rapidly changing world, the edifice stood tall against the city skyline, testament to the glamour of a bygone era.

Even now, decades after opening her doors, Hotel Ethel had maintained her looks. Rows upon rows of windows sparkled in the sunlight against the brick exterior.

"I don't think it looks haunted at all," Jen said.

They'd all read the stories, how the hotel had seen its share of suicides and even the odd murder, but wouldn't that be true of any building with hundreds of thousands of guests over its lifetime?

"Don't be a party pooper," Christy said. "We wanted a haunted hotel for our graduation trip, and that's what we're going to get! We didn't drive all this way for nothing. Besides, if no ghosties crawl out of the walls, we'll just have to bring them ourselves."

With a mischievous smile, she patted her tote bag. "My mom would freak if she knew we were going to a haunted hotel to use a Ouija board, but she can't tell me what to do anymore."

Even if Christy's comment was meant to be lighthearted, it cast a pall over the excitement. The other friends knew what a big deal it was for Christy to get away from her controlling mother, a woman who had inserted herself into every single area of her daughter's life from the moment she drew her first breath. Hell, maybe even since conception.

But that's what this trip was about—breaking away from their previous lives with one last hurrah together before they went their separate ways for college.

How Christy had managed her mother's blessing to go on this trip, let alone go to college all the way in San Francisco, was nothing short of a miracle.

Christy had made up a fake letter with a mandatory freshman orientation coinciding with her mom's big business conference, so the girls had a perfect excuse. As far as Mrs. Grimm knew, Christy was traveling solo and staying in a dorm.

Christy checked in from a payphone every day but was otherwise out from under her mom's thumb.

What was worse, though: too much mothering or not enough? Christy was heading to Stanford when Jen had only gotten into the local community college, her own mother seemingly disinterested in what she did with her life.

As long as Jen paid her share of rent and bills—effective the day after she had turned eighteen in February—her mom didn't care.

But being away from the oppressive two-bedroom apartment they shared in Des Moines still felt like freedom, even if a completely different type from Christy.

"Are we going to stand here and gape like slack-jawed fools or go inside? Come on, ladies!" Michelle marched up to the arched doorway, the wedges of her sandals slapping on the sidewalk.

As they approached, a doorman in a purple and gold uniform swung the door wide open for them. "Welcome to Hotel Ethel," he said. "I'm Shelly, proud to be at your service."

"Thank you," Michelle practically purred, throwing him a salacious wink. "I'm already loving this California scenery!"

Hours later, Michelle and Christy lay on one of the double beds, the open box of pepperoni pizza between them threatening to leak grease onto the fancy maroon comforter.

Jen liked having the other bed all to herself, the same as she'd enjoyed the roomy backseat of Christy's Toyota Corolla. Plenty of leg and elbow room, though it might have been nice just once for Michelle to offer to sit in the back and let Jen ride shotgun.

The three of them had become fast friends back in kindergarten and had stayed like that all these years. But where Christy and Michelle had stood out amongst their classmates for their academic and athletic prowess, Jen stayed more to the shadows.

Maybe she could've joined volleyball with Michelle or the debate team with Christy, but then she couldn't work as much. And Jen's mom cared more about those wages than any scholarship opportunities.

Jen shouldn't have been too surprised when people would forget that Michelle and Christy weren't a twosome—Jen was a part of the group, too. If she weren't, she wouldn't have been invited on the trip.

"I'm gonna gain, like, five pounds after all of that. And I didn't even run today," Michelle said, placing her crust back in the box. She'd already pulled off most of the cheese and sopped up the grease with a napkin, but she still wouldn't finish her single piece.

"You'll be fine," Jen said, taking another bite of her second slice. If the past few days of the road trip had taught her something about her life-long friends, it was that Michelle was weirder about food than she'd known and Christy was more obsessed with her appearance than she'd ever realized.

Sure, Christy had been homecoming queen and all that, but Jen had never really paid attention to all the primping and mirror checks.

"There's no room for a chubby freshman on the volleyball team," Michelle murmured, getting off the bed and heading into the bathroom.

Jen glanced at Christy, who was already closing the pizza box.

"So, do you think we should …?" Christy let the question hang in the air but pointed toward her tote bag.

"We've already driven on the Golden Gate Bridge, ridden on the cable cars, and seen the sea lions on the pier, and we're doing Alcatraz tomorrow. But we came here, to the Hotel Ethel, for a reason. We could've saved a bunch of money if we stayed at a Holiday Inn or something. You want to, right? Isn't that what we all want?"

"I don't know." Jen shrugged, pushing away her own paper plate, the pizza now cold and congealing.

"Maybe we could just hang out, have some drinks, and listen to music instead?"

Christy sighed. "That's what we've been doing since we left home. I think Michelle played *Cooleyhighharmony*, like, five times."

Though all three girls had been thrilled by the CD player in Christy's new car, Michelle liked R & B, whereas Christy was more of a grunge girl, enjoying bands like Pearl Jam and Nirvana.

Meanwhile, Jen didn't care—she liked it all. It was better than the endless loop of Beach Boys she had to listen to at Burger King, at least. Well, she enjoyed the music when she could actually hear it all the way in the backseat.

Michelle walked out of the bathroom, her eyes bleary. "Did someone say drinks? I think we've all earned one." Squatting down in front of the mini-fridge, she pulled out three bottles of Zima, twisting off the caps before passing them around.

The girls clinked their bottles together. "Cheers, ladies! Class of '95 rules!" Michelle said before taking a long swig.

Jen swallowed, smacking her lips at the tartness of the clear malt beverage, but at least it didn't burn like some of the other types of alcohol she'd tried.

Drinking wasn't her thing—she'd grown up watching her mother down a bottle of chardonnay almost every night, and that took away most of the appeal. Her friends had dragged her out to some parties during high school, but she'd only had a few sips of booze, not enjoying the taste.

Still, it felt like a rite of passage, sharing a drink with her friends on a road trip to California while staying at a swanky hotel.

"Remember, we have an early start tomorrow," she said, watching as Michelle drained almost half of her beverage.

"Controlling much? We're on vacation," she said, rifling through her booklet of CDs, Zima in hand. She popped a disc into the boombox and skipped ahead to the track she wanted until the opening chords of Bob Marley's "Buffalo Soldier" filled the room.

"We're about to start college, Jen. No more Capri Suns and Kool-Aid. You need to build up your tolerance so you don't embarrass yourself at parties."

Jen didn't think she'd spend too much time in frat house basements, considering her school didn't even have Greek life, but she didn't say anything.

It was better to live in fiction together, pretending her college experience would be like theirs, that their futures would be similar, and they'd all be bridesmaids in each other's weddings.

She got up and walked over to the balcony. As much as she loved her friends, spending all this time with them without a break felt like a lot.

Taking in the scenic view of Telegraph Hill for which they had paid extra, she exhaled, trying to imagine that she was one of the people lucky and rich enough to live in one of the houses peppering the cliffs.

Was that—was that a little boy playing near the edge? In the fading daylight, it was hard to tell. Jen leaned closer, her nose practically touching the glass of the sliding door, her heart pounding. "Hey!" she called to her friends.

"What?" Michelle answered between greedy sips.

But when Jen turned back, all she saw were rocks and moss. "Nothing," she said. Maybe she needed that drink more than she realized; she was starting to see things.

She plopped down next to her friends and reached for her Zima.

The friends talked for a while, drinking and occasionally singing along to the music, until the Zimas were finished. Jen didn't say anything when Michelle grabbed her third drink—the one that should have gone to her. After all, Michelle had paid for the six-pack, getting her older brother to hook them up with booze for the trip.

"Don't worry! We still have the Smirnoff!" Michelle hopped off the bed, causing her empty bottle to fall on the carpeted floor with a soft thud. "Oops! At least it didn't break!"

Jen clocked Michelle's glassy eyes, a telltale sign that the alcohol was already getting to her. She glanced Christy's way, looking for support, but Christy was staring at the ceiling, seemingly in her own world.

"Get out those shot glasses I bought today," Christy said. "First, liquid courage. Then we try to summon a goddamn ghost."

"Casper, Casper, wherefore art thou, Casper?" Michelle said before dissolving into giggles. She poured the drinks, giving them each a generous measure of the cheap vodka. "I'm gonna spill these if I try to carry them all! Come get them!"

Content to just brush her teeth and go to sleep, Jen nevertheless peeled herself off the bed and joined her friends at the small table. Michelle and Christy had taken the two chairs, so Jen stood, hovering over them, left out again.

"Jen, pick up your drink," Christy commanded. She and Michelle held theirs up, waiting.

They weren't going to peer pressure her into drinking like this was some lame afterschool special.

"Come on, Jen! Let your hair down for once! It doesn't mean you're gonna be a drunk like your mom if you have one little drink!" Michelle whined.

Christy gasped audibly and slapped Michelle's hand, just a little, not enough to spill her drink. "Rude much?"

Hot shame flooded Jen's face. She knew her friends were aware of her mom's problem, but they'd never actually said anything about it before, not once in all these years.

"Ow, Christy! Sorry, Jen. I didn't mean anything bad by it." From her seated position, Michelle looked up, her gaze wavering.

Screw it. Jen drank the shot.

So this is why people drink, Jen thought as the haze of alcohol descended over her in a pleasant fog. She didn't think she was drunk—not like Michelle was, anyway—but she felt looser, less focused. Less burdened by the weight of the world.

"I'm ready, Christy," Jen said. "Let's do the ghost thing."

They'd switched the disc to the Chili Peppers' *Blood Sugar Sex Magik*, and Christy was rocking out to all the most inappropriate parts of "Suck My Kiss." Stopping mid-lyric, she swung her head around. "Yay!" she cheered, shutting off the music and running to her bag.

Jen settled herself on the floor, cross-legged. She didn't really believe in ghosts—too many real-life things to be worried about instead of that silly kid stuff—and wasn't a fan of horror movies like Christy and Michelle, even though she'd sat through a ton of them over the years, yawning as her friends screeched and jumped.

However, there was something to be said about how maybe certain things didn't need to be messed with, if her super-Catholic grandmother was to believed, and the occult was one of them.

But it was just a game, wasn't it? Jen watched Christy unearth the board from the box like she'd once opened up Candy Land for the three of them to play. Despite the otherworldly designs in the corners, the cheap cardboard was only about as menacing as the Molasses Swamp.

A big grin on her face, Christy mirrored Jen's pose, the Ouija board between them. "Come on, Michelle! Before she changes her mind! It has to be all three of us."

Michelle slouched in one of the chairs, her empty cup on the table in front of her, a vacant look on her face. "Yeah, okay," she slurred, rubbing at her eye and smearing her mascara into a black smudge.

Taking her time getting up, Michelle traversed the six or so feet to join her friends, flopping down on the floor with none of the grace she showed on the volleyball court. She opened her mouth wide to yawn before focusing her attention on the rectangle of interest. "Should we, like, turn off the lights or something and light a candle?"

"I don't think we're allowed—" Jen started.

"Already ahead of you," Christy said, springing up from her spot and bringing out a candle and lighter from her bag.

"Is that a Yankee Candle? It's probably a fire hazard, and I don't want us to get in trouble for underage drinking or anything," Jen said, glancing at the ceiling to see if there were sprinklers.

"It's fine. I'll open the door to the balcony just in case there's a smoke detector we can't see." Christy struggled with the door, but then the sounds of San Francisco traffic spilled into their insulated room, the honks of horns and whoosh of cars gliding over pavement punctuating the silence.

Jen enjoyed a moment of calm as the cool breeze slinked into the stuffy room, airing it out. But a gasp escaped her throat a moment later when darkness enveloped them.

"Geez, chillax, Jen. We didn't even try to talk to a ghost yet," Christy said, chuckling as she sat down again, her face illuminated by the candle's thin flame. "Supposedly candles, especially black ones, can protect us from bad spirits. I always light a candle when I use it at home."

"Wait, like with your sister? Wouldn't your mom freak? She's only twelve," Jen said, picturing Mrs. Grimm screaming at the three of them when she caught them watching *Pulp Fiction* on Christy's VCR.

"No way! My mom'd kill me. I use it by myself sometimes, especially when I need something to happen, like when Mr. Harris was gonna give me a B-plus in trig. Remember? It would've messed up my chance to be valedictorian. Kelly Caldwell got that one A-minus sophomore year, so I was ahead of her, but that B-plus would've tanked me. So, I made a wish to get that A."

"Wait, what?" Michelle perked up out of her daze, her full lips contorting into an Elvis-like sneer. "You're using the Ouija board, like, what, Aladdin's lamp or something?"

Christy shrugged.

"It's not like a genie popped out or anything, but I found out that Mr. Harris was banging some lady at the bank. I asked him if we could talk about my grade after school. I told him I knew all about his affair, and then I said he'd better give me that A or I'd tell his wife."

Jen watched Christy's face, trying to see if she showed any signs of having them on. "How did you find that out? And what are you actually saying? That you blackmailed our teacher? What the fuck, Christy?"

"It's all good! That was just my leg up, you know?" Christy smiled, but her mouth turned down when she met Jen's glare. "Hey, Jen, don't judge. You'd have done it, too, if you actually cared about school."

Her mellow feelings dissipating like smoke, Jen let out a sigh and caressed her temples.

"Whatever. It's not like you took my spot as valedictorian. I'm just surprised, is all."

"Christy, who was talking to you on the Ouija board? A ghost, or what?" Michelle shifted in her seat, her demand to know the details keeping her upright despite the alcohol trying to drag her down.

"His name's Paul," Christy said. "We've been communicating for a couple of years now. He helps me, telling me things I want to know, and now it's my turn to help him."

"Help him how, Christy? And who is he, or was he? I don't even believe in this shit, but you're kind of scaring me," Jen said. She wasn't mad—Christy's mention of her lack of academic success might have been a dig, but that didn't make it any less true.

The emotions churning inside her didn't include anger; she mostly felt fear and anxiety, with maybe a little excitement thrown in.

"Paul died in the eighties. When he was only a few years older than us. And he's the reason I wanted to come here, not 'cause of any other stories about this hotel. Paul told me we could help him if we came to stay here, in this hotel, in this very room." Her voice trailed off so that it was barely a whisper.

The pleasant blur of the alcohol dissolved, replaced by the start of a gnawing headache, as Jen processed this piece of information.

"Are you freaking serious right now? We came here because you've been talking with a ghost? What about 'oh, it's our last summer to do this before we all go to college, so let's do a road trip'? And are you sure it's not just all in your head, that it's not you thinking somebody's talking to you, and it's your subconscious or something?"

"Jen, I'm going to Stanford. I think it's pretty clear that there's nothing wrong with my brain. And he knew things I didn't know, like about Mr. Harris's affair. He also told me how he died, and I looked up old newspapers at the library to verify it was true.

"Besides, staying at this gorgeous hotel in California is a lot better than whatever any of us would be doing back home."

Christy smiled at her then, but it was that patronizing one she used—Jen believed—to remind her of how different the two of them were. If they were back home, Christy would probably be shopping for college supplies with her mom and spending days working on her tan at the country club.

Meanwhile, Jen would be sweating her ass off standing over the fryer and trying to keep the drive-thru timer down so the manager wouldn't give her any trouble.

Was this really their friendship? Did they even like each other anymore? Jen cringed at the memory that inundated her consciousness. At Christy's insistence that an extracurricular would bulk up her college applications, she'd joined the science fair team their junior year.

They only met once a week for three hours, so she was able to make it work with her job. She'd always liked science and found the robotics stuff pretty interesting.

They needed to create a machine that dispensed ketchup onto French fries, a completely goofy idea that nevertheless involved quite a bit of studying and poring over manuals.

They'd stayed late at Christy's house the night before the big day, griping at each other and pointing fingers at how each member of the team had let everyone else down.

And when Christy—the very person who persuaded Jen to join the team—started picking her apart for accidentally stepping on the control switch and breaking it, even though that was Andy's fault for leaving it on the damn floor, Jen couldn't control the hot tears that leaked from her eyes, nor could she stop the red flush she knew crept onto her face.

Jen had run inside Christy's house to get her face together. When she came back about ten minutes later, the rest of the group was huddled together. She couldn't catch what Christy was saying, but the sound of her voice was unmistakable, the low singsong quality it took on whenever she gossiped about somebody.

The guilty look on Andy's face when they made eye contact confirmed they'd all been talking about her.

Christy hadn't said a word when Jen mumbled her apologies and announced she needed to head home. Jen didn't show up to the science fair the following morning, and she wasn't named in the yearbook with the rest of the team when they took the first-place prize.

Sure, it was her choice not to go, but shouldn't Jen have deserved some credit after the months they had worked to put it together?

The two friends never talked about the science fair team disaster, acting like it had never happened. But here, now, the old wounds stung, and the resentment bubbled in her blood, hot and rancid.

Michelle broke the tense quiet, her words slurred but intelligible. "So, what does Paul want us to do?"

"He said that I'll talk to him like usual, but that it has to be here, in this hotel room. He said I needed to bring two friends for, like, strength in numbers or something. It was kind of confusing," Christy admitted.

"But I really want to help him. He's my friend, and I care about him. He said he wants to move on to the next realm, and this is the only way for that to happen."

Jen opened her mouth to protest, to ask all the questions she had and explain why this was a terrible idea, but she knew it was useless. They were doing this, whether or not she liked it.

Once again, she was outnumbered. And if she refused to participate, if she said she'd go take a walk as her so-called best friends conjured the dead or whatever the hell they were trying to do, then she'd continue to isolate herself.

"Fine," she said instead. "Let's get this over with before we all fall asleep. All we've been doing is talking about it. Let's meet your ghost friend, Christy."

Christy motioned them to come closer to her, so Jen and Michelle scooted forward until they were touching knee-to-knee.

"Okay. Place your fingertips on the planchette. Lightly, Michelle! Don't lean your weight on it. Since I already know Paul, I'll be the one to talk. I want him to feel comfortable, so don't say anything dumb. Oh, and, like, try to be open-minded."

Christy closed her eyes and rolled her head, her neck cracking with an audible pop.

"Paul, it's me. Christy. I've come here, to room 624 of the Hotel Ethel like you asked. I brought my friends, and we're ready to help you. Are you here?"

In the dim light of the candle, Jen stared down at the cheap plastic device, her fingers tingling in anticipation even though she didn't really want anything to happen.

If there really was a ghost, she didn't know how she'd react.

Nothing, not even the slightest twitch. "Alright, it looks like Paul didn't make the road trip with us. Maybe—"

Jen stopped talking when the planchette yanked to the left-hand corner: YES.

"Did you push it?" Michelle asked Christy.

Jen hadn't noticed the temperature until Michelle said something, but she realized her arms had broken out in goosebumps. "It feels … cold in here. I'll close the balcony door," she said, starting to shift her weight to get up.

"No!" Christy didn't move her fingers off the planchette, but she knocked her knee into Jen's. "You need to stay. Don't break the circle. He said not to."

"Okay, okay, but he's not saying anything." The planchette hadn't moved from YES.

"No, he said it inside me. Inside my head." Christy squeezed her eyes closed and lifted her chin in the air. "No, I will. I said I will."

"What?" Jen said. "Christy, what the fuck are you talking about? You will what?"

"Guys, I don't like this," Michelle said. "We need to stop."

The planchette jerked across the board, not stopping on any letter long enough for Jen to see what it was spelling, if anything.

"I allow you. I give my body to you, Paul. Inhabit me," Christy said, breathing heavily. She pulled her fingers away from the Ouija board, her eyes remaining closed, and sat up straight.

The planchette continued spinning until it jerked violently to the top of the board, sliding off and landing with a thunk on the carpet.

Christy opened her eyes, but then they rolled up in her head as she slumped to the floor. The candle blew out, thrusting the room into almost total darkness.

As if it were a snake or something foul, Jen flung the Ouija board away and reached for her friend, shaking her shoulder. "Are you okay? Christy? Wake up!"

Lying on her side, the whites of her eyes glimmering in the moonlight that trickled through the glass door, Christy opened her mouth and began panting.

"Get some water, Michelle!" Jen commanded, crouching over Christy's prone form and slapping her lightly on the face. "And turn on the light!"

Michelle stumbled to her feet and lunged for the switch on the wall. As light flooded the space, she started walking toward the bathroom.

Jen waited impatiently, wanting that water to splash on Christy's face to try to snap her out of this… whatever this was.

Should I call 911? But what about the booze? Will we get in trouble? she wondered. The problem seemed like a bigger deal than getting a slap on the wrist for underage drinking.

She reached back down to give her friend a comforting squeeze on her shoulder and touched the floor instead. Christy was no longer lying in front of her.

The crash of breaking glass drew her thoughts away from the empty space in front of her. Christy stood by the air conditioning unit, brandishing a Zima bottleneck in one hand.

"Looking for me?"

Michelle stopped in her tracks, eyes wide. "What are you doing, Christy? Careful, you'll step on that glass! Let me hel—"

As Michelle stepped forward, full of good intentions to help her friend clean up one more in the laundry list of messes since they'd become friends all those years ago, from My Little Ponies and Barbies to the more complicated problems of boyfriend drama and various gossip scandals of junior high and high school, Christy moved as well, closing the gap between them.

In a swift flick of her wrist, she plunged the shards of the broken bottle into Michelle's throat.

A red, gaping maw opened in Michelle's porcelain flesh, spilling her life force onto her tank top. Michelle collapsed to the floor, her eyes blinking as the blood continued to flow, her mouth opening and closing like that of a goldfish as the seconds dragged on.

Then, she lay motionless.

Jen cried out in terror, wanting to help Michelle but also knowing she had to get away from Christy—whatever thing Christy had become.

Scrambling to her feet, Jen ran for the door, yanking off the flimsy chain meant to protect them from any harm that could come from outside.

But the danger came from within the room, and the Christy-thing was upon her, stabbing the bottleneck into her back as her hand grasped for the doorknob, for freedom.

And when Jen turned to face her attacker, she was rewarded with a stab of the broken bottle into her eye. It pierced her brain, killing her almost instantly. Her body crumpled to the floor.

The room was silent except for the ever-present thrum of San Francisco traffic infiltrating from outside.

Paul stepped out of the bloody clothes covering the body that was now his and turned on the shower. As the piping hot water cleansed his new skin—that of a young woman, no less, not his preference, but he'd make do—he took in a deep breath, relishing the feeling of once again being human.

He inhaled the cucumber scent of the body wash, wondering if he'd ever smelled something so fresh and exhilarating.

He rifled through Christy's suitcase, finding clean clothes. If anyone had heard Jen's screams, hotel security might arrive at any point, and he needed to be long gone by then. Not that they'd responded to his own cries for help a decade earlier.

He'd thought he'd get lucky when he met that girl at the club and headed back to her hotel room, but she hadn't mentioned anything about her jealous ex. Instead of getting laid in a hotel room, he ended up getting laid out in the morgue.

Over the last decade, he'd struggled with the monotony and limitations of the afterlife. Once he heard rumors that a return to the land of the living was possible, he did everything he could to find a way back.

A psychic in New Orleans told him what he'd need to do, and he spent years trying to convince teenagers he'd contacted via Ouija boards to come through for him. A kid from Pennsylvania made it all the way to the hotel in the early nineties, but he didn't bring any friends, so the exercise was fruitless.

Paul liked Christy, he honestly did. She was so earnest in listening to his troubles and trying to help. But the rules were that she'd need to give herself to him and that he'd have to kill two living souls for the possession to stick.

And it worked.

Christy had done everything he asked, and he'd always be grateful. Maybe Christy would find her own way back to the living some day. She was a smart girl, and Paul had faith in her.

The girls' mutilated bodies had stilled, their corpses discarded as Paul's own had once been. But he felt no remorse, not for this girl whose body he'd stolen, not for her friends whose lives he'd extinguished as easily as a candle's flame. Paul had no time for or interest in compassion. All that mattered was that he'd found his way back to life.

After wiping away the steam, Paul smiled in the mirror at his new face. From the counter, he picked up a clear tube on which the words Kissing Potion were written multiple times in pink.

Paul popped the cap and rolled the little metal ball onto his lips, dispensing sweet, sticky goo. Okay, this would take some getting used to, but that was okay—he had all the time in the world. Christy's dewy youthfulness was all his.

With a final glance back at the carnage he had left behind, after cleaning out all the cash and credit cards from the girls' purses, Paul closed the door of the hotel room behind him.

San Francisco, take two!

5th Floor – Guest Rooms
2013

Devoured By Shadows
William F. Gray

It started a few weeks after she died. That's why I'm here.

Sometimes it was a soft tap from the inside of the drywall. Others, a draft or a whisper or maybe even a touch on the arm. I think I felt that once, but I could have imagined it.

I didn't believe in ghosts before Isabel.

I think she was mostly there at night. Not one to assume, but I think that spirits are mostly nocturnal creatures. That's how we portray them, at least. Stalking the halls when all the lights are out, jangling heavy chains and moaning like a bad seventies porno. It's kind of offensive, if you ask me.

But I've always been quick to defend my wife.

In the middle of the night, I'd feel her climb into bed. The first time she did, I jumped out of bed and scrambled to the other side of the room.

It wasn't just that there was no one inside the room with me, although that certainly was part of it. No, the biggest reason that I was so terrified was because I recognized that experience. It was one that I was familiar with: Isabel climbing onto her side of the mattress. I know it sounds crazy, but I *knew* it was her.

Everyone wishes they'd gotten more time when someone passes. But I don't think they mean like this. I sure as hell didn't.

When it happened the next night, I fought the urge to flee. The following, more of the same. Eventually it didn't even faze me, or if it did, it was in a pleasant way.

You see, I think I started looking forward to these visits. Much like one can become accustomed to the sounds of the city, one can get used to being visited by the spirit of a loved one. It's all really the same, isn't it? Phantom sounds are only described as such because we don't know what they are. How is the tap of your wife's fingernail more horrifying than the noise created by thousands of strangers outside your window?

By the end of that first month, I expected her to come.

So when she didn't, it felt like losing her all over again.

As quickly as it began, it stopped. It was like she disappeared overnight. The comfort of her weight on her side of the mattress became a thing of memory for the second time, and I was left wondering what I'd done to make her leave me.

I know what you're thinking. She was never there in the first place, right? All of the things I've described are just notions of a grieving mind, a coping mechanism to allow me to get through the days. If that were true, why would I stop imagining them? Why would I put myself through this?

I need to reach her again. That's why I'm here. All the googling in the world got me nowhere. The information on the World Wide Web may be readily available, but the legitimacy of it on a subject so debated as ghosts is… varied to say the least. *Conflicting* is a better description.

But one thing seems pretty consistent: Hotel Ethel is the real deal.

Maybe I can reach her again in a place like this.

I'm not a very spiritual person, but even I can feel that there's something different about the hotel the moment I step foot into the building. The floors are polished marble that reflect the ornate chandelier hanging overhead. The heels of my boots clack on them, echoing through the stone archways that surround the lobby. A long counter with matching granite tops and delicately carved wood awaits whoever has the courage to approach.

"Hello," I say as I set my single bag down on the floor by my foot. A young, Middle Eastern woman smiles at me in response. "I have a reservation?"

"Your name, sir?"

Sir seems a little much, considering my jeans and wrinkled dress shirt, but I keep my mouth shut on that one. "Dan Oyler."

"Hmm… let's see here…" Her eyes dance across a computer screen, and I can hear his fingers tapping away just out of sight. I take note of her nametag: Adina.

"Ah, there we go. A one-bed suite for a Mister Dan*iel* Oyler."

I stifle a chuckle at the way she stresses the second syllable of my given name. Out of place doesn't even begin to describe me in *this* place. It's a good thing I'm not here to socialize, or I'd likely be shunned.

Or eaten alive.

The clerk retreats to a cabinet hanging behind her. When she opens it, she reveals a board with dozens of old metal hooks inside. Most are empty, but a few still hold ancient-looking keys.

"Mmm… here it is. Room 524, sir," Adina says as he hands me a key with the room number written in delicate script on a piece of paper hanging from the loop. "Do you require assistance with your bag?"

"No thank you," I say, looking at the key. "You guys are still using keys?"

"In the modern world, everyone is in a rush to update everything." The receptionist sounds utterly uninterested, and I get the sense that she's said these exact words a thousand times. Maybe a million. "Here at the Ethel, we believe there's a certain charm in keeping things the way they've always been."

"Good to know. Well… thanks for taking care of me."

"And thank *you* for choosing the Hotel Ethel."

I make my way to the elevator, which appears to be original to the building. Instead of a door that slides shut, an attendant closes a metal gate that looks like the latticework one might install under a deck. He never so much as gives me a glance, and I try to avoid staring at disfigured face. The flesh there is so pockmarked that it looks craterous.

The motor stutters as it begins to move, and I have to steady myself against the wall.

It takes almost thirty seconds to get to the fifth floor, and the feeling I've been experiencing since stepping foot inside the Ethel is only growing stronger. There's an energy to the air, a presence similar to when Isabel would visit but magnified. Darker, too.

I didn't realize it then, but I think I felt it from the moment I first spoke with Adina. A negative charge in the air that I can't quite shake.

Mr. Craterface only solidifies that feeling. I chastise myself for referring to him in such a callous, ugly way, but he wears no name-tag and has no other distinguishing features.

When the elevator groans to a stop and the attendant opens the gate, I'm so relieved that I nearly leap out.

"Uh… thanks," I manage, retreating down the hallway and casting nervous glances back in the direction of the elevator. The attendant closes the gate and I catch a glimpse of him right before he disappears.

From this far away, he looks almost like a corpse.

My bag feels heavier than it did just moments ago. My muscles strain to keep it from dragging while I walk down a long hall lit with sconces. The key in my other hand digs into my skin painfully, and I realize I'm holding it with a death grip.

When I reach my room, my hand is shaking so bad that it takes a few tries to slide the key into the lock. It turns with an audible click, letting me into a lavish suite. The furniture appears original to the hotel as well, beautiful pieces featuring embroidered floral patterns. Art hangs from the wall with signatures that I'm hopeless to recognize. Isabel was the art fan in our relationship.

The only thing that seems to have been updated is the carpet. Just one look at the simple beige carpeting tells me that it's not a hundred years old. After all the attention to detail and focus with retaining the authenticity of the hotel, the carpet seems so wildly out of place that I can only stand there and stare.

I think back to the old pictures that I saw in my research of this place, remember the old, out-of-fashion design of the carpet in those pictures. I don't have to wonder what would have made them rip it out. There's plenty of data online to tell me it was likely ruined by the blood.

What the fuck are you doing here, Dan?

It's Isabel's voice, clear as day. I haven't been able to call it to mind lately, so to hear it now sends a shiver of excitement down my spine. Whether or not it's because of the Hotel Ethel itself or my own mind tricking me into conjuring it, I don't care. It's here. That's what matters.

I place my bag on the bed and unzip it. Where there normally would be a couple of outfits and some other odds and ends, I've heavily focused on the *odd* category. A set of Isabel's clothes is folded neatly to one side, while the rest of the suitcase is filled with things she loved.

A red Yankee Candle reading *Home Sweet Home* is tucked into one corner, a Ouija board in the center, and then a collection of small things that were once my wife's. A hair clip, her wedding ring, and even her toenail clippers are in a small plastic bag next to a brush that still holds her hair. A single frame, eight by ten, looks up at the ceiling. It depicts the two of us smiling.

This is all I have left of her. A pathetic conglomerate of afterthoughts.

I carefully lay out each piece around the room, saving the outfit for last. This I arrange on the bed. Once I'm done, I stop and inspect my work.

When my eyes focus too long on the empty clothes, I become incredibly conscious of the wrinkles in the fabric. Isabel deserves better than a crumpled wardrobe, so I cross the room to the single wardrobe. What I'm looking for is tucked into the corner, and I pull it out with hands that are shaking so bad the leg of the ironing board gets stuck for a moment.

"Come on," I mutter, shaking it violently until it frees itself. Once it's set out, I retrieve the steam iron from the same wardrobe and look at it. It's old, without any clear branding other than PROPERTY OF HOTEL ETHEL on it.

I head to the bathroom and turn on the faucet in the basin sink. The pipes groan, sounding almost human, before clear water spills out. It only takes a moment to fill the iron, and I retreat to the main suite.

The first thing I notice is that the ironing board is moved. It's a full foot closer to me. Then my eyes wander to the bed, and I can't help but gasp.

When I'd laid out her clothes, I'd been meticulous. Legs straight down, arms crossed over the stomach. Now one leg and one arm hang off the edge of the bed, as if the clothes had been in the process of getting up.

My entire body is vibrating now.

"Isabel?" My voice cracks on the second syllable. As soon as her name fades from my lips, the picture frame showing both of us falls from its place on the dresser.

That's when I begin to cry.

I collapse to the floor, my face streaked with tears, as I try to feel her presence the way I used to. When I can't, I sob even harder.

I'm losing my mind. I'm really…

When the Ouija board box slips off the dresser and lands with a thud, I nearly leap out of my skin. The sound of the planchette clacking inside of it echoes in my ears as I slowly crawl toward it. Then I realize it isn't an echo— *something is moving around inside of the box*.

I carefully slip off the lid, fully expecting to see a mouse running across the carefully laid out numbers and letters. It would be the crescendo of my insanity, the moment when I realize it's truly all been in my head.

Instead, I watch with equal parts horror and excitement as the planchette slides on its own accord until it sits comfortably over the YES.

Yes. Yes it's me, my love.

I can hear her voice again. It fills my heart as much as it does my head. My fingers reach for the planchette with a stillness that defies what I feel. The moment that they touch it, I feel an electricity flow through my muscles. It passes through my arm before radiating outward until I can feel it in the tips of hair, the ends of my toes.

"Isabel, are you okay?"

I feel the planchette move. There's no doubt in my mind that it's guided by something I cannot see. I actually feel my fingers leave its surface for a moment before I dive after it. It moves around the board for a moment before coming to rest back on the yes.

I sigh in relief, but I don't have time to relish in it. The planchette is moving again now, so fast that I can barely keep my hand on it.

Y. R. U. H. E. R. E.

I try to piece together what I'm seeing before it finally clicks.

WHY ARE YOU HERE.

"You… you left me, Izzy. You were there… and then you weren't. I had to make sure you were okay. I… I miss you."

The planchette is moving again, so fast that I'm not entirely sure it's still touching the board between letters.

N. O. T. S. A. F. E.

"You're… not safe? I thought you were okay."

The planchette hesitates. I *feel* it hesitate, or rather the woman on the other end of it. When it moves again, it glides to the word NO before slowly making its way back across the board.

U.

NO, YOU.

"Me? I'm not safe?"

The planchette returns to YES, then lifts into the air and taps angrily over the word. I sit there, slack jawed, as it begins to move again. It leaves my hand hanging in the air over the YES on the board, hastily spelling out something else. My eyes dart after it in an attempt to absorb what my wife is trying to communicate.

N. O. T.

The planchette stops with a shudder.

"Not what, Izzy? Not what?!"

A sudden drop in temperature causes my body to shiver. On the board, the planchette begins to shake in place violently. My eyes feel like they're on the verge of falling out of my head as it finally gains an inch or two.

A.

The toy slides clear across the board in a rush. It comes to a stop at the very edge of the board before ricocheting back toward the middle.

L.

The lights begin to fluctuate in the room, and I can see my breath puffing out in front of me.

O.

"Come on, baby. What are you trying to tell me?"

N.

The lights are strobing now, almost blinding me, but I refuse to look away. My head pounds angrily.

E.

"Alone? You're not…"

The next two letters are revealed quickly, as if the hand on the planchette knows there's no time left.

G. O.

Every bulb dies in the room at once, plunging me into absolute darkness. There's not even a crack of light where the window curtains are. I sit there in the pitch black, my gaze still locked on the one spot in the dark expanse where I know the board is sitting.

NOT ALONE GO.

We're not alone here.

You want me to go.

I don't know that I could even if I wanted to.

When you stepped in front of that car, I hope you didn't feel anything. The first responders seem to think that, but I can't help but imagine you lying in the middle of the street. Gasping for air like a fish out of water. Choking on your own blood. Your ruined limbs refusing to move, so many bones in your body shattered.

Including your skull.

Your parents didn't have to see that. They got to see the real you, or at least an approximation of you. The people at the funeral home really did a good job, I have to say. I think it fooled your mother, but your father could see through the mask the same way that I could. Dress it up how you want, but death is death, and you were gone.

When I think of you, too often I imagine you on the cold metal slab. They needed me to identify you, even though you had your goddamn wallet right on the back of the phone in your pocket.

If I could describe that process in one word, it would be *cruel.*

There was no attempt to hide the destruction you'd suffered. Your skin was a nearly translucent white, devoid of all color except the places where the road ripped it away. When I first laid eyes on you, I had a moment where you looked... normal. Like I superimposed my memory of you onto the vessel you'd left behind.

Then I saw all the blood, the cuts and abrasions, the places where your bones had snapped and stretched your skin into malformed lumps, but most of all, the crater in the back of your head where it connected with the pavement.

I don't remember much after that, but I relive that first moment upon waking in my dimly lit room at the Hotel Ethel. My head hurts like I drank too much, but I know the real cause.

I'd cried myself to sleep after the lights came back on. My head on the pillow that should have been yours, my hand resting over the place where yours should be.

My eyes struggle to adjust to the darkness, the only light in the room filtering in through the crack around the door.

What even woke me up?

My answer presents itself immediately. Underneath my fingers, I feel Isabel's shirt rise and then sink in an impossible breath. I withdraw my hand as if I've been bitten, scrambling for the lamp on the bedside table like a man fleeing a wild animal. My fingers find the switch and turn it, but I've been too careless. It teeters and then falls toward the floor as I turn around to face the bed.

The bulb explodes in a flash of light, but I have a single moment where I see the familiar face of my wife smiling from the other side of the bed.

I stand frozen with the broken lamp at my heels. My breathing is ragged and shallow, and I'm confident that I'm close to a panic attack. I've only ever had one of those before, and it was the night that we buried Isabel.

My phone. My phone.

I reach into my pocket and pull out my iPhone, toggling the flashlight icon on the screen. The bright light illuminates the bed before me. I open my mouth to address Isabel, but the mattress is empty.

There are no clothes on the bed.

Isabel's outfit is gone.

"Izzy?"

There's a clack from the front of the bed. I shine the light there, revealing the Ouija board that I'd left out. The planchette is moving again. I'm about to start toward it when I notice the silhouette of a figure standing in the corner by the door, her back toward me. The soft, curly hair falling over the shoulders of the familiar red sweater makes my heart flutter in my chest.

"Isabel, is that you?"

The figure doesn't move, but her voice fills the space between us. "Dan? Dan, where are you? I can't see you…"

Just turn around, I think, but the words don't leave my mouth. There's something wrong about this whole thing that I can't quite place. It's too insidious for my liking, maybe.

But this is also what I came here for. When I look at the woman standing in the corner, I recognize every part of her. It's picture perfect, exactly as I remember it. This is everything I ever wanted.

I take a tentative step toward her when I feel a sharp pain in the side of my foot that brings me down to my knee. Blood blooms as the planchette flies back to the board and begins moving again, faster than ever.

N.O.T.M.E.

Suddenly the shadows at the corners of the room deepen. I sit riveted as the planchette finds those same five letters again and again. My blood seeps into the carpet, staining the fibers crimson.

Looks like they'll have to replace it again.

In the corner, Not-Isabel turns her head toward me. As the profile of her face appears in the pale of light of my cellphone, I can plainly see that this isn't her. The features are an approximation of her appearance and nothing more.

Those shadows in the depths where the walls meet are moving now. Shapes are congealing out of the darkness, forming more figures. I see what looks like a man, woman, and child in one corner. Behind them, there are more still taking shape. My peripherals catch the hulking shape of a tall man in the corner closest to me.

Not-Isabel's neck continues to crane, and now her head is almost on backward. The skin around her throat is as twisted as her grin, which is all teeth and no humor.

The planchette begins to spell out something else now.

T.O.O.L.A.T.E.

I feel her presence as they descend upon me before I have a chance to scream. Maybe it's just my imagination, but I feel her hand in mine as the shadows take shape, hungry and desperate.

When her hand begins to slip from mine, I realize the mistake I've made.

The veil is thin here, thin enough that she could reach me and I could find her again, but she doesn't belong here. Not only have I damned myself, I've also called her to a place she may never be able to escape.

I hear voices and names. Christy tells someone something, and that someone laughs as if she's told them the funniest joke.

As the shadows swallow me whole, I pray with my last breath that Isabel is able to return from wherever I've pulled her from. That she isn't trapped here like I fear she is.

As for me— I've traded forever for a moment.

I belong to the Hotel Ethel now.

4ᵗʰ Floor – Guest Rooms
1933

A Bath of Merlot
Steve Van Samson

Addie sat on the end of the chaise, clutching her wine glass. She was letting it hover just beneath her nose, trying her damnedest to become lost in the crisp bouquet. After a while, she swallowed a rather unladylike mouthful, realizing it was going to take a lot more than her glass currently held to get her where she wanted to go.

With a sigh, Addie looked to the sloping back of the sofa. She had never actually seen a chaise before and, aside from the elaborate upholstery, was underwhelmed. Not that a piece of furniture, no matter how fine, could have pulled her out of her current malaise. Especially not after that two-hour car ride. She looked down at the leather wallet on the far end of the seat and sneered.

Seth didn't want her here—that much was plain. And while her brother-in-law did on occasion remind her of the wriggling, crawling things that lived under flagstones, she couldn't exactly blame him. At least, not this one time.

The truth was, Addie didn't want to be here either.

Taking a sip for courage, she snatched up the wallet and shoved it between the cushions.

She could hear them arguing through the bathroom door. Her sister, Jeannine, was using that hushed voice. The one she thought didn't go through walls. Doctor Seth Chomsky, on the other hand, attempted no such considerations.

"I don't know why you're acting like this," came the hushed voice. "You know perfectly well what she's going through."

"Of course I do. It's just…" The male voice was clear as day.

"Keep your voice down!"

After a sigh, the second voice returned, in a slightly lower volume. "I'm sorry, darling, it's just… I don't understand why she couldn't have stayed at our apartment for the weekend."

There came a pause. Without thought, Addie began counting the tassels on a nearby valance. They were gold, which stood out starkly against the rich burgundy of curtains that were almost the color of wine.

Speaking of, she took another sip.

"I already told you why." Jeannine's voice was lower too. "You didn't see how I found her Thursday night. What she almost did."

As the voices paused, Addie swallowed what was left in her glass. She didn't want to hear what was coming next.

"I don't think she should be alone right now."

And there it was. The real sting of it. Her beloved sister no longer had the benefit of trusting her.

Even the idea put a sinking, pulling sensation in Addie's stomach. But that was just one more discomfort for the mountain on her chest—the one that was making a labor out of every breath.

Addie's mind drifted back to two nights prior. To how Jeannine had found her, shivering in a bath of cold water… her hand gripping a shard of broken glass.

She could admit how that must have looked. But Jeannine was wrong. She was just reading between lines that weren't there. Despite what Daniel had done. Even if he had shattered their carefully planned future… Addie simply wasn't the type to hurt herself.

She had tried to explain as much, though the tepid water had chilled her more than she'd realized. When her jaw worked, a hurried explanation of the hand mirror, which was still on the floor, had fallen past chattering teeth. It was all an accident, she assured her sister. A misunderstanding.

But there was no convincing Jeannine—her beloved older sister by just eleven months. Polish Irish Twins, they had always joked. The Tyminski sisters had decided long ago that they would share in everything. Hair ribbons, clothing, dreams… and now one didn't trust the other.

This was, in part, the cause of Addie's malaise, though the couple they'd been forced to share an elevator with certainly hadn't helped. Both had been so wrapped up in their passionate embrace, neither seemed to notice when more riders stepped on. In fact, the display had been so egregiously sickening, Adelaide had considered tossing her cookies directly into the faces of the happy couple.

As for her brother-in-law, well… this weekend at the illustrious Hotel Ethel had been planned for some time. It was a celebration that had been delayed until the good doctor had achieved a modicum of success in his practice to justify both the time and cost of three full days away with his wife.

Only, now it was his wife and her little sister. The one who couldn't be trusted and who possibly tried to end her own life in the Chomsky's roll-top bath tub, two nights previous.

The bathroom door swung open and the elder sister stepped into the living area of Room 401. As she approached, Jeannine worked on securing one of her earrings.

"Are you sure you won't come down with us?"

The woman was a vision. Gliding with her perfect red curls bouncing just an inch above her shoulders. In that moment, Addie could think of nothing more heartbreakingly lovely. The sight filled her with a mixture of emotions, and thoughts of their mother.

"Of course I'm sure." Addie pursed her lips into a smile. "I'm already intruding enough just by being here."

Finished with the earring, Jeannine looked wounded. "Don't do that."

"Don't do what?"

"Assume you're a burden. Nothing could be further from the truth. Especially not after everything you've been through this week. I'm just… happy you don't have to be alone. We both are. Isn't that right, Seth?"

Seth had also exited the bathroom, forcing Addie to suppress an eyeroll. Her brother-in-law seemed unswayed from his quest to become Douglas Fairbanks, albeit without the charm. Seth cleared his throat and began fixing the already correct angle of his bowtie.

"Of course. You know we're happy to have you along, Adelaide." Clearly impatient, he checked his watch. "Remember, darling, they're kicking off the festivities with a toast promptly at nine o'clock. Don't want to miss that."

"He's right," Addie agreed. "You don't want to miss that. Go! I'll be fine." Recognizing the guilt on her sister's face, Addie leaned forward on the chaise. "Trust me, a room full of people is the last place I want to be right now. Besides, I already ordered room service." This she said with a wink.

Still unconvinced, Jeannine bit her lower lip in the way both of the sisters sometimes did. "Alright, well… you know we're just one floor down. If you change your mind…"

"Right, I'll just throw on my spare ball gown and arrive fashionably late—the mysterious belle of the autumn ball." Addie raised a mocking eyebrow. "Just go. Stop worrying about me for five minutes and have some fun. Right now, all I want is some quiet and, maybe, to get a little plastered." She picked up the bottle of chardonnay from the floor and poured the last of it into her glass.

"Darling," called Seth, a note of annoyance in his voice. "The toast!"

Jeannine rolled her eyes. Then she plucked the wine glass from her sister's hand and took a sizable gulp.

Unable to stop herself, Addie giggled. In fact, she held the smile until both Jeannine and Seth Chomsky were out of the room.

Only when the door clicked shut did she finally exhale. The breath left her slowly and seemed to go on forever. When she inhaled again, Addie's lungs were filled with the crisp bouquet which drifted from her glass. Unable to savor it, she took another mouthful, even less ladylike than before.

After removing her shoes, she tossed them somewhere and picked up the empty bottle. According to the label, the wine was from Chile. She took another, smaller sip and let the liquid wash over her palate—tasting it with both sides of her tongue—the way Daniel had taught her. He was the wine expert, and he always drank white.

This thought made her feel like crying again… but she was tired of doing that. Tired of thinking of Daniel and of what had happened between them. She took another sip, hoping to push these things away. The wine was alright, but it didn't fit. Somehow the taste was too full of light. And, despite what she wanted her sister to believe, Addie's mood was far too dark for a chardonnay.

It was for this very reason, when she had called for room service, Addie ordered something her Daniel would never have approved of.

First was the audacious cut of meat—a porterhouse. Not well done, but as far in the opposite direction as the chef would go. Bloody was the word that had passed into the handset with a jolt of defiant glee. And with this rarest of meals, another bottle of wine. Nothing specific, she had told the man on the phone… as long as it was red.

The knocking made her jump.

When she opened the door, the attendant gave a shallow bow. He carried a tray supporting a dish with a domed silver cover and a bottle of the deepest, darkest wine Addie had ever seen.

"Oh," she said at last, moving aside so the room service attendant could enter the room. "Right there on that little table is fine. The one beside the chaise."

The attendant entered the room, laid down the tray in the indicated spot, and removed the cover. The fragrant steam filled the room quickly and nearly buckled Addie's knees.

"A twenty-ounce porterhouse, rare, with asparagus and smoked sweet potatoes. Paired with a bottle of Château Latour a Pomerol 1929." The man spoke with pride, as if he had prepared the meal himself. "Shall I open it for you?"

Though flustered, Addie managed a nod. Once the bottle was uncorked and set back on the table, the attendant offered, "The wine should be permitted to breathe for no less than thirty minutes."

Knowing she was not going to be doing that, Addie quietly cleared her throat. "Pomerol? Is that this type of wine?"

The question seemed to confound the attendant.

"Oh, no, Madame… Pomerol is a place. A small region just north of Bordeaux… in France. Merlot is the variety." The man looked like he intended to stop there, but added, "A most beautiful choice, Madame."

"Mademoiselle," Addie corrected with a tight smile that did not touch her eyes.

Feeling that she should at least tip the man, she picked up her handbag. Unfortunately, her coin purse was extracted with such force, something unintended came with it. Something which Addie had wanted desperately to hold all evening, despite knowing the damage it might cause.

The man saw only a small silver disc, no larger than a nickel, fly out of the bag and hit the floor. With horror, Addie watched the object bounce once, then roll across the carpet. Making a perfect beeline for the only wall that sported a nine inch brass floor vent.

There was nothing to be done. It all happened in the span of a breath or two. One second it was there, then it wasn't. And as the small, coin-like object dropped into the unknowable blackness of the vent, so too dropped Addie's heart.

Glumly, she placed two coins in the hungry palm of the room service attendant.

"Give us a ring if you need anything—" The door shut before the man could finish.

Addie turned to look at the far wall—specifically where it met the floor. She strode past the chaise and lowered herself to peer into the ornate vent. Like everything else in the Hotel Ethel, the vent cover was a work of art. Long and sweeping openings formed a floral scene and were just large enough to permit something roughly the size of a nickel.

"Shit."

Addie was unable to see anything but shadows beyond the brass. Even at home, she had known bringing the object was a bad idea, but losing it like this was too much. Without wanting to, she pictured it flying through the air again—feeling the impact of it bouncing off the carpet deep in her stomach. It was the sort of mistake that could have happened a million other ways without ending in tragedy.

Frantically, she ran her fingers along the edges of the vent, testing to see if it were perhaps kept in place by gravity alone.

But when she noticed the tiny screws, Addie swore again. There were four, one in each corner. All made of the same metal as the cover plate. Seeing them made her want to cry again. Either that or scream.

With a defeated sigh, Addie picked herself up and sat beside the lovely meal, which was sized, rather generously, for two. Feeling more miserable than she had all evening, she snatched up the bottle of merlot and poured. Then, for a few minutes, Addie sat on the end of the chaise, not knowing what to do with herself.

She picked up the glass, brought it close, and inhaled. The merlot was everything the chardonnay had failed at being. It was rich and complex. It smelled of the earth. Of roses and spiced plums and perhaps something deeper, older. Blood and sex and the sweet agonies of birth. The bouquet hit Addie's brain like a kind of passion. Forgetting her myriad woes, she lifted the glass, losing herself in the act of emptying it.

This was her first taste of red. A delirious joy she now knew had been denied for so long by the so-called refined palate of her former fiancé. Now she wished she had more—enough to fill herself up and an entire bathtub besides.

The second glass went down slower than the first. Partway through, Addie could feel a delightful weight pressing on her brow. It seemed that the six glasses of wine she had already tucked away were finally starting to assert themselves.

Remembering the food, she picked up the fork and skewered a piece of orange potato. It was good. But surely the porterhouse would be better. Still chewing, she picked up the knife and sliced off a small four-sided bite of meat.

As she bit down, her eyes rolled back into their sockets.

After many mouthfuls more, Addie looked down at what was left. She couldn't come close to finishing, but somehow, this was exciting too. Being wasteful was wrong. Sinful, maybe. But Addie no longer cared. Because being right was all she was ever told to be.

Right then, she wanted to take Daniel's locket and throw it out the window. Maybe the damn thing would crack the ground open when it hit. The thought made her giggle. But… she no longer had Daniel's locket.

The vent.

Addie blinked in the thing's general direction, then sighed. Her hand reached for a drink but moved slowly, clumsily, like that of a marionette. Quite by accident, her fingers brushed against a piece of silverware, causing it to clink against the domed metal lid of the serving tray.

Those fingers curled and the knife was lifted instead of the glass. Uncertain why, she began studying it. Her eyes sliding up the silvery length that still dripped with the enticing juices of her unfinished meal.

The point was sharp.

It gave her an idea.

After swallowing a mouthful of red courage, Addie got on her hands and knees, then crawled across the carpet. It felt as if her brain were floating behind her as she went.

When she reached the brass cover, she had to fight to bring the first of the tiny screws into focus. Again, she looked at the end of the knife, wondering if perhaps she was too plastered to problem solve… but she forced herself to be serious. To focus only on a little brass screw. The first of four.

It was removed more easily than she had guessed. First one, then two. The third was a little stripped, but she muscled through it and went on to the last.

Almost unable to believe what she had just done, Addie drew a hand across her forehead and licked her lips. The ornate brass cover was removed with relative ease and placed to the side.

The revealed darkness was complete. Even sober, she wouldn't have been able to tell how far down the opening went. It could have gone six inches or straight down to the basement for all she could see.

Feeling a flicker of doubt, she looked back, seeing the wine glass on the table. Another swallow of courage might help... but that would mean moving again, and the glass looked very far away.

Addie shook her head, then took a deep breath and held it. Her hand moved fast. Plunging into the uncovered vent—disappearing almost to the elbow. Furry, scurrying thoughts attacked her mind, causing her stomach and jaw muscles to clench.

Moving frantically, she discovered that there was a flat surface down there. A place that had collected more secrets than the one she had lost. She felt something flat and folded. A greeting card, maybe. And on top of that... something else.

Her eyes lit up.

Addie pulled away from the vent so rapidly she fell on her duff. Remembering to breathe, she opened her hand and let the objects fall flat on the carpet. Then, wincing at the stale smell, she clapped the prodigious dust off her hand.

"Oh, God." She began to cough.

Fearing she might become sick, Addie ran to the bathroom. Fortunately, after a few minutes, her breathing had returned to normal. After washing her hands, she emerged back into the main room and strode barefoot across the carpet.

She emptied her glass in two quick swallows and the merlot did its good work—drowning her malaise, or at least, dulling it the slightest bit more.

It took almost a minute before she opened her eyes again. When she did, Addie looked at the carpet. There, right where she had dropped it, was her recovered property.

Daniel's locket was round, flat, and about the size of a nickel. Padding over, she picked it up and frowned. The thing held no chain, only a poison photo that had been calling to her all evening. Now though, whatever sway the object contained was easily ignored. For there was something else on the carpet which was far more interesting.

The second object was an old envelope. It was smaller than standard—sealed with wax and warm to the touch. Surely this last part was due to its time within the vent, she reasoned.

After carrying both objects back to the chaise, Addie refilled her glass almost to the top. Then, with no particular reason not to, she dropped in the locket—watching as it slowly sank, reaching the glass's bottom with a high-pitched *tink*.

She turned the envelope over in her hand. It looked as if it belonged to another age. The paper was thick and rough to the touch. Though covered in dust, the work of one thumb revealed its color to be a rich oxblood. Once cleaned, she could see the surface was not the uniform perfection one might procure from a specialty shop. It was mottled, as if it had been dyed by hand.

Turning it again, Addie could see something was written on one side. After blowing more dust away, she could see the letters were definitely foreign. Perhaps Chinese, or Hebrew, maybe.

She turned the envelope back to the side with the seal. In the ink-black wax was the depiction of a hand with two thumbs and an eye in its palm. As she gave up trying to remember why she knew the text and the symbol, something else came to mind.

The paper's residual warmth seemed to be increasing. Entering her fingertips and pulsing there. Realizing the impossibility of this fact, part of her wanted to drop the old envelope, or just throw it away. But this part was small and rapidly shrinking. The plain fact of it was, something about the curiosity was a comfort to her. Almost as if the paper begged to be touched, held, opened. Not by just anyone, but by her.

And why not?

If it weren't for her actions and for Daniel's stupid locket, the envelope might have gone undiscovered for the next hundred years. Besides, whomever the contents had been meant for, they certainly weren't here. Inside was almost certainly a letter—no, a love letter. Lost and undelivered.

This handmade object had been crafted, folded, stained, and sealed by someone with the utmost of care. Even the envelope's color spoke of passion. Those deep, reddish hues. Almost as if, in preparation, the paper had been allowed to soak in wine. Perhaps a bath of merlot.

Picturing this very act, Addie reached again for her glass and took some of the rich liquid into her mouth, allowing it to drain slowly down her throat.

Yes. Of course it was a love letter.

As she turned the envelope once again, a feverish excitement thrummed in her breast. Suddenly she wanted nothing more than to be lost in what she was now convinced was unread poetry. The unfiltered contents of someone's heart. A man, she decided. Someone who wasn't called Daniel or Seth. A man whose devotion knew no bounds. Who would never dream of breaking off a two-year engagement just weeks before his wedding.

She looked at the bottom of her glass and frowned. The locket seemed too small, too insignificant to have power over her. And so, right there, she decided that it no longer did.

For what he had done, Addie could find only the purest distilled loathing for her dearest Daniel. In fact, she rather wished he was dead. Not as a result of some random accident either, but after many torturous hours, wallowing and weeping over what he had done to her.

She could picture him now, lying naked in a bathtub with the undersides of both forearms gaping darkly from wrist to elbow, like sideways mouths.

Addie looked at the knife in her hand. At how sharp the edge was.

Without thought, the knife that had been brought to her on a silver platter flew, slipped inside, and opened what had been sealed for so long.

Her eyes widened when she saw what she had done. The envelope gaped—raggedly sliced along its top edge. Though, to her own shock and confoundment, she saw that it was quite empty. Inside, there was no poetry, no declaration of love… only one thing.

Heat.

The wave that was released was sudden and intense and it slammed Addie full in the face. With burning lungs, she shot backward, struck by some invisible force.

As she flew, time distorted—seeming to stretch and elongate. In that distended moment, she became aware of an intense wrongness. The presence of something trying to force its way inside. But before she could consider this, the back of her head struck a hard edge and all went black.

After that, Addie was aware of nothing at all.

The thing inside gasped. Breathing truly for the first time in decades. With a long sigh, it stretched—adjusting to its new self like fingers in a too-tight glove.

When the woman's form rose from the ground, blood was released from where it had pooled beneath her open skull. The vertigo which would have been Addie's was relished by the thing inside. For even discomfort was better than the absolute void of sensation it had known for so long. Imprisoned in that box—the fucking rabbi's prison of paper and wax.

But all of that was over now.

This was a new beginning. The most recent of many.

While the thing had lived many lives, most were hard to recall. Like the fragments of dreams, they existed only as flashes. Occasional insinuations. But right now, there was this. These hands, these eyes. The thing inside had been a woman before… it remembered that much.

As its head turned, joints in the neck cracked, producing small, pleasant pops. As it stretched, a fair bit more blood dribbled out the back of the skull—its skull. This wasn't important though. Blood wasn't what it needed, only the flesh. That's where the memories were.

Hiding there amidst the soft grey folds, a life was laid out like a well-stocked buffet. Full of joys, yes, but also the woman's fears, her sorrows, and her guilt.

Yes, that most of all. To the thing inside, there could be no finer vintage than the wine of regret. And inside the shell that was once Adelaide Tyminski, it drank. Gorging itself on unspeakable hypocrisies. Acts even her beloved sister did not know. Could never know.

Suddenly, the thing reached out a slender hand, steadying itself on the arm of the chaise. There came a rosy flush, both to cheeks and chest, as well as an expression that bordered on the postcoital.

When stolen eyes opened, the thing inside tried to bring the blurs of shadow and light into focus. After some effort, it could see that the room was quite opulent, reflecting a level of excess and sophistication it had no appreciation for.

Sweeping its gaze around, the thing focused on the small end table. Specifically on the bottle and the mostly full glass beside.

With deft control, it lifted the receptacle in a graceful sweep. Then it drank, this time with lips that could experience the cold of the glass and the alluring tang of the liquid. When the glass was empty, the thing wanted to do more with those still warm lips. Much, much more. But first, there appeared to be something on its tongue.

Fingers reached past the lips to retrieve what was there. Something small, only about the size of a nickel.

The thing inside looked at the locket with curiosity. Then it remembered. Donning a wry smirk, it triggered a hidden clasp, opening the object like a tiny clam shell. Held within was a photograph. The woman whose face it wore and a man. The memory freed a trapped pocket of emotion that was so powerful, the thing had to sit down. Ecstasy arrived as it was hit by wave after wave of wonderful, rapturous regret.

"Why Addie... you little devil," said the thing inside, immediately enamored by the music of its own voice.

Suddenly, there was a sound at the door. A hurried, discontented sound.

Something was inserted, turned, and then, the door opened to reveal a man. The woman had known Seth Chomsky, and so too did the thing inside. He looked flustered. With long purposeful strides, he crossed the room. Ignoring Addie at first, he began patting down the far end of the chaise. Finding nothing, he met her eyes.

"Where is it?"

"Where is what?" replied the thing with Addie's voice.

"You know very well what." Seth was clearly agitated. "I just waited twenty minutes in line at the bar only to discover I had forgotten my damned wallet... and now I'm missing the toast!" He sighed. "The bartender had already poured our drinks and everything. I've never been so embarrassed in all my—"

Addie was moving—gliding across the carpet leaving a trail of red drops behind. Seth didn't see these, however. His eyes were locked on hers. Eyes which held plenty of nervousness, some fear, and a healthy portion of the thing's favorite spice.

The woman fell into the arms of the man. Her lips meeting his—parting, feasting. When the kiss ended, the man was out of breath. Then, he forced her away.

"No—this is crazy!! We can't. Not here!!" He turned to check the door. "What if Jeannine—?"

"Jeannine!" hissed the thing inside. "Ah… my sister. My sweet…" It searched the memories as if trying to locate a specific passage. "Polish Irish twin? Doesn't exactly roll off the tongue, does it?" The smile was too large for the woman's face. "Let her see us, then. After all, a gal's laundry is meant to be aired."

Seth recoiled. "What?! No… you can't mean that."

"And why not? You'll recall we've already been caught once. If your Jeannine runs as fast as my Daniel did… you and I will finally be—well… why put a label on it?"

The horror on Seth's face grew. "Adelaide… why are you talking like this?" He looked at the bottles and the empty glass beside. "How much wine did you drink? Jesus, you're three sheets to the wind!"

The thing inside threw the woman's head back and laughed. The force caused more drops of red to fleck the carpet and this time, Seth saw.

"My God… and you're hurt!"

In fact, Seth remained so entranced by the not-inconsiderable amount of blood on the carpet, he didn't see Addie's hand. How it reached for and gripped the handle of the wrought-iron fireplace poker.

"Not hurt. Not drunk. Just free."

The swing was hard and swift, and it struck true.

Doctor Seth Chomsky didn't even see it coming.

Some time later, Seth opened his eyes. His brain felt heavy, and when he tried to speak, he found parting his lips took a monumental effort. He was in a sitting position, but could not for the life of him figure out where he was. All he knew for sure was that he was very, very cold.

Suddenly, there came a crisp sound like the striking of a match, and with it a bright flash of heat and light. Seth looked up with eyes only, for turning his head proved too difficult. He could see someone there—a woman he could almost place. In her hand, something was burning. Something that might have been an envelope.

"Adelayy…" Seth trailed off, his words separated by a deep, undeniable shivering, "Wha… did… you?"

The woman turned toward the voice. She seemed so tall, so high up. Or perhaps it was that he was so low.

"With us again, lover?" The grin she was wearing was wider than ever. "Didn't mean to wake you. Just taking care of some old business."

The mass of flames was tossed in Seth's direction. His eyes, wide with fear or perhaps only curiosity, followed it down. When it hit the surface of the liquid at his chest level, the flame winked out.

He was sitting in a bathtub, he realized. His back pressed against one end, with both arms up on the sides.

Though he strained to move, Seth's body refused. Panic surged as he fought to wiggle even a single finger, but this too was a wasted effort. His bare chest heaved as he looked down at the remains of what had been tossed. The old paper had been doused, though a wisp of smoke was creating dainty loops in the air.

Nothing made sense.

As Seth scrambled for some semblance of mental purchase, he could feel himself slipping. The coldness around him was all encompassing, even if his shivering had stopped. He tried to speak again. To ask why the bath water was such an odd color… or why the undersides of both his forearms had been opened from wrist to elbow.

Instead, he just lay there. Watching as the woman—his sister-in-law, his secret lover, approached. Slowly lowering herself to his level.

Demurely, she reached out and dipped a finger in the bloody water. Tracing playful circles there before tasting it.

"To be honest, this wasn't even my idea," she said. "This girl, little… Adelaide? Her mind is quite full of surprisingly unspeakable things. Urges and ideas you wouldn't believe. Case in point…"

Before Seth's eyes, a small locket appeared.

"She was obsessing about this all night. This trinket… a gift from her beloved."

The locket was forced open on its tiny hinge, revealing a photo. The woman was Addie herself, but covering her Daniel's face was another that did not belong. The edges of Seth Chomsky's photo were hard to notice at first—so careful had been the cutting and gluing. Still, there was something about the angle of the doctored photo that made the alteration undeniable.

"Pretty bold, wouldn't you say?" The thing wearing Addie grinned. "She did this months ago. When your little affair had yet to be realized… carnally speaking."

Right then, as his slipping mind tried to process the barrage of information, Seth understood only one thing for certain. Somehow, the woman who was holding the locket was not his sister-in-law.

With a shrug, Adelaide—for Seth did not know what else to call her— raised an unseen bottle and drank. When finished, she went on in a voice that became more distant with each passing moment.

"Do you recognize the original photo, Seth? It was Adelaide and Daniel at their engagement party. Do you remember the French restaurant? The menu? The blessed couple shared bland roasted chicken and vegetables that night—his choice, as always. Even then—even by his side on their special night… she yearned for you, Seth. Not because you were more successful or charming or beautiful than her sweet Daniel… but because you were something that she couldn't have. Something that belonged to one sister alone. And as was decided at the ages of six and seven respectively… the Tyminski girls were supposed to share everything. Hair ribbons, shoes, fears, dreams… and of course their playthings."

Adelaide smiled again. "Don't you wonder how Daniel will react when your sweet Jeannine arrives at his door? Jilted by the same affair that caused him to call off his own engagement? Can't you picture them? Or should I say, us? "

The thing inside stopped talking.

"Seth? Are you listening, Seth?"

Addie's face turned into a scowl. Admittedly though, as the rest of the Château Latour a Pomerol was poured over his head, Seth Chomsky was too dead to notice.

Still more satisfied than not, the thing stood with long, smooth legs, tossing the empty bottle into the bath. Ignoring the splash, it strode out to the living area, finding the wrought-iron poker, right where it had been left. This it picked up, admiring the bit of brain on the far end.

With a contented sigh, the thing lowered itself—sitting first, relaxing second—upon the elaborate upholstery of the chaise. And there it waited.

The other sister would return soon and discover the cause of her husband's delay. When she did, the thing inside would have to be more gentle. Though Adelaide had proved a veritable font of inspiration… her corpse was already starting to smell.

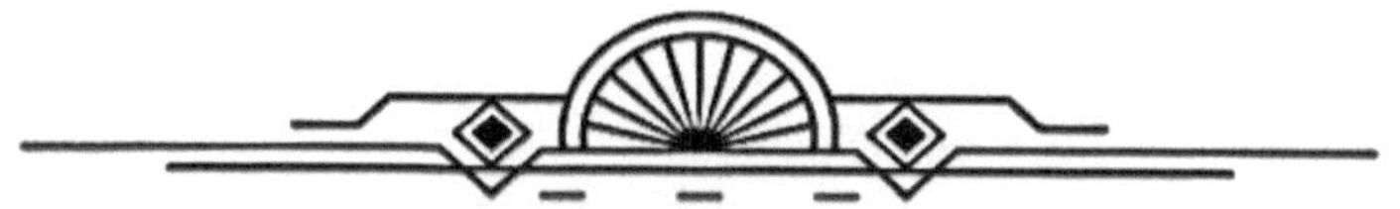

Service with a Smile

Oh, goody, there you are!

Paul didn't try to hold you up, did he?

No? Excellent.

Such a menace, that one.

Anyway, look! You've made it!

Here's your wine.

No, none for me, thanks.

No, I didn't think to get a glass. Just drink from the bottle. Yes, the whole thing is for you. Drink up now.

So, let me tell you about the last few floors, because they are my *favorites*.

As soon as you finish your wine—drink up, darling—I'll show you the ballroom. It's just there, across the hall. Hear the music? It's a fantastically grand space, if I do say so myself. Always some kind of party going on there. Just, um, make sure you don't overstay your welcome, alright?

Are you hungry? One floor down is the Golden Bell; it's the Ethel's fabulous restaurant. You can get any kind of food you like there, day or night. Lobster. Steak. Heck, a peanut butter sandwich, if that's what you want. Everything a body could need. Or a body growing a body. You know, whatever.

After that you'll reach the Lobby. You can go ahead and check in while you're there. Make sure you sign the right ledger. No, not that one. *That* one.

Do say hello to Shelly for me, will you? He's the doorman, and he's infamous for finding lost things.

And you, sweetie... you're as lost as they get.

Hmm? Nothing. Just thinking out loud. Don't mind me.

Anyway, I know, I know... you don't really need to see the basement floors, but since we've come this far together, why not?

Get checked in and then sneak on down to the Maintenance floor. Tell Willy that I sent you. He'll make sure you're comfortable. Nice and warm.

Only one floor after that—the Vault. I'll meet you there after you've had a chance to poke around a bit. Not many people get to see that floor. It's full of wondrous things, I assure you.

You'll see the girls down there. The Circle. They make the most fantastic tea.

But first, darling, finish your wine. Yes, the whole bottle.

No, no, I won't hear of you leaving a single drop.

Drink up.

More.

More.

Good. That feels nice, doesn't it?

Let the stress of life just slip away.

It's far too overrated anyway, life.

Listen. A new song just started in the Ballroom.

Go on.

I'll see you soon.

3rd Floor - Ballroom
1999

Left Behind
Christopher Badcock

The ballroom was bustling with the pompous energy and sassiness of youth. Girls and boys popped and locked their way across elegant parquet, all to the sound of "Scrubs" by TLC.

It was Prom night for the kids of Westlake High.

He wasn't here to dance though. And he wasn't here to fuck his way toward a higher sense of self-worth or popularity. He wasn't here to smoke dope either, or even trade Pokémon cards with the nerds huddled together in a shaded corner of the room, away from all the commotion, happy to be forgotten.

He moved throughout the crowd for an altogether different reason. Something far more important than the trials and tribulations of adolescence.

How unfortunate it was that none of them had any idea of what awaited them.

It was all laid out. Hell, his business was set in stone, as were the fates of all those here tonight.

He consumed his surroundings.

The whole situation was a delicious juxtaposition synonymous with the era. In an age of music videos featuring punk metal bands performing in quiet assembly halls, boy bands in haunted houses, and the most popular rapper in the world being a white guy, here was a majestic Art Deco ballroom, exuding a timeless opulence, filled with crazy teenagers and Hanson's "MMMBop" now escaping through the speakers.

He reached the far side of the dance floor seemingly unnoticed. This was how it often was; he always seemed to just fade into the background of any situation. He wasn't sure if there was some intentionality on the part of those around him to disregard his presence, or if it was just simply how things were supposed to be for people like him. Either way, he didn't mind. He liked it.

It made his work easier.

On this side of the ballroom the oak parquet floor gave way to an elegant navy-blue carpet patterned in golden Art Deco motifs. This area stretched along the entire far side of the room, and was lined with floor-to-ceiling mirrors that were so expertly polished it was hard to tell where reality ended and reflection began.

This space also played host to an arrangement of tables adorned in white linen. Cushioned chairs with ornate backrests sat mostly empty while the music played, except for a few occupied by those too shy to bust a move, or those without dates.

He spied two such specimens to his left. A couple of stoners in baggy grey suits and black crew-neck t-shirts. One of them had his face buried in a Nokia 3210—no doubt playing Snake—whilst the other sat backwards in his chair, arms crossed over the backrest, watching the party unfold on the dance floor through glazed eyes.

Behind them he could see the sound area; a small room-within-a-room built into the far corner to house the DJ and their equipment. The builders had done well to integrate it into the overall design. Its two plaster walls had been decorated with an elaborate fresco of overlapping circles that reminded him of peacock feathers. At each corner, a small pilaster rose up from the floor to match those set into all four corners of the ballroom.

Try as they might to hide it, he could still see the white cable running out of the roof and up to the three-tiered ceiling above, where it connected with the first of many speakers that had been installed throughout the venue, all carefully drilled into the stepped ceiling.

Enough observation for now. He knew where he needed to be.

The man turned and headed away from the potheads, weaving his way throughout the tables toward the southern end of the ballroom. The next song came on and, much to his surprise, the once-empty dining area suddenly filled with all of the excited teenagers who weren't in the mood for a slow dance to Savage Garden's "Truly Madly Deeply."

His panic at the swift change in proximity to others was short-lived though, and he simply lowered his head and continued on toward the kitchen doors, being careful to avoid touching anyone. He hated contact.

The conversations were a cacophony of judgments and envious observations on what people were wearing, whatever college acceptance letter they'd received in the mail that week, and how unbelievably hot Freddie Prinze Jr. had been in *She's All That*.

He eventually reached the swinging doors that led into the kitchen. As with everything else in the room it was clear that special care had been taken to create an authentic Art Deco design true to the original ballroom. A gilded checkerboard had been set into the dark mahogany behind brass plates that were polished so pristinely that they showed no sign of the many hands that had pushed the doors open over the years.

Now *he* pushed them open.

As was always the case, he found it easy to sink into the background of a busy environment, moving between smartly dressed staff poised for the plating of food. Chefs presided over hobs and grills, shaking pans and checking timers whilst others tossed salad in glass serving dishes. He reached the pantry at the end of the commotion, opened the door, let himself in, and closed it behind him.

Blake narrowed his eyes, looking out across the dance floor, perplexed. "No frickin' way. Dude. Check it out. Did Travis Lieberman show up dressed as Austin Powers?"

Kevin looked up from his phone. "Are you kiddin' me?" He scanned the ballroom, slack-jawed and hazy-eyed. He laughed when he spotted Lieberman. "Dude, how high are you right now?"

"Obscenely," Blake replied proudly.

Kevin laughed. "Dude, I can see Lieberman, and he ain't dressed like Austin frickin' Powers, man."

"I swear he is, look." Blake nodded toward the crowd. "He's out there, bro, I'm tellin' you. International Man of fuckin' Mystery," he chuckled.

Kevin shook his head, eyes now fixed back on his phone. He put a hand on Blake's shoulder and leaned in. "Hey, check this out. Tell me what song this is." He held his phone up to Blake's ear and a monophonic jingle erupted from the tiny speaker.

Blake began to nod along, a stupid, stoned grin on his face. "No way, man."

Kevin laughed and sat back in his chair. "Yes way."

"That's Pearl Jam."

"Damn straight it is. This monophonic shit is tight, I'm tellin' you, man. I can make my own jams. There's this internet page and it tells you what buttons to press and you can make 'em all. And get this, when someone calls me, it plays."

Blake stared at him, wide-eyed. "Dude, that's like, some futuristic Matrix shit right there." He rested his chin on his arms and exhaled. "What a time to be alive, man."

Kevin snorted. "Dude, in like, I don't know, what month is it again? Like, six months or somethin', it's the year 2000. Like, holy shit, can you believe that?"

Blake looked at his friend and shook his head. "Know what's even wilder than that?" He didn't wait for a reply. "These damn munchies, bro. I am ravenous as fuck right now, where's the food at?"

Kevin chuckled, his phone still playing the worst cover of Pearl Jam's "Alive." "Dude, we've been here for like, a minute. They ain't servin' shit yet."

Blake stood up and straightened his jacket, swaying.

"What're you doin', man?" Kevin was almost hysterical now.

Blake stepped over the chair and stumbled forward. He turned and fixed his eyes on his stoner composer friend who he'd known since first grade. "I'm on the hunt. Like one of those Neanderthal dudes. Gotta catch me some fried chicken and fries. Or, like, I don't know. A donut, or some fish tacos."

He stepped away and left Kevin to work on his next ringtone masterpiece, moving through the now-crowded table area with the gracefulness of a sea lion.

"Dude"—a shout from behind.

He turned back and Kevin was now standing. "If you see any Pringles, can you get me some Pringles?"

"No problem." Blake winked and gave him a thumbs up.

As he moved around the tables, he amused himself with mumblings of incorrect lyrics to the Savage Garden track now playing.

"Boobie doobie geeky chew."

He bumped into Austin Powers but didn't notice. His eyes were fixed on the kitchen doors.

After what felt like an eternity, he reached the entrance and opened the door with his middle finger. "Open sesame."

He was greeted with the same commotion any other visitor might've experienced, but his razor-sharp stoney-senses helped him get a fix on the pantry at the end of the room, and he glided forward.

"Hey, you shouldn't be in here."

He pulled out his bus pass and flashed it in someone's face. "Health inspector, let me do my work." He stashed it back in his pocket and moved on.

"Moron."

He chuckled, now at the pantry door, and stepped inside.

Darkness.

He placed a hand on a shelf, and as his eyes adjusted, the dark slowly turned to grey. He could just about make out the rows of shelves on either side of him, leading off into the darker depths of what he hoped was a treasure trove of munchies.

"Garlic, onions, mustard." He moved along the shelf, looking for something more appetizing.

"Caviar?" He chuckled. "Why not?" He grabbed a jar and began to twist it open, but a shuffling in the darkness further along startled him and he dropped it. As the glass smashed on the floor he could hear the Backstreet Boys in the distance.

"Yo," he called out, amused, but the hint of a tremor in his voice. "Someone back there?"

More shuffling. And a form in the darkness now, moving forward.

Moving toward him.

"Hey, sorry about the caviar."

No reply. But the clear outline of a person was now visible, and still moving toward him.

Incoherent mumbling from the darkness. Words, but nothing Blake had ever heard before.

"Me no speak that language, bro," he laughed, but it was forced; something didn't feel right about this. He hated it. He hated how high he suddenly wasn't feeling anymore, he hated the dark, he hated that there was no fried chicken. He hated this whole situation and wanted out.

A gleam in the blackness, like glass, or steel. Another noise, but he didn't know what it was. And now the menacing shape in the dark was a man, a tall beast of a man in a trench coat.

Blake stepped back and stood in the shattered glass and caviar, nearly slipped, but grabbed a shelf and steadied himself. A weapon, he needed a weapon, this didn't feel okay, this felt far from okay. Maybe he was hallucinating, maybe this was all in his head.

Maybe it wasn't.

He reached out and grabbed the first thing he found.

A carton of marinara sauce.

He held it out in front of him like a sword.

"Don't make me use this, man."

A voice now. A reply.

"I'm sorry I have to do this."

Another flash in the dark and he felt something wet hit his face.

He wiped his eyes. "Dude, what is your problem?"

The figure began to slowly retreat into the darkness, uttering more of those strange words. Blake turned to leave, but before he could reach the door handle the burning started.

It tingled for a second, like that mint leaf shampoo he liked to use. But only for a second. Then it turned fiery. He cried out, clawing at his face.

"What the fuck, man. What the fuck did you do to me?"

He wiped a hand across his cheeks and felt parts of himself fall away. Panicking, he tried to rub whatever it was out of his eyes, but his knuckles sank straight through into his sockets. The world suddenly turned darker as he felt his hands begin to tingle.

He could still hear the Backstreet Boys, but nobody in the kitchen heard his final cries for help.

Amanda winced as she rubbed her stomach. She'd taken some Tylenol before Jared had picked her up, but it wasn't helping. It was just her rotten luck that what her mom often referred to as Aunt Flo had decided to show up just two days before prom.

She felt like her entire life had been ruined.

Worst of all, she'd planned on going the whole way with Jared tonight. They'd been dating for seven months, and he'd been surprisingly patient with her about it. Most guys wanted it all on a plate after a few weeks, but she hadn't wanted to give herself up so easily. She loved him, and she hoped he loved her too. That meant something. It did to her, anyway.

"You okay, babe?" Jared put his fork down and leaned in close. He kissed her on the cheek and put a hand on her thigh.

"No, Jared, no I'm not. This sucks."

He sighed and went back to his plate. "You should've just stayed at home."

She turned to him. "Are you serious?"

"Yeah. I mean, come on. Look at you. What's the point?"

She was seething. "You're being a real dick about this. I said I was sorry, okay?"

"Yeah sure. It's just, you know?"

"Know what, Jared?"

"You know. Tonight was supposed to be *the* night. Me and you." He shoveled some fries into his mouth.

She grimaced. "Is that honestly all you care about? Isn't it enough that we're here together?"

He dropped his fork on the plate. "Maybe it's not. Am I not allowed to be pissed about this too?"

"Okay, settle down, love birds." Erin appeared at the table holding her disposable camera and fell into the chair next to Amanda. She leaned back and held the camera up. "Now, show me some teeth."

Forced smiles all around.

Click.

"There we go." She leaned in and stole some fries from Amanda's plate, which had remained untouched since being served.

Erin had been her best friend since fifth grade, even though they were complete opposites. Amanda was shy, prissy, and had always been intensely focused on her studies. Erin, on the other hand, was always the loudest in the room, had already slept with God-only-knew-how-many boys—and even a college guy last month—and she was lucky to have been accepted to Florida State.

As much as Amanda kept telling herself it was all about the right time and being in love, there was a small part of her that wanted to put an end to Erin's constant commentary on her sex life, or lack thereof. In fact, commentary was probably the wrong word; it had been criticizing. Erin had been on her back about it more than Jared. Persistently reminding her that it'd be social suicide to go to college a virgin.

So tonight was a double-edged sword; Jared seemingly devoid of all patience now and being the most unsupportive boyfriend a girl could ever wish for when Aunt Flo visits your vagina. Plus, the best friend who would—despite being a girl herself—probably show no sympathy and continue the barrage of anti-virgin slurs Amanda had been subjected to over the last two years.

Suddenly, the Spice Girls gate-crashed the silent dance floor in the wake of Savage Garden, telling everyone what they want, what they really, really want. Erin grabbed Amanda's arm and forced her up. "Come on, Shark Week can wait for three minutes. Girl power, Mandy."

She hated it when Erin called her Mandy, and had told her countless times, but she stood up and followed her friend to the dance floor, the cramps still feeling like a bag of nails had split open inside her abdomen.

"Erin, I don't know if I can do this."

"Of course you can, it's prom. Anything is possible tonight."

Jared followed close behind and joined them, not really dancing, just moving his hips from side to side and wanting to remain a part of things.

Amanda looked up at the chandelier and tried to ignore everything she was feeling. Not just physically, but in her heart too. Why was she still hoping? Hoping that Jared felt the same way. Wasn't he disproving that tonight? Was she so stupidly in love that she couldn't see reality?

She'd never liked the Spice Girls. She preferred All Saints.

This was hell. And she wasn't even sure why she was going along with it.

The first was taken care of. But there was more work to be done tonight.

He passed tables that were once again empty and headed for the main entrance. He kept telling himself this wasn't a bad thing he was doing. He had to.

That poor boy in the pantry, he'd passed over in pain. Real pain. The kind of pain people weren't supposed to feel. But it was needed. It was a necessity. They had to feel the pain. They had to cry, and shout and scream. They had to know it was the end.

He pushed through the doors and found himself back in the hallway, where earlier on tonight he'd needed to take a moment to compose himself. The ballroom was the centerpiece of this floor, and surrounding it was an elegant hallway lined with gas burners and laid with a crimson carpet patterned with yellow silhouettes of the Golden Gate Bridge.

He moved down the hall with conviction, passing the first set of restrooms, then the second set at the end of the walkway. He turned to the right and followed the corridor past meeting rooms that had once been suites where the high society of San Francisco and beyond had spent their nights sleeping, or indulging in all manner of other wakeful activities. Now they were high-end corporate hosting spaces, where local businesses wined and dined potential clients, or held boring meetings for their staff, who tolerated it just so they could eat free food and tell their family and friends they'd attended an event at the prestigious Hotel Ethel.

He stopped at Meeting Room 4B and let himself inside.

"Okay class of '99, it's time for another slow dance. If you ain't got a date then get a seat, because this one is for the princes and princesses, the wannabe kings and queens. Ladies and your gentlemen, it's time to show everyone else why you're winners and not losers."

This was the last thing Amanda wanted right now. LeAnn Rimes telling her to question how she could live without this selfish jerk in front of her, still moving his hips like he was dancing to the Spice Girls.

She didn't know what to say to him; she could barely think straight through the pain. Erin ushered her forward and shot Jared a look. He slowed his rhythm and stepped toward her, looking deflated. Looking uninterested.

Lucky him, all he had to deal with was the disappointment of nothing more than an intimate encounter with his right hand later that evening. Amanda wouldn't even get that. Self-pleasure was entirely off the cards when the dreaded Aunt Flo came along; it made her feel sick if she did anything like that.

Jared held out his hands and she took them, even though he didn't deserve it. He gently pulled her in close and placed her hands around his neck, dropped his hands to her waist, and they began to sway in rhythm with the music.

Erin left them to it and returned to the dining area to find someone else to dance with, Kevin Dillinger perhaps. The guy was a stoner who could barely string a proper sentence together most of the time, but he was cute, and she'd never been that interested in what boys had to offer intellectually.

Jared sighed. "Look, I'm sorry, okay?"

"Sorry for what? Do you even know what you're apologizing for?"

"Sure I do." He paused. "I'm sorry for how I've acted this evening. I'm just, I don't know."

Erin looked up at him. "Just what?"

"I don't know, like, is this even gonna happen, Amanda?"

"*This*? And what's *this* supposed to mean?"

"You know what I mean. We got summer break in a few weeks and my parents are taking me to Europe. Then we go to college."

"And?"

"Oh, come on, Amanda. You know what I mean. You'll be in Florida, and I'll be at Penn? They're like, a thousand miles apart."

Amanda pushed him away. "So what, that'll be it then? Are you seriously doing this, tonight, of all nights?"

"Doing what?"

"You know what you're doing, Jared. Don't play dumb. You're going to break up with me, aren't you?"

"Well, don't act all surprised, I mean, Florida and Pennsylvania. It's not exactly a walk down the street, is it? You must've been thinking this too."

"I can't believe I've been so stupid." Her voice caught in her throat, and she could feel tears forming. Her heart felt like a jackhammer, and the cramps down below were still agonising.

She turned and ran for the door.

"Amanda, wait."

She ignored his half-hearted plea and moved through the crowd of couples, some noticing her tears and whispering.

As she reached the door, she felt a sudden hot gush between her legs that stopped her in her tracks.

No, not now, please not now.

She felt the tickly trickle of blood begin to run down her inner thighs. It had been a big one, too much for the pad to handle. She needed to get to a toilet, fast.

She passed through the doors and turned down the hall, picking up her pace as she moved. There were girls coming in and out of the first bathroom. She bolted past them toward the one at the end of the corridor. There'd be more chance of a cubicle being free down there, she thought.

As she got closer though, a group of girls stumbled out of that one, laughing and cursing, one of them swigging a bottle of peach Schnapps. She decided to carry on past them too; there had to be other toilets on this floor that weren't so busy.

She swerved around Alyssa Franks, who was stumbling backward, the other girls pointing and laughing as she slurred her words. None of them seemed to notice Amanda run by.

She took the corner and could see another bathroom sign at the end of the corridor. It was all meeting rooms down here; surely nobody would've walked this far to take a piss. She looked down and could see lines of blood on her ankles. She had to clean herself up, just clean herself up and put on a new pad; everything was going to be fine.

She could hear Ricky Martin singing about "Livin' La Vida Loca." The drunk girls behind her started singing along.

This was such an awful situation.

She reached the bathroom and almost fell through the door in her haste to try and salvage this nightmare of an evening. She moved to the bank of sinks on her right and turned on one of the taps, then pulled a wad of paper towels from the dispenser beside the mirrors and held them under the warm water for a few seconds. She pulled her dress up and began to wipe the blood from her legs, relieved that the flow had at least stopped.

Once she was finished, she pulled down her underwear and removed her pad, dropping them both in the trash along with the paper towels. She reached for another handful to clean the rest of the blood away from her private parts.

She reached for her handbag. She always kept spares of everything in there during this time of the month.

Her heart sank.

"No. No, no," she cried. "Shit. Shit."

She'd left her handbag on the table.

The tears came in floods now as she realised what this meant. She leaned back against the sink and buried her head in her hands.

She suddenly heard voices approaching. A girl laughing.

"You've got to be kidding me."

She turned off the tap and retreated into the last cubicle, locked the door behind her, and sat down on the toilet cover, feet pulled up and praying nobody would find her in this state.

Jared was back at the table, staring at Amanda's handbag and cracking his knuckles. Erin sat down beside him. "What did you say to her?"

"All the wrong things," he replied blankly.

"Where did she go?"

"I don't know, she just left."

Erin sighed. "I'm bored. These guys are all losers. Dance with me."

She was already slowly gyrating her hips in her seat to Mark Morrison's "Return of the Mack."

He looked up at her now. "Are you serious? You wanna dance with me after your best friend just ran out of here?"

"Oh, don't act all high and mighty." She put her hand on his thigh. "We've done plenty more than just dance."

He brushed her hand away. "Now's not the time, Erin."

She huffed. "Fine, be like that." She picked up the handbag. "Might as well go and find her then." She got up to leave and Jared followed.

"I'm coming with you."

"Whatever. She probably just went to the bathroom."

They left the ballroom and followed the corridor down to the toilets. Erin told him to wait while she pushed past another group of girls and disappeared inside. Two minutes later she reappeared, still holding the handbag. "Nothing behind Door Number One."

"Maybe she's at that next one down there." Jared nodded toward the end of the hall.

"Or maybe she just decided fuck you very much and took her ass home."

"Let's just check the next one, okay?" Jared began walking and Erin decided to follow him, knowing full well that Amanda wouldn't have strayed far from the crowds. She'd almost certainly gone home.

They reached the second bathroom and Jared waited outside again. After a few moments Erin returned, the handbag still in her hand.

"Looks like you're all out of luck, Romeo," she laughed.

Jared ran a hand through his hair and sighed. "Damn it."

Erin looked beyond Jared toward the end of the next corridor and smirked. "Might be another bathroom down there for us to check, or some other dark room."

She brushed past him and he could smell her perfume; the same stuff she'd been wearing the first time they hooked up, and the second. And the third.

He followed. Hating himself just a little, but feeling a swell in his pants.

She turned back and gave him eyes, sultry eyes. He couldn't help but grin. She laughed and carried on, pulling up her skirt to reveal a lacy red thong tucked neatly between what many referred to as the finest cheeks in Westlake High.

She chuckled loudly now as they passed the other restroom without noticing. She opened the next door, a meeting room, 4B printed in black on a gold plate set into the mahogany.

She turned and placed her hands high on the door frame, her skirt still hitched up. "You have a very important meeting you need to attend."

He didn't hesitate. He moved forward and she moved back into the darkness, forcing him to follow. He closed the door behind him and could barely make out her form moving around the table, still giggling to herself.

"You'll have to catch me if you want this bonus."

Amanda was the furthest thing from his mind now. Erin had always had this effect, and it's why she was such a bitch. He began to unbuckle his belt as he moved around the table, and he could see she was making no effort to continue the chase. When he reached the other side, she was already sat on the tabletop, removing her thong.

As he descended on her she brushed aside notepads and speakers to make space. He thrust his hips against her and their mouths met. In the heat of the moment he didn't feel the splash against the back of his head.

In some cruel—or perhaps lusty—twist of fate, he could hear Will Smith in the distance, "Getting Jiggy Wit It." He could feel her smiling against his kisses, probably realising the irony of it too.

Then the heat of the moment was replaced with another heat.

"What the fuck?" He stopped for a second, reaching round to wipe the back of his head.

"What is it?" she asked.

He felt the skin pull away like cheese from an overloaded slice of pizza.

He pulled out of her and stumbled away from the table, the back of his head on fire now. Another splash—this time he *did* feel it, something hitting his neck and the spot behind his left ear.

He turned and saw a figure looming in the corner. The light on one of the speaker phones caught something the man was holding and for a second Jared saw red. He thought about those spy films where the hero had to traverse a room of lasers. It was funny, the things that popped into your mind when you were dying and didn't really know it.

"What the fuck is happening?" Erin sounded like she was in another room entirely. He reached for his ear, but it was already sliding down to his shoulder.

He tried to talk, but couldn't. The heat in the back of his neck was now in his throat and he could feel his breath catching. He began to choke and fell back toward the table; something was in his mouth.

It was his tonsils. Whatever had burned through his neck had found its way right through to his gullet and melted them away, leaving them lodged in his windpipe.

He fell onto Erin and the back of his head connected with her nose, splitting it on impact.

She screamed.

"Get the fuck off of me." Blood gushed across her lips and chin as she struggled to push Jared aside.

"Get off of me, Jared."

He was already dead.

Her eyes began to swell from her broken nose, and she could barely see, in the dark, a shadow—larger than any of the football players she'd spent too much time with that senior year—standing above her.

She heard words, but had no idea what they meant.

Then she felt the splash too. Something wet and immediately warm against her face and shoulder.

Suddenly, the broken nose was forgotten. Replaced with some other pain. Something fierce and unbearable. She struggled, trying to push away Jared's dead weight. An awful burn across her face now, and not the broken nose. Something worse.

Then nothing. After a few seconds it was gone, and so was everything else. She couldn't even feel her own head, her own face. She managed to push Jared's head away from hers and had a brief moment of opportunity to let her fingers caress her skin.

She screamed.

Everything she touched caught her nails and came away with them. She peeled away her skin and felt chunks fall away and hit the table behind her.

But there was light now; the door had been opened.

Help had arrived. Surely.

But then the light was gone. Her eyes burned for a second, then just like her face, there was no pain, and only the dark. No feeling. No help arriving.

Just someone leaving the room.

A dreadful man in a trench coat, his business done.

He didn't enjoy what he was doing.

But it was necessary.

He closed the door behind him, ignoring the girl's whimpering, and headed back toward the ballroom.

As he moved along the corridor he meditated for a moment on his mission. Because that's what it was.

A mission.

Sometimes you had to be cruel to be kind. Sometimes, the only thing that could set you free was pain. And these kids—four of them on his list— needed to feel it. They needed to feel the pain.

He knew where the last one was. She'd hidden herself away in a bathroom.

No way out for her.

Poor girl.

But it was necessary.

Amanda could hear shouts nearby, a few rooms down maybe. She was sure it sounded like Erin.

She was trying to figure out what to do. How to get out of this situation. Jared was her only ride home. Her phone was in her bag though, if she could just get to her phone, and get outside, she could call her dad and have him come pick her up.

She tried to play it through in her mind. Just run back in, straight to the table, she knew she'd left her bag on the table. Get the bag, and run straight out. Don't look at anyone. Come back here and sort herself out. Take the stairs instead of waiting for the elevator. Call her dad on the way and ask him to pick her up from the corner so she didn't have to wait outside.

The bathroom door opened and somebody came in.

She pulled her feet up closer, bringing her knees to her chest.

Below the sound of heavy footsteps against the tiles, she could hear Alanis Morissette, but it was muted, like music underwater.

"Ironic."

What a perfect song, she thought.

It's like red rain, on your high school prom day.

Heavy footsteps. Not a girl's footsteps. This was someone big.

This was someone to fear.

She heard the first of the doors swing open and bang against the cubicle interior.

Then the second.

She fought back tears and tried to hold her breath.

The third door.

The fourth.

She suddenly thought of *Scream*, that horror movie she wasn't supposed to see but had snuck in with Erin and Jared anyway. But this wasn't a movie, this was real life.

A pair of wide black boots stopped outside her cubicle, and she could hear muttering. Something incoherent. Something that sounded drunk, or deranged.

She spoke up. "Whoever you are, just leave me alone, okay? My boyfriend's on his way. He's big and he plays football."

Nothing.

"So you better leave right now. I'm being serious."

Before she could register why one of the boots had suddenly disappeared, the lock was taken off its hinges and the door swung violently inward.

She screamed.

This was supposed to be the part where the heroine managed to get away. Somehow ducking and diving out of reach and escaping to safety before a final confrontation later on.

But not this time.

The man was huge. Dressed in a black trench coat and fedora that cast a shadow over half of his face. He took up the entire doorway.

"Please, please don't hurt me."

He reached inside his pocket and brought out a small glass bottle, something that looked like fancy perfume.

He removed the lid. Still uttering incoherent words.

A flick of his wrist and she felt something hit her face and arms and knees. Something wet.

She cried out, jumping up and charging forward. Deciding she had no other choice.

He stepped aside with an unexpected gracefulness, and she fell forward toward the sinks. A glimmer of hope now as she realized she could make a run for the door.

Before she could though, she glanced up and saw herself in the mirror.

She squealed.

Her cheeks were dissolving like one of those bath bombs she'd gotten from her mom for her birthday.

The pain was excruciating.

She fought back the urge to claw at her face and made a break for the door. Before she could get there, her knees gave way and she fell down; her face hit the tiles, not with a thud, but with an awful squelch. She turned over and looked at her knees.

They were almost gone.

The white of bare bone shone through blood and flesh that was already pooling on the floor around her.

She could still hear Alanis Morissette.

Then nothing.

As her vision began to fade to black, she saw the man standing over her. He looked sad.

The last thing she saw was his hand moving to his head, then his chest, then both shoulders.

The Holy Trinity.

He left the bathroom and made his way toward the elevators.

His work was done.

As he waited for the doors to open, he heard the DJ announce the final song of the evening.

"Okay, Westlake seniors, you've been great tonight. Now grab your dates and head to the floor for our final song. It dominated the charts and our hearts, and we all know there was plenty of room on that door for poor old Jack."

He grinned. Of course. He remembered it well.

As the doors opened and he pressed the button for the reception, he could hear Celine Dion begin to sing.

He crossed the foyer and approached the front desk, pulling out his iPhone and checking for any messages from his wife.

I hope everything worked out ok honey. I made the stroganoff. We can heat it up when you get home.

He nodded at the young man behind the desk, who didn't say a word, just motioned for him to head straight into the Manager's Office.

Mr. Fenton sat behind his desk smoking a cigar. As he entered, Fenton quickly stood up and straightened his hair.

"Mr, Miller," he said, somewhat flustered. "I trust everything has been taken care of."

The man parted his trench coat and took a much-needed seat. Mr. Fenton hesitantly sat back down.

"Yes," he replied. "The smoking entity in the kitchen pantry. The poltergeists in Meeting Room 4B, and the bleeding walls in the female restroom on the south side."

Fenton rested back in his chair and sighed. "Thank God. So there really were ghosts? Honest-to-God actual ghosts? There's always been rumors at this place, but seriously? This was the real deal?"

Miller nodded. "Yes. But these were different. I don't come across this sort very often."

"What do you mean?"

Miller nodded toward the cigar. "You got one to spare?"

"Sure, sure, of course." Fenton fumbled with a box on his desk and pulled one out; he clipped the end, his hands shaking. He passed it over and lit a match for Miller.

"Cubans. The real deal, like your ghosts." Fenton feigned a laugh while Miller took a puff and settled in the chair.

"What you had up there were not ghosts. I did my research." He took another long draw on the cigar. "They were left behind."

"What do you mean?" Fenton looked perplexed as he wiped beads of sweat from his brow.

"These kids didn't die. In fact, they were the only survivors. They were the only ones not in the ballroom for that final song when, well, you know what happened to everyone else that night in '99." He took another puff. "They're probably alive and well to this day, God willing."

Fenton stirred in his seat. "But how then? How are they there if they aren't dead?"

Miller frowned.

"It's not always the dead that stick around, Mr. Fenton. In some rare, tragic circumstances, those who survive die a little inside, and they leave their dead parts behind. They have to. You know? Sometimes we have to leave a part of ourselves. It's like paying a fee to balance out the trauma."

"But—but what about the rest of them then? The ones who *did* die."

Miller shrugged. "They're up there. All of them. Every last kid and teacher. The DJ too. But they're fine. They're enjoying themselves. They all know they're dead."

Fenton shook his head. "No. No. That's not good enough. What if that changes? What if they all decide they want to start haunting my guests like those others? It's not good for business, Mr. Miller."

The exorcist grinned. "They'll be fine. And if anything *does* change, you have my number."

2nd Floor - Restaurant
1967

The Cost of Motherhood
Briana Morgan

Dawn stares down at the dead fly on the hotel windowsill. The insect sprawled on its back, its legs curled close to its body, its unseeing red eyes turned upward.

Is that all *her* life amounts to? Trapped, alone, waiting to die without ever having left a real mark on the world?

Suzanne nudges Dawn's shoulder. "You ready?"

Dawn puts on some lipstick. Suzanne does, too. This feels like magic somehow, or like gearing up for war.

As the sisters head down to the hotel's restaurant, The Golden Bell, Dawn's heart flutters. Is she making a mistake? All her life, she's been careful and lonely. Watching her sister thrive—chasing dreams and lovers, Dawn wanted to be like her.

Nothing could bring them any closer than this.

Suzanne told Dawn all about the Hotel Ethel. She told her about Nancy. She instilled Dawn with hope.

It was the hope that convinced her.

Maybe if her husband weren't away in Vietnam, Dawn wouldn't waver so quickly.

Robbie.

God, she misses him. She misses him more than she ever dreamed possible.

Robbie.

His name conjures up the warmth of his hands on her arms, fingers brushing away her tears, soft mouth reassuring *everything will be okay.*

She is changing the narrative. She *will* give him children.

"Be careful what you wish for," someone says into the payphone as they pass.

Dawn tries to imagine the other half of the conversation, as she often does, but this time comes up empty.

When they get to the restaurant, Suzanne tells the hostess they're waiting for someone. Dawn peers over the hostess's shoulder and locks eyes with a slight brunette woman at a table.

The woman, whom Dawn doesn't know, winks at her.

"There," Suzanne says. "We'll be joining her. Thank you."

Nancy grins as they approach. Her teeth are so white, so sharp, they don't look real.

Dawn and Suzanne sit across the table from Nancy. Dawn finds the table unexpectedly long, seating more than she anticipated.

Dawn leans close to her sister. "You didn't mention any others."

"Only two more," replies Nancy.

Dawn's goosebumps tighten. How can she have heard that? The din of the restaurant and commotion from the nearby kitchen should smother any whisper into nothing.

So lost in her uneasy thoughts is Dawn that she misses when the girls come in. Nancy waits until they have settled, her hands folded neatly on the table. When she speaks, her voice is soft, almost apologetic.

"I'm so glad you made it," she says. "I know how hard it is to wait for something that never comes."

Dawn forces herself to look at the saltshaker instead of Nancy's face.

The two women at the table shift slightly. One of them, a muscular

Black woman with a shiny beehive hairdo, wears an eyepatch over her left eye. She sits tall and still, like a soldier waiting for orders.

"This is Jolene," says Nancy.

"Jo," Jolene corrects her.

The other woman, a willowy Vietnamese girl with dark hair styled in a sleek bob, lowers her gaze to the table. Her green eyes catch the light, sharp as an emerald.

"And this, my dears, is Melody."

Suzanne and Dawn introduce themselves to the new girls.

Nancy continues. "What I'm offering isn't science. It's older than that. Simpler."

The girls lean in. Dawn's pulse pounds against her ribs.

"No hormones. No knives. Your body already knows how to do this. It only needs a little... encouragement."

Nancy's words turn Dawn's stomach.

"You'll be pregnant before the next moon. And the child will be yours. Completely."

The word *completely* coils tight inside Dawn like a worm.

Nancy tips her head. "But there's a price. You must never tell anyone how it happened. Never speak of this meeting. Never speak of *me*."

Her voice, so gentle, barely cuts through the clatter of plates and kitchen noise. And yet Dawn hears every syllable, as if Nancy were whispering right against her ear.

"Secrets keep the magic clean." Nancy smiles wide enough to show them all the sharpness of her teeth. "Secrets protect what's growing."

Jolene scratches at the side of her neck with her nails. Melody presses her lips together. Suzanne waits. Dawn listens.

"If you can keep that promise," Nancy says, "you'll get all you've ever wanted."

Dawn's skin prickles. She looks to Suzanne, hoping for a sign, an anchor. But Suzanne's already nodding.

"Dawn?" Suzanne asks.

Can she go through with this? What if Nancy is wrong? The certainty in her voice is beyond any certainty Dawn has ever heard.

Robbie wants her to have babies. He wants them to be a picture-perfect American family with two bright-eyed children.

Robbie will understand. If he shows up, he will tell her he does. In her mind's eye, she watches him take her hands in his and press his lips to her knuckles.

"You did this for us," he'll tell her. *"You sacrificed so much for our little dream."*

"Exactly," Dawn will answer, sated by his understanding.

"What do you say?" Nancy's voice snaps Dawn out of it.

What does she have to lose?

"I want that," Dawn answers.

Nancy's smile sharpens. She reaches into the folds of her coat and pulls out something small, cradled in a piece of black cloth.

Dawn stares at the object in her hand. It's small, smooth, and unmistakably delicate. The cracks across its surface seem to pulse as though something is alive inside.

"What's this?" Dawn asks.

"Pretreatment. Just take it."

Dawn stares at the seed.

"Swallow it," says Nancy, her voice as calm as ever, but there's a flicker of something—anticipation, maybe?—in her eyes. "It knows where to go."

Dawn's fingers curl around the object involuntarily. *Pretreatment.* Her pulse quickens. A seed... a pill... it's everything and nothing.

"But what is it?" Dawn demands.

Nancy doesn't flinch. "It's the beginning," she murmurs. "It's what will make everything else possible. You've heard the stories of women who dream of motherhood and wake up to find that dream real, that miracle blooming inside them."

She stands and steps closer, leaning over Dawn's hand, her breath cool on Dawn's skin. "This is your miracle, Dawn."

The words are laced with something dark, something sweet and terrible. Dawn's hands curl into fist. This is it. *The choice.*

The restaurant closes in on her. Everything feels hazy and far away, and yet, the weight of the decision presses on her chest. She's never been so certain of something and yet so terrified in her entire life.

Her fingers move of their own accord, pulling the cloth away from the object, revealing the small, cracked seed inside. She shudders. Her heart pounds in her ears. She can't shake the feeling that something is wrong.

But then she thinks of Robbie. What if this is her only chance to make the life they've dreamed of?

Dawn snuffs out her fear. "Fine," she says. "I'll do it."

Nancy's smile is sharp and knowing. "Good."

The moment the seed touches her palm, Dawn feels it—an unnatural warmth spreading from her fingertips, a pull deep in her bones.

She raises her hand slowly. What if this is a mistake? But it's too late for doubts now, isn't it?

The air shifts around her, thick with something strange, something that stirs beneath her skin. Her body hums with the promise of change, and a sense of inevitability wraps around her heart.

Dawn takes a deep breath. This is it. There's no going back now.

She lifts the seed to her lips, feeling the cool texture against her mouth. Nancy watches with quiet satisfaction.

Dawn hesitates, then swallows.

The next day, golden sunlight filters into the Hotel Ethel. Dawn steps out from her room, her pulse pounding in time with the beat of her shoes on the floor. The air in the hotel is thick with the smell of polished wood and antiseptic, sterile in a way that doesn't comfort her, but rather unsettles.

The elevator ride to the penthouse suites on Floor Nineteen is slow, too slow. The tall, ghastly elevator attendant with the pockmarked face says nothing the whole way, not even *hello*. His gaze makes Dawn shudder.

By the time the doors slide open, Dawn's hands are slick with sweat. She forces herself to step out, to follow the long, quiet hallway toward the suite Nancy had told her to meet her in.

The door is already ajar.

Inside, the room is dimly lit, the light cool and clinical. An aroma lingers in the air, a blend of incense that reminds Dawn of hospital waiting rooms, and something deeper, almost like earth itself. It's calming, in a way—but the calm is deceptive. The entire room feels like an operating theater, a place where the boundaries between the natural and the unnatural blur.

Nancy stands by a narrow table in the center of the room, her figure eerily still. The instruments laid out before her are meticulous—all gleaming, all clean. Needles. Small vials. Thin, silver tubes. And, in the center, an unmarked jar of something that shimmers, caught between colors.

Dawn stops inside the door.

There's a shadow on the wall—bleak, unmistakable—a huge, hunched figure with two horns.

Dawn blinks, and the shadow is gone.

"You're here," Nancy says, as if Dawn's arrival is something inevitable. "Good."

The door clicks shut behind her, louder than it should be.

"I—" Dawn stops herself, throat tightening. She should be asking questions, but she can't find her voice.

Nancy turns, holding up a slender syringe, needle gleaming in the low light. "You understand, don't you? This is all very... natural." Her smile is small, reassuring, too practiced. "It's science, Dawn. Don't be afraid."

Dawn nods, though the word *science* feels hollow in her mouth. It feels like something darker—something older.

"You're sure?" Nancy's voice pierces through the haze of doubt swirling in Dawn's head. "Once we begin, you won't be able to turn back. This... will change you."

Dawn thinks of the girls back in the restaurant, their faces lit with desperation. Jolene's steady gaze. Melody's anxious eyes. Suzanne's eager smile. She swallows again, deeper this time, and nods.

"Yes."

Nancy's smile widens, a thin and strange thing that doesn't quite reach her eyes. "Good." She steps forward, the air shifting around her. "Then let's begin."

Dawn lays down on the table as instructed, the coolness of the surface a sharp contrast to the heat crawling up her spine. The room feels smaller now. Nancy's presence holds her still.

The needle slides into her skin with a quiet precision, the sterile metal entering her vein without resistance. Her vision blurs at the edges. The smell of incense fills her lungs.

Throughout, there is no pain.

Nancy moves around her with smooth, practiced motions. Her hands are cool, unshakable. The instruments gleam like they've been waiting for this moment—for Dawn.

Each action is deliberate, measured, but there's something strangely graceful about it, like a ritual, not a medical procedure. Dawn feels the drug start to work its way into her bloodstream, a heavy, slow pull dragging her further from reality.

The air around her feels thick, dreamlike. Her eyelids flutter, the world outside the room slipping into a blur of gray shadows. She can almost hear the hum of something deep beneath the floor, something ancient, calling to her.

The horned shadow appears again. It flashes before her eyes, then vanishes just as quickly.

It's just a procedure. *It's just science.* Isn't it?

Nancy's voice breaks through the fog, soft but firm. "How are you feeling?"

Dawn blinks, trying to focus, but the words float like wisps of smoke. She can't form a full sentence. She tries to sit up, but her body feels foreign, sluggish, like she's underwater.

"I'm... fine," she whispers. The heaviness in her chest grows.

Nancy tilts her head, as if she's studying Dawn. "Good," she says, "You did so well."

Dawn watches Nancy pack up her instruments. The ritual is over, but the feeling it's only just begun gnaws at her.

As the darkness at the edges of Dawn's vision deepens, she can't shake the sense she's crossed a line. She's made a choice she can't undo.

It's just science. *Just science*, she repeats in her head, the words more of a prayer than a truth. But the room feels too cold now, too empty. The weight on her chest grows.

She hopes that when the baby comes, she'll still be herself.

Dawn doesn't know when it happens exactly—the shift, the change—but over the days following the procedure, she feels an unspoken connection between her and Jo.

The other woman sits across from her at the Golden Bell for their new post-check-in ritual. Jo's a few years younger than Dawn, though she acts ageless and unshakeable. There's something magnetic about her, the way she keeps going even when the world feels heavy.

Over the past few days, they've bumped into each other during the mandatory check-ins, their awkward silences turning into the tentative beginnings of a friendship. They've exchanged glances in the hallways of the hotel, lingered over coffee in the mornings, and laughed about how strange the whole thing is—this procedure, this promise of babies.

Today, Jo is different.

She's still smiling, but the corners of her mouth turn downward. The vibrancy in her eyes has dimmed, though she tries to mask it with exaggerated cheer.

"Another day, another weird doctor visit," Jo says, her voice light, almost dismissive. She swirls her coffee in a mug the size of a small bowl, staring into the swirling dark liquid. "Who knew trying to have a baby would be so... strange?"

Dawn smiles in return, though the edges of her lips feel stiff. "Yeah, it's... a lot more than I expected."

Jo glances up at her, and for the first time, Dawn sees something raw in her eyes.

"Honestly? I don't even care anymore. I'll sell my soul if it means I get a baby. Hell, I'm not even sure what's in this 'pretreatment' they gave us"—she gestures at her mug—"but if it works, I'll do whatever it takes."

Dawn laughs, but it's hollow. She wishes she could be as flippant as Jo about it.

"Yeah," she says anyway. "I feel that too."

Jo shrugs it off, giving her a wink. "If it works, we'll all be happy little moms before you know it."

But Dawn isn't so sure anymore. There's a heaviness in Jo's words, an undercurrent of something not entirely hopeful. As if the desperation behind those words is all too familiar.

As if it's not just about babies.

The conversation drifts away. Jo's hand trembles as she brings the coffee to her lips, and Dawn wonders—

What if it doesn't work like they think?

The next morning, when Dawn runs into Jo in the hotel lobby, something's off. Jo is pale, her face drawn in a way Dawn hasn't seen before. There are dark circles under her eyes, and her usually bright smile is nowhere to be found.

"Hey," Dawn says, stepping closer. "You all right?"

Jo's lips curve in a weak imitation of a smile, but her eyes are glassy. "Yeah, just tired. Side effects. You know... it's a lot on the body, all this *magic*, or whatever."

Dawn's gaze flickers over Jo's thin, trembling frame. She doesn't believe her, but she doesn't know what to say. Instead, she nods.

"Okay," she says, though she's unsure. Dawn wants to say more, to ask Jolene if she needs help.

But she doesn't.

The gnawing emptiness wakes her. Dawn groans, rubbing her face with the heels of her hands. The hunger feels different today—darker, *deeper*.

In the bathroom, she catches a glimpse of herself in the mirror. Her skin, normally smooth, is marred by faint, dark lines winding like root systems under her flesh, the veins crisscrossing her arms like spider webs. They pulse black and jagged beneath her skin. Dawn touches her wrist.

It's just the procedure, she tells herself, *just side effects. It's part of the miracle.*

She inhales deeply. The veins are getting worse. She should tell someone. But who? Suzanne, who's as enmeshed in this as she is? Nancy? No, no. This is normal. Nancy said this would happen. Dawn's adjusting. That's all.

After a long moment, Dawn pulls her sleeve down to cover the marks. The mirror won't help her. Not today. Not now.

The rest of the morning is a blur of forced normalcy. Dawn goes to the market and buys baby clothes. Little onesies with animal prints. Soft cotton socks. She lets herself smile at the sight of them, even as a strange flutter stirs in her stomach. The hunger claws at her insides again, this time more urgent. She feels the overwhelming need to eat, and she can't help but give in. She picks up a pack of granola bars, eating one in the car before she even leaves the parking lot.

The food doesn't satisfy. Not anymore.

Her stomach feels like a black hole, demanding more. She drives through fast food places on autopilot, ordering a burger, fries, anything to fill the void haunting her.

At night, she curls up in the hotel's plush bed with a pregnancy book, its pages filled with hopeful promises about the wonder of new life, the beauty of motherhood. The pictures are soft—round bellies, glowing smiles, radiant mothers holding their newborns. Dawn's eyes trace the words, her fingers running over the pages as if absorbing their meaning.

She writes another letter to Robbie, careful to keep the tone upbeat, cheerful. She finally mentions her pregnancy, how she's excited for their future.

She doesn't mention the changes.

⚜

But the changes don't stop. They escalate.

Her nails grow longer, sharper. Her skin becomes oddly sensitive, tender to the touch, as if the air itself is too thick. She can't walk into a room without the scent of food assaulting her senses, too sharp, too overpowering, making her stomach churn with need.

One morning, she notices the veins are darker, more pronounced, twisting along her legs like something alive. She presses her fingers against them, the sensation almost... comforting, Maybe she should embrace them.

This is all normal, isn't it? This is part of the process. This is part of the miracle.

She continues shopping for baby clothes, picking out soft blankets, more onesies, a tiny pair of shoes. The changes keep coming, but she doesn't stop. She won't stop. She refuses to stop.

By the time she sits down to write another letter to Robbie, her fingers tremble. The paper shakes beneath her hands as she writes the words, careful and precise.

The black veins on her wrists catch the light as she writes, but she doesn't look at them. She can't. If she looks, she might see something she doesn't want to see. Something she's afraid of.

Her breath hitches but she pushes forward, finishing the letter with a flourish. She tells herself this is a phase. It will pass. Once the baby is here, everything will be perfect.

The hunger comes again, fiercer now. She stands, taking the elevator downstairs on autopilot, double doors sliding open to reveal the Golden Bell. The smell of food fills her senses, overwhelming, suffocating. Her hands shake as she grabs a menu and asks for her usual seat. She eats one of everything on the menu without tasting it, chewed meat and vegetables sliding down her throat, the hunger never satisfied.

That night, she dreams again.

The baby is in her arms, but its eyes aren't human. They're hollow black voids, staring at her with a cold emptiness. Its tiny hands reach for her, and its teeth sink into her skin.

She wakes with a scream, sweat pouring down her face, her heart racing in her chest. The hunger claws at her once more, stronger than before. She tries to ignore it, but she can't. She's too far gone.

This is the miracle. She needs to believe it. She needs to believe it even though she knows—this isn't right.

No matter how desperately she clings to hope, the truth is creeping closer.

Dawn sits on the edge of the hotel bed, feeling the soft comforter beneath her fingertips, the only thing tethering her to reality. The room feels too quiet, the air too still. Outside the window, the city hums, oblivious to the strange undercurrent pulling her further from herself with every passing day.

She adjusts her posture, attempting to appear more composed than she feels, though the edges of doubt are creeping up around her like smoke.

There's a knock.

Dawn straightens, stands up. Her heart skips a beat, an unsettling mix of excitement and unease swirling in her stomach as she walks toward the door.

When she opens it, Nancy steps inside, her presence filling the room with an unsettling calmness. Her eyes gleam with a knowing warmth, as though she's been waiting for this moment for a long time.

"You're looking well, Dawn," Nancy says, her voice soft, almost too smooth. She brushes past Dawn with the quiet grace of someone who knows exactly how to take up space without seeming to.

She's wearing the same coat she wore the last time they met, though now there's something even more deliberate about her movements—like she's performing a ritual without needing any incantations.

"Thank you," Dawn murmurs, stepping aside to let Nancy sit in the armchair by the window. She closes the door, the click of the lock echoing too loudly in her ears.

Nancy settles herself, her fingers trailing over the armrest. "How are you feeling?" she asks.

"I'm… I'm fine," Dawn answers, though the word feels strange on her tongue. She's never been good at lying to herself, but something about Nancy's presence makes her want to say everything is going perfectly. She feels the pressure to make things seem easier than they are.

Nancy's eyes narrow. "Everything is going perfectly," she says with quiet assurance. "Your progress is incredible. It's rare to see someone adapt so quickly."

Dawn swallows, unease bubbling in her chest. *It's rare to see anyone adapt at all*, she thinks, but she keeps the words locked inside. She's seen the changes in her body—how her stomach is starting to swell, the faintest curve beneath her clothes, how the hunger that bites her never subsides. And there's the strange, darkened veins beneath her skin, creeping inch by inch, as if they're part of her now.

"You should be proud of yourself," Nancy continues, her voice a soft lull, coaxing Dawn into a state of calm. "This is all going as it should. Your body knows what to do. The baby will be here soon, and it will be... perfect."

Dawn nods, but her fingers tremble as she rests them on her stomach. The sensation of life inside her is still so new, so overwhelming, but it feels like the only thing that's real anymore. She touches the slight curve of her belly, her breath catching as she feels an unmistakable surge of hope.

Soon, I won't be alone, she thinks, letting the thought settle deep in her chest. For the first time in months, she feels something close to peace.

"You're doing everything right," Nancy says again, her voice almost too gentle. "Everything's as it should be."

Dawn shoves aside the nagging sense of doubt that lingers at the edges of her mind. She should be thankful, shouldn't she? This is what she wants. This is what she's been waiting for—her body, her life, aligning in the way she's always imagined.

Her thoughts drift to Jo. The woman had been full of nervous energy in the beginning, her jokes about "selling her soul for this" still echoing in Dawn's mind. She'd brushed it off then, but now, the words feel different. Heavier. And Jo is sick. It's a quiet sickness—unnerving because it's so unpredictable. The doctors can't figure it out. They won't.

Dawn opens her eyes, her fingers tightening on her stomach. But she isn't sick. She's *fine*.

Nancy's gaze sharpens. She seems to sense Dawn's distraction, the shift in her mood. She leans forward, her grin more knowing, more dangerous.

"Don't worry about Jo, my dear. Not everyone can handle the sacrifice. But you? You're different. Stronger."

Dawn doesn't question her. She doesn't question the way Nancy's words seem to make the room feel colder, like the air itself has thickened, pressing in on her. *No.* This is the price. This is the price of everything she's wanted. This is the cost of motherhood.

"What sacrifice?" Dawn asks, her voice barely above a whisper.

Nancy watches Dawn for a long moment, her eyes glinting with quiet understanding.

"The sacrifice is worth it," Nancy says, her voice low, smooth. "You'll understand when the baby is here. You'll understand when you're holding your child in your arms."

Dawn nods, but her stomach churns. It's the same hunger that's been gnawing at her for days, only now it's mixed with something else— something deeper. Something darker.

Nancy stands and moves toward the door, her steps light and sure, as though nothing in this world could ever shake her. "I'll leave you to rest. The time is drawing near. I'll check on you again soon. Dawn, everything will be worth it."

The door clicks closed behind her, and Dawn is left alone in the room, her hand still resting on her stomach.

Everything will be worth it.

For the first time since the procedure, the words sound hollow. Something inside her stirs uneasily, but she buries it deep, hoping it'll disappear.

It doesn't.

But she pushes the fear away, touching her stomach again. Soon, she won't be alone.

The room smells sterile, the faint scent of antiseptic mixing with the heavy, metallic tang of fear. Dawn stands at the door of Jo's makeshift hospital room in the penthouse suites, the quiet hum of the machines almost mocking the silence between them.

Jo is pale—paler than Dawn has ever seen her—and lying perfectly still in the bed, her dark skin drawn tight across her bones, her chest rising and falling with ragged breaths.

Dawn steps in, her footfalls muffled. She'd come here to check on Jo, to comfort her, but now that she's standing here, she doesn't know what to say. She's never seen someone look this way—this close to the edge, to the finality of death.

Jo's eyes flutter open. There's no smile this time, no quick-witted joke, only the weariness of someone who has fought too long, too hard, and finally lost. Her lips twitch, but it isn't a smile.

"You look like hell," Dawn says, the words too sharp, too strained.

Jo manages a weak laugh, a sound that doesn't reach her eyes. "I feel like hell, too," she mutters, the words barely a rasp. "Guess I'm not cut out for this miracle thing after all."

Dawn's stomach clenches. Jo's bones press against her skin, her body losing its fight. It's like something no one can see but everyone can feel is draining the life from her.

"You're going to be okay," Dawn says, though the words sound hollow in her ears.

Jo looks up at her, her eyes tired but sharp. "I don't think I am. I don't think any of us are."

Jo closes her eyes one last time. The machines continue their soft beeping, but the sound has changed. It's softer now, slower. As if the world outside is catching up with the stillness inside this room.

Dawn steps back, her heart heavy with the weight of Jo's passing, and yet... part of her is relieved. At least Jo is out of the pain. She won't suffer anymore.

The relief is short-lived.

As Dawn exits the room, the air feels thick, as if it's holding something out of reach. Dawn closes her eyes, takes a shaky breath, and promises herself she'll make this right. But as she walks away, she feels a growing unease. If it could happen to Jo... what if it's already happening to her?

Melody's baby shower at the Golden Bell is meant to be a celebration, a time for laughter, for joy, for the anticipation of new beginnings. The decorations the hotel staff put up are sweet—soft pastel balloons, cakes shaped like little onesies, games where everyone's guessing the baby's weight and hair color. It should feel festive. But it doesn't.

Dawn watches the women chat, their voices rising and falling like the gentle hum of a lullaby, but her stomach churns. Her hands are sweaty, her breathing shallow. The changes in her body are getting harder to ignore. Her skin feels tight, stretched thin. The veins underneath it seem darker now, more pronounced. And her teeth... they ache, like they're being pulled out from the roots.

She should be happy. She should be excited. She should be glowing. Instead, she feels like an imposter—like the baby growing inside her doesn't belong to her.

The child will be yours. Completely.

Then Melody cries out.

It's sudden, sharp, and impossible to ignore. The room falls silent, and all eyes turn toward her. Melody claws at her stomach, her breath coming in short, desperate gasps. Her face is contorted in pain, her eyes wide with fear.

The women rush to her side, but it's too late. Red blooms at the crotch of Melody's dress. Dawn can't look away as the blood seeps through Melody's clothes, pooling on the floor around her. It's a violent hemorrhage—too much, too fast.

The Golden Bell erupts in chaos. Women scream, some try to help, but it's clear—Melody isn't going to make it. Dawn stares, paralyzed. There's nothing she can do. She feels a terrible, helpless stillness inside, like the world is shifting around her, and there's no safe place left to stand.

Melody's green eyes lock onto Dawn's for a brief second, full of horror and confusion. But then they dull, and her body goes limp, and Dawn is left standing in the middle of a room that's suddenly too small, too suffocating.

A silence fills the restaurant, broken only by the sobs of the women around her. Dawn doesn't know how long she stands there, staring at the blood-soaked floor, the sounds of the room muffled in her ears.

She's not sure who calls for the paramedics, or when they finally arrive, but she knows one thing for sure—this is not a *miracle*.

This pregnancy? It's a nightmare.

Hours later, Dawn's fingers tremble as she presses the cold washcloth to her forehead, pushing away the nausea that rolls through her in waves. The baby shower had been a blur of faces, awkward smiles, and strained conversations. She should have been thrilled. She should have felt the joy of being surrounded by women, the hope of new beginnings hanging in the air.

She stumbles into the hotel room, her breath shallow, a dull ache pulsing through her abdomen. It's been happening for days now—the pain, the pressure—but tonight it's different. She can't tell if it's the strain of the day, the stress of the gathering, or something worse. She can't remember the last time she felt *normal*.

The room feels too hot, too small. She kicks off her shoes and sinks down on the bed, her hand on her belly. It's still there, faint but persistent—

the thought that everything will be worth it in the end. That she'll have the family she and Robbie dreamed of. That *he'll* be here to see it. They'll raise their children in the little house they've talked about, with a swing set in the backyard, their laughter echoing through the halls.

But as she settles into the bed, her vision blurs. The pain in her abdomen flares, sharper now, as if something inside her is pushing against her from within. She gasps, pressing her hand to her stomach. It doesn't help. The room tilts, spins, and her body sags into the softness of the mattress.

Someone knocks at the door. Dawn barely has the strength to get up, but she does. Suzanne stands in the hallway.

"Hey," Suzanne says softly, her voice trembling enough to make Dawn sit up. "You okay?"

Suzanne didn't go through with the procedure. Dawn almost resents her for it.

Dawn nods, swallowing against the dryness in her throat. "I'm fine," she says, though the words feel like they don't belong to her. "Just… tired."

Suzanne doesn't move, doesn't step into the room, as if unsure whether to cross the threshold. "You don't look fine, Dawn. You—"

The telephone rings on the nightstand. Suzanne's hand shakes as she answers it, her voice low, tight. "Hello?"

Dawn watches her sister's face as she listens to the voice on the other end of the line. Something shifts in Suzanne's expression, her eyes widening.

The silence stretches for a moment too long.

"Robert Phillips," Suzanne whispers.

Dawn's heart stops. Her breath catches in her throat.

"Robbie?" She tries to push herself up, but the room spins again, a tidal wave of dizziness crashing over her. "Suzanne, what happened? What is it?"

Suzanne hangs the phone back on its cradle. For a long time, she doesn't look up at Dawn.

"Robbie… he was… he was killed." Suzanne chokes on the words, like they're too heavy to say, too impossible to bear. "In combat. They came to your door, but you weren't home. That's why… that's why they called here."

The room goes dead silent, and for a moment, Dawn doesn't understand. It doesn't make sense. It can't be real.

But then the weight of the words settles over her, crushing her. Her body goes cold. Her stomach lurches, and she pulls her knees up to her chest, trying to hold herself together, but the devastation is too much. The cold emptiness of it settles deep in her bones, in her very core.

Robbie.

Her Robbie.

The man she was building a life with. The man she dreamed of having children with. The man she thought she was making this sacrifice for.

The thought that had kept her going through everything—the promise that she would finally give him what he wanted, what they both wanted—vanishes. *He's gone.*

Dawn's breath comes in jagged gasps as the tears finally break through, spilling down her cheeks. She doesn't try to stop them. She doesn't know how to stop them. The world feels impossibly distant, like she's watching it from underwater.

She wanted this. She wanted to be a mother, to build a family with Robbie. But now…

Now she's…

Alone.

Suzanne steps closer, murmuring, but Dawn can barely hear her over the roar of her own thoughts..

"What do I do now?" she whispers.

After a while, Suzanne goes outside to smoke. The hotel room is empty except for the hollow echo of Dawn's breath, deep and ragged. The walls seem to close in on her as she stares at her reflection in the mirror, her eyes wide, pupils dilated, skin pale. She barely recognizes herself.

Her body, once so full of promise, is failing. She can feel it—every painful pulse, every snap of skin, every shift inside her that shouldn't be there. The life growing within her feels wrong. It's an infection. It's tearing her apart.

Dawn's legs buckle beneath her, and she sinks to the edge of the bed. She clutches at her stomach, a deep, jagged pain slicing through her body. She gasps for breath, her skin slick with sweat. Her body trembles, holding pieces of a life—a dream—already shattered.

The baby. The… thing inside her, it's not the dream of motherhood. It's a curse. An unholy consequence of her need to feel complete. If she survives the birth—if she survives *this*—what's left? Her body will be a hollow shell, worn down by the toll of this nightmare. A reminder of all she's lost.

She presses her hands to her temples, trying to stop the thoughts, but they keep coming.

The dead fly from the windowsill flashes in her mind.

That's what she is now. That's what she's become. Trapped, struggling, *dry*—ultimately forgotten.

Was it worth it? Was it ever worth it?

The question hangs in the air, but the answer is already clear. It was never worth it. Not the sacrifice, the lies. She's been a fool, and now she'll pay the price.

Dawn presses her face into her hands, the tears falling faster now, but she doesn't wipe them away. She lets them fall, feeling each like a release. A *surrender*.

It takes her hours to stop crying. Dawn's fingers tremble as she holds the phone to her ear, staring at the wall. The silence closes in on her.

Her hand shakes as she punches in the number she had hoped she'd never need to dial. But here she is, desperate. Terrified.

The phone rings once. Twice. Three times.

Finally, she answers. "Dawn?" Nancy's voice is soft, but there's something beneath it—a certainty, a coolness that lifts the small hairs on Dawn's neck.

"I… I need to see you," Dawn says, her voice cracking. "I don't know what's happening. Something's wrong."

Nancy's silence stretches on the other end of the line. Dawn hears faint murmur of distant noise—voices, clinking silverware, the hum of a busy kitchen. Is Nancy answering from the restaurant? That doesn't make sense.

But nothing makes sense now.

"I told you, Dawn," Nancy finally says, her voice gentle, *maternal*. "I promised you this would work. You are well on your way."

"But..." Dawn cuts herself off, takes a steadying breath. "But something's wrong. Jo... Jo's dead. Melody's—Melody's dead, Nancy. And I—"

She chokes back a sob, pushing it down before it overtakes her. "I'm next."

There's a long silence, and Dawn fears Nancy has hung up on her, but then Nancy speaks again, her voice unwavering.

"Come meet me, Dawn. You've come this far. All I can offer you is the next step. Meet me at the restaurant. I will make you feel much better."

Dawn closes her eyes, tears slipping down her cheeks despite her best efforts to hold them back. She shouldn't trust Nancy, but she doesn't know what else to do. The world is unraveling around her, and all she wants—all she needs—is someone to tell her it will be okay. Even if that person is Nancy.

"Okay," she whispers, her voice hollow. "I'll be there."

The commotion of the Golden Bell hums softly around Dawn, its warm lighting and comforting atmosphere making the cold knot of dread in her stomach that much more pronounced.

She's done. She can't endure it anymore. Not the growing sickness, not the lies, not the hollow promises that kept her tethered to Nancy and this madness. The taste of death is bitter on her tongue, but it promises an end.

Nancy sits across from her, colder now, her presence more calculating. There's no sympathy left in her eyes—no warmth, no understanding.

"Dawn," Nancy says, her voice even, detached. "This isn't just about you anymore. I warned you before. There are consequences to turning back now. It's too late to undo what's been done."

Dawn's breath catches. There's nothing left to lose. "I don't care. Take it out. I can't live like this."

Nancy doesn't blink. "You should have listened." She stands, slow, deliberate. "But I'll give you what you want."

Dawn follows her through the restaurant into the kitchen. No one pays them any attention, so Dawn assumes Nancy has been here before. Nancy opens the door of what seems like a closet, but is actually a small storage room turned operating theater. The faint smell of antiseptic fills the air, mixed with ancient odor of moonshine, and Dawn's stomach lurches. This is where it ends. The sharp chill of the metal tables, the sterile lights overhead—they all blur together, a quiet, oppressive silence that deepens the fear rising in her chest.

Nancy works with a practiced precision. Dawn barely notices the first sting. The cold of Nancy's touch spreads through her, an unnatural chill that crawls under her skin. It doesn't hurt at first, just a pressure, a pull that feels wrong—like something inside her is being tugged out, something that should never leave.

But then it's worse. Much worse. Her insides contort, twist, and tear. Dawn can't breathe. She screams, but the cold air swallows it.

Nancy works in silence, detached.

The pain balloons inside Dawn until it explodes. Blood, hot and thick, pours from between her legs. The world blurs, and for a moment, she wonders if she's dreaming. If this is some twisted nightmare she can still wake up from.

Nancy's hands never falter. Her focus is complete. There's a cruelty to it, but also a strange, detached satisfaction. "This is what you wanted, isn't it?"

Dawn's chest heaves as she gasps for air, her body on fire. It's almost over. It's almost—

Oh.

But then, a flutter. It's subtle at first, an unnatural movement in the core of her being. It contorts her body as it moves, curling her legs up like the dead fly's.

Nancy's face looms above her. Her smile is sharp as ever, not sympathetic, but satisfied. Dawn sees it now—Nancy is pleased. She's *happy* with this outcome.

"Congratulations, Dawn. You did exactly what we needed."

Dawn's body gives out, but the flutter continues.

Lobby
2010

The Black Ledger
Patrick Tumblety

The doorman at the Hotel Ethel picks up a penny and holds it to the sky. His eyes widen, and his mouth opens to unleash a gasp as he reads the date.

"Find something good, Shelly?" shouts the doorman from the adjacent hotel, the Bartholomew, over the beeping horns and conversations of the busy San Francisco street.

"Nineteen-fifty-four. One of six I'm missing."

"What are the odds you'll ever collect them all?"

Shelly shakes his head in disbelief as he rolls the coin between his thumb and forefinger. Items he's missing are less likely to appear within his ten-by-ten-foot red concrete plot outside the Hotel Ethel as the years pass, or end up in the hotel's lost & found.

"You stand in one place long enough, everything comes back to you, eventually."

"Why don't you just go online?"

"There's no fun in that." He laughs. "It's the searching that makes the finding worth it."

"I'll take your word for it!" the other doorman shouts before a truck's horn drowns his voice.

A white limousine pulls up to the curb. Shelly drops the penny into the gold-rimmed breast pocket of his purple uniform and opens the door. Veiny feet in high heels step out as a hand reaches up for help. Shelly takes it and pulls the woman out of the vehicle.

"Thank you, my boy," Madam Sperry says with a cheery voice, raspy with age. Shelly smirks at her business suit, which she is pulling off despite her elder frame. Madam finds joy in adapting to changing fashions.

"It's always a pleasure." He lifts her hand to kiss it and cannot help but notice the blue veins on its back and the thin, pockmarked skin.

"It's time for my annual rejuvenation," she sighs, reading his mind.

"You're always perfect in my eyes," Shelly says.

"And you're always a kiss-ass," she scowls.

"That's what you pay me for." He steps to her side and lifts his elbow. She wraps her skinny arm around it so he can escort her to the door.

"Dare I ask the question, my boy?"

Shelly purses his lips and thinks carefully about the way he replies. "Tonight is the night, Madam. If you'll allow it, of course."

"What makes this year different than last year, or the year before last?" she chides.

Shelly does his best not to let her skepticism irk him. He owes his life to her, but she is anything but a benevolent soul. He opens one of the two glass doors leading into the hotel.

"I can take it from here," she says. "We have a new investor arriving soon who will be presented with an award at the ball tonight. I need you to ensure his stay is worth the money he paid."

"Of course, Madam." Shelly releases her arm. She takes a few steps and then turns around.

"What kind of monster would I be to save you from a prison just to put you in another? I will have no ill will towards you. Hell, I'll even wish you the most fulfilling life a single soul can earn. If you want to leave, you have my blessing."

Shelly wonders if that's true or if she's testing his loyalty, but does not dare to let that question show on his face. "I will forever be grateful for your hospitality," he says with a bow.

She stares at him without betraying any emotion or thought. "If you choose to leave, do so knowing that my hospitality will never again be offered." She turns away before he can think of a response to utter.

He closes the door and turns his face to the sun, waiting for the cold to leave his body. He has worked for Madam Sperry for fifty-five years, the gatekeeper for her hotel and its secrets. He is one of the select few who have witnessed her soul turn a darker shade over time. Not until recently did that sight begin to be bothersome.

What makes this year different?

The cold that seeps from her and the hotel takes longer to leave his body, and if he stays, he might never again feel warm.

A black limousine stops at the curb. Shelly stands straight and forces a smile as he approaches the vehicle and opens the door. A salt-and-pepper-haired man in a blue polo exits, followed by a younger woman in a skin-tight white dress and large, dark sunglasses. A daughter, he figures, until a young boy slides out, immersed in a portable gaming device, his thumbs wildly clicking its buttons.

"Good afternoon, sir." Shelly bows. "And welcome to the Hotel Ethel."

The man looks up at the breadth of the building. "I thought this place was supposed to be a hundred today."

"She is, sir. But she gets reworked every few years to look brand new."

"She can relate." The man thumbs at his female companion. He laughs and checks to see that his audience is laughing as well. Shelly offers a smile and nothing more.

In another time, he would have placated the man's misogyny with a hearty guffaw, eager to please any guest and not judge the unique personalities they carry. Enough time has passed to prove that the same handful of personalities show up at the door, rarely offering unique perspectives or experiences.

Meeting new people used to bring him excitement. The Ethel is known as a residence for the elite, the wealthy, and the influential. Being in those categories used to come with an air of worldliness, experience, and knowledge, but the quality of stories that guests carry has exponentially diminished.

He often wonders why and assumes that the change is due to technology and how easy communication has become. The smaller the world, the fewer opportunities for broadening experiences.

He used to meet adventurers who saw the most incredible sights, but now all he gets are conversations about in-flight movies and terrible food. Nowadays, the wealthier the person, the less time they have for adventure. Hard work used to mean hard play, but now it just means more work.

"My name is Shelby Petrovich, but guests call me Shelly. Please allow me to escort you to our check-in counter. I will send someone out to retrieve your belongings."

The family follows him through the doors and into the grand entranceway. A rotunda with an elaborate fountain of Dionysus, the Greek god of recreation, graces the center. Above it is a multi-layered gold chandelier that hangs from a dome ceiling.

Long rectangular desks surround the walls in segments, separated by walkways branching to other lobby areas, including a seating area with sofas and a fireplace. Colorful tapestries hang from the ceiling, and historical paintings and photographs of the hotel's most notable events and visitors cover the walls.

Amongst the decor and patrons, Shelly sees the outlines of other figures. Former visitors and victims of the hotel and its owners and patrons.

The Hotel Ethel is one of the oldest and most prestigious hotels on the West Coast, and its history is as infamous as it is famous.

Royalty from all walks of life have resided in the hotel for almost a century, either raving about the luxury at the end of their stay or not surviving by their checkout time.

A former President's mistress was found in the honeymoon suite, hacked to pieces after a weekend rendezvous. A mob hit inside an elevator during Prohibition. A ritualistic sacrifice on the roof to resurrect a Hollywood legend.

The stories are endless and continuous, but the hotel is never held accountable. The stories become rumors, then die, and the hotel keeps its five-star status.

Rumor has it that those with the authority to investigate such matters also benefit from the hotel's discretion. Discretion must be the only reason the Hotel Ethel has not been shut down. People are okay with corruption as long as their corruption is included.

These memories have always been just beyond his sight, never solidifying when he tries to concentrate on them, but lately, they are clearly in his vision, and the details of their forms are more defined.

What makes this year different?

He escorts the family around the fountain to the desk at the farthest wall. Behind it hangs the largest photograph in the room.

"The six women in the photo are the hotel's founders, along with every worker who built this magnificent place, dressed in their finest, at the opening ball on October thirteenth, nineteen-ten, exactly one hundred years ago tonight."

"I don't get it," the man says, his brow furrowing as he looks at the photograph. "This was taken a hundred years ago?"

Shelly smiles, delighted that the man will read it as polite instead of deceptive. "You are referring to Madam Sperry. This is her mother," he lies. In truth, she could be her great-great-grandmother or any of the Sperry lineage. "A spitting image, is it not?"

"I wouldn't have turned that down." He laughs again and slaps Shelly on his shoulder. If his wife is offended, she doesn't let it show. His son continues to mash buttons.

A woman of Middle Eastern descent stands from her chair behind the desk to greet the family. "Dr. Elliot Roach, I presume?" She holds out her hand for a shake. "I'm Adina."

The man's eyes alight, and his mouth opens. "Lovely to meet you." He twists her hand over and kisses the back. Adina feigns politeness. His wife continues to stand unbothered by her husband's actions.

"Would you like me to escort you to your room, Dr. Roach?" Shelly offers, hoping to pull the man from his lecherous gaze and his hold on the young woman's hand.

"No, Shelly, I'll take it from here," the man says, letting go of Adina's hand and taking his eyes from her slowly enough to make the movement awkward. "I'll see you around," he tells her, and his tone implies more than a salutation.

"Have a great stay," Adina's voice sings. She waits until the man rounds the corner with his family toward the elevator bay to lean on the desk and say, "Surgeon," with a mouth full of disdain.

Shelly leans on the desk and matches her inflection, "Jerk."

"You don't know the half of it." She reaches underneath the desk to pull out a black item and place it on top.

The cold returns to Shelly's body. Then, voices fill the lobby. The ghosts haunting his peripheral vision stand around him as clearly as if they are alive, speaking in a language that sounds like Latin but is accompanied by a guttural base that resonates from a place not found in the living realm.

Shelly doesn't know what a ghost has to be afraid of, but those semi-translucent eyes are full of terror. Perhaps it's the memory of how they became ghosts. If there is any evidence remaining of their untimely demise, it is documented inside that black ledger.

Shelly's fear for the young boy grips his heart, but he must word his question carefully or risk seeming too curious. "Dr. Roach earns a place in the ledger? What's his story?"

"Oh, Shelly," Adina says, rolling her eyes like he is a child asking for an extra dessert after dinner. "You know it's better not knowing. At least it's not the other ledger."

He lifts his hand to say, "Just curious, is all," in his aw-shucks doorman persona, and hopes that Adina doesn't notice that his hands are shaking. She's correct, at least it isn't Sperry's ledger. That one is hidden in a place he has yet to discover despite his many years living inside the hotel. Though the lines inscribed in it are few, the poor names that are added to that one... he is too terrified to imagine.

She opens the book and flips through the pages.

The unintelligible ghosts raise their voices in a crescendo.

He turns away from the desk and walks across the lobby to his outside post, keeping his eyes toward the marble floor as he passes through the cold veils of the dead.

In 1952, a group of Nazi soldiers smuggled the corpse of their former commander, Heinrich Heiden, out of Germany and sacrificed themselves in the basement of the Hotel Ethel to ensure he would carry their mission into the future.

As a product of the hotel and as one of its benefactors, Heinrich was allowed privileges within its walls. On a Friday in December of 2009, the commander arrived with a group of young men for a seminar about the legacy of the Nazi party, only to be sacrificed to the hotel to keep Heinrich young.

Shelly was not privy to this information, but his curiosity got the best of him when he saw a man arrive with a group of people half his age and leave without them two days later. That was the first time he read the black ledger. He has not been the same since.

Despite some of their darker dealings, the hotel and its owners do good things. The hotel hosts fundraisers for good causes and donates a percentage of earnings to progressive political parties and charities for San Francisco's underprivileged youth. Sometimes, questionable compromises need to be made to maintain the good deeds.

It is the ultimate life form that way. It takes away and provides without prejudice. At least, that is how he justified his compliance. Once he read the black ledger, he understood that compliance was just another word for ignorance.

No wonder Nazis hate books.

Shelly thinks about this as he irons his tuxedo. After his fortieth year in the hotel's service, when he first had the gumption to consider retiring, he had the suit custom-made for the annual ball. Purple wool with gold buttons to honor the Ethel. It was the biggest expense he ever made for himself.

Since his world is the hotel, from the food to his room, he's never needed to spend a dime. Most of his minimum wage goes to homeless shelters and charities around the city that the younger employees, like Adina, help him find over the internet.

A knock on his door, followed by Adina's voice as though the thought of her had conjured her to him. "It's me."

He reaches into his closet to grab a hotel robe to place over his pajamas before answering the door. Adina smiles at him, which is beautiful despite Shelly also being able to see the disfigured skin beneath the veneer. Her hands rest on the shoulders of the boy he had met earlier that day. He's still holding his gaming device, but his eyes are averted to the ceiling.

"Good evening, Shelly. This young man forgot his gaming charger at home."

"Ah," Shelly exclaims with excitement. "Come in, young man, and I'll see what I have."

Optimism seeps into the boy's eyes. Adina takes her hand from his shoulders as he follows Shelly into his room.

"I'll take him back to you when I've found what he needs," he tells Adina.

"Good luck." Her voice is a melody that echoes long after she closes the door.

"Let me see." Shelly holds out his hand for the device and then flips it around to find the charging port. He turns toward the desk to pull out a drawer full of cables. "I'm sure I have something that fits this gizmo. The lost comes to me to be found."

"Whoa," the boy says, looking around the room in amazement. "Is this all from the hotel?"

Bookshelves, curios, and shelving racks take up every inch of space, holding various objects without categorization. Jewelry boxes, books, stuffed dolls, compact mirrors, and makeup kits. Glued between them and across the ceiling are coins, paper money, and pictures in various formats and physical conditions from different ages.

The boy lifts a crystal ashtray from Shelly's desk and turns it over.

"That belonged to Sidney Jolson, one of the greatest jazzmen of the nineteenth century. A lifetime of smoking cigars gave him a deep vibrato. A bad habit, but the best artists sacrifice themselves for their art. Or so I hear."

"He left it here? Looks expensive."

"I collect memories that others leave behind," Shelly says, sifting through the cables.

"How long have you been here?" the boy asks.

"This will be my fifty-fifth year at the hotel, but I'm retiring tonight at the ball."

The boy is quiet, then says, "Dr. Elliot is fifty-five. You look like you're thirty."

Shelly winces. He has been so excited about helping the boy that he forgot to lie. "Good genes run in my family," he says.

"Is that you?" The boy points at a picture on the desk.

"That's me and my mother," he answers.

He pulls out a cord and compares its shape to the hole in the device. "It's a match!" He sits on the bed, plugs the charger into the wall, and the other end into the game. The outline of a battery with an electric bolt appears onscreen.

"That's awesome." The boy looks relieved as he sits next to Shelly. "Thanks!"

"My pleasure." He raises a hand, and the boy slaps him with a high-five.

"You have a tattoo?" the boy asks. Shelly is confused by the question until he realizes the cuff of his robe has dropped beyond his wrist to the numbers written on his forearm. His face flushes with heat, and he drops his arm to his lap.

"Have you learned about the Second World War in school?" he asks.

The boy thinks and then shakes his head.

"How old are you?" Shelly figures that if the boy is too young to know which year the war started, he most likely won't be able to do the math.

"Eleven."

"I was ten years old in that picture," he explains, pointing to the photograph on the desk. "It was the last day I saw my mother. The enemy kidnapped us and took us to a camp where they… would make us work for them. My mother bribed enough people to sneak me out so I could escape to the States. Fifteen years later, I met the owner of this hotel and have been living here ever since. Collecting all these things helps me stay in touch with the world."

"You never take a vacation?"

"I was always afraid to."

"Afraid of what?"

Shelly takes a moment to answer. A child should stay ignorant of the evils of the world until avoidance of it becomes impossible. "I was only in the camp for a week, but I saw horrible things. Evil things that people do to each other."

The boy's inquisitive eyes fill with sadness and turn toward the floor. Perhaps this boy has seen more than Shelly suspected. "Have you seen people do bad things?"

The boy shrugs.

"Is it your dad?"

"He's my mom's friend," the boy spits.

"I see," Shelly says. "Does he hurt you?"

The boy's reluctance to answer says more than words could.

"It's okay to tell someone," Shelly says, to which the boy remains silent.

"Did you know this hotel has magical powers?" Shelly asks.

The boy turns his face back toward him.

"It's true. I've seen some amazing things here. If you ask it for help, it just might answer."

The boy opens his mouth to speak, and then turns his gaze down again. "Will it take the man away?"

"I don't know, son, but you can ask."

"What if it doesn't answer?"

"If it doesn't answer you, I will. If you need some company, come see me. You can teach me how to use that little gizmo you're holding." Shelly leans over and unplugs the charger from the wall and then places it on the boy's lap.

"I can have this?" the boy says, surprised.

"Sure can," he says.

"What if you need it?"

"I doubt that. Besides, if you stand in one place long enough…" Shelly shuts his mouth, the implication of what he is about to say stings his heart and sends the dead cold back into his body. The history of this place, its nature, means that anything this boy has will most likely make its way back to him.

"Let's get you back to your mom," Shelly says. He escorts the boy out of the employee area and into the lobby, where ghosts that the boy can't see continue to linger with more clarity than Shelly is comfortable with seeing.

"Would you mind taking the boy back to his room?" he asks Adina as she shuffles papers at her desk. He indicates his evening dressing.

"Of course," Adina smiles.

His eyes see beyond her jovial facade to the burnt, damaged skin underneath, reminding him that Adina is another of the hotel's servants. If she steps beyond the grounds, her true face will be revealed. It keeps her compliant and loyal to its dark dealings, just as it keeps Shelly.

If that bothers her, she doesn't show it. She might even prefer this existence of servitude, as Shelly once did. The compromise he made with Madam Sperry, with the hotel, is worth its shelter from the pain and horror he experienced. He never expected to regret that decision, but the passage of time is another type of pain. As the years progress, the deeper regret seeps into his soul.

He hurries around the desk and pulls out the black ledger, shuffling through its pages until he reaches the last entry. The ghosts in the lobby once again stop their mingling and turn to stare at the book with terrified eyes.

He reads the last entry.

Dr. Elliot Roach. Written in red ink.

Each ink color is a code that employees learn after pledging their fealty to the hotel.

Black ink is required for all standard VIPs.

Green means they're paying to stay for longer than a month.

Blue means they're hiding, and staff are to play ignorant if questioned by authorities.

Purple means the client should not be disturbed for any reason, even by staff.

Red is reserved for the guests who need the hotel's services for one singular purpose.

Hotel Ethel never contains more life than on the day of its annual ball. This year is no exception, as over two hundred guests dressed to the nines pass by an equally adorned doorman.

"You could have taken the night off," he hears Madam Sperry say from the lobby. He keeps the door open against his back and turns toward her.

"This is the last opportunity I'll have, and I get to do it dressed in the finest, for the finest."

Once again, her expression does not hint at her thoughts. "We'll see," she says, and then turns to mingle with the crowd.

Yes, you will, he thinks, even though he supposes her to be correct. There is no reason he should leave the safety of the hotel to be out in a world that has only brought him loss and pain. If he is ready, he should be in the ballroom eating, drinking, and dancing. Not standing at the doors he has been haunting for over half of a century.

"Shelly!"

He turns toward the sidewalk and recognizes a middle-aged man in a brown suit and top hat. Bile rises from his stomach, and his hands shake. He is too frightened to respond.

"A pleasure as always, sir," the man says, tipping his hat and walking past him. As he crosses the threshold into the lobby, Shelly sees beyond his middle-aged face to the rotting flesh beneath.

The line outside the hotel dies. Shelly mingles with the guests until they move out of the lobby and toward the elevator bays or up the stairways leading to the third floor from the other lounges.

For an hour, he sits on the fountain's edge in front of the main desk and listens to the muffled orchestra through the lobby's ceiling, along with the partygoers' rhythmic stepping and joyful cheers.

He should walk through the ballroom doors, accept his award from Madam, leave the hotel, and let the rest of his life start spiraling toward its end. Instead, he sits and looks at the ever-shifting reality that is his home.

As the coldness of the dead seeps into him and the ethereal becomes commonplace in his existence, more details in the facade become clearer. The paintings show the scarring from the fire that nearly destroyed the hotel. Cracks appear in the walls from earthquakes that threatened to swallow the building back into Hell. Scribed in blood across the ceiling are the words "The Vampire of Hollywood lives," and he has several theories about who was bestowed such a title.

"Mr. Shelly?" A high-pitched voice calls his name from the hallway leading to the elevator bay. He squints beyond the veils of the dead to see the boy he had talked to earlier that night. The gaming device remains in his hands, still tethered to the white charging cord. The other end of it is wrapped around the boy's neck. His irises are bloodshot, and his skin is pale.

Shelly bounds forward and drops to his knees in front of the boy. "Son, what happened?" he asks while unwrapping the cord from the boy's neck.

"He hurt my mom," the boy replies, his eyes glazed over and emotionless, in shock.

"Get back here, David." Dr. Roach says as he appears from the elevator bay around the corner. He wears the hotel's purple robe with gold trim, dripping with blood that trails behind him on the white marble. A surgical scalpel pokes from his fist, its tip caked in dark viscera.

Shelly stands between the boy and the man.

"What are you doing?" Dr. Roach scowls and stops a few feet away. "Give him back to me and get all this cleaned up. I have a ceremony to attend."

The man's request dumbfounds Shelly.

"Isn't this what you people do?" The doctor meets Shelly's expression with equal incredulity.

The implication causes a surge of rage in Shelly. He turns around, picks up the boy, and hurries into the lobby.

"Hey!" the man screams and gives chase.

"What are you doing, Shelly?" Madam Sperry stands by the fountain, questioning him like he is a boy who just got caught with his hand in a cookie jar. The ghosts that surround her bow their heads in sorrow.

"I can't let him kill this boy."

"How is this time different than any other time you looked away?"

The question stings his heart, yet his thoughts return to the walking corpse in the brown suit.

"Heinrich Heiden," he says, and the words leaving his body feel like dropping a thousand-pound weight from his shoulders.

For the first time, Shelly witnesses Madam Sperry's face appear surprised. Then, it returns to a blank slate. "We make no compromises, Shelly. You know that."

Shelly's rage boils. "Neither do I. Not anymore." He walks past her and around the fountain.

"Aren't you going to stop him?" Dr. Roach cries. "Do you know how much…"

Shelly hears Madam sigh, followed by a deluge of liquid spilling across the floor.

He is almost at the door as she commands, "Shelly, you stop right there."

Since she is the only authority he has had since being taken away from his mother, he stops and turns around. The boy squeezes him harder, so he pats the boy's back and whispers, "It's going to be okay," even though he does not believe that to be true.

"You just cost the hotel a lot of money. It will want compensation." Terror contorts her face, as though she cares about his life or death. A flash of his mother comes to mind, crying as two French soldiers take him from her arms. He watched his mother collapse to her knees in sorrow, and then never saw her again.

Icy fingers grip him, and he is surprised that the sensation is borne from normal fear that would affect any person, not the chill of death that has been seeping into his soul.

"I'll take whatever is coming, but I'm not letting it get to this child." He turns and walks through the hotel doors, leaving Madam Sperry to cry over his fate.

"You're going to be okay," Shelly says as he exits the Ethel, not knowing if he is telling that to the boy or himself.

The first step he takes off the ten-by-ten red brick area outside the hotel, he starts to feel his body change. Muscles weaken. Skin sizzles. Throat burns. By the time he reaches the end of the street, his body has aged fifty-five years. He tries to place the boy down, but his grip does not loosen, so he kneels slowly and cradles the boy in his arms.

"Show me how to play that gizmo," he tells the boy in a strained, elderly voice, "until someone comes by to help."

The boy plays his game as Shelly waits for his borrowed time to expire.

Shelly closes the door behind a young couple and sees an object lying on the ground. He picks it up and turns it over. Had the couple dropped it?

He hadn't seen one like this in quite some time, maybe ten years, maybe more. They looked too young to have anything that needed something this old.

"Find something good, Shelly?" shouts the doorman from the adjacent hotel, the Bartholomew, over the beeping horns and conversations of the busy San Francisco street.

"I think I used to have one of these," he shouts.

"Maybe it's the same one," the other doorman laughs.

"I wouldn't be surprised. You stand in one place long enough, everything comes back to you, eventually."

A strange sensation overtakes him.

Since his resurrection, he doesn't feel much of anything other than the joy of meeting new people and collecting whatever items they leave behind. He looks through the glass doors and sees humans and spirits mingling in the lobby, but nothing out of the ordinary. He then looks up and down the street, having the eerie sensation that someone is watching.

He stares at the white cord in his hands. It's familiar, like something he saw in a dream he can't remember. Seeing it brings him another feeling he has not felt in a while, relief.

He shrugs and places the cord into the gold-lined pocket of his purple uniform. He'll remember one day.

Everything comes back to him, eventually.

Sub-Level 1 - Maintenance
1918

Boiler Room Hot
Jason Daughrity

Boiler room hot. Willy liked the way that sounded. Actually, Ol' Willy *loved* that particular saying. It had… what was the word? A lot of… a lotta connotation. That phrase really had a lot of *connotation*. Real meaning to it, that's what it was.

To Willy, those words both captured the atmosphere of the sub-basement that the big, rumbly boiler was in and added their own flavor to the type of heat in the room that he was all too familiar with. Boiler room hot. Yessuh. That's what it was.

You see, Ol' Willy loved it in there. He *loved* it. Loved the heat, the sounds, the boiler pipes creaking, the steam rushing through them, the hard work of keeping the boiler going day in and day out. The routine of it all; the familiarity of the place. The importance of it. Keeping hot water flowing through the pipes was the lifeblood of ol' Ethel.

He loved all of it. It wasn't so much that he had been working and sweating in the boiler room of the beautiful Hotel Ethel since it was built eight years ago so much as a special kind of heat that just seemed natural. And… and just *right* to him.

Willy looked around the boiler room and took it all in. Just as it always was, which suited him right down to the ground. The big, darkened room had a *life* to it. Yeah, it was dimly lit. A sub-basement that was always all the time loud and soggy, humid and HOT.

The yellow-orange glow coming through the door grate of the furnace at the front of the boiler put out the only light besides his lantern on the desk in the corner. But it was enough to see around the room, once you got used to it.

His homespun cotton shirt clung to his skin, soaked with sweat, some of which dripped from his forehead in a steady stream down both sides of his head. He had to take his shirt or his newsboy hat off every so often and wring out all the perspiration they accumulated when he was working the long hours required. He was a regular soaker, he was.

Not one of them plantation boys back east, but he worked damn hard enough. Hard work, tending the fires of the furnace, shoveling coal, portin' it around town and patching the pipes if they had too many leaks.

The steam had some of the pipes red hot, pipin' hot, coming from the central furnace of the boiler and going out to the walls, then up many floors. There were small jets of steam from some of the pipes, heating up the reservoirs of water for the guests to use throughout this somewhat-latest addition to the San Francisco skyline.

THAT had seen enough new buildings go up in the last few years that the Ethel was ascending into adulthood before his very eyes. He swore he'd seen the damn place grow another story or two since he'd been workin' there.

The pipes were coming out at all angles from the central boiler furnace, looking like nothing so much as a gargantuan black spider with its legs spread all around the room and one glaring eye in the middle of its squat, bulbous body. A demon's eye that was akin to the entrance of hell, he reckoned, being the mouth of the furnace like it was.

The heat was intimately intense. A living thing. It permeated the environment Willy was in. It cooked the air that he breathed. But he didn't pay it no mind nor heed. That's just how it was in the boiler room. Didn't bother him none.

No, not Ol' Willy. He had been working hard his whole life and had got hired on here at the Ethel a little bit before it opened back in 1910.

Eight long years he had been carting coal from the railroad along the foggy, early morning San Francisco streets, dumping it in the chute hole in the alley and watching the black chunks of coal flow down to the bin on the inside sub-basement wall, then going inside and shoveling it into the open door of the furnace.

All to make sure that the upper crust folk staying above visitin' the city had hot baths and shaving water a-plenty. He was a regular institution, he was. That's what his pa used to say. If someone was around a place long enough, and worked long enough there, they were a regular institution.

Ol' Willy's pa had come into California back in 1849 during the Gold Rush after they found a few nuggets of the yellow metal at Sutter's Mill. That news got spilt by some worker at the mill and it spread like wildfire across the whole damn world, seemed like.

The Rush was incredible, according to his pa. He had lived through it. Thousands and thousands of hopeful immigrants, prospectors and settlers, poor sharecroppers and rich businessmen alike, had descended on San Francisco and turned a simple mining town into the biggest boomtown ever in the space of a few months.

Prospectors would show up in droves, coming by land or sea to the Bay Area used as a base camp for most, then make their way up into the hills, panning for gold, fighting off bandits and Injuns and even Army deserters and other prospectors to try and find the mother lode.

The city exploded with people, with those that came to seek their fortunes rubbing elbows with Chinamen, prostitutes, sailors, porters, and merchants along with their families, coming there to support those going into *them thar hills*, with the more savvy of them setting up shops and stables and essentially building a massive port and economy overnight. The unwashed masses had laid claim to the land around San Franciso and brought every conceivable way of life with them.

Jason Daughrity

It was a regular sophisticated city now. He remembered when it weren't nothin' but a growing Bay town and port getting bigger by the day. Now it was awful tony and posh. He was still too young to have the rough memories his father had of the Gold Rush in '49, but he grew up with the resulting economic boom in the area and all the glorious traffic and trade that people from across the world brought with them.

Ol' Willy had grown up with all of their loves, their languages, their cussing, their smells.

That most of all. The smells of the city and the food that people cooked. The curry, the rice, the peppers, the vegetables and soups, meats and baked goods, the sharp smell of many kitchens cooking on a hot Bay night. They mingled on the air, scents and aromas mixing in the wind like a tempestuous stew.

Their cultures, their *lives* were in those smells, along with tastes and sounds imprinted on Willy's brain while growing up in the last forty years of the 1800s and the past eighteen in the new century.

He could recognize any part of the city with his eyes closed based on the smells alone. San Francisco was a hodgepodge of all the peoples of the world, it was.

So much went on and through the city daily. The imports of other lands and continents shipped in on the great merchant vessels, or overland from the surrounding states, with the latest fashions or furniture sold off a wagon fresh from the docks or stables. You could catch the latest European opera at the Civic Auditorium or get a cheap seat at a nickelodeon down a side street on any given night.

And the smell of sourdough bread, the specialty of San Francisco, was always on the air. It saturated the area, mixing with all the smells of the city and all the different kinds of people. There were as many variations of sourdough bread as there were people that made it.

They had come from their countries and their cities, moving to the Bay Area wearing a jar with their sourdough starters, some generations old, around their necks or on their belts. The chewy, crusty bread was a regular institution, just like Ol' Willy himself.

Willy was fifty-eight, Irish on his pa's side and a mix of Italian on his ma's, God rest her. She died from dysentery when he was but a toddler, but at least she went real fast.

His pa had come with his first wife and their children, two older girls named Maddie and Lisbeth, during the '49 Gold Rush, and after his first wife and the baby had died during her third labor, his pa met Willy's Italian mother at the docks one day and his brother Andrew and him the youngest had come along not too long after.

After his ma's death, his pa hadn't remarried anything but the drink. It took him in 1872. The two oldest girls took to raising Willy and Andrew, until they got on with different families as scullery maids and died as old biddies.

His brother had died about ten years ago after a wagon he was driving had overturned. So, it weren't nothin' but Willy in the world. He didn't have nothin' or nobody and so applied himself diligently to his work.

Willy was close to six feet tall and lanky, with sinewy arms and shoulders, corded muscles bunching and stretching from shoveling coal all day. He could work all day and night if he had to. His leathery skin was permanently marked with black specks from working with the coal for hours on end, and frequently sweat trails would mark small pathways down his arms and legs through the coal dust.

Willy didn't have a hair on his head and always wore an old newsboy hat to cover up that fact. His beard was grey and brown and hung down to the middle of his chest, somewhat scrawny and thin like the man that wore it.

He was stooped from a long life of labor but still had a strong back. None of the young bucks down at the port bars could arm-wrestle him and win very often. He'd have to be deep in the drink for that to happen.

Willy always wore that newsboy hat, even when down in the boiler room hot, to help with the perspiration that seemed to be perpetually pouring down the sides of his head. The hat stunk of old sweat, but it kept the stinging stuff out of his eyes at least. It had been his pa's, and he'd worn it ever since it had come to him from his dead pa, when Willy was a wiry and scarecrow-thin lad of twelve.

His cotton shirt and pants, held in place with suspenders, were always blackened with coal dust and wet, so he kept a bucket with water in it close to the door of the boiler room to dump over himself whenever he was done at night.

He'd finish his days around an hour or two before midnight, with the furnace banked and ready for more coal early the next morning. He didn't have many days off but that didn't hurt his feelings none.

Sometimes they'd send down Curtis the bellhop to shovel and give him a day to himself, so he'd walk around and look at all the people and new worksites and scaffolding popping up around the city. He'd visit Chinatown with all its myriad scents and sights, then go down to the port to look at the big ships coming in or berthed at the docks.

Ol' Willy liked to watch all the different kinds of people that came to the city seeking their fortune, and he liked to drink with the sailors down at the port.

Most nights he'd take his pay and go out to one of the bars down that way. He'd stop off in the little room he maintained next to the boiler room, clean up a bit, and then head down the hills of the city for a drink or two, drying as he walked.

Sailors coming off the many merchant and military vessels in the Bay would always make the bars a rowdy place, with hootin' and hollerin' and catcalls filling the air, laughter and jokes and the occasional bar fight over a woman or imagined or real insult livening up the place a little bit.

Ol' Willy would go down to one of his favorite watering holes and spend a couple of hours playing poker or backgammon, or maybe a faro game if he was feelin' lucky.

Most times, though, he would sit at the bar and talk with whomever was sitting next to him, about whatever was going on in the city at the time. The main topic of conversation these days was war and the outbreak of sickness in the city.

It seemed that all anyone talked about these days was the goddamn Spanish Flu. In fact, the previous night, when Willy was at the Maidenhead, most of the patrons had on some kind of cloth mask over their faces hoping for some protection from the highly contagious disease.

San Francisco was in the middle of a pandemic in 1918, and the city governors had put up notices and sent around town criers and constables enforcing a mask ordinance. It was supposed to prevent the spread of the Spanish Flu but didn't work out so well, and quite a few people had died of the disease in the last few months. You could say it was on everyone's mind.

Willy walked over to the door of the boiler room and picked up his bucket of rainwater next to the exit. He dumped it over his head to help wash off the sweat and most of the coal dust, then went out the door and into his little room on the right.

He didn't have much in the room in the way of personal possessions; just a cot and a locker for what little clothes he owned. There was a chest at the end of the cot with some odds and ends he had gathered over the years and saved from his pa and sisters, and a small mirror and washbasin beside the bed on a stool.

He would go outside to the water closet whenever he needed to and would go bathe in one of the servants' restrooms in the hotel once or twice a month to get the worst of the stink off.

The soap the servants used wasn't like the fancy French stuff they used upstairs. It was coarse and would sting a little bit from the scrubbing. But Willy didn't mind. It got him clean.

But not tonight.

Tonight was going to be one of *them* nights. He was in one of his moods. He didn't do it often, but he would spend all day feeding the flames of the boiler just thinking about things. His life, his pa, his ma (what little bit of memory he had of her), his brother and sisters, and growing up in this city. He'd remember all the good things, the good times with family. But there was always a dark cloud of bad stuff on the edges.

He'd feed it all into the flames.

Every good meal around a fire, every hug from his ma when he was not even three years old, every prank by his brother and him on his sisters inevitably ending in fits of laughter from all involved.

But also, every atrocity committed against him and his family by other prospectors and "native-borns," fights against local gangs and Chinese and even the Mexicans that came up from the south. He was a mix of Irish and Italian, and people didn't like that.

He'd think about all the bad crimes in the city and gang beatings, all the stench of hate that accompanied the sweet aromas of food and sourdough bread in the festering city that he loved.

All his memories would go into the licking, cleansing flames of the boiler. He would lose himself in his work; the hypnotic, chaotic dancing of the fire and the steady grating slide of his shovel into the pile of coal, lift, shovel it into the boiler mouth, repeat.

It was his ritual, his *religion*. If he was an institution, then being boiler room hot and doing the hard work was his sermon. His congregation was so many lumps of coal, which in Willy's opinion weren't too far off from what was in the churches these days anyhow.

The thoughts and the flames mixed like the scents on the air and created within Willy a purpose, a connotation if you will, that would build up and build up until he had one of those nights and had to get it out of his system.

It was his therapy, his *release* for all that he did and had been put through. His pa dying from the drink, stinking so bad and feverish and sweating gin. His brother crushed by a wagon he was driving that overturned while going too fast, his head split wide open, his brains scattered all across the cobblestone street for the passing city folk to gawk at.

His ma, weak and pale and the bedding she was laying on covered in the bloody flux as she took her last breaths (from what little he could remember). His sisters passed and no one even blinked an eye that they were gone. Him having to work so damn hard his entire life and never amountin' to nothin'.

Being harassed and bullied for being an Irish and Italian mutt, and never really fitting in with any of the cultural groups in the city had taken a long, hard toll on Willy. His back was knotted up with a lot more than just the hard coal shoveling he did every day.

It was about a half hour after midnight as Willy was walking down the hilly streets to the Maidenhead. He knew he wasn't going to drink that much tonight but needed the routine to help calm his nerves.

He took long strides going downhill until he got to the rowdy port bar, lights blazing through the windows at the front and the salty spray of ocean water in the air.

Willy poked his head inside the bar and took stock. Sailors and dock workers, whores and scullery maids, soldiers and farmers and prospectors were all inside the bar, with music from a local band (a hand-painted sign saying *Frisco's Incredible Dixieland Originals featuring Sidney Jolsen!* was propped up in front of them) filling the night air with the occasional off-note, that lead singer wailing his head off. Laughter and yelling filled the rest of the night with all the rest of the normal bar sounds. It was perfect. Willy stepped inside.

He walked up to the dirty bar and sat down on a stool toward the end. He pulled out a few coins and put them on the bar, and Rufus the fat old barkeep perked up at the sound and came down to get Willy's drink order.

Rufus never bothered to stay and talk, or memorize drink orders, but that suited Willy just fine. Kept hisself to hisself, his pa would say. He liked Rufus but never really talked to him. Willy settled down to drink and looked around the bar.

It was the usual type of ruckus. Whores were sitting on the laps of sailors and Marines returned from the war overseas, their bawdry goods spilling out of tight corsets, and cheap perfume mixed with the smell of sweat and beer.

Merchant mariners and other San Francisco natives were drinking in groups and yelling over each other, rowdy laughter and cries filling the room. Porters were getting drunk at the bar, big men smelling of fish and salt and every smell in between. There were even a few uppity types, in suits and ties, chatting and drinking by the fire in the hearth.

Masks were in evidence everywhere, pulled aside to quaff thin beer or covering the faces of sailors negotiating prices with a lady of the night, oil light and firelight from the hearth glittering in their eyes, husky breathing to make their chests heave to spice up the barter.

Willy loved all the sounds in the bar. It wasn't just noise; it was tinny and thin, loud and boisterous and sweet to his ears. Willy looked around for someone that was close to passing out from drinking.

He found a young sailor, slumped and head nodding, at the other end of the bar. It looked like he had been drinking all evening with beer and some vomit sloshed down the front of his white uniform. Willy noticed that that was none too clean to begin with. If the man had friends, they had left him to sleep it off at the bar and gone on without him. Perfect.

Willy took his drink and went over to a table right next to the dozing drunkard. He didn't look at the sailor but watched the room and kept hisself to hisself. He needed to drink a few more and wait until the right time of the night, which was fine by him. He quickly quaffed the thin beer and called for another from Rufus.

A few hours and about six beers later, Ol' Willy figured it was about time. People were starting to pass out around the bar, and Rufus usually just let them sleep it off where they fell. Most of the patrons were starting to leave, however.

When no one was watching, Willy got up from his small table and went over to the still-dozing sailor. Willy put a hand on his shoulder and shook him until the sailor's half-lidded eyes opened, reddened with drink and smoke and in a daze.

The sailor had sandy blond hair and wasn't too big or tall, so Willy reached down and picked him up by putting his hands underneath the shoulders of the sailor and heaving him up onto his feet. Willy looked around. No one was paying him any mind.

"Let's get you back to your berthing, sailor. What ship are you stationed on?" said Willy.

The sailor mumbled something unintelligible and drooled down his neckerchief onto his dress whites.

"Alright then," said Willy. "Let's get you back to it."

Willy pulled the sailor's arm across his shoulders and helped the stumbling seaman navigate through the tables and other passed-out patrons in the bar until they made it through the door and into the salty night air.

Willy breathed deep. This was the hard part of the night. But he was tough and wiry, and he could do it. They started walking, not toward the docks but back the way Willy had originally come, toward ol' Ethel. It meant going up hills and switch-backed roads, and over some slick cobblestone, but Willy was strong and steady holding up the inebriated man.

A light rain began to fall.

As they walked, with the sailor barely conscious, Willy talked. "I grew up here, in the city. Weren't much back then. You would never even recognize it, back how it was when I was a young'n. So much has changed. And not all of it for the better.

"That tall building there? It was built a few years back and I think only twenty men or so died building it, so that was somethin'. Usually, it's a lot worse. You smell that? That's a bakers shop around the corner that's got some of the best sourdough bread you've ever had the pleasure of eatin', and that's sayin' somethin' around here. Watch yer step there, buddy."

The last was said as the sailor slipped on the wet cobblestones of the street. Willy kept up his string-of-consciousness talking but the drunk sailor obviously wasn't listening at all.

Ol' Willy guided the inebriated man up the roads toward the Ethel until they got even with an alley a few blocks away from the hotel. Willy stopped for a moment to catch his breath and set the sailor down against the wall, where his head slumped forward and drool mixed with the rain coming down his face.

Willy stood there and looked the man over and liked what he saw. "You'll do just fine," he said into the wet night air.

Willy looked around the street and up in the windows but didn't see anyone or anything passing by this late at night and in this weather.

He stepped over to the sailor and pulled him away from the wall a little bit by his shoulders, then turned him and hooked his hands under the almost comatose man's arms from behind and stepped back into the alley, dragging the seaman's heels over the cobblestone.

It couldn't have been a more perfect setup, his best catch since he started doing this ritual every so often a few years back. Willy and the young man disappeared into the darkness of the alley, the patter of rainfall masking all sounds.

Willy dragged the sailor several feet in until they got to a darker lump in the night, parked against the wall of the building about fifteen feet inside the alley. Willy bumped against the waist-high object, and it rocked back on squeaky wheels, with some shifting of the coal inside it adding whispers of their own to the night air.

It was his coal cart, still in the exact location he had left it earlier in the evening, with coal dust and rainwater mixing on the bottom.

Willy stopped and dropped the sailor's arms, with him propped up against the cart and nodding off again. Willy looked at him in the dim light of the moon for a few moments, then stretched his lanky arms overhead, popping his knuckles and yawning. He stretched his back and squeezed his hands into fists, then stood shaking them out.

He looked down at the drunk sailor, rain causing the man's sandy blond hair to droop and the water running down his face. Willy breathed in a few quick, deep breaths and closed his eyes for just a moment.

Then Willy reached down and picked up the large brick that had been propping up the wheel of the cart to keep it in place, pulled his arm back and struck the sailor as hard as he could on the side of the head with the makeshift weapon.

The sick crunch and squelch of meat never meant to see the light of day was the last thing the sailor heard, as he crumpled with only a slight grunt and release of breath making an *oomph* sound, and fell down to the ground beside the cart.

The man's brains, chunks of skull and skin and lifeblood poured out of the ruin that used to be the side of his face, and the sailor knew no more.

Willy dropped the bloody brick into the cart and stepped back, his face looking to the sky, eyes closed and leaking tears that mixed with rain. He pulled off his newsboy cap and wrung it in his hands, letting the rain pour on his face and wash away all sin. Retribution was his, this night.

Then it was time for the cleanup.

Willy put his hat back on and reached down and again hooked his hands under the shoulders of the body, heaved up and got the sailor half into the coal cart, careful not to let any of the man's fluids get onto his clothing. He knew that he would have a hard time explaining that to the ladies that did the laundry at the hotel, when they washed his meager belongings while he bathed in the servant's bath. Ol' Willy refocused on his task.

Willy reached down and picked up the unfortunate sailor's legs and hefted them into the cart, folding the man in half. He made sure all the parts of his victim were in the cart, then went around to the back where a pile of coal and his shovel were waiting to cover up his crime. He started shoveling coal into the cart on top of the dead man.

When he finished, he knew that there was still coal dust and blood and brains on the ground that could be pretty incriminating, so he took the bucket he had staged next to the cart as well, stepped to the mouth of the alley, dunked it into a rainwater barrel there and came back and sloshed it all down in the alley floor.

The gore wasn't too noticeable in the dim light of the moon and with the rain washing away the evidence of his crime out into the gutters and sewers along with the rest of the offal of the city, Willy felt pretty confident no one would notice that anything bad happened here. Except one more smell to add to everything else, he reckoned.

Willy put the shovel into the hooks on the side of his handcart like he always did, put his hands on the handles, and walked out of the alley and into the wet street, the scene of his damnation already behind him and being forgotten.

He made his way to the side street of the Hotel Ethel and opened up the coal chute, then dumped his load with its unwilling and uncaring addition down the chute and into the sub-basement. The body and the coal fell down through the chute with a large thump and the tak-tak-tak of all the coal falling down around him.

Willy spent a few moments with his bucket and some nearby rainwater cleaning out the bottom of the cart but knew you couldn't see much with the coal dust in the bottom soaking everything up.

He was cautious anyway.

He had never been caught nor had there even been a rumor about what he was doing, the tricks he was pulling with the cart and coal, and he didn't want to take chances. This man's shipmates would probably think that he'd run off with some port whore, which happened all the time with these guys coming back from the war.

Jason Daughrity

Willy put the cart, shovel, and bucket into the small shed off to the side and went through the side door of the hotel and down into the boiler room. It was still hot inside and dried his wet skin and clothing quickly in the dim glow from the boiler gate. He stepped over to the coal chute.

Willy looked at the body of the young sailor that had fallen haphazardly into the chute amongst the lumps of coal. The coal dust had mushed into the gaping ruin left of the man's head and soaked up most of the blood, which was fine by Willy.

He pulled the young man out of the bin and put him down onto a spare piece of canvas he had set down on the floor for this purpose. It was time for the final part of his cleansing ritual.

Ol' Willy knew, deep down, that this was the only way to atone for what was done to him and his growing up. All his tension, his stress, and his hatred for those awful memories he had, he fed into the fire. Every beating, every terrible circumstance, every horrible smell was burned away by the dancing flames.

This was owed him by God, this chance at retribution.

But the fires always seemed to need something more. Something tangible. He had to do something terrible and satiate the fires of the boiler.

So, a few years prior to this night, he had found a dead body (likely from some illness) in that same alleyway while going to get his early morning load of coal, seized the opportunity, and brought the body back to the boiler room, where he promptly fed it into the flames.

The release of emotion and his grudge toward all this awfulness around him had been instantly sated. He couldn't believe how cathartic it was to feed the flames, and decided that was what he needed to do from now on when things got too bad.

So, Willy had willingly become a murderer.

Oh, it wasn't so bad as all it was made out to be. Most of these people would never be missed, or they were drunkards that never even felt the killing blow. Doing them a service, really.

A lot of people were dying from the Spanish Flu, or in fights or accidents or some other crazy way here in the west, so it was a grace really, killing them quickly.

And the boiler was always hungry.

The familiar sensation of catharsis began to sweep over Willy. It was tangible, and he could feel the tingling in his fingers and toes as a wave of release started. He knew it would only finish when he fed the beast.

So, he used a long poker with its hooked end and opened up the boiler fire gate. The blast of heat felt like an oven being opened to check on sourdough bread, and Willy breathed it in. Boiler room hot. He loved it.

Willy had had a rough time at first, trying to figure out the best way to put his bodies into the boiler, but after a few singed arms and hands had prompted him to stay far away from the heated metal, he figured out a way.

He had run a chain and pulley up into the rafters and, using a spare piece of canvas with holes cut into it, rigged a system to lift a body up and get them close enough to the boiler door grate and start sliding the body in.

It was tricky, but he could generally slide the body in far enough that with a good push, it wouldn't take the canvas with it and the body would slide right in.

The smell was pretty potent, kind of like burned pork, but it was late enough at night and in an area where few enough people came to that he felt reasonably safe from prying eyes.

Willy had taken the canvas out of storage and set it on the floor in front of the boiler before he had left to the bar.

He used this method now, pulling the young sailor's body over to the canvas and getting it in place with the head and shoulders sticking out past it, then folding the ends over like he was wrapping up a body to be buried at sea.

Then, he was hooking the chains to the canvas and using the pulley to lift the body up, and it was just a simple matter of moving the body close to the boiler, slide the head and shoulders of the young man into the open furnace mouth, rest the body on the lip of the grate, catch his breath, and then, with a big hard push, slide the body out of the canvas and into the mouth of hell.

Willy lost his balance a little bit and struck the side of the open grate mouth, singing his left upper arm, but it wasn't too bad. He stumbled back and watched the body start to burn.

The smell was intense, and the body burned fast in the incredible heat. That smell.

Human meat had a sweet kind of smell that he never really got used to. He had heard it described as being called "long pork" by some of the sailors down at the bar, regaling those in attendance with tales of meeting Marquesan tribesmen in their travels, cannibals known for eating the bodies of their enemies.

The uniform crisped and shriveled, the hair and skin started to burn away and then muscle and fat and bone. Willy used his hooked tool to reach over and close the grate.

Suddenly, a wave of *release* burst over Willy, something akin to a fancy lady's fingernails lightly brushing over his bald pate but all over his body. The feeling sent shivers down his spine and his breath came in ragged gasps. He bent over to exhale deeply with a great woosh of air coming out of his lungs.

It was done and all was right in the world.

Willy dropped to his knees on the dusty floor near the boiler, hands balled into fists on the side of his face, eyes squeezed shut and tears streaming out, matching the sweat trails tonight's work had made in the never-ending coal dust that coated his face. His body shook and shuddered, but he never opened his eyes.

This was the tenth time that he had done this, the ninth time that he took matters into his own hands and killed. He *needed* this. This was the culmination of his sermon, with splashes of blood on his congregation demanding that they too be thrown into the cleansing fires of the boiler.

He opened his eyes and looked into the grate door that he had closed with his hooked tool, watching the thing that was once a man burn to cinders and ash, and knew it wouldn't take long to burn away all evidence of his crime.

Willy breathed it in and reveled in it. He had done it. He had gotten all the rotten shit of his life out of his soul with this one despicable act and knew he had gotten away with it. He was euphoric and somewhat dazed but stayed kneeling on the floor.

He had worked. He had murdered. He had gotten rid of all evidence and knew that he would continue to do this into the future, and he would feel amazing afterward until all of life caught back up with him, at which point he would just repeat the cycle over again.

After all, there were always plenty of sailors and sinners who would never be missed in a bustling port as big as San Francisco.

He looked around one last time, didn't see anything else that could incriminate him and what he had done tonight, and went to lay down in his cot, mind clear and conscience clean.

He had done what he needed to do.

Willy woke up with a start, in a dim orange glow and darkness around it. He didn't know if it was still night or day, and his mind was all fuzzy. He knew he had lain in his cot for a while thinking about everything he had done during the night, and finally drifted off to sleep.

He had felt good before going to bed, but that hadn't been what had woken him up. No, he had come awake after hearing chains rattling right over him.

Wait. *Dim orange glow*?

Willy shook off his tiredness and tried to rouse and realized that he couldn't move his arms or his legs. In fact, he could only move his head.

He looked around him with wide eyes and realized that he wasn't in the little room next to the boiler room, in his cot. Instead, he was back in the boiler room somehow and he couldn't move his arms and legs. He was wrapped in something.

Oh God. He was wrapped in the canvas that he had used to move the sailor's body. What's more, the chains from the pulley above were also wrapped around Willy, binding him tight. What the hell was going on? How did he get in here, and how the hell did he get wrapped in the canvas? Was he sleepwalking? Was someone playing a prank on him?

Then, he saw them. There were shapes, human-sized shadows all around him and somehow he knew that it was *they* that had wrapped him in the canvas, with the chains wrapped around *him*.

"What the FUCK is going on???" Willy screamed.

His eyes adjusted to the glow coming from the grate of the boiler, and he saw what the shadows were. And he couldn't believe his eyes.

They were… ghosts.

They HAD to be. They were outlines of people, and most of them were wearing sailor uniforms. They were bloody and had smashed-in holes in their heads, with blood and other ghostly fluids dripping down on to the uniforms they wore.

Oh God. He recognized them. He goddamn recognized them. They were the shapes and outlines of the people that he had killed each and every one of his retribution nights.

He recognized the older sailor from a year before, his throat slit with Willy's knife and blood soaking the front of his dress blue uniform.

He saw the young man from earlier tonight, his head bashed in with a brick, standing right next to him.

He could see all this because Willy was suspended in the air, right around waist height for all the ghosts in the room. Right where he had lifted the body of the younger sailor earlier, whose ghost was standing close by the boiler.

Willy sucked in a breath to scream.

And promptly let it out with a guttural "taa-huuuuh" as he saw what was lifting him into the air. *The boiler had come alive*. IT WAS FUCKING ALIVE.

The squat body was up off the floor, and a pipe had moved to pull open the grate cover of the furnace. The open grate of the boiler mouth was just in front of him, and he saw that other pipes had come away from the walls and floor and ceiling and were supporting the boiler like some gigantic chitinous beetle or, no… it was like a huge, bulbous *spider*.

The boiler creature had the pipes pulled from the walls, bits of concrete and wood still attached to the ends, angled down and supporting its fat body off the floor exactly the way a spider would.

The insane nightmare was using several pipes, supernaturally moving in ways that Willy couldn't understand, horribly jointed and creaking, pulling the chains of the pulley and heaving him into the air.

Willy's blood turned cold, and he released his piss into his pants; the stink of his sweat and the coal and blood from the ghosts was all around him.

Willy screamed and screamed and screamed.

The ghost of the boy that Willy had just killed came up to him and leaned down close.

In a deathly whisper that Willy could barely hear, it said, "You bastard. You goddamn piece of shit. I had the rest of my life ahead of me. I was celebrating coming back and surviving the war, and you took all that away from me. You took that from all of us. You fed us into the boiler; you took our lives to feed your fucking sick habit. Well, welcome to our hell, you son of a bitch. We're all in the boiler now."

The ghost sailor chuckled and stepped back.

Willy began to shiver uncontrollably. His eyes bugged out, and his breath came in faster and faster through his flared nostrils and gritted teeth. The stench of sulfur filled his nose, and he saw the boiler spider pulling his chains to draw him closer and closer to the gaping, fiery maw of the furnace.

Willy started thrashing in his canvas shroud, rattling the chains and causing his newsboy hat to come off his bald pate and fall to the floor.

The pipes were moving Willy closer to the furnace opening. The heat was unbearable; he felt the skin on his bald pate start to redden and blister, then deeper searing pain as he got closer. The top of his head was only a few inches from the open grate and the heat made his eyes water and he felt his bowels unclench as he screamed even louder.

Surely, surely someone would hear his screams and come to help him. Someone would come pull him from this nightmare. Someone would come to save him. This wasn't going to happen. This wasn't how Ol' Willy ended. Not bad like this, like his brother, his pa and ma and family. Willy was supposed to pass on quietly with all his sins burned away! Surely, surely someone would hear him and come rescue him!

No one did.

Ol' Willy's screams cut off in the middle of his loudest one as his entire head disappeared into the fiery hell of the open grate. A hissing gurgle replaced it, and Willy's body shook uncontrollably as a seizure took hold.

His juices started to boil, and his skin started to burn away from his face. He felt his eyeballs pop and melt into his skull.

The rest of his body followed, swallowed into the flaming belly of the unnatural beast, until the swinging grate door slammed close after his feet went in, with a loud and resounding *thud*.

Ol' Willy, who had been an institution at the Ethel, was gone.

One by one, the ten ghosts standing in the boiler room winked out of existence, and the boiler settled back down to the floor, the pipes moving back to their original locations, plaster and concrete and wood sealing them in place like nothing had ever happened.

"Willy? You down here, man?" called Curtis the bellhop as he came into the boiler room. "Where you at, old man?"

Curtis looked around the room and didn't see the old coal stoker. That was odd. Ol' Willy was always down here and hadn't missed a day in all the time that Curtis worked at the hotel. He didn't even go off very far whenever he got a day off and Curtis had to shovel coal in his place.

Curtis didn't like it very much down in the hot and dark room, and frankly, the boiler was kinda scary if you got to thinking about it too much.

Curtis looked around the room but didn't see anything out of the ordinary. The room that Willy lived in was untouched, and the handcart and shovel and bucket were up in the little shed.

There was plenty of coal in the bin, meaning that Willy had gotten up early to go get his normal load from the boxcar warehouse he always got it from, but of Willy himself there was no sign.

If he would have bothered looking closer, he would have maybe noticed the old newsboy cap on the ground, stuck part way underneath the boiler.

The bellhop shrugged and went out the door to go upstairs and tell management that Willy was nowhere to be found, and to change clothes because he knew he was going to get told to get down to the boiler room and shovel coal until Willy showed up. Damnable man.

Oh, well. It beat having to greet all those people wearing masks, coming in and out of the Ethel's doors. He wouldn't be exposed to the Spanish Flu, thank God for small favors.

As he walked out, Curtis didn't notice the shadow that stood away from all the rest in the room. Tall and lanky, it would have smelled of coaldust and sweat if he had gotten close, but that's how everything smelled in the room.

The shadow looked with sullen eyes at the bellhop leaving, and resented the fact that he, Ol' Willy, was a ghost now. He was stuck in the boiler room and couldn't interact with anything at all. He had tried yelling and waving his arms in front of Curtis, who had seen absolutely nothing.

In fact, there was only one thing that Ol' Willy could do now, only one thing that he could feel: the heat from the boiler. It was with him all the time, only now it wasn't the comforting, suffocating heat that he had known before.

Willy had burned and burned and burned until nothing was left, nothing to touch with or see with or smell with, but he could damn sure still feel that heat, even as a ghost.

This heat was intense, didn't like him, and punished him. That was his fate, he reckoned. He knew he couldn't leave this boiler room, couldn't interact with anyone who came in like how he tried to get Curtis to notice him.

He was going to burn for eternity, burn for his sins, burn for what he had done. He knew this and still screamed even though no sound came out of his ghostly mouth. He knew this heat, knew what was in store for him.

Before his ghostly form faded away, only one thought remained. Ol' Willy had always liked the boiler room, and the heat in there.

But now, his fate, his eternity was going to be hell. No, not hell. It was going to be a different kind of heat. A heat that used to be friendly, but had now burned everything Willy was away, and was a sinister, punishing heat.

Jason Daughrity

A pulsating heat. And only one phrase came to Willy's mind as his ghost disappeared.

His damnation?

It was gonna be *boiler room hot*.

Sub-Level 2 - Vaults
1910

The Recipe Book of Lillie Hitchcock Coit
Heather Daughrity

The massive earthquake of 1906 nearly destroyed the great city of San Francisco. Between the earthquake itself and the subsequent fires that swept the city, four out of every five buildings were destroyed. No one knew for certain the final count of the dead, though estimates placed it in the thousands.

In the wake of that great upheaval, however, a group of shrewd and clever women came together to form a plan.

A plan that would require immense wealth, great sway with the city leaders, and sacrifice.

The women had the first two requirements aplenty.

They had no qualms about procuring the third.

The maître d' at Carrington's, a restaurant blocks away from the soon-to-open Ethel Hotel, bowed as the procession of women made their way through the crowded dining room.

The patrons of the restaurant halted, staring, forks lifted halfway to their lips, at the line of well-known socialites that threaded purposefully through the tables. These women commanded an air of respect, of deference, as they made their way to the private room kept ready for them at the back of the establishment.

Whispering filled the air as the ladies passed, names murmured in quiet tones.

Lillie Hitchcock Coit. Independently wealthy. Patron saint of firefighters. A woman in trousers—*trousers*!

Louise Erni Boudin. Wife of Isidore Boudin, owner of the famous Boudin Bakery. She trailed the scent of sourdough wherever she went.

Alma de Bretteville Spreckels. Wife of Adolph Spreckels, owner of the Spreckels Sugar Company. Alma stood taller than most men and was equally as frightening as any if crossed.

Maud Younger. Living nicely off her late mother's inheritance. Known for going undercover as a working woman to help further the cause of women's rights.

Corrine Carrington. Wife of Richard Carrington, though it was clear to all that the money was hers. A member of the *nouveau riche,* mysterious in origin. Owner of the restaurant in which they now sat.

Ethel Sperry Crocker. Wife of William Henry Crocker. Wealthy in too many ways to count. A patron of the Arts with a stern countenance.

They made quite a group, the six women who seated themselves at the round table in the curtained room in the back.

They had been seen together often these past few years, sparking rumors aplenty and earning them the tongue-in-cheek name the *Baking Circle* in the society columns—an allusion perhaps, to the numerous interests the women had in flour, sugar, and fruit companies.

Or perhaps a thinly-veiled insult meant to imply that the women—clearly no mere housewives—*ought* to be at home baking when they were obviously out doing something far more nefarious.

Not that a single member of the so-called Baking Circle would have paid the slightest attention to the insult, if that's what it were.

No, the ladies of the Circle had far more important things to discuss—and plans far more nefarious than anyone could imagine.

The plans had started one dark night in 1907. Now, three years later, as they neared their completion, the ladies were filled with both excitement and fear.

The building itself was finished. Situated just on the edge of the earthquake's damage zone, tucked neatly into the crook of towering Telegraph Hill, and mere blocks from the gently lapping waves of San Francisco Bay, the new hotel stood tall, proud, and almost ready to accept guests.

The name of the hotel had been a subject of heated debate among the Circle, but Mrs. Crocker had won out by virtue of having donated the largest sum of money to fund the building's construction.

Thus, the Ethel Hotel came into existence, built of the finest marble and mahogany, fitted with indoor plumbing, heated water, electric lights, and all the lavish comforts a well-heeled traveler could desire.

The women made sure to have their hands on every part of the hotel's plans. Every choice, every decision—the lettering of the signs, the carpets that ran the long length of the hallways, the daily specials in the restaurant, the frescoes on the lobby walls—had been made by the collective group.

This was *their* hotel.

And to make sure the hotel prospered, the fine ladies of the Baking Circle had turned to a source more powerful than the banks or the politicians.

It was Lillie who first suggested it. An off-hand remark. A joke.

"Perhaps we should just sell our souls and get it over with."

It was Corrine who had taken the idea and run with it.

There is little in this world, be it material possessions, influence, or knowledge, that money cannot buy, and Corrine Carrington had plenty of expendable income.

She spent it on knowledge.

Dark tomes full of strange languages. Cryptic drawings.

Diabolical promises.

It took her some time to find someone to translate the old Latin phrases, to explain—for academic purposes, of course—just exactly how the rituals worked.

It took even longer for her to convince the other members of the Circle to join in her dark plan.

But, as most women who wanted more than anything to succeed in a man's world, the ladies of the Circle eventually came to the conclusion that any price was worth the promised reward.

It wasn't so bad, really. One small sacrifice to ensure the Ethel's prosperity. One measly little life to bring benefit to thousands. It wasn't much to ask for, in the big scheme of things.

All for the greater good.

It wouldn't be hard to find someone. The streets teemed with people no one would miss. Prostitutes. Criminals. Vagrants. San Francisco was full of lost souls.

So that was the plan, and that was the subject of the discussion that took place across the round table in the back room of Carrington's.

There were only five days until the grand opening, and to celebrate the occasion, a party had been planned in the richly appointed Ballroom on the third floor. Of course, most of the illustrious guests would also stay a night, a week, or more in the hotel.

It was during the late hours of this great gala that the six women of the Circle would slip away, sneak down the back stairs to the vaults, two floors below ground, and enact the ritual that would ensure the Ethel's success.

With every plan solidified and Corrine chosen—much to her annoyance—to lure the unwitting sacrifice to his doom, the ladies finished their tea and went their separate ways.

Corrine didn't have far to go. She waited until the others had left, then snatched her silver teapot off the table and made her way up the hidden stairs to her apartments on the floors above.

The teapot had been her mother's—the only thing she had left of the woman who had died when Corrine was only four. She had carried it down with her to the first official meeting of the Baking Circle—such a ridiculous name—in the hopes of impressing the ladies.

Of course, they had assumed the teapot belonged to the restaurant and hadn't paid it the slightest bit of attention.

Still, there was something in Corrine that made her carry it down to each and every meeting.

A bit of her mother to give her confidence among so much old money, perhaps.

Or a fear that the other ladies might see the plain ceramic pots used in the rest of the establishment and turn their nose up at them.

Either way, that silver teapot had borne silent witness to plans and promises that would bring about the downfall of each and every one of them if they ever came to light.

A maid bobbed a curtsy and hurried out of Corrine's way as she entered the rooms above the restaurant.

At the end of the hall, the nanny was just closing the door on the nursery. She glanced up at Corrine and smiled as she put a finger to her lips.

Good. Rose was asleep.

Corrine was not the type to take naturally to mothering. Perhaps it was the fact that she had grown up without a mother of her own. Perhaps it was simply her personality. Either way, she didn't have the patience right now to deal with the child, lovely though she was.

And where was the girl's father? Where was Richard?

Corrine sighed. She could make a dozen guesses where her useless husband was, each one as likely as the next. Wherever he was, he was surely either sleeping off a hangover or working on creating a new one. There were plenty of dirty bars and gin palaces about.

She'd had suspicions, lately, that those weren't the only places he was frequenting. He often came home with the slightest whiff of strange perfume about him, or smudges against his lapels that looked an awful lot like lipstick.

And then there were the mornings he came staggering in, smelling of cigarettes and booze and the musky cologne of other men.

But she mustn't think about that right now.

The Ethel must be her focus. At least for the next five days.

Alma de Bretteville Spreckels paced through her lavish mansion. At six feet tall, the top of her head barely passed beneath the arched doorways that led from one room to another.

She didn't like what they were about to do, not one bit.

And now there was something else to worry about.

Her old friend, Agnes, who she had grown up with, had come to visit.

That wouldn't have been so bad. She could have kept her own secrets well enough, even with Agnes about.

But now she had Agnes's secrets to deal with as well.

On the way home from her meeting with the ladies of the Circle, she had happened to glance up and out the window of the car when the chauffeur stopped at an intersection, and she'd done a double take.

There, silhouetted in the doorway of the Ruby Goose, was her friend Agnes, held tightly in the arms of none other than Richard Carrington.

Corrine's husband.

Should she say something? To Agnes? To *Corrine*?

Why couldn't things just be easy for once?

Thursday, October 13, 1910.

The Grand Opening of the new Ethel Hotel.

The doors were to open at eight o'clock that evening.

Just two hours away.

The ladies of the Baking Circle stood in the ballroom, watching nervously as the Ethel's staff put the finishing touches on the room's décor.

Golden tables clustered in three corners, surrounded by chairs covered in purple velvet. A raised dais in the fourth corner held chairs for the band that had just arrived and begun to set up.

At one end of the enormous space, a gold-topped bar stood in front of a wall of glittering liquor bottles.

Richard Carrington, never one to miss a party—or a steady supply of booze—leaned against the bar, chatting up the bartender, who graciously kept Richard's whiskey glass topped off. Corrine had sent Richard away after his millionth exclamation about how gorgeous the ballroom was and how much money they would make.

It would be a party to remember, that much was certain.

But the ladies weren't truly focused on all this activity

Their thoughts were on another space, another set of preparations.

One by one they slipped away, gathering once more a few minutes later in the cold and dark of the vaults. The table was ready. The knife gleamed in the sputtering candlelight—no electricity in the basement floors.

"Did you bring it?" Ethel's voice was cold, curt, as she addressed Lillie.

"Of course I brought it," Lillie replied, picking up a square parcel wrapped in black satin. She unfolded the fabric with a flourish.

A book.

A simple thing, covered in red linen. Across the front, gold letters spelled out:

The
Recipe Book
of
Lillie Hitchcock Coit

It was a ruse, of course. The book contained not recipes, but spells, copied down carefully in English by Corrine's translator friend, alongside drawings painstakingly reproduced from the accompanying archaic texts.

The recipe book held the steps for the ritual.

Corrine stared at the book. She understood why they'd chosen her to lure in the sacrifice—she was the youngest, the most likely to be able to easily lure in a man with promises of a secret rendezvous, but she still didn't like it.

Once she had convinced their victim to follow her down into the vaults of the hotel, the instructions in the book were quite clear.

The victim must lay willingly upon the sacrifice table—they'd make easy work of that by plying the poor man with alcohol beforehand. Then the proper words must be spoken as the cuts were made. The sacrifice's blood must flow freely into the building's foundation—into cracks left purposely between the stones for this very act.

It was simple enough.

If they'd only had to do it once, it might not have been so bad.

But, according to the calculations cited within the spellwork, calculations that the Circle had checked and double checked, in order to keep the Ethel in tip-top condition, the ritual would have to be repeated.

Once every twenty-three years.

Best not to worry about that, though. They needed to focus on tonight.

The heavy doors of the Ethel's lobby opened at eight o'clock sharp. A horde of well-dressed revelers entered, gasping in pleasure and nodding in approval at the beautiful lobby. They rode in groups of six or eight in the gold-plated elevators only to be even more surprised and impressed by the grandiosity of the lavish ballroom.

The ladies of the Circle mingled among their guests, accepting all the proffered compliments and congratulations on their new venture. The band played; the people danced. Liquor flowed freely from the open bar, and Corrine Carrington was the only one to wince at the thought of the tab.

By ten o'clock, the party was in full swing, the guests growing louder and rowdier by the minute—with enough alcohol, even the most refined and proper of the gentry would loosen up and make fools of themselves.

One man in particular was making a bigger fool of himself than usual.

Corrine watched with clenched fists and narrowed eyes as her husband made his rounds, throwing back glass after glass of whatever liquid was put into his hand. He stood dangerously close to too many people, men *and* women, making some uncomfortable but raising blushes of desire in others.

She made up her mind. First thing tomorrow morning—assuming they survived tonight—she was shipping him off to one of those classy resorts that the rich and scandalous sent their black sheep to for treatment. They'd send him back to her sober and repentant or they'd better not send him back at all.

But before all that, she had to do her part to ensure the success of the Circle's venture.

Corrine looked slowly around the ballroom. She locked eyes with each of her sisters-in-crime, one by one, each giving her a small nod of the head or a tightening of the mouth that might have been a smile.

It was time.

Slipping out was easy enough; spirits were high in the ballroom, and no one could be bothered to care about what she was doing.

Corrine took the back service stairs and exited the building in the narrow space between the outer wall and the cliff face that rose overhead. She pulled her beaded shawl around her shoulders and set off into the darkness, her heels clicking against damp pavement as the night's fog descended on the streets.

She didn't have to walk far. A couple of blocks from the hotel, Corrine heard the shuffling, uneven steps of a drunk man. A moment later, the shape of a sailor emerged from the mist.

A few whispered promises and a steady shoulder to lean on were all it took to convince the man to accompany her.

Corrine stopped for a moment once they were safely back inside the hotel. The man was becoming heavier, dead weight against her. She leaned him against the stair rail. He slumped down onto the steps while Corrine caught her breath.

She checked her watch. 11:30. She should have plenty of time to get him down the two flights of stairs to the vaults.

If only she could pick him up.

The sailor snored softly, his head against the wall, arms and legs out at odd angles.

She tried to lift him. The man was easily double her weight. She heaved and panted but it was no use.

"Shit."

Corrine looked around. The service halls were dark and quiet. She'd have to find help, but who? She couldn't ask anyone outside the Circle. Would the ladies all be down in the vault already? Could she chance leaving the man here, hope that no one else would stumble upon him before she returned?

She didn't really have a choice.

Cursing under her breath, Corrine peeked out into the lobby. Maybe she'd get lucky and spot one of the ladies hurrying down from the ballroom on her way to the vault.

No such luck, but she did spot something.

Someone.

Two someones.

The sight was enough to boil the blood in Corrine's veins.

Her husband and another woman, locked in a tight embrace, lips pressed together.

A quick and deadly plan flashed through Corrine's mind.

She steeled herself and started forward, the staccato tap-tap-tap of her heels announcing her arrival in plenty of time for Richard Carrington to look up and realize just how much trouble he was in.

The Circle was almost complete. Lillie, Alma, Maud, Ethel, and Louise stood in silent anticipation, waiting for the sixth member of the group and the sacrifice she would bring.

A clatter on the stairs, followed by a woman's cry, made them all turn.

Five pairs of eyes widened, Alma Spreckels' most of all, at the sight that greeted them.

Corrine Carrington marched down the stairs, her arm around the neck of a young woman who only Alma recognized, a knife held tight against the woman's throat.

Clattering along behind them came Richard Carrington, holding tight to the rail, unsteady on his legs, clearly halfway to blackout drunkenness.

Richard's words ran on endlessly, a litany of begging pleas and promises growing more grandiose by the second.

"Corrine!" Lillie scolded. "What on earth is going on here?"

Corrine pushed the woman—Alma's old friend, Agnes—down the last few stairs. The young woman stumbled and sprawled face-first on the stone floor, her dress hitched up around her thighs.

Richard rushed toward her, but Corrine sidestepped and planted herself between her husband and his most recent mistake.

"Change of plans," Corrine said, kneeling down to grab a handful of Agnes's hair. She yanked the young woman's head upright so that Agnes's tear-streaked face looked out at the group.

"We'll use this one," she said. She then gestured toward her helpless husband. "And then that one. Surely two are better than one."

The other members of the Circle looked from one to another. What on earth did they do now? Time was running out. They wouldn't have a chance to lure anyone else down here, not before midnight.

The Recipe Book stated clearly that the sacrifice had to happen at midnight. It was almost time.

Lillie cleared her throat. "Alright then. Ladies first."

Corrine moved toward the group, toward the table, dragging Agnes upright as she moved. Agnes let out a whimper.

Alma stepped forward. "No."

Everyone in the room froze.

"No?" Lillie said, her tone sharp.

"Not the girl." Alma's voice allowed no argument.

Corrine argued anyway.

"Yes, the girl."

A cacophony of voices rose then, each member of the Circle voicing her own opinion, until above them all rang Richard Carrington's voice, strangled and high-pitched, like a prepubescent boy's.

"I don't know what the hell is going on here." He gulped in a great breath of air, tears running down his face. "But I won't let you hurt her. Leave this alone, Corrine. Leave her alone, or you'll be short one husband."

Corrine's eyebrows furrowed as she tried to make sense of his words.

Richard's arms moved, and that was when she saw it.

The fool had made a sloppy noose out of a length of rope coiled up in the corner and had looped it over the stair railings.

While the others watched in disbelief, Corrine simply laughed.

"You idiot," she spat, releasing Agnes and starting toward Richard.

Richard dropped the noose around his own neck and pulled as hard as he could, the rope straining against the metal railings and pulling taut against his throat. He choked and coughed but did not release the rope.

Corrine looked on, speechless, at the man's stupidity.

After a moment in which Richard continued to gag and splutter, his feet actually managing to lift an inch or so off the ground, Louise—sweet, quiet Louise—called out, "It's almost time! We have to do it now if we're going to do it at all!"

"Oh, for heaven's sake!" Corrine cried. "Alma, help me!"

Alma, relieved to see that Corrine's attention was focused on Richard and not Agnes, rushed forward to assist in dragging the man, rope and all, across the room and toward the table.

"He has to lie down of his own free will!" Louise reminded them.

"Richard," Corrine said, standing with her face mere inches from her husband's, "if you want me to leave that little whore of yours alone, you will lie down on this table right now. Do you understand?"

Richard nodded, not comprehending the true essence of what was happening but guilty—and drunk—enough to play along.

He climbed up on the table and stretched out along its length. The noose still hung loosely around his neck, the rope trailing off the edge of the table and snaking across the floor.

Agnes sobbed in the corner.

The six members of the Baking Circle gathered around the table and began the chant they had memorized months ago. A vibration started in the stones beneath their feet; a low hum reverberated along the walls.

As the others continued the chant, Lillie—their *de facto* leader—took up the ceremonial knife. She hesitated for the briefest of moments, her eyes on the small clock on the wall ahead.

As the minute hand clicked over, marking the stroke of midnight, she plunged the knife into Richard Carrington's body.

Agnes let out a howl of rage and grief and fear.

Lillie paid the girl no mind. Her arm rose again and again, the knife's sharp blade puncturing Richard's body over and over until his blood ran thick along the edges of the table and onto the cracked stone below.

A surge of electricity infused the air around them. The walls and floor shuddered, and a biting wind rushed in circles around the room. The blood that had reached the floor was sucked downward with an audible slurp, and a blast that was both a boom of sound and a vacuous silence sent all the women stumbling backward.

For a moment, no one spoke. No one moved. The only sound was Agnes's continued sobs.

Finally, Maud managed to whisper. "Is that it? Did we do it? Is it finished?"

"I think it's done," Lillie said, looking around, expecting the walls to look different than they had moments before.

Everything looked the same.

Stone floor. Stone walls. Arched doorways. The sturdy foundation of the great Ethel Hotel.

Richard Carrington, dead on the table.

And one loose end to tie up, crying in the corner.

It didn't take much convincing to quiet the girl. Alma took her friend in hand and told her in unquestionable terms just exactly how horribly they would torture her if she breathed a word of what had happened that night to anyone, but also just how handsomely she would be rewarded if she kept her mouth shut.

They'd keep her close, of course. Maybe put her up in the hotel itself. Keep an eye on her.

She was young and stupid, easily swayed.

Corrine stood over her husband's body. They'd already made plans to dispose of the body, though of course at the time they hadn't known it would be such a familiar one.

She stood looking down at Richard's face, the pale skin already purpling around his eyes. Inside, she was a mix of roiling emotions. He'd been a cad, a faithless, lying man-whore, but he'd also been her husband. They'd had good times together in the beginning.

Corrine huffed and wiped away a tear with the back of her hand. Something in her compelled her to take her husband's hand in her own, one last time.

The hard onyx of his cufflinks pressed against her skin. She turned his arm to look at them. Gold serpents with ruby eyes, biting their own tails—her present to him on their fifth anniversary.

With practiced motions, she removed the cufflinks and hid them down the front of her dress. She'd not let him go to his eternal reward—whatever that might be—with her gift still on him.

Several floors above, drunken businessmen and tipsy socialites stumbled out of the ballroom and into the elevators, making their way to the fine accommodations they had booked for the night at the Ethel Hotel.

A young bellhop discovered a drunken sailor sleeping soundly at the foot of the service stairs and promptly ousted him into the fog-shrouded night, locking the back door firmly behind him.

Behind every wall and beneath every floor, the aftermath of the Circle's ritual surged and grew, spreading tendrils into the masonry and woodwork, the plumbing and the wiring, and the Ethel came alive with a dark and deviant power.

Three Months Later

The Ethel raked in more money in its first quarter than its founders could have imagined, with no sign of slowing down.

Of course, there was always good with the bad. While the hotel attracted wealthy and even famous guests, people known for their discretion, rumors did begin to spread. Nothing too scandalous—sex and violence were the daily norm for people of that level—but enough small scandals to make Agnes Roberts take notice.

They had welcomed the young woman into the Circle in the most ancillary of ways. Not a member, exactly, but an acquaintance, nonetheless. To pay for her silence, Agnes had been set up in her own plush suite on the sixteenth floor, which was where she was sitting the day she opened the newspaper to startling news.

Corrine Carrington, young, beautiful, and rich, the beloved darling of the socialite circles, in her grief over her husband's disappearance and assumed death, had killed herself with an overdose of pep-up pills mixed with vodka.

She left behind one daughter and a whole lot of money.

"Grief," Agnes snorted. "More like guilt."

She rubbed her hand along the burgeoning swell of her belly. "Don't worry, little one, your mommy is made of stronger stuff than that. Stronger stuff than any of them will ever know."

A sudden wind stirred the pages in Agnes's hands, a breeze heavy with the scent of tea leaves and Corrine Carrington's floral perfume.

Agnes froze for a moment, then laughed and said, "Blow all you want, Mrs. Carrington. Hang around and haunt me if you like. Haunt this hotel forever, for all I care."

She laid her head back against the fluffy pillows that surrounded her and closed her eyes. She was tired, which was of course to be expected of a woman in her condition, not to mention the lack of sleep she'd had due to strange and vivid dreams these last few weeks.

She wouldn't think about that now. She'd focus on happy things, like the baby growing inside her. She hoped it would be a boy, felt sure that it would be. He would live with her, here, inside the hotel, for the next few years, until he was old enough to need a room of his own.

She supposed that when that day came, she'd need to buy a larger home—the Circle would help with that. But the suite was hers to keep for as long as the hotel stood, so she could bring little George—or Georgina—for visits when they got tired of other places.

Maybe one day she'd even have grandchildren to visit the old place with her.

The thought made her happy, and she drifted off into dreams of baby carriages and bottles…

…and blood, and violence, and horror.

The walls of the Ethel shifted and groaned around her, the darkness inside the old hotel hungry and growing as swiftly and surely as Richard Carrington's baby in Agnes's belly.

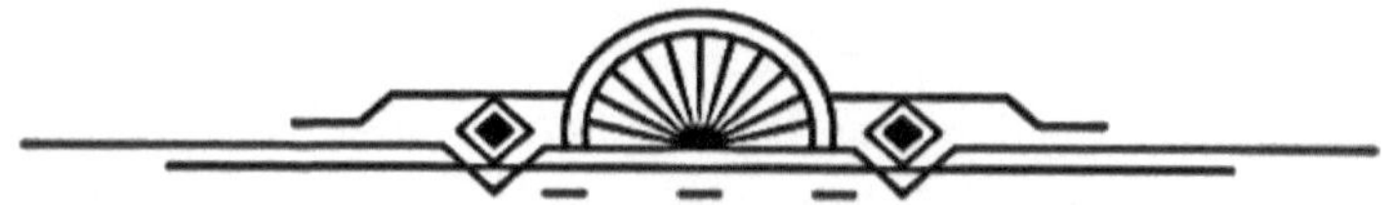

Farewell

Oh, there you are, you scrumptious little tart.

Tarts and tea, get it?

Ah! The girls are here. I thought they would be. Let me make the introductions.

Louise.

Maud.

Alma.

Lillie.

Ethel—the lady, not the hotel!

Ahem. Corrine.

We're so glad you're here, really.

Our own little Founders' Day Celebration.

I did good, didn't I, ladies? Please say I did. Please. I don't—I don't want to be in trouble again.

Yes, I did? Oh, thank you.

Damned uppity women. Not so much as a "thank you, Richard" or "good job, Dickie-boy."

Oh, yes, and YOU. You did quite well yourself. Made it through all the floors. Met all the gho—ahem, people.

Drank all that delicious wine.

It's going to your head a bit now, isn't it? Alcohol will do that.

Especially alcohol with a little something extra added.

Now, now, come sit at the table. Let the ladies pour you some tea.

Yes, that silver teapot is quite old. A little tarnish never hurt anyone.

Or a few bloodstains.

Delicious, isn't it? Darjeeling—Alma's favorite.

Darjeeling and a touch of digitalis, ha!

Nothing, nothing, shh.

Drink, dear, drink.

Good, good. Now let's get you straight to bed.

What's that? You forgot to check in up in the Lobby?

No worries, darling.

Just through here, we have the perfect place for you to lie down.

It's not the most comfortable place to pass out—and trust me, I would know—but you'll soon be beyond caring about such things as life's comforts.

No, don't mind the rumbling. It happens from time to time, when Ethel—the hotel, not the lady!—gets impatient. Sometimes she lets herself crack. Once she burst every pipe in her walls. There was an incident with a fire one year—but we don't talk about that.

This year she's being a bit more dramatic. Earthquakes and sinkholes, indeed. Pfft.

No worries. We'll have everything sorted by the morning and the Ethel will be back in tip-top shape.

There you go. Easy does it. Now close your eyes and try to relax.

No, no need to speak. We know you're grateful to be here.

We're quite glad to have you, too.

New blood for the foundation.

The Circle must endure, you know.

The Ethel must endure.

Raise it up, ladies.

About the Authors

Christopher Badcock

Chris works as a Marketing Consultant by day, and by night pursues his passions for procrastination and writing scary stuff. He lives in Nottingham, in the United Kingdom, with his 7-year-old daughter, Aubriella.

His debut novel, *Those You Killed*, was published in 2021 and garnered rave reviews before being discontinued.

He's currently working on a collection of short stories entitled *Hummingbird and Other Iniquities*, which he hopes will see the light of day in 2026.

Craig Brownlie

As the pandemic wound down, Craig Brownlie went to a lot of clubs to hear local bands, especially when his son's band, Turkey Blaster Omega, played. His first bigger concert happened to be Arturo O'Farrill and the Afro Latin Jazz Orchestra at Birdland in Manhattan. If you see Craig at a convention or really anywhere, let him know if you were there also.

Craig recently edited the anthology *Five Raging Hearts: Splatterpunk for the Soul*. Look for other work in *Metalhearts, Demons and Death Drops, Wands: Year of the Tarot*, and *Unspeakable Horrors 3*. He has three books out in his Little Books of Pain series: *Hammer, Nail, Foot; Thick As A Brick*; and *A Book of Practical Monsters*. These are in addition to the re-release of his middle-grade novel *Comic Book Summer*.

His first collection of short stories, *A Touch of Silence & Other Tales* was released in 2017, followed by *The Basement of Dreams & Other Tales* in 2019 and *Within the Flames & Other Stories* in 2021.

Rebecca Cuthbert

Rebecca Cuthbert writes dark fiction and poetry. She loves ghost stories, folklore, Gothic settings, and anything that involves nature getting revenge. Her books include *In Memory of Exoskeletons*, *Creep This Way*, *Self-Made Monsters*, *Down in the Dark Deep Where the Puddlers Dwell*, and *Six O'Clock House & Other Strange Tales*.

For additional information, with links to free stories and more, visit https://linktr.ee/rebeccacuthbertwrites.

Heather Daughrity

Heather Daughrity loves all things macabre, dark, autumnal, and horrific. She writes Gothic, psychological, and grief horror. In her spare time, she works as an editor of speculative fiction for dozens of independent authors.

She lives with her husband, author and publisher Joshua Loyd Fox, their extended circus of children and pets, and more books than any one house can hold.

Heather is the author *Knock Knock, Tales My Grandmother Told Me, Echoes of the Dead*, and several short stories in various anthologies.

She is also the curating editor of the HoH anthology series, including *House of Haunts, Hospital of Haunts*, and *Hotel of Haunts*.

Jason Daughrity

"Doc" Jason Daughrity is a former US Navy Hospital Corpsman of Marines and an Iraqi War veteran, working in Florida as an Industrial Construction Safety Trainer for the largest solar company in the US.

Besides stints as a paramedic, state health inspector, night club manager, and casino security, Doc Jason goes all over the country teaching First Aid and other classes to construction workers.

He is the brother of author Joshua Loyd Fox, and brother-in-law to Heather Daughrity. At home he has a beautiful fiancée and five dogs as well as a cat or two. He loves fantasy novels and sci-fi movies, and writing has always been an aspiration.

He has written short stories for the anthologies, *Hospital of Haunts*, *Hotel of Haunts*, and *George Watertower and Other Childhood Terrors*, all from Watertower Hill Publishing.

Savannah R. Fischer

Savannah R. Fischer is the permanently exhausted pigeon in charge of two well-loved chaos gremlins. When not with her family, she can usually be found in her cave, wrapped in an oversized blanket and dreaming of spinach puffs. She wants to show her gremlins that they can do hard things, even when it's scary, like pulling the wrong lever and ending up in a pit of alligators. No llamas were harmed in the making of her works of horror.

You can follow her on Facebook as Savannah R. Fischer and Instagram as @s.r.fischerauthor. Signed copies of her books are available at https://srfischerauthor.bigcartel.com/

Savannha's works Include: *Incantations of Blood*, *The Broken Cord*, and *Phobophobia* with Jyl Glenn.

Douglas Ford

Douglas Ford's short fiction has appeared in a variety of anthologies, magazines, and podcasts, as well as three collections, *Ape in the Ring and Other Tales of the Macabre and Uncanny, The Infection Party and Other Stories of Dis-Ease,* and *Let's Cut Up Dad! and Other Stories of Transgressive Madness.* His longer works include *The Beasts of Vissaria County, Little Lugosi (A Love Story), The Trick,* and *Who Dies First.* He lives on the west coast of Florida.

Joshua Loyd Fox

Joshua Loyd Fox is the author of several novels including *I Won't Be Shaken, Had I Not Chosen, Amongst You, To Build a Tower, One Becomes a Thousand*, and *Unto This Mountain*.

He is also the author of the upcoming *Shaken the Worst*, the sequel to his breakout autobiography, and Book VI of the ArchAngel Missions, *Least of These*. His short stories, *The Book of the Tower and the Traitor* a companion series to The ArchAngel Missions, can be found on Amazon Vella.

He is also the editor of the local urban legend horror anthology, *George Watertower & Other Childhood Terrors*.

Joshua Loyd Fox is an old-fashioned boy from West Texas who now spends his time in NE Oklahoma, with his wife, author and editor Heather Daughrity, and their children, friends, and as many pets and books as they can surround themselves with.

He is also the owner/publisher at Watertower Hill Publishing, LLC, under his legal name, Joshua Daughrity.

See everything Joshua is up to **at www.watertowerhill.com.**

Emma J. Gibbon

Described by NPR as "Shirley Jackson meets Johnny Rotten," Emma J. Gibbon is an award-winning horror writer and poet. Her debut fiction collection, *Dark Blood Comes from the Feet*, was one of NPR's best books of 2020 and won the Maine Literary Book Award for Speculative Fiction. Her stories have appeared in *The Dark Tome* and *Toasted Cake* podcasts, various anthologies, including *Wicked Haunted and 13 Haunted Houses*, and magazines such as *Reactor* (formerly Tor.com) and *Unnerving*. Her poetry has been published in magazines and anthologies, including *Strange Horizons, Kaleidotrope,* and *Under Her Eye*, and she has been nominated for the Rhysling twice. Emma was part of the writing team behind the Realm "heavy metal werewolf" podcast drama, *Undertow: Blood Forest*. Her latest story on *Reactor* was edited by Ellen Datlow and was collected in *Some of the Best from Reactor: 2024 Edition*.

Emma lives with her husband, Steve, and four exceptional animals: Odin, Mothra, Hamlet, and M. Bison (also known as Grim) in a spooky little house in the woods. You can find her at emmajgibbon.com.

William F. Gray

William F. Gray is an author living in West Virginia. He has released three novels, a novella, a short story collection, and has appeared in the various anthologies. In his free time, he enjoys reading , playing music, and outings with his wife, son, and daughter.

Justin Holley

Justin lives somewhere on the Cass Lake chain of lakes and when not writing, he is boating, golfing, or possibly investigating the paranormal.

He is the author of *Unseen Gods, Hellweg's Keep, To Cut a Man, Blood From the Stars, Tethered to Darkness, Seven Cleopatra Hill*, and the 3-book *Bruised* series.

Justin loves to hear from fans. Please check his writing out at www.justinholley.com.

Caleb Jones

Caleb Jones is the horror and thriller author of *Red Hill Paradise* and *The Eliza Test*. He lives in Hampton Roads, Virginia with his wife, two daughters, and hound dog. When he isn't writing he can be found watching scary books and reading spooky movies. Those two teachers provided his education in the macabre and are highly responsible for the stories he produces today.

Bert Lestrange

Bert was gifted his father's horror and fantasy collections at age 9 and never looked back. He met his wife, Marie, on a flight to Europe and they fell madly in love. He writes just as much to elicit emotion as tell a story. Bert writes like a charcuterie board; spicy, psychological, thriller, high fantasy, cosmic, traumatic, folk, and his most popular: naughty bathroom graffiti.

He is currently the assistant to the assistant regional janitor of Crimson Curiosities.

Bert loves international exploration, truly excellent dining opportunities, and staring at Marie while snuggling their beautiful spawnling close.

Follow Marie to find him. He doesn't understand technology…

Marie Lestrange

Marie Lestrange is a true multipassionate badass. Her fascination with the macabre, true crime, and occult practices fuels her intricate research for captivating gothic historical novels, including *Crimson Cobblestones* and *The Devil's Colony*.

After fourteen years dedicated to teaching special education, Marie has seamlessly transitioned her diverse skills into the entrepreneurial world. She's currently the CEO of Crimson Cult Media and the proud owner of Crimson Curiosities Bookshop and Oddities Store.

When she's not immersed in her many ventures, Marie (also an oil painter, sculptural artist, and musician of eight instruments) enjoys traveling with her husband, fellow writer Bert, and their eight-year-old Hobbit, exploring beyond the mountains of East Tennessee which they call home.

You can learn more about Marie's work at **linktr.ee/lestrangebooks** or follow along on TikTok!

Sirrah Medeiros

Sirrah Medeiros is an award-winning author, editor, and anthologist, and the Editor-in-Chief of Tundra Swan Press. She is a Marine Corps veteran, staunch LGBTQ+ ally, and began writing horror, poetry, and dark fantasy while a member of the Vicious Writers consortium in 2009.

She recently partnered with Vince A. Liaguno to co-edit *Don't Ask, Ghosts Tell: An LGBTQ+ Horror Anthology*. The anthology was published in June 2025 and supports the charity, Modern Military Association of America.

Other works include The BookFest award-winning charity anthology, *The Haunted Zone: A Horror Anthology by Women Military Veterans,* and *The Malediction Plague*, a zombie novella, both published in 2024. Her debut novel, *Secrets of Mother*, from the Cristiane Bradford series, won the National Association of Book Entrepreneur's Pinnacle Book Achievement Award for Best in Fantasy.

She lives in Northern Virginia with her husband and two energetic, playful rescue dogs. She takes pleasure in supporting causes, mentoring writers, hiking with her pups, drawing on occasion, and uniting experienced authors with new voices in genre fiction.

Sirrah's short fiction and poetry are found in numerous anthologies.

Visit her website to learn more at SirrahMedeiros.com.

Briana Morgan

Briana Morgan is a horror writer, editor, and author *of The Tricker-Treater and Other Stories*, which won a Godless 666 Award for Best Audiobook.

With more than a decade of experience scaring herself and others, Briana has a fresh voice that shines through in her latest book, *The Reyes Incident*, which has sold more than 16,000 copies to date. Her other books include *The Mouth Full of Ashes, Unboxed: A Play*, and more.

Briana has a BA in English and Creative Writing from Georgia College & State University. She is also an active member of the Horror Writers Association.

When not writing, Briana loves reading disturbing fiction, playing video games, and spending time with her husband and cat.

Susan H. Roddey

Susan H. Roddey writes dark speculative fiction and serves as Art Director for Watertower Hill Publishing. She is also a freelance book formatter, cover designer, and developmental editor.

Susan is a voracious reader, wanna-be chef, crafter, and amateur gamer who lives in the Piedmont area of South Carolina with a house full of humans, cats, books, and yarn, and spends entirely too much time yelling at her sewing machine. She is also very food-motivated and can easily be bought with cookies.

Find her at https://linktr.ee/shroddey

Cassandra O'Sullivan Sachar

Cassandra O'Sullivan Sachar is a writer, editor, and English professor in Pennsylvania who teaches creative writing, composition, and composition theory courses. She received her Doctorate of Education with a Literacy Specialization from the University of Delaware and her MFA in Creative Writing with a focus on horror fiction from Wilkes University.

She is the author of the Regal Summit Book Award-winning dark suspense novel *Darkness There but Something More* (Wicked House Publishing), the short horror story collections *Keeper of Corpses and Other Dark Tales* (Velox Books) and *Prepare the Coffin* (Screaming Scorpion Press), the middle-grade mystery *The Hidden Diary* (Baynam Books Press), the horror novella *Close the Door* (Baynam Books Press), and the young adult mystery *Lake of Secrets* (Horrorsmith Publishing).

Additionally, she is the editor of the Bram Stoker Award®-nominated multiauthor volume of horror scholarship *No More Haunted Dolls: Horror Fiction that Transcends the Tropes* (Vernon Press) as well as the fiction anthologies *Wicked Universe: A Wicked House Publishing Anthology* (Wicked House Publishing) and *Dark and Dreary: A Basement Horror Anthology* (Screaming Scorpion Press).

Read her work at https://cassandraosullivansachar.com/.

Cat Scully

Cat Scully is the queer author-illustrator of *Below the Grand Hotel* from Clash Books and *Jennifer Strange* with Haverhill House Publishing.

She is the illustrator of over thirty world maps, including Zoraida Cordova's *Labyrinth Lost* and Beth Revis' *Give the Dark My Love*, and the picture book *The Mayor of Halloween is Missing*, written by Emily S. Sullivan.

When she's not writing and illustrating, she works in marketing and lives just outside of Salem, Massachusetts.

Katherine Silva

Katherine Silva is an ace Maine horror author, a connoisseur of coffee, and victim of cat shenanigans. Her favorite flavors of the genre mix grief and existentialism which she combines with her love of the New England wilderness in her works.

She is a three-time Maine Literary Award finalist for speculative fiction. Katherine is also editor-in-chief of Strange Wilds Press.

You can find out all about her work at katherinesilvaauthor.com.

Ali Toothman

Ali Toothman lives in Southern Illinois with her loving family and four-legged friends. You can usually find her buried in a book or singing along to Hamilton.

Ali grew up on nineties horror movies, which led to her love of the genre and writing career. She has taken her trauma and real life demons and processes them through the fictional worlds she creates.

Ali Toothman has been featured in various anthologies and is the author of the revenge/psychological thriller, *Libby Lives*.

Patrick Tumblety

Patrick Tumblety is an author of horror, science fiction, and poetry. He has been featured in numerous anthologies, including *Tales of Jack the Ripper* from Word Horde Press, *The Dead Inside* from Dark Dispatch, and *Sincerely, Departed,* created by Cat Voleur and Angel Krause.

His premier horror novel, *Come Out & Play*, debuted in September 2024 from Uncomfortably Dark Horror and has been reviewed as "A poignant look at how our trauma bleeds into every part of our lives. My heart didn't know whether to break or race" by Laurel Hightower, Bram Stoker Nominated Author.

Steve Van Samson

Steve Van Samson is the author of the novels *The Unpleasant Mister Snif, Mark of the Witchwyrm, The Bone Eater King,* and *Marrow Dust*, the short story collections *Year of the Rattlesnake* and *Black Honey and Other Unsavory Things*, as well as numerous published short stories.

A fierce proponent of character diversity & of avoiding cliché like the plague, his writing tends to be on the pulpy side—intermingling genres like horror and dystopian with dark fantasy and adventure.

When not tapping the keys on his Chromebook, Steve co-hosts the *Retro Ridoctopus* podcast and watches entirely too many black-and-white monster films.

Also on his resume are the weird western *Trade Your Coffin for a Gun* and the coming-of-age terror novel, *The Country Girl's Guide to Hags, Hexes, and Haints*.